Tempus

by

A.D. OCIEN

ISBN: 979-8326-6588-83
First Edition

For the Claires

prologue

In the back room of a carpenter's workshop, in the town of Naples, sat a handmade desk. Commissioned by a nobleman, the desk had an extra, important, albeit small, feature that only this carpenter could create. Nobody knew where his talent had come from, only that he had a gift for making wood do things that others couldn't. The desk, along with its special, little feature, was completed three months after its commission and there it sat - waiting to become a fixture in the memories and history of a nobleman who had a vision and a plan. It would be in the background of every recollection. It would hold secrets and schemes. Upon it would be written great plans which, the nobleman was confident, would end up in history books alongside images of the ambitious leader in the different stages of his rise to great power. This desk, felt the nobleman, was destined for greatness that only a throne could surpass.

Three weeks after the desk was delivered to his opulent home, that nobleman died without merit or lasting memory.

The desk was sold at auction to pay off debts and was bought and sold and traded hands from one ambitious man after another. There was the Kingmaker who purchased the desk for his new castle when he successfully married his daughter to the barely-legitimate teenager he put on the throne. When that throne was taken by force, by another would-be king, the desk had been the only surviving piece of furniture when that castle was set ablaze by the new king's army. From there, the desk was again bought and sold and bought and sold until it ended up in the penthouse of a steel tycoon's eldest son who wanted nothing to do with steel. Instead of the business dealings his father wished for, the son only wrote poetry while sitting at that desk. There were twenty-seven poems in total and upon completing the last, that steel tycoon's son disappeared, never to be heard from again.

Around the world, the desk traveled, carrying secrets and schemes, love letters and ideas, dreams and even nightmares. Its special feature was used and the secret of it guarded by every one of its owners. Its original stain was long forgotten under the many layers atop it and it bore little scars from every trade of hands. If one knew where to look and had enough light, they might see a tiny hand print on one of its drawers. Made by the grandchild of a man who bought the desk for his enterprising brother, the hand print was never fully removed and the ambitions of the man's brother never realized. Such was the story of every owner of this desk until it made its way to an unassuming antique shop across the ocean, some would say, lifetimes, after it was made. Not a single photo of the desk graced the pages of a history book. Not a single scheme written upon its olive wood top would come to fruition. It was meant to be a quiet and steadfast fixture in the lives of men who were meant to become what boys, with sheets pinned about their necks and paper swords fisted in their tiny hands, dreamed they'd become.

The desk sat in a window of this antique shop and was used to display seasonal, featured items, sale signs and even the occasional discarded coffee cup. Its journey had seemingly come to a lackluster end. That was, until the day its surface was grazed by the manicured fingers of an elegant, designer-bag-toting woman, no less ambitious than the men who had so before her.

"Oh, Raymond, honey," Nadine Cielo said in her lilting voice. "This is it. This is the statement desk for your office. We simply must have it."

As it happened, the life this desk was meant to impact wasn't ever going to be that of some great and powerful man, but that of a young woman who had no intentions for greatness at all.

part one

a secret found

a layer of dust

what you have done

knocking is just a formality

If a picture was worth a thousand words, a layer of dust over a once-priceless desk could be worth two. With that melancholy thought, Claire slumped into her father's large, caramel-leather office chair and dragged her palms down her face with a sigh. Regret settled in her for having agreed to organize her father's neglected office. It was far too big and far too grand, as was the whole of her parents' lifestyle. It was a lifestyle into which she never did quite fit. Her eyes roamed over the seven desk drawers in front of her; three on each side and a longer, shallow one in the middle. She then contemplated which one she'd get lost in first. Her mind slipped away for a rest as she allowed herself this moment of peace in the quiet office. She listened to cars and birds in the distance, seeing but not focusing on the sunbeam-illuminated dust waltzing by.

The moment brought Claire back to a time when she'd been sitting at another desk in a library on campus; stacks of textbooks and scribbled notes were in front of her. At the time, she hadn't imagined that two years later, she would be wishing for the sleepless, caffeine-fueled nights of binge studying during finals week. There was a time when all she worried about was maintaining honor grades and staying on her professors' good sides for when she'd eventually ask them for recommendation letters. She'd dreamed of finally getting out there in the world. Determined to pay her dues, she joked with friends about having a closet of an apartment over some Mom-and-Pop restaurant downtown while she toiled away as an intern at a floral boutique. Her five year plan would end in her eventually owning one of her own in the city. It was a simple dream for a simpler time she thought may very well never come true now.

Her eyes dropped at this thought and snagged on the intricate details of the desk drawers in front of her. Filigree borders were carved along the drawers' edges with some parts inlaid in gold. Its copper drawer pulls hung like pendants and made a very distinct, muffled clank against the leather-covered wood when opened. With a deep breath, she leaned forward to start opening. The first drawer, filled almost completely with business cards, yielded nothing of value. Each drawer was similar; old magazines, trinkets from decades of world travel, receipts, bank statements, gifted pens, golf balls, cigar boxes, note pads. The desk had become a mausoleum for the memories belonging to a man who now barely knew they were even his.

When Claire got to the bottom-right drawer, however, she noticed the pattern of the sweeping vines and leaves all leaned toward one edge. When she compared it to the other drawers, she wondered why it hadn't been more noticeable before. The chair groaned as she rose and crouched in front of it to look at the curious design. There was a button around which the intricate details were carved. She pressed it. The drawer made a small *click* and then opened slightly on its own. She yanked it open, but it caught on something. Shifting to get a better angle to peer in, she saw that a small compartment had opened slightly in the back, revealing what seemed to be a wooden box. She reached in and tried to pull the little box out, but the compartment's door, hinged at the bottom, was stuck and prevented it from getting free.

She grabbed the little door and tried pulling on it, wiggling it from side to side, back and forth. She closed the drawer and pressed the button again, but the inner door remained stuck. She slammed the drawer shut and yanked it back open in hopes of shaking it loose, to no avail. Frustrated, she stood up and opened the middle drawer of the desk and searched around.

There wasn't anything of use except the ornate Fabergé letter opener she had seen her father use dozens of times before. The handle was carved from a single piece of jade and was wrapped with a carved sleeve made of gold, inlaid with little rubies and diamonds. The cap of the handle was a half-sphere of deep-red enamel and had a tiny golden egg sitting at the very top. The blade was polished brass, fashioned to a point and had an unusual, knife-sharp double- edge. It would do. With the opener in hand, Claire grabbed the stuck little door of the secret compartment and then jammed the letter opener along the bottom of it. It caught on something and Claire gave the little door one more good push and pull; it swung open suddenly as it became unstuck. The letter opener, free from where she had it jammed, sliced the side of her finger before she knew what had happened.

Cursing, she tended to her left index finger that bled enough for her to wonder if she might need stitches. She was about to stand up when she remembered the small, wooden box. From the back of the drawer, now wide open, she pulled it out. It was simple, oak, with no markings or carvings. The small box had only a thin varnish on it, without any lock or closure. Claire, with her non-injured hand, opened the box to find a parchment letter inside, folded up and tied with a bright red, velvet ribbon.

Having realized she was about to invade her father's privacy, Claire stopped short of untying the ribbon. She remembered this particular parchment. Her father handled it with care and could often be found just reading from it. One memory in particular stood out. It was a time she was much younger, playing with dolls, sitting on the floor of this very office. He had read from the parchment and stood up suddenly, startling little Claire. He had stared at her and his wide eyes had bounced back-and-forth between her and the parchment before he sat back down. His expression, she would later understand, had been hopeful.

She sat on the floor, pulled the letter into her lap and tugged loose the ribbon with her good hand, dismissing any feelings of impropriety. The ribbon fell away from the letter, flowing over her lap and onto the floor. Confusion and a bit of disappointment washed over her as she found the parchment blank. It unfolded to a rather large size; larger than the average sheet of paper, at least one and a half times the width and twice the length. She flipped the parchment to look at its back - nothing. Then, she flipped it back over and merely studied its emptiness.

Claire sighed deep and with frustration while rolling her eyes. She went to stand up and lost footing, almost falling backward. Instinctively, she grabbed the blank parchment with her injured hand, leaving a large, bloody streak across almost half of the bottom edge. She swore, convinced she'd just ruined something, that was an antique collector's item moments ago, but worthless with her blood smeared across it now. As she scowled at its ruin, a shadow passed through the room. Claire looked over her shoulder out the large, bay window behind her to see a crow land in the window's flower box. He cawed --seemingly at her-- and they studied each other long enough for her to feel uncomfortable. When she stood to leave the office, the crow's gaze followed her out.

II

Leaving her father's stuffy office, Claire breathed in the perfume of the towering, twin magnolia trees that stood sentry in their front yard. Sun rays turned into fat drops of raining light through their blossom-heavy branches and their sweet scent was invited in through the open front windows. Tucked safely beneath her arm was the little rudimentary box and parchment within. There was a bookstore downtown, she remembered, that did restorations and sold first editions and other antiquarian collectors' items. She'd go there to see if they would be able to safely clean her blood off of the page. She made plans to go as she strode toward the back door, in the kitchen, where she'd head outside to her converted carriage-house apartment.

As she approached the kitchen, her parents' voices floated out as they chatted over their morning coffee and pastries. Their conversation topics usually ranged from gossip to world news while taking in the view outside the bay window under which the breakfast table sat. Claire walked in to the sound of her mother's soothing voice. It guided her father's attention away from a conversation that she knew her mother had no patience to deal with.

"Oh, that reminds me, darling. We should call someone to come out and trim up the magnolias," said Nadine.

"I wasn't talking about the magnolias. I was talking about the man I saw yesterday. He's one of those demons, Nay, I know it. He stood right under our tree and watched me through the window," protested Raymond.

"Darling, it is no wonder you thought a man was out there, those sagging branches make all sorts of shapes in the dark. I will call someone to come take care of them and you'll see," she said, delicately balancing acknowledgement and dismissal. She went on to talk about the branches being a safety concern and how trimming them would give them a better view of the sidewalk.

What was I talking about, he thought as he listened to his wife prattle on about some landscaping concerns around their house. It *was something about the trees. Damn it. It was important.* I... And then the thought left him. It left him like so many thoughts had in the past two years - quickly and without warning. Enough times to make him want to rage, Raymond felt like he'd just woken up but couldn't remember going to sleep.

His attention peeled away from his wife to the peculiar movements of his daughter, who had walked more quietly through the kitchen than usual.

He watched her with narrowed eyes from under his lowered brow as she shifted about like she was uncomfortable with the air around her, her face mostly turned away. His frustration rose as he felt a wave of confusion crest and loom, ready to wash away this brief moment of lucidity. A small sense of comfort settled over him when his gaze floated to the back door out of which she was about to walk. Over it, hung one of three plaques engraved with symbols to ward against demons. There was a traveling psychic who made a show of seeming like it was a great sacrifice for her to sell the supposedly-precious spiritual plaques. She'd let them go to him, he said, for the small sum of a thousand dollars. He was happy to pay and she was happy to oblige, despite her reluctance which had evidently assured Raymond of their value. One of the other plaques hung above the front door that opened to the street, and the last above the door leading into the house from the vestibule.

Neither Claire nor her mother shared Raymond's enthusiasm for the plaques. He knew what their tight-lipped smiles and sideways glances to each other meant when he'd proudly shown his family the protective etchings. He could see how much they misunderstood him, but felt vindicated in the weeks after he'd hung them above the doors. He soon felt safer and more calm at home knowing his new plaques would keep unwanted visitors away. He noticed how much more calm and relaxed his wife and daughter had become as well.

Claire opened the back door and a puff of warm, late spring air wrapped around her. She had still not acknowledged her parents as she usually would; Raymond wanted to ask her why, but he'd learned that when he was quiet and still, so were his thoughts. So often, he chose silence over speaking –over thinking too much– as he was always painfully aware of the undulating confusion that dared him to disturb it.

"Claire."

Nadine Cielo's regal voice interrupted her daughter's near-perfect exit.

She was the only person Claire knew who could make putting down a coffee cup look ethereally graceful. In the wake of her husband's illness, Nadine's entire way of life had shifted into something for which she never thought to prepare. Despite this, her long, black hair lay beautifully over one shoulder in a purposeful way as if she'd just finished getting ready to go to a garden party.

"What are you doing?"

"Just gonna grab something from my room," Claire replied, and made sure to stand at an angle where the box, tucked under her arm, would not be seen.

"I hope you'll be finished with that office soon. It's abysmal," Nadine said with a small shake of her head.

"It certainly is. I wonder how it got that way," Claire replied and turnedto walk out again.

Nadine had every ability to at least help her daughter organize the office.

She just had chosen not to. She just chose not to do a lot of things anymore.

It wasn't that she was unable to, like her husband, and it wasn't that caring for her husband was so all-encompassing that it made anything outside of doing so impossible. She'd just decided that any inconvenience, however small, was not for her to deal with. Because of this, the vast majority of household responsibilities fell upon Claire to manage. Whether her mother was aware of the halt this had all put on her daughter's life, Claire didn't know; if her mother knew and just didn't care, Claire didn't *want* to know.

"Claire."

It was her father's voice, now, that blocked her attempt at an exit a second time. He was sharply-dressed in pressed trousers and a button-down shirt and light sweater vest. He had a freshly trimmed three-day beard and slick, combed hair, once raven-black all over, now a classic salt-and-pepper. Both Claire and her mother waited for him to finish, but he seemed to struggle.

"I seem to have, um..." He trailed off.

"It's okay, Dad. Mom, I'm going into town to run some errands later. Want me to bring anything back for you?" Claire hoped her mother wouldn't ask to go with her. She did not want to have to explain her trip to the bookstore. "I can pick up some things for you, too, Dad. Just let me know," she continued.

Nadine merely looked at her daughter blankly, as if to say with her eyes, *you should know what to get.*

"I'll just get whatever I think you two need," Claire finished, more to wrap up the conversation that felt one-sided anyway.

Her father palmed his beard and looked out the window suspiciously now. His paranoia was manageable most days - nothing more than a question or a longer look out of a window. On the "bad" days, his paranoia seemed to be triggered by anything from the knock of an unsuspecting solicitor or his wife receiving a phone call. Sometimes, a mere change in temperature could send him into a days-long tirade about his "demons." Often, Claire's mother would defer the handling of these episodes to her daughter. It would cause her great distress, Nadine would claim, then she'd sequester herself in their bedroom for the rest of the day.

Claire often thought of the day she received the call from her mother to come home. Finals week had been upon her and she was on her way out to join a study group to prepare for the hardest exam of the semester.

"I can't handle him anymore, Claire. I need you home. You need to come home. Come tomorrow," Nadine had been nearly sobbing when she'd called her daughter for help.

"Mom, what happened? I can't just drop everything and go home," Claire had tried to reason.

"Nothing happened! He lost that hideous pendant he always wore. I don't know. Maybe I misplaced it or something. It was so dreadful to look at. But it's gone now and he wants it. He says the demons will come back without it. Claire, he's gone completely mad without it. Please, please come home and help me," her mother had begged.

"Mom, can this wait? Can you ask anyone else for help? Things are really busy here and I can't just leave," Claire had tried to reason some more.

"If I had any other option, I would, Claire. Please," Nadine had insisted.

"I'll just come for the weekend and see what I can do, but I have to make it back in time for my final on Monday, Mom."

"Okay. Good. I need you here. Please come as soon as you can. Leave tomorrow," her mom had instructed, as if it might be something easy for Claire to do.

"Just for the weekend, Mom. I only have one semester left before graduating and it's going to be a hard one, so I really need to be back here to focus," she'd added.

"Sure, sure. I'll see you when you get here." And her mother hung up. Thanklessly, as she typically was.

When Claire had finally made it home, the house had been quiet and calm. She'd walked in the door to find her parents outside lounging on the back patio. At first glance, nothing had seemed out of place in the house. Upon closer inspection, however, the signs of her father's illness and her mother's denial of it had shown. Unpaid bills had been piled up in the office. The refrigerator had been empty save for takeout leftovers. Their housekeeper had clearly not been by in what looked like months. Her mind had gone straight to an old documentary she'd seen about a mother and daughter who had been wealthy socialites but somehow ended up living in a run down mansion in the Hamptons. They'd seemed oblivious to the squalor in which they lived with their dozens of feral cats and raccoons living in the attic. She'd thought this is what it must have looked like for them before the first cat moved in. Things were still nice, they'd just had a layer of dust over them. For Claire, it had been more telling than anything else.

She never returned for her final semester.

Finally in her apartment, Claire searched for a purse that would be big enough to hold the little box. Once she found one, she changed her clothes and properly cleaned and bandaged her finger before making her way back into the main house.

"Oh I don't know, darling. I'm just not in the mood for anything too fancy this evening. Let's wait to see if Claire's made dinner plans for us," Nadine said with a bored sigh.

"What about dinner?"Claire asked as she grabbed her keys from their hook beside the refrigerator.

"I was just explaining to your father that I'd rather have dinner at home tonight. If I have another French something-or-other dish, it would be too soon."

Claire pitied her mother for all the effort she had to put into still feeling like any of this new lifestyle was her choice. She was often torn between just telling her mother that what she was doing was obvious or letting her continue with the little lies she told herself and those around her.

"I was hoping to try out a new recipe tonight if that's okay with you two."

If Nadine knew the lie for the favor it was, she didn't show it. She simply turned to Raymond and shrugged a little, "Maybe tomorrow night, darling," and soaked up the loving gaze offered to her by her doting husband.

Nadine was always well aware of the power of her beauty - especially the power it had over her husband. Claire had always been told that she was the spitting image of her mother, but for all the similarities the pair shared, however, there was one glaring difference. They both shared the same slight, upward tilt of their almond-shaped eyes, but it was the color of Claire's that was remarkable. Unlike the chestnut brown of her parents' eyes, Claire's were a bright, emerald green with flecks of jade that were stark against the nearly black ring that framed the jeweled irises. When gemologists called rubies or emeralds "fiery," for the way they captured light and forced it to do their bidding, they could very well mean the same thing for Claire's eyes.

She watched her parents go up the stairs before she left. Her father had complained of a headache and her mother suggested he have a nap while she read her new book. Claire planned to leave before her mother had a chance to change her mind and want to join her. Outside, as Claire passed by the bay window of their living room, she noticed how beautiful her flower arrangement looked perched perfectly-centered, on display for passers by. A mosaic of hydrangeas sat heavily in the vase with pink and blue larkspur fanned out amongst them. White and pink dried limonium peppered the flower arrangement like a handful of powdery snow. All the pastels were hugged by fat green leaves.

If anything, she thought to herself with a self-assured grin, *I've got this.*

The uneven brick sidewalk just outside of the Cielos' home was covered in grass clippings and budding little weeds between the bricks. Claire enjoyed this and all the little details along her walk that made the town seem livelier in the late spring and early summer. Boats were back in the water, tourists had returned and outdoor vendors, with their unique wares and talents, brought life to the streets. The town had two main attractions; docks for boat lovers and more notably, the military academy that was just a few blocks away from Main Street. It was normal to see young students of the academy wandering about town in full uniform. Often, they would be seen giving tours to their visiting friends and families. "Ego Alley" was where boat owners docked to show off their wealth and carefree lifestyles. The small food market right off of Main Street beckoned to passers-by with scents of all the different foods awaiting inside.

Ahead of Claire was a woman who merrily chatted with a raw-oyster vendor. She held a freshly-shucked oyster while the vendor shook a local, favorite seasoning over it and topped it with a few drops of hot sauce. She quirked a nervous smile as he assured her she would love it.

"Do you *promise* I'll love it? I'll be very upset with you if I don't!" The woman nearly sang her words with an accent that seemed to come from everywhere at once. She held the oyster close to her brightly-smiling mouth and made a show of deciding whether she would eat it or not. People closeby encouraged her with broad, reassuring smiles.

Nearing the small crowd around the woman, Claire made her way to cross the street. As she walked by, she noticed the glint of the woman's signet pinky ring as she held the oyster. It was made of yellow gold and was set with jade. It had a gold relief cast of some ancient-looking coin. Then she took in the rest of her. The woman was statuesque and dressed like someone who regularly sat in the front row of fashion shows. Every part of her commanded attention and even a bit of awe - even her hair. Stick-straight and sable-black, it gleamed like glass and draped down her back past her bottom, stopping just short of the back of her knees. The woman had sun-drenched, olive skin and hazel eyes that seemed to sparkle with every color of eyes there ever were. Everything about her looked youthful and glamorous, but something about her just seemed older. She moved, talked and interacted as someone who watched others in their awe, but rarely experienced her own. It was as if she'd known this world and everyone in it for much longer than the years on her face would suggest.

As Claire crossed the street, she could hear a small applause from the handful of people who were encouraging the enchanting woman to try her first raw oyster. Claire reached the other side and looked back. The woman was looking directly at Claire as she wiped the corner of her mouth with a thumb. The crow from her father's office window flashed in Claire's mind as the woman's hair shone in the sun. Her brows edged toward each other as neither she nor the splendid woman looked away. It would be the second time that morning she returned the gaze of a mysterious creature. The raw oyster vendor tapped the woman on the shoulder. Before looking away to acknowledge him, the woman seemed to flash Claire a little smirk.

Claire couldn't quite remember where the bookstore was, so she picked a direction and started walking. She walked leisurely through the age-worn streets and slowed her rush to find the bookstore. There were buildings that maintained their original, early 18th century forms while others bore the nips and tucks of the dozens of facelifts they'd had since. The storefronts ranged from modern to historic and the mix of old and new had its own unique sort of charm. Along her walk through the architectural history, she'd finally gotten to the block that the bookstore was on after cutting through an alley and finding herself back on Main Street.

The bookstore was nestled between an ice-creamery that was often voted "Best in town" and a gift shop that sold handmade knickknacks. Hand-painted on its glass door was its name: *East Water Books & Antiques*. As she approached it, Claire noticed several crows perched along its hunter-green awning. She wouldn't have noticed them if not for the crow she'd seen at her own window just hours ago. And almost as if her very thoughts beckoned them, they all seemed to look at her as one stood out. It almost seemed like acknowledgement was in his small caw.

Claire walked up a ramp that met the sidewalk and sat flush with the entrance of the bookstore. The brass doorknob looked like it hadn't been changed in decades. It felt like it, too, as Claire turned the knob and its aged, inner mechanisms creaked in protest. A string of little brass bells hung over the door and clanged as Claire walked in. *If the feeling of being forgotten had a scent, this would be it*, she thought to herself as she took in the scent of old leather and dusty attics. Walking fully into the bookstore, hearing the door close behind her, somehow made her feel unnervingly separated from her own time. She had only the whine of old floorboards under her feet for company.

The bookshelves in the store seemed to come in sets and from different centuries, with ornate, gothic details giving way to the clean lines of mid-century modern. On tables scattered around the store were various featured books and collectibles. Several glass display cases held first-edition books and more valuable antiques. Claire was surprised to see that there was an antique teller's window farther in the store. It seemed to be from when the building was first a bank, complete with glass windows and a dark-stained wood frame that stopped about two feet short of the ceiling. A small ramp led up to the entryway of the teller's window where sat a scowling man she assumed was the shopkeeper.

Much of her view of him was blocked by a column of the teller's window, but she glimpsed his profile. His neatly-cut hair was the type of red that leaned brown and he had an equally kept beard that was more red than his hair. He had on a simple, gray cardigan and white t-shirt and sat straight-backed. In front of him was a ledger positioned on a high shelf at his eye-level. She thought it odd that he wore a pair of small, round sunglasses that fit snugly to his face. They were tinted dark enough that she could not see his eyes behind them.

He didn't acknowledge Claire right away and it made her feel awkward and wary. She was about to say "hello" when the man murmured something and a large paw of a hand reached over his shoulder to turn the page of the ledger. Though floorboards groaned under her slow steps, announcing her presence, he did not look her way. She approached the side opening of the teller's window to get his attention and took in the rest of him. He sat in a high-backed wheelchair, his hands purposefully placed on the armrests. He still hadn't acknowledged her when he murmured again and his companion turned another page for him. Claire edged past a display stand and cleared her throat, politely. As she waited for the shopkeeper to acknowledge her, she pulled the wooden box holding the parchment from her purse with hope it could be salvaged.

"I am not in the market for any new books at this time," he said. His voice was gruff and his tone was more terse than Claire was expecting. When he spoke, he barely shifted his face in her direction, ready to dismiss her.

The shopkeeper's companion straightened at the sight of her. Dull, blue eyes flicked in her direction. He was a rather tall and large man who took up so much space, it was a surprise Claire hadn't seen him when she walked in. His weathered face looked like it might have once been menacing. Now, as if in juxtaposition to his size, the man's countenance seemed almost meek.

"Oh I--" Claire would have stammered through some explanation about why she was there, but was cut off by the clanging of the shop bells, tumbling through the silence.

The shopkeeper looked away from his ledger for the first time since she arrived as a man and woman walked in, deep in conversation. They had no interest in the books and antiques around them as they made their way to the back of the store. The sharply dressed man seemed closer to Claire's age, maybe older by only a few years, and was listening intently to his companion. The woman, silver-haired and stout, seemed deep in some explanation or directive. Neither of them acknowledged her as they walked past.

"What can I help you with, then?" the shopkeeper said as he drew Claire's attention back.

Her cheeks warmed as she realized she'd been distracted by her study of the pair who had just walked in.

"Oh. I'm so sorry," Claire almost squeaked out as she pulled the wooden box out of her purse. As she opened the box and held it out to the man in the teller's window, she explained further, "I heard you restore first-editions and antique documents here. I was hoping you could help me with this parchment. I'm afraid I've damaged it."

"I need to see it up close," the shopkeeper said as his large companion made to step down the ramp and approached Claire.

"May I?" The shopkeeper spoke more softly this time; almost soothingly.

In concert with the shopkeeper's request, the large man, now towering over Claire, reached out a calloused and scarred hand. In that moment, it seemed as though everyone in the bookstore studied each other and with as many reasons as there were sets of cutting glances. Even the man and woman, who had no previous interest in her, now paused their murmuring to lend attention.

"Sure. Of course," Claire said as she pulled the parchment out of the box and held it out, albeit nervously to the shopkeeper's companion to whom she had yet to speak directly. The large man brushed her bandaged finger with his own when he took the parchment and paused. He looked over his shoulder at the shopkeeper and then back to her finger.

"What happened to your hand?" the shopkeeper asked without taking his eyes off his ledger. The large man only loomed over Claire, waiting for the answer. They both studied her bandaged finger as she told the story about how she'd found the box that belonged to her father and cut herself trying to free it from its drawer.

"Give it here," the shopkeeper ordered. The large man gave Claire a small nod as he turned back to deliver it.

The red ribbon looked dainty in his pinched fingers as he untied it while walking back up the ramp to hold the parchment in front of the shopkeeper. The smear, when the parchment was opened, had been across the top left corner. The shopkeeper jerked his chin, slightly, in a tilt motion and the large man turned the parchment so that the smear was on the bottom right. It was in the same way someone would turn a letter that had been opened upside down. He studied the parchment as if he was reading from it. He looked so engrossed that Claire did not want to interrupt, despite her growing confusion over the fact that it was blank. Even the man and woman there had moved closer to the teller's window, practically leaning into the opening. Claire hadn't even noticed their approach, studying the shopkeeper and the parchment as if it was as much their business as it was hers.

She felt a rush of panic and discomfort as she began to apologize and excuse herself. "I'm sorry. I think this was a mistake," she said nervously.

She began making her way to the window with an already-stretched-out hand and the shopkeeper's attention fell back onto her. The large man pulled the parchment toward himself and raised a bear's paw of a hand in what was supposed to be a reassuring gesture. It only served to frustrate Claire as her face contorted into a scowl.

"Is your father able to come see me?" the shopkeeper asked, drawing Claire's attention from the parchment.

"Why do you need to see my father? I just need to know if you can remove the blood or not." Claire's frustration fell away to confusion as she searched the shopkeeper's face for an explanation and her polite tone shifted into something more curt.

Part of her attention caught on the man and woman who were now opening a door that was partially hidden by a display case. The woman entered first. The man held the door and looked over his shoulder at Claire. Eyes the color of mountains in the distance met hers just before he disappeared behind it. The town was so old and had so much history, things like hidden doors in the back of shops were no surprise to Claire. Stories of secret societies and generation-sold mysteries haunted the town as much as its famous ghosts. They kept its age on display and celebrated an unwillingness to move too far forward with the times. The stories would be easier to dismiss as folk lore, exaggerated for tourists and haunted bar crawls, if it weren't for things like that door and the people now on the other side of it.

"I cannot undo what you have done," the shopkeeper said with a small frown.

Claire would have allowed herself to become angry and demand the parchment be given back had the man not chosen such curious words.

"Why did you ask about my father?" It was the only question that Claire could articulate through her confusion.

"This is his, is it not?" The shopkeeper raised his brow at the parchment and then looked at her.

The large man came around the shopkeeper and held the parchment beside the ledger so both were in view. He then flipped through the ledger with his free hand, pausing at each page, awaiting instruction. Claire watched as the shopkeeper glanced at the parchment and then to the pages as if using one or the other as a reference.

"My father won't be able to speak to you. He isn't well and hasn't been for some time. Why do you need to speak to him?" She walked closer wishing for a better angle to see the ledger and discern anything from the pages. Her gaze flicked back to the shopkeeper and when she spoke to her own reflection in his sunglasses, it unnerved her even more.

"It looks like you were actually reading from that thing and there's nothing on it." Claire's voice shook a little as she realized just how strange it all had quickly become and how desperately she wanted answers.

"I was," the shopkeeper said flatly.

Claire stared at the men incredulously as she tried to find words, but had none.

"I am sorry. I know you are confused."

"You just told me that you were reading from a piece of paper that clearly has nothing written on it. I'm more than confused and I think I just want it back now so I can leave."

The shopkeeper looked as though he might refuse, but didn't.

"Okay," he said. And he moved his chin in the direction of the large man. Claire hadn't expected him to oblige so easily, but was relieved nonetheless.

"The page is not blank. You just cannot see what is on it. I also understand you are having difficulty with this, but at this very moment, this is all I can offer you. You will have all the answers you seek very soon," the shopkeeper said, cutting off the string of questions that would have begun to spill from Claire.

Her hands slackened to her side. Her mouth opened and closed with questions that fought for priority and became stuck at the bottleneck of her frustration. She mostly figured this had to be some kind of joke - that these men enjoyed toying with unsuspecting people who wandered into the shop. But there was such seriousness about the men, so heavy was the air in the shop that she couldn't bring herself to just laugh this off and call them crazy.

The shopkeeper looked at her from the ledger and pointed at the front door with his chin. Claire studied the shopkeeper's sunglasses, imagining the eyes behind them, noticing the permanent scowl lines etched between his brows.

"Okay. This has been...not what I expected," she said with a resigned tone.

Those scowl lines deepened. A small glint drew Claire's gaze from the shopkeeper's face to his necklace; hanging from it was a ring. It was gold and had a striking similarity to the signet ring worn by the mystifying woman from earlier. The shopkeeper's was set with black onyx with a gilded quill printed on it.

Claire turned toward the door and balanced herself under the weight of her confusion and what had just happened; she felt nervous, maybe even scared.

"Thank you for your help," she paused, then continued, "I guess."

"Good luck," he said, looking at the door as if to encourage her departure.

With nothing else to say or dare ask, Claire pushed out the door, bells clanging noisily behind her.

The town outside still looked the same. It still sounded the same. Tourists still milled about and locals still sold their wares, but it felt as if the world had shifted ever-so-slightly to one side for her. It was an enjoyably mild day in the picturesque town, but Claire barely noticed as her mind strained for understanding.

Finally back home, Claire trudged inside, the day having caught up to her. Her father was already up from his nap and lounging in an armchair that had the best view of the front door. Her mother sat on the couch adjacent to him, reading a book. She couldn't help but stare, hopeful that she might get answers from one of them. She decided she would tackle the office once again to try to find anything that could lead to answers there. She'd planned to do it after they'd gone to sleep.

The afternoon had come and gone. Claire had made dinner and afterward, a pot of chamomile tea to encourage her parents' early retirement for the evening. She had to make a conscious effort not to pace, waiting for them to get tired enough to head upstairs to bed. She tried to be interested in a newspaper article as her parents lounged in the living room with their tea, quietly conversing. There was finally some hope in the form of her father's long yawn and slowly blinking eyes.

She took in a breath to make her suggestion that they go to bed, but she didn't get the chance to as a knock at the front door barreled through the quiet of the house.

In one moment, the house and its occupants were at peace, ready to sleep for the night. In the next, Claire was watching as her father fell to the floor and gripped his right hand in pain. He screamed in agony and fear. Her mother was on her knees beside him in an instant, hands on his shoulders.

"What is it?! What's wrong with you?! Are you having a heart attack?!"

Nadine frantically searched Raymond's face and body as if she could find signs of a heart attack there.

Around them, the sounds and howls of a baying hound shook the house, assaulting them from all quarters. Instinctively, all three of them covered their ears and searched for the beast from which the howling came. Raymond's eyes were wide and trained on the front door. Claire frantically tore through her fear and confusion and placed herself between her parents and the threshold of the room in which they now cowered.

"*He's here, he's here, he's here, he's here. He's here! No! I need more time! NO no no no no no!*" Raymond babbled as he stood up, pushing Nadine aside, and turned in a circle as if searching for a hiding place.

Claire and her mother looked at each other, wide-eyed. They both started as yet another knock, louder this time, stopped Raymond where he stood. Nadine went to him and the two shared a knowing and fearful look. Noticing it, Claire looked on at the both of them, bewildered. Raymond held up his right hand where, on the side, just below his pinky, was a burn wound that was not there moments ago. The burn was small, about an inch long. It was an angry red and had already begun to blister.

"Raymond, your hand! Let me see," Nadine demanded, pulling his hand toward herself as the wound continued to fester. "Raymond. What have you done?" Her voice was shaky, her eyes wide and accusatory, welling with fear.

"Dad. There is--" Claire kept looking at his hand and forced herself to keep speaking as her reality fractured before her. "Dad. That wasn't there. That wasn't there a minute ago! What is happening?!"

She couldn't make out what the brand was but that it had a clear outline and looked like it was just stamped onto her father's hand. Some type of feather or oddly shaped leaf. She looked around the room for what could have burned him as if there could be a logical explanation for any of what was happening.

Another knock, less demanding this time, startled all three of them into stillness.

"I have to answer it." Raymond spoke clearly, if not fearfully; his face leached of color.

"Who cares about whoever is at the door?! Your hand, Dad! What happened to your hand?!" Claire managed between heavy breaths.

Another knock.

"WAIT," Claire bellowed the command in the direction of the front door, fear and confusion be damned.

The knocking stopped and she turned back to her parents who were now standing side-by-side. They looked prepared to run, but to where? She had no idea where she'd take them and she had no idea from whom they'd even be running. She just knew that everything in her told her to. Every bone in her body ached with the instinct to just go and escape to as far away as possible and never look back. She lunged for the phone and told her parents to stand back as she began to dial the police. She would ask for an ambulance for her father and hoped that the approaching sirens would scare away whoever was at their front door. While she didn't know who was there, something deep inside her knew it was someone to be feared.

"Mom, I'm calling an ambulance. We need to get dad to the hospital," she said as she picked up the phone and brought it to her ear, only to pause just before dialing. She looked at the phone, pressed the hook several times and looked at it again. There was no tone.

"The phone isn't working," she said, less surprised than she thought she should be. "Okay, we're going out the back. Come on. We'll call an ambulance from next door," Claire ordered as she grabbed for her purse and made to usher her parents out of the room.

The purse slipped from her grasp in her haste and fell, spilling its contents on the floor. She hurried to shove everything back in it, but as she reached for the little box holding the parchment, the end of her father's cane was atop it.

He moved his cane and stooped down to pick up the box.

"You found it," he said, a note of relief in his tone, and opened it. He let the box drop to the floor as he untied the ribbon and opened the parchment. His cane fell, too, as he lifted his branded hand to his mouth. He repeated himself from behind his hand as his eyes fell upon the smear of blood. "You found it."

After another great howl split the air, Claire was certain she could hear something sniffing and pawing at the door. As if he didn't even hear the howl, Raymond straightened the chair he fell out of and sat down. His eyes never left the blood stained page in his hand. It was as if the past several minutes hadn't happened at all and it was an invited guest at their front door.

This wasn't the time for another one of his episodes. Claire needed him lucid, able to answer questions, able to run if she could just come up with a plan for them.

"Dad. We need to go. We don't have time for this! Mom, get your bag. We're going out back. Dad, let's go," Claire barked the orders as she went to grab her father by the wrist and drag him out if she had to. She meant to tear that confounded sheet of paper in half and step on it on their way out, but their escape was again interrupted.

Knock... Knock... Knock.

The pause between each knock sounded like a patient reminder that there was someone still waiting there.

"Let's **go**," she said one last time, pulling her father out of the chair and shoving her mother forward to get all three of them to the kitchen door.

Though confused, Nadine did as instructed, grabbing her bag and heading out the room. Raymond seemed to finally snap out of it and followed. Claire, leaving the parchment on the coffee table, looked over her shoulder to make sure her father was following and turned back around to see striking dark-gray eyes meet hers. The stranger had gone from waiting patiently outside, to now standing in their foyer, as if he'd been there the entire time. It was the sharply dressed man from the bookstore. Claire recognized him right away and he recognized her. Her mother screamed and stumbled toward the kitchen, pulling on Claire's sleeve, but a low growl stopped her in her tracks. They could see nothing in the hallway leading to the kitchen, but they could feel it there, hear it, smell the distinct must of fur and the earth that dirtied it. Its presence felt enormous. While the growl was low, the sound of it came from eye level. They were trapped.

"*Seir. Relax*," said the stranger with a small shift of his face toward the hallway.

The walls of the hallway shuddered along with the sound of something that seemed to fill it entirely, dropping its weight to the floor. It let out a deep groan and the warm air of a huff blew past Claire's and her mother's legs. They both frantically took in the hallway that, except for how it felt, smelled and sounded, *looked* completely empty.

"Pardon the intrusion. I waited for some time outside. My name is Niran and I am here to see Mr. Raymond Cielo," the stranger said to Claire.

She and her mother were now backing into the living room. Nadine gripped Claire's arm so tightly, the pain radiated up her arm and into her shoulder. Claire realized her mother wasn't pulling her toward herself, but pushing her in front as a shield. Her panic was broken, for the briefest moment, by the shock and hurt of it. Her mother had been ducking and eyeing the stranger called Niran with no concern for Claire's safety.

"How did you get in here?" Claire asked him shakily. "And what the hell is in the hallway?!"

"Knocking is really just a formality," he said as he walked past her and her mother to where her father had staggered back into his chair, stunned and wordlessly shifting his gaze between the plaque above the door and Niran who now stood before him. "And that is Seir in the hallway. He is with me," he informed them, as he followed Raymond's line of sight to the plaque behind him.

"Lovely place you have here, Raymond," he drawled with an undertone of sarcasm. He found his place at the couch and sat down with a small sigh, placing an ankle over a knee.

"Now, let's take a look at what we've got here," he said as he grabbed the open parchment from the coffee table.

That god damned paper, Claire thought to herself as she pulled out of her mother's grasp, leaving her still frozen in fear. She dared a couple steps closer and glanced in the hallway that now sounded of light, rhythmic breathing.

Interlaced with the sound of that breathing was another sound, like muffled screams echoing deep in the woods. It was faint, but nonetheless discomforting. Despite everything around her that made no sense, she still thought if she could just get the police on the line.

"I've called the police," she stammered. "I'm sure they're on the way. You don't wanna be here when they get here." She poured every ounce of confidence she could into the threat that was also a lie.

"You probably don't want to hold your breath on that. Even if the phone did work," he said with a knowing glance. "And you were able to get them over here, I don't believe there would be much they could do to help you." He scanned the parchment --reading from it in the same way the shopkeeper did earlier that day-- and gave a nod in the direction of the hallway. "So try not to worry. Seir won't harm you."

"But you will? And what is it about that stupid paper?" Claire asked, exasperated. She wanted answers, but also hoped the questions would buy her time to come up with another escape plan. She dared several more steps closer and stood behind the armchair that sat across the coffee table from her father who, strangely, wouldn't acknowledge her. Arms crossed, she stared at the side of her father's face, as he seemed to strain under the weight of it.

"This 'stupid paper' meant a great deal to your father at one point, didn't it, Raymond?" Niran said as he leaned back comfortably on the couch as if he'd sat there a thousand times before and continued to read from it as if it was just the Sunday news.

"Raymond, you sly dog, you. Did you plan this all out?" he asked, smirking and raising his brows.

"I don't... I'm not sure what you're talking about. I didn't..." Raymond stammered.

"*Don't do that.*" Niran's tone went from cavalier to flat and almost threatening with those three words. He leveled a look at Raymond that cut through him and the old man gripped his cane, as if the wood and metal would protect him any more than his worthless plaques. He dropped his eyes and he bowed his head as if in submission.

"You know exactly what you did and so do I," Niran said and finished his scan of the parchment and placed it back down on the table.

Claire could barely breathe as she felt the air tighten around her. She continued looking at her father who continued making a point not to meet her eyes.

"Can you please tell me what's going on?" she asked, weakly now, all of her anger and frustration having left her with only exhaustion and dread in their wake. She looked to Niran for answers, down at the parchment where her smear of blood still stained it, and then back at her father, who seemed apologetic, deferential - why, Claire didn't know.

"Soon enough." Niran didn't look at Claire as he said this, rather at Raymond. And he didn't have the calm, cavalier tone he had just moments ago. Nobody spoke. Neither Raymond nor Claire seemed to even breathe.

"I hope you didn't think this would be easy for you, Raymond." The relaxed air had returned to his tone as he spoke with a dark smirk.

Raymond lifted his chin slightly, seeming to cling to some former version of himself that was once confident and commanding. His hand trembled upon the carved top of his cane as he dared eye contact with Niran. Though he was sharply dressed and composed, the look he speared through Raymond's facade was feral, demanding.

"I don't... I don't know what you mean," Raymond, once again, denied.

In one swift movement, almost too quick to follow, Niran stood up and was upon Raymond. He snatched the shaking hand Raymond had on his cane and gripped it at the wrist. Niran caught the falling cane and threw it aside. It clattered to the floor as Raymond held his free arm across his face and began sobbing.

"What are you doing?! *Stop*! I'm calling the police!" Claire lunged for him, ready to fight him off of her cowering father.

She was stopped short as he held up her father's hand and turned it to look at the brand on his skin, which had begun to glow as if a fire burned underneath it. She could make no sense of what she was seeing, though her mind worked furiously in an attempt to. Its radiance revealed an intricate design of the head of a wheat stalk, not that of a feather or leaf, as she had previously thought. If his sobbing was any indication, the brand was causing her father intense pain as well. In her awe and confusion, Claire had forgotten she meant to defend him.

"I can't do this! I can't do this!" Nadine exclaimed as she stumbled toward the front door. She shrank slightly, at the large shuffling that came from the hallway - seemingly in response to her outburst. There was a deep sigh and another shuffle before the sounds and movements from the hallway stilled again.

Niran ignored the screeching woman and only stared daggers into Raymond who was on his knees now, at his feet. Her parents' wails snapped Claire out of her confusion and brought her back to the chaos around her. She looked to her mother who seemed prepared to leave her at the mercy of this stranger. She looked at her father, more pathetic and broken than she'd ever seen him. And she looked at Niran who calmly held Raymond at the wrist.

No wailing, no sobbing, no threats of police or even a locked door would stop this man from doing what he'd gone there to do. Claire ran through every way she might stop all of this and came up short. She covered her face with both hands for a moment and forced herself to stop; forced herself to meet Niran at his level, or at least the level at which she perceived him to be.

"Please. Whatever he did... Let me help figure out a solution." Claire's forced calm somehow made its way past her mother, over her father, and to Niran. He turned his head slightly in Claire's direction before speaking.

"There's nothing you can do for him now," he said, his gaze still fixed upon her father.

Nadine let out a fresh, new wail that unnerved Clair to hear. She had been trying to open the door, but could not as she slid down to the floor, still grasping the doorknob. Claire turned her face away and squeezed her eyes shut at the sight and sound of it. Raymond crumpled before Niran, protests choked out between sobs. He'd gripped his pant leg and Niran derisively shook him off.

"Whatever it is, I'll handle it! Does he owe you money? I can get it for you. If it's anything else, I'll take care of it somehow. Just talk to me. Let him go. *Please*," Claire begged, forcing herself to speak as calmly as possible.

"Let him go! Let me out!" Nadine's voice broke as she wailed her plea to Niran.

"This debt is only for Raymond Cielo to pay," he said and yanked on Raymond's wrist causing him to twist to his side. He fell awkwardly, grabbing at the air.

Claire's eyes stung as the tears she'd been holding back threatened to betray her. She could feel her heart pounding harder than it ever had. Her legs were shaking and her breaths were uneven. That small part of her, the part in everyone that still thought like a child, was sure it was all just a nightmare. Niran knelt down to be eye-to-eye with the weeping man in his unforgiving grip. Raymond only cowered, eyes squeezed shut, and tried to turn away as he felt his face so close to his own that his breath warmed his cheek.

"As per your agreement with my associate," he hissed, "I've come to collect what you owe." Niran, whose face up until this moment had been placid, somehow managed a look of simultaneous disgust and satisfaction. when he said it.

"You've got it wrong! It should be her! I made sure of it. Check the contract! Check for her blood! I made sure she would find it," Raymond exclaimed, still cowering.

Silence fell over the room like the darkness of a blackout. Niran's grip on Raymond's wrist tightened painfully for a moment longer and then let go. He stood up and took a step back as even Raymond quieted to the sound of what he'd just admitted. Claire focused on him, his words, the implications. Niran said nothing, did nothing. He only stood with hands in his pockets, looking down at Raymond whose face was now buried in both hands. It could have been seconds or minutes the four of them lingered, trapped in that soundless control.

Though what Raymond had just said may have had no effect on the world as a whole, it shattered Claire's like a rock through a window. *He made sure I would find it*, she thought. Time for Claire had slowed to a painful drag of every jagged-edged emotion over her thick, muddy thoughts. She heard the words over and over again as the pieces of this puzzle slowly made connections along the edges. *It was supposed to be me? He made sure of it?*

Even the sounds of large shuffling and another huff that came from the hallway seemed not to register. Nothing about her relationship with her parents had ever been much more than their keeping her clothed, fed and educated. There were, of course, small affections here and there, but they were never very close nor sentimental. Yet, she'd loved and cared for them and believed they'd loved and cared for her, too, despite the coldness of their relationship. It must have been a thousand little times one or the other had let her down, and it was always okay. It sounded and it felt like a betrayal... *It can't mean what it sounds like*, Claire thought to herself. The weight of her father's words pulled Claire's face down into an anguished frown as she finally took her eyes off of him and looked at Niran. She could barely find her voice as she began to quietly ask him, "What?"

It was the only word, from every single one in her vocabulary, that she could speak. "What" was asked as a lifeline between herself and her father - an opportunity for what she heard to be wrong. She asked "what" in the only way and from the only place in her mind and heart that any words could come from. It wasn't only a question; it was a *plea*. She couldn't rewind time to before any of this happened, she couldn't take it out of her head and just not know it anymore. This "what" was the first singing shatter of her breaking heart. This was the kind of "what" that she wouldn't wish on her worst enemy to ever have to ask.

She sought answers from her mother, but she was too preoccupied with her own safety and her own escape to even acknowledge what was said. That, in and of itself, was another heartbreaking disappointment for Claire.

"What does all this mean?" Claire fought herself to ask more clearly.

At the sound of her voice, Niran looked to Claire and softened slightly.

"I need to complete my business with your father before we can get to the answers to your questions," he said plainly, yet gently.

Raymond got up to gingerly sit back in his chair, his head down as he averted his gaze from his daughter. With no other direction or course of action, Claire returned to her seat directly across the coffee table from her father. Her mother merely slumped at the front door, still trying weakly to open it.

"Claire, I-" Raymond started.

"--No, no," interrupted Niran. "You've said and done quite enough," he finished with a look void of sympathy or respect.

Raymond looked as though he might argue, but instead just let his head drop in another submissive bow. Claire could only stare blankly at the parchment, the eye of this dreadful storm she could neither understand nor escape.

Niran studied the small family for a long, quiet moment. Nobody spoke. They didn't even look at each other. They were like the inscrutable characters of a painting that could be interpreted a thousand different ways.

"We're going to need some privacy," Niran said, looking between Claire and her mother.

"No," Claire shakily replied. She looked at Niran resolute, though fearful.

"She still protects you, Raymond. A snake in the grass like you, she still protects you." Niran stood over him, one hand out of his pocket, toying with a signet ring he wore on his right hand.

"I don't care. Whatever he did, we'll figure it out. I can't just leave him here with you. You could hurt him."

"I assure you, Miss, since the first drop of your blood touched that," he said, locking eyes with Claire while motioning to the parchment, "I cannot touch him. Well, not in any way that would matter." With that, he cut his eyes to Raymond.

Claire looked at her father who was once a proud, confident man, now reduced to this pathetic, whimpering thing before her. She looked to Niran for some kind of reassurance that he was telling the truth, and had no plans to hurt her father.

"Nothing is going to happen to him." His tone had become even again, impatient.

"Please, listen to me, Claire, you'll have plenty of time. I swear. You'll have time, just like I did," her father proclaimed.

Niran stopped toying with his ring and turned all of his attention back to Raymond.

"Do any of you people actually read the contract?" His look of pitiless disdain bore into Raymond.

"I've read it," Raymond insisted.

"You didn't read a word of it, *snake*." Niran shook his head slowly as he huffed. "Do you really think you were the first person to try to outsmart us? What kind of unchecked hubris have you allowed to govern your life? You had six months left on your contract. *Six months*." He stood beside Raymond's chair and with one hand on the back of it, leaned in close to Raymond's face and directed his attention to Claire sitting across from them. "Now, I want you to think about the deadline at the end of those six months and to whom it will transfer." Both Niran and Raymond now looked at Claire.

"It can't be. It said in the contract that I could--"

"You're all the same. Come on, now. I haven't got all night," Niran cut in.

He reached over the chair, grabbed Raymond by the back of his shirt collar and pulled upward. The motion forced Raymond to stand awkwardly and Claire turned her face away. Nadine covered her mouth with a hand to stifle a cry. Niran positioned himself so that he and the cowering man would be face-to-face. Claire reached out to protest, to try to help her father, to try to understand anything that was happening.

"I can't let you do this," she said shakily, as she made to put her body between her father and Niran. She felt her father's hand on her back as if to accept her protection and the touch was abhorrent. She jerked just out of his reach, but stood her ground with Niran.

"I'm sorry. You will let me do this," he said with a hint of pity.

Claire's mouth dropped open as her body betrayed her will and she easily stepped aside for him. He gave her a slight nod as she continued to back away, leaving plenty of room for him to access her father.

"Raymond Cielo," Niran said as he looked down at the pinky ring he turned on his right hand. "I release you from your contractual obligation," he finished, his voice dripping with impatience and disdain.

With that, Niran reached for a handshake. Raymond only looked down at the awaiting hand and then at Claire. All she could do was stare, barely breathing. Without warning, he gripped Raymonds hand. At the same time, Niran's invisible companion entered the room. Movement could be felt, indirectly, in the same way the beast's true, enormous, form could only be seen out of the corner of their eye. It padded toward Niran and then circled the room as a sentry would. Raymond's eyes widened and his mouth dropped open. His entire body shivered violently as Niran's gaze seemed to pour into Raymond's eyes.

Though the darkness of night had already fallen, everything seemed to get even darker. Silence constricted itself around the vocal cords of Claire and Nadine like a python; Claire had the same, pinned feeling of a night terror in her bones. Neither could move. Neither could speak. Claire could see, but couldn't remember what she saw from one moment to the next. Raymond dropped to his knees as drool began to seep from the corner of his frightful, open mouth.

Niran continued to hold the handshake tightly as he pierced Raymond with his glare. Though nothing immediately perceptible had changed about his appearance, he had become not wholly of this world. He had become something they not only saw, but also felt in their bones and in their chests. It was as if discomfort, and frightening unease wafted from Niran in tendrils. The feeling of him had *become* him, and was taking air from the room in giant gulps.

Niran stood calmly over Raymond and his eyes emptied of color, life, humanity. To look into them was to fall on your back onto the floor of unfathomable depth and the darkness within them. Time bent to the will of Niran's unleashed power as the small family remained locked within his invisible grip. Mere seconds had passed but if someone had told the Cielo family that they had been trapped, frozen in those positions for days, they'd have believed it. Even the tears going down Nadine's face merely trailed lazily like cooled molasses. And for every terror, every choked scream, every agony the three felt, there was not a single sound in the room.

Through the nightmare, Claire was feeling with every fiber of her being, she could hear the wind blowing through the magnolia tree just outside the window. She knew that she'd never truly had a nightmare. She knew that she only ever thought she did. This moment, this unending silence that held her within a phantom grip was what nightmares grasped at, limited still by the imagination of the sleeper. This transcended even dreams, for Claire could never have imagined any of this. She could only watch as Niran finally released her father from that baneful handshake. He slumped to the floor and curled into himself. His eyes were vacant, wild from whatever he'd just returned from.

Niran then turned away from her father and took a step toward Claire. It was as if undiluted fear stepped aside to introduce her to incomprehensible terror. His eyes were so black, they swallowed light from around his face. Another step and Claire could see specs of dark gray within the swirling. Another step toward Claire and the light-swallowing blackness had become mere wisps of shadow snaking over his furrowed brow. By the time he was before her, looking down at her, his eyes were clear again, as if she had imagined it all. He sat on the edge of the coffee table and faced Claire. Seeing her terror, he dipped his chin slightly as he looked away from her.

As if he somehow plugged the hole that was emptying horrors onto the family, Claire felt herself lighten, breathing in deeply. She was still fearful, but it wasn't the agonizing fright from moments ago. He took in a cleansing breath and held his hand out to Claire in the same way he did for her father. She did not move. She only continued to stare into him.

"I'm going to need you to take my hand," he said more softly than he'd spoken since his arrival.

The two searched each other's faces and Claire was the first to look away. She looked down at Niran's open palm and loosened the grip her hands had on each other, lifting her right hand ever-so-slightly. Her whole body trembled as she resigned herself to whatever fate she imagined had befallen her father. In that terror-filled silence, Nadine made a tiny, distressed sound and Claire suddenly remembered her.

"My mother," Claire said, barely above a whisper. "She's--" Claire paused as she looked at her mother then. "If I'm like him, she won't be able to..."

Niran curled the fingers of his right hand into a loose fist and finally acknowledged Claire's frightened mother, still slumped in front of the door. Though the rest of her body remained frozen, Nadine's eyes were wide and wildly moving between him and Claire.

"Nothing is going to happen to you right now that will change anything about you," he said, reassuringly to Claire. "I promise you."

Claire's confusion was clear as her mouth parted, in search of a question for which she didn't have the words. Niran rested his now-clasped hands in his lap as he took in a breath to explain.

"My father-"

"--Is fine. I assure you." Niran looked over his shoulder at Raymond who was still on the floor. He lay in the fetal position with his hands covering his head. He was unnervingly still, but was breathing calmly, almost as if he was Asleep.

"Many years ago, your father made an agreement with an associate of mine. The terms of the agreement were drawn up in this contract." Niran turned and picked up the parchment from behind him.

To Claire's shock and awe, it now had words on it. The smear of blood was juxtaposed against the elegant script of the document which had now revealed itself. She didn't blink as she watched the words shift about on the page to reveal more of itself to her. Sentences became paragraphs and then shifted back to sentences. Paragraphs expanded from one to five and back to one. The script changed sizes from large and perfectly readable to so tiny, Claire couldn't even make out the words.

"The agreement," Niran continued, "was sealed with a handshake." He paused to let Claire take in what he was saying. She listened, intently. "Much like any other contract, my associate agreed to give your father certain things, for which he agreed to pay with, for all intents and purposes, *his soul*. A contract can be transferred from one individual to another," he said as he brushed a thumb over Claire's smear of blood on the page, "with a blood signature and another handshake. We have your blood signature right here - we just need the handshake now. I strongly urge you to take it." Niran paused to allow the information to settle within Claire.

The hush that fell over the room this time was different. Claire only stared at her streak of blood while her mind raced through every confusing and surreal moment of the day.

"How can this be real?" Claire asked. She shook her head slowly, dubiously, as part of her wondered if she truly wanted the answer to the question. Niran opened his mouth to speak, but Claire held a hand up to cut him off. She bowed her head into the palm of her other hand and continued.

"Do you get what I'm saying?" she scoffed, lifting her head from her palm to face Niran. "Are you trying to tell me you're the devil or something? My father sold his soul to you for what," she said as she looked around the room, gesturing around her; "for this?" she finished with a scoffing laugh. "And now, what? So I cut my finger and got my blood on that stupid paper," she said, her voice rising as she leaned forward to challenge Niran. "Now it's *my* soul that belongs to you? What is supposed to happen to me in these six months that I apparently have left?" Her look was sharper than her words as her breath quickened.

Niran did not try to answer her questions, but he did not dismiss them either. As he listened to her, he folded the contract back up and held it in his lap. Claire pressed her lips together and clenched her jaw as she reined herself in, looking past him at her father, who still lay on the floor.

"What's gonna happen to him now? Hm? He's free to go?"

"Yes," Niran answered succinctly.

Claire laughed. She laughed heartily and with a smile that was too bright, too big for what was happening. A small part of her was surprised to know that this would be her reaction to these unimaginable events taking place. She wasn't giving up, but it felt like she was giving in. She looked at her mother and continued to laugh and then to her father on the floor. The sight of him turned her bright, big smile to a small grin. It was then that she finally understood why some people say, "It's better to just laugh than to cry."

"Right." Her grin dimmed to resignation.

With that, Claire held her right hand out to Niran. Her heart raced and her breaths were quick and shallow. She lifted her chin and in her best impression of Nadine Cielo, looked down her nose at him. Her defiant glare cut through his empty one as she waited for him to take her hand and bring her to whatever hell from which her father had just returned.

"I acknowledge your claim to this contract, made by blood signature."

Claire's breath caught and she squeezed her eyes closed as he grasped her hand in his own. She swallowed and took in a sharp breath as she felt his hand squeeze hers firmly, yet gently. The world stilled. She felt the air flowing through her nose and into her lungs, smooth and cleansing. With each exhale, she felt heaviness leave her. Again, she heard the rustling leaves of the magnolia trees outside. The sound draped over her and blanketed her in calm and understanding.

She knew. She *understood.*

She'd never felt such clarity before. Though it did nothing to take away the fear and anger she was feeling, it provided her with solid ground upon which she could stand. Moments ago, the screaming *why* and *how* in her mind had her descending into a free-fall. Now, however, those screaming questions were quieted.

This was, indeed, real. Life, as she knew it, would end in six months.

The sound of Niran clearing his throat jarred Claire into returning to her surroundings. She looked down at her hand, feeling as if she'd just woken up from a very long sleep. The understanding remained, but the calm and the peace that had come with it had left her entirely.

"I thought--" She cut herself off, not wanting to say what she thought.

Niran stood up carefully and adjusted his pinky ring as he said, "I'll need you to come by the bookstore first thing in the morning tomorrow. Your contract has yet to be written, recorded; all things that will be explained to you. You'll need to bring this with you," he told her, dropping the parchment back onto the coffee table. He looked back at Raymond, who had begun to stir from what seemed to be a deep sleep. "He should be fine when he wakes up," he said, waving his hand in Raymond's direction.

Claire dismissed her father completely and stood up to follow the man as he made his way to the front door. They both walked past Nadine who quickly shuffled aside and averted her eyes. "You're just going to leave? Mr. Niran, I--"

Claire was stopped mid-sentence as he stopped just at the threshold of the living room and turned to face her.

"Please, it's just 'Niran,' and, yes. There's nothing left for me to do this evening."

Claire opened her mouth several times to speak words she didn't have. There was nothing. Niran waited for Claire to find her words and when she didn't, he turned to continue out the door. He put a hand on the knob and turned to her again.

"Please go straight to the bookstore first thing in the morning. It is imperative you go straight there. Make no stops. Speak to no one," he instructed again.

"I- okay," Claire said with a resigned huff.

"Seir," he beckoned. And Claire looked back into the living room as she felt the large creature move past her and out the door Niran held open.

Nadine let out another distressed sound at the sight of the door opening easily for him.

Claire had no idea what she should do other than follow Niran and the invisible Seir outside. She caught herself and stopped on the steps of the front porch as he continued to walk away. He didn't acknowledge that she had followed him as he reached in his pocket and pulled out a small notebook and pencil.

"Will you be there?" Claire's voice broke through the night's stillness. It was louder and more desperate than she wanted it to be.

Niran stopped and turned around to face her. He had every intent to answer Claire, but instead studied her face for longer than necessary. He opened his mouth to speak.

"I mean," Claire continued. "I don't know who I should speak to when I get to the bookstore."

She looked down at her feet to steady herself and looked back up at Niran. His face was obscured by darkness. Claire saw a flash of his unearthly face from earlier. The only movement she could see was him slipping a hand back into his pocket. Niran took a step forward to answer her. His face was then visible again under the dim light of the street lamp. There was peace that surrounded them in that moment that neither of them hurried to escape. Niran's face was unreadable. Claire, for all that she'd gone through, breathed steadily and waited patiently for his answer.

"I will be there," he answered plainly.

She looked out into the street in the direction of the bookstore as if she could see it from where she stood. By the time she looked back at Niran, he'd begun walking again. She didn't stop him this time. She only watched him until he was a small silhouette disappearing into the distant dark. She did not know how long she stood there looking at nothing, and it was tiredness that finally took her attention from the end of the street and called her inside. As she closed the door behind her, Claire peered into the living room and found her father sitting again in his chair, head in his hands. Her mother was nowhere to be found. She only continued walking to the back of the house and to her apartment.

There was nothing left for Claire to feel but heavy exhaustion. It dragged her into a deep, dreamless sleep.

part two

a handshake

terms

the first to arrive

a gasp for air

Just before the light of dawn rolled over the dark of night, Claire rose from her brief respite. She'd gone through her morning routine as if it was the start to any other day; as if the evening before hadn't happened. As she finger-combed her damp hair she caught a glimpse of her right hand in the mirror. She thought she might have the same brand her father had on his, but saw nothing.

On her way out the front door, Claire walked back into the living room to grab the contract from the coffee table. Part of her hoped she didn't see it there - that it had all been some kind of nightmare. But there it sat, exactly as it had been left. It wasn't a nightmare. *Perhaps the nightmare was just beginning*, she thought. Whether her parents were awake or still asleep or even in the house, Claire didn't know; she didn't care. The only thing she could steady herself with was the task she'd been given to go to the bookstore first thing in the morning. That small task was the only thing keeping her mind in one piece. It was the only thing that stood between her and the abyss of dark and terrible thoughts she could have easily fallen into.

Every consideration had crossed her mind as she made her way to the bookstore. The thought of every kind of escape, every kind of bargain, every kind of new reality had her wholly distracted. She was so distracted that she almost didn't notice the woman leaning against the lamp post just ahead of her. It was the same woman who was with the oyster vendor the day before. She was focused on Claire almost as if she'd been waiting for her. The sun shone off of her crystal black hair as she dipped her head ever-so-slightly in Claire's direction. It seemed like a nod of respect, of all things. The gesture made Claire uneasy as she didn't know what to make of the woman who had, twice now, found herself in Claire's path. She slowed and looked around her to see if the woman's focus was on someone who was perhaps behind her, but there was no one else around.

The woman's attention cut from Claire to an apple she was holding. The deep red of it was stark against the woman's all-white ensemble of a silk blouse tucked into wide-legged trousers. Claire did her best to seem casual as she continued past her. To her relief, she was ignored as the woman took a bite of the perfect apple. Once past her, however, Claire couldn't help but look over her shoulder, and some part of her was not surprised to see the look returned with a grin. Too distracted to think much more about the encounter, Claire focused on every step closer to the bookstore, which felt like bricks in a wall between her and the life she had known. She didn't dare look back because there was too big a chance that she'd *go* back. She turned the corner and entered the busier streets of town; around her, there were only early-morning joggers, the occasional early-bird tourist and workers preparing for the day ahead.

She savored the normality that surrounded her. She knew her world was turned upside down but she wanted to know she could at least walk through town and pretend it hadn't. She'd almost found herself having forgotten why she was even walking through those beloved streets that morning until she was met with a heart-sinking thought: the stranger from the bookstore, whom she learned was named Niran, said something about her having only six months left on the contract that was now hers to honor. The normality of her surroundings fell away as she turned over details of her conversation with Niran the night before. Nothing was mentioned about what would happen at the end of those six months - or until then, for that matter. However, *judging by the terror of the night before, it had to be unimaginable*, she thought.

Claire felt like her blood had cooled. How long had her father been pointing her attention to that contract? How many ways had he planned to have her "sign" it with her blood? She found herself imagining every way she could have avoided doing so. But perhaps, she thought, with anger and hurt beginning to boil, she may not have even had a choice in the matter.

Stretched before her, Main Street seemed menacing now. How could a place she loved so much hide something so dark? The sound of cobbles under car wheels, the cheery storefronts, the beautiful architecture all seemed like an elaborate lie. She'd fallen for it like she'd fallen for every lie told to her by her father. He'd stood there, looked her square in the eyes and lied to her every single day. She felt her face begin to warm under the anger rising within her. Everything had been taken from her - *everything*. He'd taken her future, her life, her love of this town, her ability to trust, and for what? She thought of all the grandeur, the excess in which her parents lived and loved. They'd enjoyed it all without so much as a glance toward the impact their choices would have on their daughter who hadn't asked for any of it.

Claire's breath had quickened along with her steps. She tucked her chin a little and felt the sting of tears about to form. It was going to consume her right there before she even made it to the bookstore to learn her fate. Just as she was about to stop walking and give up, she heard a crow's call from behind her, close enough to startle her. She froze as the crow flew by her so closely that the tip of its wing brushed her arm as it passed. Almost immediately, her anger, which had begun to boil over, eased a little. She watched the crow make a swoop upwards and then land on the green awning of East Water Books and Antiques. It hopped a few times along the edge before settling on a corner, facing Claire as she approached.

As the sound of the hourly bells rang through the town, inexplicably, always two minutes late, Claire found herself feeling small again, childlike. Her instinct was to wish for her parents, but one of them was why she was there in the first place. She shook off the thought and made her way to the entrance of the bookstore. Approaching the door of the shop, she noticed it was still closed. She reached for the knob, but changed her mind, quickly turning around to leave. As she turned, a caw echoed through the entryway and before her was the crow, standing on the ground between her and the exit. They looked at each other and for the first time, Claire understood the interaction between herself and the crow as something intentional.

"It's closed. I can't go in," she said to the crow, as if it could understand her; and could see the excuse it was to not have to face what awaited her within.

The crow hopped closer to Claire and made a small squawk. She retreated a step back toward the door and scowled.

"Fine," she said to the crow before turning back around and putting her hand on the doorknob.

Looking over her shoulder at the crow as she touched the doorknob, she watched the meddlesome bird merely turn its back on her to face the street. A couple passed by just as the crow hopped out onto the sidewalk and it squawked, startling them before it hopped back into the shade. At her touch, the door opened seemingly on its own. As she quietly walked in and pulled it closed behind her, she noticed the sweet, melodic tune the little brass bells made. It was a stark difference from their noisy clanging just the day before.

As she stole a glance out the front window. A part of her was saying, "goodbye." Another part of her was saying, "good riddance" and it broke her heart a little to know to whom it was directed. With that thought, she stood, just inside, clutching the contract that she just pulled out of her back pocket. She didn't bother putting it back into the box and the red velvet ribbon was also discarded. Just the day before, the parchment was treated like a priceless antique. Today, she treated it like shared midterm notes from one of her college classes.

There was nobody in the bookshop that she could immediately see. The curt gentleman in the wheelchair was nowhere to be found and no one came from behind the door at the back of the shop. Claire didn't move from where she stood. The only sounds were her own breathing and her heart that she realized was pounding. A loud squawk came from behind her, startling Claire enough that she dropped the parchment. She whipped around to find the crow with its neck craned to look inside at her. She bent to pick up the parchment with a scornful glance at the bird.

"There's nobody here. I'm just gonna come back later." When she grabbed the doorknob to walk out, the crow squawked and flapped at her, forcing her to retreat a step.

"What is your problem?!" she barked at the crow who only tilted its head at her words.

"Who are you talking to?" a deep, mellow voice came from behind Claire.

She was startled again and turned around to meet eyes with Niran. When she didn't answer, he looked past her out the front of the store.

"There's a crow. You know what? Nevermind. Here." Claire held the wrinkled contract out to him, frustration clearly splayed across her face.

"You learn to ignore them. And that goes to Jacob," he said, eyeing the contract Claire still held out to him.

"Who's Jacob?" she said, returning the contract to her back pocket.

"You've met him. Wheelchair, sunglasses. Hangs out over there." Niran gestured to the teller's window in the middle of the shop.

"Should I wait for him?" Claire asked as she looked past him at the empty teller's window.

Standing there, Claire was struck with images of what had happened the night before and had to look away. Just then, the hauntingly melodic tune of the front door bells rang. The sound was like nothing Claire had heard before. It should have sounded random and jarring. Instead, they harmonized. The melody was melancholy - beautiful and sad.

The large man from the day before was walking into the store backwards, using his back to hold the door open. He gingerly wheeled the shopkeeper --Jacob, she had learned-- into the shop. Claire shook off whatever thoughts held her in place and went around the large man to hold the door open for him. He merely nodded to her as he walked past her. No sooner than he crossed the threshold, the shopkeeper next to enter, did the bells fall completely silent. She looked at Jacob and then up at the bells, now still as death, that seemed to command silence from around them.

The large man brought Jacob to his window, where he had sat the day before; Niran followed, gesturing for Claire to join them.

"It has been a very long time since I have sat across someone in your position," Jacob began. "Unfortunately, it has been far less time since I have had to deal with someone who thought they could outsmart us. But a contract is a contract. And it must be honored." He paused. He had her full attention and she was surprisingly calm, so he continued.

"I have done a lot of traveling in my time. And in Spain, I picked up a rather charming word: *cobarde*. It simply translates to 'coward' in English, but I like the sound of *cobarde* more." Indeed, as the word left his lips did it sound caressed by them. "When the Spanish said it, they said it with *heart*. They wielded it like an ax to a tree. They watched men fall as the word cut through them. This is the title I would give to your father, as it were, but he is not here to receive it. As such, the unfortunate honor of this contract falls to you." The large man began moving ledgers and parchments about. Jacob's face only shifted slightly to see each action.

Claire looked away. The last thing she would ever expect was for her father to walk through that door to take back what he'd done. Here she stood, awaiting a fate that was thrust upon her by her father who was supposed to protect her from things like this; her father, who, if he *had* to do this, should not have ever considered her. When she turned back to Jacob, his lips were pursed in what she thought could have been a sympathetic smile. He shifted his head slightly in the large man's direction who then paused his task of sorting papers and headed toward Claire to retrieve the contract in her hand. Her attention on the large man was broken by Niran entering her periphery as he moved toward the door in the back of the shop. She'd forgotten he was even there, he was so quiet.

"Niran," Jacob quietly said. "Stay close. I will want to talk with you a little later." He dismissed Niran with a switch of his chin, turning his attention back on Claire. "I am certain you have many questions. I will answer them, but let me get a few things out of the way to save us some time." He gave a small nod as if to confirm agreement she hadn't yet expressed. "It would behoove you not to attempt the same maneuver as your father. It did not end well for him. It will not end well for you." At that, Jacob leveled a grave look at Claire. She only nodded.

"Not that I would," Claire said, "but my father seemed fine, you know, after he..." Claire said, gesturing to the mysterious door; Jacob understood she was referring to Niran.

"Ah." The dull smile returned to Jacob's face. "Have you ever had one of those dreams in which it felt as if you had lived a lifetime?"

Claire's own countenance became grave as she recalled her muted horror from the night before. She and her mother had sat for mere moments that felt like days. Her small nod was confirmation enough for Jacob to continue.

"The first thing you will learn in this process is that there are absolutely no winners whatsoever. There is only losing a little less if you play your cards right." Jacob made a small motion for the large man to place Claire's contract in front of him. "And your father, well, he did not play his cards right," he told her, raising his brow. "Here is hoping you will, yes?"

Claire tensed as she considered how it seemed, more and more, like her father's wish had been granted by a monkey paw. In that moment, a wave of fear washed over her again, as she considered fleeing from the bookstore. She looked at the front door, and Jacob let out a scoff.

"You are well past the point of being able to run from this, Claire," Jacob drawled from behind his sunglasses.

"I wasn't going to," she replied. The world beyond the front doors mocked her with its normalcy and casual disregard.

She spent the next hour looking at the titles of what seemed like every book in the little store. The only sounds were of Jacob's murmuring to his companion as the large man wrote between the ledger and a parchment that looked similar to Claire's father's. For a place where so much had caused Claire to be in disbelief, the books it sold were surprisingly normal. There were poetry books dating back hundreds of years. There were autobiographies written by little-known rulers from eras past. There were first editions and reference books, diaries and planners. It was a store that chronicled the lives of people one would have to dive deep into research to know. As she perused, the back room door opened suddenly and she started. Niran emerged along with his companion from the day before. They acknowledged each other with a swift glance, the gruff woman edging past him.

"Claire," Jacob said firmly.

She stood up and walked toward the teller's window where the large man plucked the parchment he'd been writing on and passed it to her. Before her, in a script that was so elegant and expressive of how gently it was written, was her own contract. The ink, as the saying goes, was not even dry, yet the words shifted about the page in the same way those on her father's contract had.

The contract, though a single page, easily held enough information to fill a book. The part written about her remaining time stood out the most as it changed with every second that passed; a countdown clock for her life written in elegant script. As she skimmed, the words on the contract shifted about the page for her, as if it predicted where her eyes would fall and what she meant to read. There was enough information that she could only skim it to get a general idea. It seemed to only expound upon information that had already been shared with her. She took in what she could but almost immediately let it go as she found herself focusing more on how she was feeling, rather than what she should be learning from it.

She felt alone.

She didn't count the minutes she'd quietly studied it before feeling all eyes on her. When she looked up, it was toward the large man who was moving in her direction. There was a loneliness in his eyes as well and she was sure he saw hers. It was like a secret they shared in that brief gaze.

"I will need you for a moment, Claire. Reid will need to help us with this," Jacob explained.

"Reid?" Claire asked quietly as she and the large man stood before each other. He merely nodded. Claire accepted the friendly nod as his way of formally introducing himself to her.

The teller's window was less cramped than she'd perceived it to be from the other side. There was plenty of room where she stood aside, waiting for Reid to turn Jacob's wheelchair so they could face each other. She watched as he gently took Jacob's right hand and turned his pinky ring so the top of it was now palm-side. He held Jacob's hand and then stood aside as he gestured for Claire to come closer.

"Tempus," he began. "Tempus est solucionis."

"Time is money," she replied.

"Close. And I can see why you would think that. Time is *payment*," he corrected without a hint of condescension. "Time has *always* been payment. Over the centuries, too many men with too much hubris and misguided ambition have twisted this crucial phrase into 'time is money.' Now it is some watered down mantra for people who have put a price on what they believe to be theirs."

"So you're saying that I will pay with time," Claire deduced.

"Yes. It is the only form we will accept. When the payment of this contract comes due, time will be the currency and only your soul will have enough of it to satisfy us," he answered. When her only reaction was a small nod of understanding, he continued. "I accept your offer to assume the contractual obligation formerly belonging to your father, Raymond Cielo."

As he said this, Reid held Jacob's hand out to Claire. Staring, again, at her own eyes in the reflection in Jacob's sunglasses, she placed her hand in his. The cold of his pinky ring bit into her skin. Never breaking the eye-contact she guessed she had, Claire felt Reid close Jacob's fingers around hers. He enclosed their grasped hands in his own, his hands engulfing the both of theirs.

When he opened his palms, Claire still gripped Jacob's hand and she felt Reid's gentle fingers part their handshake. She fought the curiosity in her to look at the side of her palm to see if there had been left a mark there like she'd seen on her father the night before. But she let her hand drop to her side instead.

"And we are in agreement," Jacob said, flatly.

Without waiting for dismissal, Claire gave a small, polite smile to Reid as she walked past him. He towered over her, but there was a peaceful stillness that seemed to emanate from him. As she made her way back to sit, she spied

Reid folding her contract in the same way he'd folded her father's the day before. He even used the same type of red velvet ribbon to tie it off.

She glanced toward Niran, who'd entered into deep conversation with the woman who had little interest in Claire, if any, then back to Reid who had just placed her neatly-folded and tied-off contract on her side of the teller's window shelf. Jacob had already begun instructing Reid for another task and in that moment, Claire, once again, felt the isolation of her new circumstances.

"I guess I don't know what to do now," she said with a little more trepidation than she wanted to show.

All four of the individuals in the bookstore stopped what they were doing and looked at her. She looked at each of them and felt the familiar sting of confusion and embarrassment.

"What? For the love of... *What?*" she said with impatience and resignation.

Jacob only smirked before asking her, "You don't know what to do now? You do anything you want, Claire Cielo," he told her, tilting his head. "Granted, you only have six months to do it, but the time does belong to you. And we will be here to answer questions," he continued with a nod in Niran's direction, "but the process is pretty self-explanatory."

Claire's mouth parted to state or question words to Jacob that got lost on their journey from her mind to her mouth. Neither Niran nor his friend offered more than the same silence as Jacob. Reid, with his gentle, but giant figure, was the only one who seemed to have any hint of concern. Because she was alone in this; because she understood that whether she remained in that store or walked outside or went back to her parents' house, she would be alone in all of this; she saw no reason to filter her thoughts. She had only one feeling of which she was certain and so it would be shared among these people who seemed to be more fascinated with her ignorance than concerned with her well-being. She looked down to her feet before finally, quietly speaking.

"It's just that... It's just that I don't think I can bring myself to go back to that house." When she finally got the words out, instead of meeting the gazes of those people whom she was certain would judge her, she looked out the small alley window.

There was nothing said for a too-long moment before Jacob finally said, "Then make a wish." When Claire's confusion did not relent, he continued, "Claire. There are two parts to the contract of which you are now obliged to honor. In the next six months, you will learn the details of your obligation. In the meantime, however, this contract is obliged to honor you. Did you even read it? Or were you too busy admiring Reid's penmanship." He turned his face toward Reid and murmured, "I keep telling you, they look at your handwriting instead of reading the terms."

"No, I..." She didn't finish and she fought the urge to grab the contract and start scouring it.

"It is okay," Jacob said, with understanding. "Your father's original contract was pretty straightforward. He wanted wealth, power, influence, all the same things most people ask from us. For decades, we obliged. He had all of those things in the exact way he wanted them. Our end of the bargain was held up. He wished it, he received it. Claire, dear, now all you need to do is wish it and you, too, shall receive it."

Her lips parted as she stared into her own reflection in Jacob's sunglasses. The implications of what had just been explained to her trickled over her in droplets of realization that became a deluge of understanding. For the next six months, Claire would have access to every "stroke of luck" or "chance meeting" or "fortunate turn of events" that made her father the man he was in his prime. Almost as quickly as the understanding came to her, did one glaring question form.

"But, my parents. They can't just wish for anything, they're practically destitute now."

"Ah," Jacob said with understanding. "You see, this contract is a part of you now. It is tied to your very soul. It will demand your integrity in honoring it. If you do nothing else with any integrity, you will honor this contract or it will balance the scales for you. I would wager the moment your father reached the point-of-no-return in his decision to trick you into assuming his debt, was the same moment his good fortune began to wane. You see, Claire, in this dealing, when you bite the hand that feeds you, that hand will simply pull out your teeth."

Claire said nothing as she allowed this information to settle within her. She grappled with her nature --which was to work and earn-- and what had just been laid before her. The idea, that she needed only wish, momentarily made her feel even more detached and more willing to accept that the last twenty-four hours had been an elaborate prank. But it certainly wasn't. She was there. She experienced the terror.

"Do you understand?" Jacob's impatient interruption snapped Claire from her thoughts.

"Yes."

"Good. Um..." he trailed off. "Niran will get you up to speed on all the things you can and cannot wish for. It should not take long."

"It's ok, I can't see myself asking for mu--" She was cut off by Jacob's laugh.

"You will. You will adjust to the new world you live in and it just so happens that that world will be tough for you to ignore. So Niran will help you. The list of things you cannot ask for is long, but necessary. Have fun." With that, Jacob turned back to Reid and resumed their work together.

VI

Back out on Main Street, the morning was in full-swing. Coffee shops and restaurants that served breakfast already had their flow of customers to serve. The beauty of the day was not lost on Claire, though she did nothing to outwardly acknowledge it. In the bookstore, she'd done nothing while she waited for Niran and his brusque friend to finish a hissed exchange. When Niran stalked through the bookstore, and muttered, "Let's go," as he passed, she'd merely followed without question.

The sun warmed Claire and the slight breeze soothed her as she walked without purpose. She didn't know where she was going, only that she was to live the next six months as she pleased. "How" was the question that occupied her mind so much that she hadn't noticed the world that had already begun to shift around her.

"You should have something to eat." Niran's voice reached from behind her to remind her she had a companion on this walk. She was so lost in her own isolation that she hadn't immediately realized the statement was meant for her.

"Claire," he tried again.

She stopped, so abruptly that he almost ran into her, and turned to face him. She looked at Niran's scowled face as she waited for the statement to register.

"Yeah, but it will be a little bit of a wait. It's the weekend," she said as she gestured to the lines of people outside of the more popular restaurants. Niran lifted his gaze from her and looked in the direction of Claire's sweep of the arm.

"Good time for your first lesson." He made sure to have her full attention before continuing. "Pick one."

"What lesson?" she asked.

"On how this all works," he answered.

"One of the restaurants...to eat at right now?" she clarified. Niran only nodded.

"I guess I'll pick the one with the shortest line."

"No. Pick where you want to eat," he said.

"Fine. That one." She pointed to the restaurant that seemed to have the longest line.

He looked at it, nodded, then held a hand out for her to lead the way. With a slight furrow of her brow and a sigh, Claire began walking toward the restaurant. As soon as she took a step toward it, the couple at the front of the line simply walked away. With her next steps, the father of the family of four, who waited behind the couple, recognized someone in line at another restaurant. The two children squealed with delight as the four of them left the line to join their friends across the street.

Claire's steps slowed as she eyed the next group in line, three well-dressed women, begin walking toward the door. Two of them chatted as the third dug through her purse, looking for something. Claire couldn't hear the conversation, but she saw the third woman beckon the other two and explain something to them. One friend placed a comforting hand on her back as the other directed them to follow in the direction where she pointed a thumb.

At that, Claire looked to Niran who only kept his eyes trained forward. The last group in line was six college-aged friends who began walking to the front. Claire had reached them and made to stand in line behind them. Someone from the group turned to Claire and said, "you two can go in front of us. We're waiting on one more person."

"Thanks," Niran said with a small nod and he and Claire made their way to

the door. Just as they were within arm's reach of the door, someone from inside opened it and looked around.

"It's just you two," the host of the restaurant asked.

"Yes," Niran replied.

"Great! A two-top just opened up. Follow me," the host said, two menus already in-hand. Behind them, people began lining up again to be seated.

Claire looked over her shoulder at Niran, who walked behind her, as she followed the host to a booth next to a large, front window. She shook her head and gave a small sigh. Once seated, Claire's eyes didn't leave Niran's face as she waited for the host to walk out of ear shot.

"This is my favorite spot in this place," she said, certain that Niran somehow already knew that.

"Good," he replied as he began to look over the menu.

She looked at him for a moment longer before going back to her own menu. They exchanged very few words in the time it took to choose and place their order with the server. It wasn't until the server walked away from the table that Niran finally relaxed, readying himself for a long conversation.

Claire looked out the window, seemingly uninterested in learning more about how the next six months could go for her. The slight warmth of the morning sun coming through it was a much-needed comfort. For everything she'd been through in the last twenty-four hours, she'd held herself together. Niran studied her for a moment and then looked out the window to where she'd been focused. There was nothing of note there. She faced him then and for a moment, they just looked at each other as two people, who'd been thrust together under the most uncomfortable circumstance, would.

She took in a deep, heavy breath and let her head fall back to rest against the high back of the booth. "Do you mind if I just sit for a while," she asked.

"Not at all," he answered.

So they sat in a silence that was neither comfortable nor uncomfortable. It was an understanding. Claire greedily took in every sight and sound as if she could stack them between herself and the truth of her circumstances. After a time, she finally spoke.

"I can't really remember what I was doing six months ago," she sighed. "I can't really remember the time passing between then and yesterday." She pursed her lips into a tight smile as she looked at Niran and continued. "Anyway," she said as she shook off whatever had begun to weigh on her, "I guess I need to know what the rules are."

"Sure," Niran answered, just as their server arrived with their food. He eyed Claire as she looked, blankly, at the plates being set down and then gave the server a polite smile.

Niran had a simple dish of two fried eggs and two slices of toast with butter. Claire, on the other hand, had three plates before her; one with two Belgian waffles, the next had two fried eggs and a pile of crispy hash browns and the last had avocado toast.

"We can start by going over your contract, if you'd like," Niran said as he used his fork and knife to place one of his eggs on a slice of toast.

"Okay," Claire said as she paused her slathering of a thick layer of butter on a waffle.

She reached into her back pocket and pulled out the freshly-written contract and set it down on the table before Niran. As he untied the red ribbon and began to unfold it, he watched as Claire put equally thick layers of butter on the other waffles. He took his time looking for a place to start as he split his attention between the contract and watching Claire drench the plate in syrup and then begin cutting the first slice.

"I don't usually do this. Normally, it would be another associate who explains these things to you - like the person your father worked with for his contract." He laid the page down on the table next to his plate so he could read from it while he made even cuts in his toast with egg. His eyes shifted between Claire and the server, a table away, to whom she had now been gesturing *bottle* with her hand and mouthing out, "Hot sauce." The server gave her a thumbs-up and Claire smiled in gratitude.

"That's fine," she said as she punctured the yolks of her eggs and mixed them with the hash browns. She thanked the server for dropping off a small bottle of hot sauce, poured a generous amount of it over her eggs and hash browns and followed it with the salt and pepper. With a sigh almost too small to be noticed, she finally looked up at Niran from beneath her lashes.

It was hard for him not to study her eyes which were brilliant to him. They weren't just green, he noted, as they seemed to create their own light. They were like shards of emeralds and jade encased in crystal-clear ice, capturing light like a prism. He was the first to look away, unsure of just how long he'd spent fixed on the gaze which commanded so much attention.

"So, you just experienced a small example of how the terms of your contract will work for you. I'm certain you've seen the same type of things happen for your father."

"What happened to him? I mean, what happened to Jacob?" The mere thought of her father made her stomach turn, so she asked about Jacob instead.

He knew the answer and, for a moment, he considered telling her the whole of it. This crowded breakfast bar, however, while she drowned her waffles in syrup, was neither the time nor the place. So he told her what he'd told countless people to begin and end the conversation quickly.

"He dove into waters he shouldn't have."

"Does he always wear those sunglasses," she asked.

"Day or night, rain or shine. Always." With that, he leveled a gaze at her that told her it was time to stop avoiding the conversation they were meant to be having.

Claire seemed to concede to that and took one last look outside before focusing on the contract between them.

"Okay," she said simply. And took the first bite of her food.

"Like I mentioned before, this isn't something I usually do. Under normal circumstances, you'd have someone else to go over all this with you. And you and I," a small gesture to her and then himself, "wouldn't meet again until..." He trailed off, shifting his eyes away from her.

"Until you do to me what you did to my dad - except, I die," she said with a small shake of her head.

Niran waited for her to follow with the line of questioning he'd grown accustomed to hearing from people in her same position. He waited for her to ask him if there was a way out or if she could negotiate a different contract. He studied her as she looked out the window and chose her next words. He already knew how he would answer.

"It's wild to think that in six months, I'm going to be just... *dead*," she said, shaking her head again.

"Of the things you may end up being in six months, Claire, 'just dead' won't be one of them. 'Just dead' would be a gift to anyone in your position. And, unfortunately, that is a gift no one in your position receives." A look of pity flashed across his face, there and gone so fast, it might not have even been there at all.

"You have a rare and unique opportunity, however. Because of the nature by which you have come into your contract, you get something very few people in your position have." He turned it around to face her and slid it over to her side of the table. He then pointed to the sifting paragraph toward the middle. Claire started to read where he'd pointed.

"It says that I," she read it again to make sure she understood correctly, "It says I have-"

"–A choice," Niran finished.

She paraphrased from what she read, "A choice of how I will pay the debt of this contract," she said, slumping in her seat, "and for how long." She skimmed some more and turned it over to look at the back even though she knew there was nothing there. "It doesn't say what my choices are. This whole thing reads like," she paused as she searched for the words, "like every word matters, yet none of them do."

"Jacob will be the one to tell you what your choices are. I can only tell you the rules for how you spend the next six months with what we are obliged to give you. As far as the language of the contract is concerned, why do you say none of the words matter?" Niran inquired, genuinely curious.

"Because no matter what it says here --no matter what I gain in the next six months-- no matter the choice I make, I lose." She skimmed the contract once more. "And the only thing I have a say in is how badly." She shook her head and sat back.

"You're probably right," he said. "And you should have had a lifetime to reap the benefits of this agreement, or at least the choice to refuse it." He watched as Claire finally showed something more than just resignation and continued. "So what I suggest is that you learn the rules of this forsaken game and play it, as best you can, for the next six months," he urged as Claire just ate.

She stabbed at her food less politely than she had been moments ago. "Do you know what choice it is I'm supposed to be making?"

"Yes."

Claire waited for him to continue and when he didn't, she prodded.

"What kind of choice is it? A choice between what and what?"

"That is a complex answer that I cannot give you, but I assure you, Jacob will be able to answer all your questions when the time is right. I understand your frustrations."

"But do you? Because not twenty-four hours ago, you seemed to enjoy what you did to my dad. I don't think you understand *any* of my frustrations. So I'm just gonna go. Thanks for the breakfast." With that, Claire began to scoot out of the booth.

"What you have fallen into" --Niran began, looking out of the window and not at Claire who was motioning to leave-- "is not something that is simply governed by happenstance or coincidence. This isn't just you. And it isn't just Jacob or me. It isn't even about who lives and who dies." With that, he looked at her and she stared back at him. "What you are now a part of is far more complex than can be understood in a lifetime, let alone over..." he said, gesturing to her three plates of food. "We each have a role to play in this and giving you the answer to that question, with the breadth and width required to do it full justice, is not a part of mine. I do, Claire, understand your frustrations. The time is going to pass anyway. You might as well spend it reaping the benefits for which you will pay so dearly."

Claire didn't finish getting out of the booth, but she didn't move back to her original position either. With a deep sigh and without breaking eye contact with Niran, she forced out the word "*fine*" with barely enough breath to voice it or movement of her mouth to pronounce it. Niran could have continued looking into her deepened stare that had become a dark ocean under an angry sky - the emerald and jade of her eyes just moments ago now sunk beneath those waters.

Noting her need for some semblance of control over what was happening to her, he turned his attention to the busy street outside, a concession. They didn't speak for several moments - another painting, replete with a pent-up intensity of human emotion that would have impressed itself upon any viewer. Somewhere in the back of her mind, Claire was always conscious of who may or may not be noticing her in public. This habit, one that she disliked about herself, was something she learned from her mother. She stared at her contract as she wondered how a person might be conjecturing about her life in this moment. Part of her was still able to feel a small amusement at the thought that the truth of this tableau was something they would never guess.

"You said there were rules. What are they?" she finally asked.

"They're simple," he said in return, adjusting himself for the conversation to come. Before Claire could ask another question he continued. "We'll call things 'wishes,' for lack of a better term. To start, you can't wish for anything that would change the will of another person. This would include things like making someone fall in love with you or anyone else or changing a decision they've already made. You can't make, say, a less-than-desirable father turn into a better person." He gave her a small smile to soften the truth of that last example, which she ignored. He continued. "You can't wish for anything that would cause harm or death to another person unless it was in self-defense. The only exception would be a contract written for an act of revenge for the wrongful death of a loved one. Obviously, this doesn't apply to you."

"When you say 'wish,' what am I supposed to do? Like, do I say 'I wish' out loud or..." she asked.

"You need only desire it with purpose," he answered.

"How does one desire with purpose?"

"Big or small, desire what you want with the knowledge and acceptance that it will be done for you. You don't have to speak it or say 'I wish.'"

"I see," Claire breathed, with a small furrow of her brow. She had a look of concentration that could have been mistaken for the rise of another question, but she remained silent. She turned her head in a seemingly random direction and slid her glass closer to the edge of the table. Just then, their server walked up with a pitcher to refill her iced tea. Niran looked at the server, then to Claire; she smiled politely in gratitude and slid her drink glass back in front of herself as she noticed his stare.

"Well, that's nifty," she admitted.

"Indeed," Niran agreed, slightly amused by her little test.

She sipped on her tea as she considered both the reality and potential of her circumstances. Niran continued, seeing she did not seem to have any other questions.

"Finally, you can't wish for anything that changes nature. Many things are under the umbrella of this rule. Nature grants you a certain body, certain talents, a mental capacity that reaches a certain level. You cannot wish for anything that would require any of these things to change." He watched as Claire considered, but still asked no questions. "You can't time travel or make money appear out of thin air. You can't create the cure for cancer if you know nothing about medicine. You can't dunk a basketball if you haven't the athleticism or height. You can't make a mountain appear in the middle of the woods or teleport to a villa in Italy." With that, he paused to give Claire time to ask a question. She didn't, so he continued.

"But say you wanted someone to fall in love with you. You could wish for opportunities to spend meaningful time with them and in ways you both could enjoy. If you wanted to change someone's mind, you could wish to learn all the compelling arguments that would help you do so. If you wanted riches, you need only choose how you want to come by the wealth and you would have every opportunity to earn it that way. It can be illegal, but there's hardly any point as you can more easily obtain it legally."

"That's what my dad did," Claire interrupted. "He wanted money and influence and this lifestyle. It seemed like everything he wanted to happen just kinda came to him through luck and coincidence," she mused.

She was suddenly met with the realization that her father hadn't been very imaginative. He hadn't used his wishes to their highest potential. They could have lived anywhere. He could have made so much more money and had so many more accomplishments. In the same way her mother had squandered the last of their wealth, he squandered the potential of his contract.

"He was so stupid," she huffed while shaking her head. "Unbelievable. He was so damned stupid. He could have made anything happen."

Niran pursed his lips into a tight twist and Claire saw the look in his eye as someone who knew, all too well, how easily the potential of these contracts gets wasted on the wishes of thc unimaginative.

"So what you're telling me is that I shouldn't expect magic, but maybe just a lot of coincidence. Maybe a lot of luck and opportunity, and that's about it?" she asked.

"That's about as correct an assessment as I can agree to without getting into the finer details of things, yes. It is the type of contract that you have. Of course, people have asked for bigger or more complex things in the past and those are the kinds of contracts they had. Yours requires far less of the world around you." He answered.

"My father," she began, followed by a pained pause, "sold me out for a contract he didn't even take full advantage of. It wasn't even on purpose, he was just that simple."

"It happens more often than not. I wouldn't say he was any more 'simple' than the next person."

"No. He *was*," she interrupted. Niran made no reply as she seemed to have another thought balanced on the tip of her tongue. "But I'm the one paying for this contract, not him, so what does that make me?" she said, and turned to look out the window.

"It makes you," Niran began as Claire anticipated an equally harsh assessment, "the daughter of a fool," he finished. Almost as soon as she heard the words, she realized she had no taste for reassurance - a deep breath being her response and a signal to move on from the comment.

"Okay," he acknowledged. "If there is anything else you want to know, I will answer to the best of my knowledge," he told her softly.

After a long moment of looking out the window, Claire finally answered, "I do. It's just a lot."

"Sure," he said to the side of her face as she continued to look out the window. "You know, you don't ever have to go back to that house. You don't have to do anything, at all, that makes you the least bit uncomfortable. Just wish it and these six months can be the best of your life."

For the second time in less than twenty-four hours, Claire laughed heartily and with a smile that was too big, too bright. The laugh was too full and sounded too joyous. Claire had seen hysterical laughter before. This wasn't it. It was more like pity, not for herself, but for *him*. For someone who, she assumed, had seen humanity's heights and depths, he seemed not to understand the simplest desires of a person.

"The best of my life," she said with that smile and a condescending nod. "Thank you so much for your perspective, Niran. I appreciate it." That tone of pity, clearer now. Somewhere in the back of her mind, she recalled memories of her mother behaving similarly. Nadine Cielo had a way of using pity for others to buoy her in the moments when her optimism could not. Niran had no response, so she continued, "I am not interested in having six of the best months of my life only for them to be the final months of my life. I would have lived quite happily in mediocrity for the next seventy years. So I get it. I can have anything. But what I want is my *life* back. Can you do that for me?" she asked forcefully.

"No."

"Of course not," she said with that smile and a tilt of her head. She took in a long, cleansing breath and let the smile fade.

"I'm sorry. I know you're only trying to help me," she said sheepishly.

"Please, no apologies. This must be a lot for you," he answered with a small gesture of dismissal. "There is one more thing," he continued. "You will never be able to speak about us, your contract or anything you may see or experience regarding it - with the exception of others who have contracts."

"Or I'll be punished or something?"

"No. You are just unable to. If you try to speak of it, write about it, draw it, or anything else people have tried to do in the past, it will fail. You may think you're telling someone about your contract and to them, you'll be informing them about a news headline or giving them a recipe for a casserole. And if you keep trying, then you will get hurt. I've collected souls from people who've lost their tongues to infection or had their hands mangled in a terrible accident, gone blind, gone deaf; all because they wouldn't stop trying to talk about it."

"I wasn't planning on it."

"That's good," Niran answered and waited for Claire to sort through what she'd just learned.

"When you say you've collected souls, what do you mean?" Claire finally asked.

"I make sure the debts are paid in full when they are due."

"By doing the same kind of thing you did to my dad? Or was that different because..." She trailed off, gesturing to herself.

"It is different for each person. The collection process is as varied as the people carrying the debts."

"But my dad passed his debt to me," Claire said, as much a question as it was a statement." What exactly happened to him? Does this mean you will be collecting on my debt in six months? And what happened to me and my mother? It felt like I'd never move or breathe or even ever feel joy again." The string of questions and the confession of her feelings leapt from Claire's tongue as fast as they flew through her mind.

"What you and your mother suffered was an unfortunate side-effect of the experience I chose to give your father when I separated him from his contract. It can be a somewhat intense process that can... *leak* outside of the individual who is experiencing it. Like smelling the food coming from that kitchen." He gestured across the restaurant to the kitchen area. "You're not the cook, you're not even seeing it. But you can smell it and if you didn't already have all of this in front of you, you could say that it would have also made you more hungry than you were before you walked in. It's similar. What leaked from your father's experience with me caused you and your mother to feel what you did."

"It felt awful."

"I know."

After shaking off the still-fresh feelings from the night before, Claire went back to eating, though she found herself enjoying it a little less than moments ago. She couldn't bring herself to ask if he was going to give her a similar experience to her father's.

"I also remove debts on the extremely rare occasion. Transferring one is even more rare. I haven't done one before you and your father. What you witnessed was your father's debt being removed. That experience, too, can be as varied as the individual," he explained.

"We were the first transfer of a contract you ever did?" she asked.

"Indeed," he said.

"What do you mean when you say you give them an experience?" she asked.

"May I?" Niran asked, reaching for an empty appetizer plate in front of Claire. He then grabbed the salt and pepper shakers from the condiments tray at the end of their table and unscrewed the tops of both; he began pouring salt onto the plate.

"We'll call this your life. Your body. Your experiences. Your physical connection to this world." He poured about a tablespoon of the salt and then began pouring the pepper on top of it.

"This, we will call your soul. It is both more and less of everything. Like your physical being, your soul is not one solid object, but a countless collection of every feeling you've ever had, every dream and nightmare, every connection you've ever made and every thread tied to you by someone else." He then poured about half the amount of pepper as he did the salt, took his spoon and began swirling the salt and pepper together as he continued. Specs of pepper were now dotted throughout the salt.

"It is the part of you that exists without all of *this*," he said, sweeping his eyes up and around. "Many believe that your soul is the voice in your head. That voice, however, is made up of your thoughts which are made up of your experiences and the influence the world and people in it have on you. Your soul is most absolutely not that voice," he said.

"If my soul is not that voice, then what is it? How do I know..." She trailed off, not knowing how to word her question.

"It is not the voice in your head. It is who *hears* it." Then he took the back of the spoon and spread the new mixture of salt and pepper on the plate and continued.

"Isn't that the same thing?" Claire asked, setting down her fork.

"It would be if your thoughts didn't cause you to feel different things," he answered.

Claire looked as if she'd ask more about it, but decided to let him continue.

"Collecting someone's soul requires me to reach into their being and seek out each and every piece of it within them. It is everywhere. It is in their physical body. It is in their thoughts. It is in their memories and dreams. It is everywhere in the entire timeline of their life and every place they've ever been. Pieces of it need to be pulled back from the darkest places some memories are locked away, the threads they've tied to other people, in the walls of rooms where they slept. As this happens, I exist in every part of their life and being that their soul does. That existence can be anything from silent and unnoticeable to incredibly loud and impactful and everything in between. It's my choice. And this," --he tapped the contract with a finger-- "think of this as being tattooed onto your soul, every bit of your soul, everywhere that it is. You've already experienced it being attached to you. Unseen, unheard. Removal can be just as inconspicuous if I so wanted it to be. Or it can be like reliving every nightmare a person has ever had, each one the length of a lifetime. All of which can happen, within the span of a handshake."

The two merely sat, staring at one another as Claire seemed to look for the real Niran standing in the black of his pupils. He broke the silence with two little taps of the spoon on the plate. The salt and pepper were perfectly separated. Claire looked down at the plate and couldn't help raising her eyebrows.

"Hell of a party trick you've got there," she said with a reluctant smile. Niran's only response was a weak grin.

"What happens to the people once you're done..." she began to ask, fishing for the right words but couldn't land on any that didn't sound ridiculous to her, "doing your thing with them?"

"Usually, they die." His matter-of-fact tone jarred Claire, but she tried not to show it.

"Do you know what happens afterward? Jacob said you all basically own our souls. What happens to our souls?"

"That, too, is a different experience for each person. Typically, we already know what will be done with each individual. But like your contract states, you will have a choice and you'll know your choices when the time comes to decide."

Claire thought to argue and demand he tell her what he knew, but she didn't have the strength for the fight. She didn't know if she ever would again. The finality of her circumstances weighed heavier and heavier on her with each new bit of information she learned. Instead, she decided to focus on the near future since the near future is all she had. There was a time, she realized, when the next six months was her near future, but now she had to shift her perspective to it being the next six days.

When the bells at the front door of East Water Books and Antiques rang, the song was of anguish and perfection. The tragedy and beauty of it drifted through the air and landed like rose petals at the feet of the woman whom it introduced. She'd been all smiles and enjoyment just the day before, drawing a small audience around herself and a raw oyster vendor. This morning, however, that infectious joy was dimmed to a pull of her lips so slight, it couldn't quite be called a smile. She looked around and her ghost of a grin turned to delight as she spotted her old friend, Reid.

"Honestly, Jacob. It's dreadful enough you've imprisoned yourself in this little shop, but must you also torture yourself with these bells at your door?" the woman said as she breezed through the bookstore toward Reid, who was making his way toward her.

"Reid, darling. It's been too long," she said sweetly as she held out her arms to him.

When he embraced the splendid woman, his arms nearly swallowed her whole. He inhaled deeply, as he held her for several moments, taking in her scent of gardenia and fresh snow. He then took her by her shoulders and backed away so that she was now at arm's length. Worry overcame him.

"I know, darling. I know - and I promise I've been okay," She gave him a reassuring smile and little twist, left and right, as if to provide proof of her good health.

Reid studied her intently and gave her a once-over that let her know he'd trust her word, but wanted to verify for himself. He took her slim arm in his bear-paw hands and held it up, looking at her arm and then to her eyes, concerned. She could not help but laugh.

"Reid! I'll have you know I am perfectly healthy, thank you. I'm not too thin, you're just a giant," she argued playfully. "So, would you please wipe that terrible look off your face and just be happy to see me?" She pulled her arm out of his hands and slipped it in the crook of his elbow. She gave him a disarming smile and nodded her head in Jacob's direction as if to ask Reid to walk her there.

With a heavy sigh and a refusal to ease his concern for her, he obliged and turned them toward the teller's window where Jacob sat, patiently waiting for them to finish being reacquainted.

"To what, dear Vera, could I possibly owe this pleasure?" Jacob said with a small smile.

"Come now, brother. Do I need a reason to see you?" She teased as she tugged Reid along to walk her into the teller's window.

Reid hesitated and made distressed gestures as if trying to slow her down or stop her, but she plowed ahead.

"Vera, there is something you should know," Jacob tried warning her.

"I should say there is a lot I should know, Jacob. That's why I'm here," she said as she strolled toward him, arms out, as if demanding a hug. "Don't look at me like that, I know it's been a long time, but I'm here now," she said, wiggling her fingers with her arms still outstretched, waiting for Jacob to stand and embrace her.

"Well, don't just sit there," she said with a hint of frustration.

Vera stopped as she took in the sight of Jacob in his wheelchair, moving only his head to speak to her. Her breathing quickened and her smile faltered as she searched for her composure and her eyes began to glisten. She felt the gentle tap of Reid's heavy fingers on her own nudge her away from her spiraling thoughts. She looked up at him, searching for something in his countenance to tell her that what came next would be okay. As if he could read her mind in the same way she could read his face, the gentle giant gave her a solemn nod and turned to Jacob.

"Jacob," she said. "It really has been too long." She knew she was forcing her eyes to stay locked on his face and only his face, narrowing her vision to the only part of him that still made sense.

Jacob gave her a sympathetic smile and a small tilt of his head. It wasn't for what she had said - it was a reminder that she hadn't yet answered his question. She finally looked past his chin and to the rest of his body. The rhythmic rise and fall of his chest was the only part of it that wasn't painfully still. She lingered on the stillness as she worked to come to terms with it.

"But-"

"We can talk about your questions once you have answered mine," he said, firmly and with understanding.

Vera slipped her hand out of the crook of Reid's elbow and gave him a small pat on the shoulder. He took a step back as she edged closer to Jacob and finally answered his question without actually answering it.

"You know why I'm here."

"Reid," Jacob interrupted. Vera's eyes shot to her friend who had already begun following her. "It has been a while, I would like a drink before you leave," he said coldly.

She felt the sting of the small indignity as Reid squeezed past her to reach Jacob's cup. He did not make eye-contact with her as he passed her again to leave. Pity pulled down the corners of her mouth as she watched the rounded shoulders of Reid's back retreat behind the back room door of the shop.

"How long are you going to punish him?" she asked quietly, still looking at the door.

"As long as I want."

Vera winced at the unapologetic cruelty. Whatever hope she'd had, years ago, that it was merely a temporary reaction, died in this moment. She thought time would help to unravel the anger which brought it about, but it had only weaved it more tightly into his being. The unshakable faith she'd had, that he would not be lost to her, finally shuddered. It shook loose the last memory she had of Reid as a whole man. The memory overcame her.

"You don't have to do this," Vera had exclaimed to Reid. His trembling hand held the quill he would use to sign the contract on the table in front of him. "Jacob, stop it! You're taking this too far. Stop!" She'd insisted.

"I am not doing anything," he'd answered with a cavalier tone. He'd casually motioned to the contract with an upturned hand. "I cannot write the contracts and sign them, too. Reid has decided that he wants to enter into this agreement, so who am I to argue?" He'd shrugged as he sat with a hip on the corner of the table, never taking his darkened, merciless eyes off of Reid.

Vera had not known how to handle this new feeling of desperation. She'd all but splayed her own body across the contract so Reid couldn't sign it, but he'd made his decision.

"You can tell him to stop, Jacob! He had no idea when he told him about that woman! Reid, you do not have to do this!" She'd started crying then. She had been powerless to stop her closest friend from damning himself to a fate she'd considered to be worse than death.

Jacob had spent from sundown to sunup in conversation with Reid. He'd unfurled his forked tongue and poured molasses-thick poison into Reid's ear for hours. Jacob drove wooden wedges into every crack he knew existed in Reid's sense of self. Every word was water poured over those wedges, swelling them until each crack was burst open. By the time Jacob had finished with him, the unusually large man was laid mentally and emotionally prostrate. He would have done anything Jacob suggested as long as it meant he could turn away from the punishing mirror held before him.

Reid had looked into Vera's eyes as she had him by the shoulders, begging him not to sign. They were bloodshot, having been crying for hours.

"I have to. This is all my fault."

"Reid, no it's not, You didn't do it to her, we–"

He'd looked down from her eyes and the unmistakable sound of quill scratching across parchment stopped her mid-sentence. Time slowed as she had been pushed aside by Jacob who had snatched the contract with his left hand and grabbed for Reid's right hand with his own.

"I happily accept the terms of your contract," he'd said, the words neutral, but the tone venomous.

Vera had turned in time to see the handshake that had bound the contract to Reid forever. Jacob had straightened to his full height and let go. Reid had only sunk further into his rounded shoulders. Sad eyes had looked up at Vera who could only stand before him, slack-jawed with horror.

"Vera," Jacob said, who had now been standing over Reid who only sat looking up at him. "I want you to meet my new man," he'd said with a cruel smile she'd never seen on his face before. Reid's lips had parted to say something to Vera, but Jacob had continued, "He doesn't speak."

The pair had locked eyes as she could only witness the realization that fell upon Reid. He'd opened and closed his lips but could not release the words trapped behind them. Had he known they would be the last words he'd have ever spoken, he might have chosen something less painful than, "This is all my fault."

Tears had streamed down Vera's cheeks as she frantically searched Reid's face as if there were some cure for his lost voice that she could have found there. Reid had only closed his lips into a tight smile and had put a reassuring palm, gently on her cheek.

Back in the present, Vera stared blankly at nothing as she raised a hand to the same cheek Reid had so gently touched all those years ago. Her mind and heart slowly returned to the present as the fog of the awful memory lifted from her.

"No. I do not know why you are here." Jacob's voice, sharper than it had been earlier, snapped Vera back from the faraway place she'd gone. "How about we make each other a promise? I will promise to be attentive if you promise to be concise." She only looked at him, so he continued. "So tell me. Exactly why are you here, Vera?"

She pushed off the wall she'd been leaning on and walked over to Jacob and half sat, half leaned on the desk facing him.

"Do you want to know what makes me so certain that you know why I am here?" She didn't give him time to answer, "Because, Jacob, after" --she bounced a thumb off each finger as if to count-- "the past ten years of hopping around the globe, avoiding each other, you're not *surprised* that I'm here, that we're *both* here now, at the same time."

"I guess I am not," he answered plainly.

"I guess you're not," she parroted.

After a long stare, she finally shared what she had spent the last several years trying to avoid acknowledging.

"I felt it, you know. When it happened. It was seven years ago, but I remember how it felt like it was yesterday. I remember it *every* day." She fidgeted with the things sitting on the desk around her as she spoke. "I think I wanted too badly to believe that it was anything else - anything but this," she said as she gestured to his still body. "It took from me, too. And I think that's why I stayed away from this place even though I was always just down the street. I didn't want it confirmed." She looked at Jacob with sad eyes then.

"Do not concern yourself. Nobody else came to see me either when it happened. We all knew it would have one of these days," he said, dismissing her sorrow.

"But there's no avoiding it now, I guess," she said with a shrug.

"I suppose there is not," he answered.

Neither of them were prepared to give anything else away, lest one knew something the other didn't. What they hid from each other, they each knew, would be life-changing, even for beings such as themselves. Vera leaned in closer to Jacob and her hair slipped over her shoulder, shielding half her face with a curtain of black, silk strands. She lowered her voice as if the books themselves might overhear the secret she was about to share.

"You don't have to tell me anything. I doubt you'll be able to hide it anyway, but do consider that I am not the only one who knows what happened yesterday. I'm just the first to arrive."

Jacob's eyes merely switched from the ledger before him to Vera's challenging gaze. A muscle tightened in his jaw. It was as brief and as small a reaction as anyone could have, but she still noticed it.

"You couldn't possibly have imagined Father and our sisters wouldn't have felt it, too. How small have you let your world become, Jacob?" She wrapped the statement with a pitiless, downturned smile.

"If I recall correctly, the size of my world or how I move --or do not move in it-- was not any large concern to you, Vera." Jacob, with no hesitation, and almost out of instinct, aimed his response at the heart of one of her only vul-nerabilities.

"Five hundred years ago, Jacob, that might have landed. I suggest you save that charming wit for when Father and our sisters find their way into this quaint little store of yours. You will need it." She looked away after making sure her point was heard. If she let him look into her eyes for a moment longer, she feared, he would learn that what he said *had* found its mark.

For all that had been said and all that had been dredged up, the pair sat in appreciative silence together. Being in each other's company once again brought back a sense of completion that neither had felt in all their years apart. It wasn't until this moment that Jacob realized that their absence had been his constant companion - both a shadow and a reminder of them.

The bells at the front door mumbled a dissonant song, whose sounds fell rather than floated. Both Vera and Jacob looked toward the door with rapt anticipation; an audible sigh came from the both of them as they saw who walked in. It was a sweet-looking lady, hunched over a small cane. She could have been five feet tall in her youth, but the decades of her life took inches from that and it showed.

Vera let out the smallest sound of approval. She then popped herself from where she was posted at Jacob's desk and brushed invisible flecks of dust from her trousers.

"I guess I can see the appeal of having the bells," she said as she grinned at the sight of the wholesome little woman. "The bells never tell a lie. How very interesting her life must have been for them to sing such a song for her." Her delight was clear as she murmured her commentary to Jacob.

After realizing the person who entered the bookstore was not anyone he'd feared it would be, Jacob lost all interest in the woman and had already gone back to reading his ledger.

"Well, I suppose we should continue this conversation another time. I have a few things that need attending. So I'll be on my way, then." Vera touched her fingers to her lips and then to Jacob's forehead and smiled.

Jacob jerked his head away and Vera outright laughed at the familiar reaction. Neither spoke as she breezed back through the bookstore the same way she came in. As she passed the woman who had begun browsing the antiques, she gave a little wink. The woman offered a Mona Lisa smile in return. Delighted, Vera leaned on the door to open it and turned back to bid Jacob farewell.

"I'll be back before you know it, dearest brother," she nearly sang before leaving.

"I know," he said.

Jacob was left alone, again; their brief reunion replayed for him in his head.

"*...do consider that I am not the only one who knows what happened yesterday. I'm just the first to arrive.*" The words echoed in Jacob's mind.

He did consider this. He had been considering it since he felt the Earth fall from beneath him just the morning before. Only one other time had he felt that kind of shift in energy. It was as significant then as it was now. The only difference was that the first time he felt it, it had brought him to his knees - from where he stood, on his own, poised and powerful. This time, it was as if he hadn't spent the last seven years feeling nothing at all. It was an eruptive blaze that started in his core and then spread to the tips of his fingers and toes. Every nerve in his body danced as if they'd been hit with a tuning fork. And in its wake, all that was left was the uncertainty of whether he was ready to have felt it at all.

Recalling Vera, sitting before him, lost in her own churning sea of deep and dreadful thoughts, he knew that he had felt it. They'd all felt it. And it was only a matter of time before the bells at his door sang for the others in their troubled family.

In her new apartment and alone with her thoughts, Claire had lost all sense of time. The irony was not lost on her as she knew, more than ever, the great waste it was for her to let day-after-day pass by while she remained broken. She was broken by what her father had done to her. She was broken by the realization she was now a part of something that obliterated everything she thought she knew about the world. She was broken by the utter loneliness of her new circumstances. If it had been a bad breakup or a fight with her parents, she had people she could have called. There was nobody she could tell about this; she couldn't tell it even if she wanted to. She'd read before about the five stages of grief, and sometimes she thought she might be in one stage or another, but she ultimately didn't have the energy to try to confirm or try to see daylight from the bottom of this chasm she'd fallen into. A week went by and the only thing she'd used the power of her contract for was to get food delivered to her faster. After three weeks, she'd gotten it down to a science.

She kept her contract open on her coffee table - the elaborate countdown clock, upon it, on full display. She'd spent entire days watching the seconds tick down in silence. Sometimes, she'd bring the contract to bed with her and fall asleep watching it. Seconds turned to minutes; minutes to hours; hours to days. The countdown was her only companion.

"This is where you live?" the delivery boy asked as he handed Claire her dinner and admired the building.

"Yes," she answered, more gruff than she'd ever heard herself.

"That's really cool. I wanna get a place like this someday. Maybe when I'm in college or something. Anyway, thanks for the tip. Enjoy your dinner," he said merrily.

When the boy left , Claire didn't immediately go back inside. She merely stood in the doorway and watched the boy bike away to the next stop on his delivery route. What he'd said reminded her of a time she would have rejoiced to live in an apartment just like the one she lived in now --but had not truly *lived* in-- for the past three weeks. She stepped out of the doorway and looked up at the building, trying to see it through the boy's eyes.

It was small and perched so precariously on the edge of her sanity that it could lose footing at any moment, but it was there: appreciation. She recognized it and she clung to it for her dear, shortened life. She clung to it because she realized that it was a gasp for air as she drowned in those dark waters of defeat; she was gasping for air, and it meant that she *wanted to live*. Maybe she wouldn't live as long as she thought she would, but she wanted her life for as long as she could have it. She clung to that tiny appreciation for how perfect the apartment was and how easily it had come to be hers. What she didn't know, because she hadn't learned yet or even cared to learn, was just how much had happened to ensure she'd have it.

It began with a toast:

"Now let's all raise a pint to my baby sister!" Marshall slurred his toast to a raucous pub full of friends and family. "Jenny! We are going to miss you while you're off doing big time barrister things in London! I think it's rubbish you have to leave us, but I'm also probably too pissed to be giving this bloody speech anyway." With an arm wrapped around his giggling sister's shoulder, he guzzled the rest of his twelfth beer.

Jenny was set to move to London after landing a position as a junior associate at one of the city's most prestigious law firms. It was her dream job and nobody was happier for her than her brother who made sure the festivities of her going-away party closed down their favorite pub.

"*Marshall.* You're coming home with me. You are *mad* if you think I'm going to let you drive home," Jenny told him. Drunken laughter and shushing echoed off of the surrounding buildings as the last few friends, who made it to the end of the celebration, helped the siblings into their cab.

"Don't forget he's got work in the morning, so you'll need to get him up early so he can go home and get ready. I've got a lot riding on this match. Don't let him cock it up!" a friend reminded Jenny as their cab was leaving.

Several hours later, thunderous booing and chants for his removal were magnified by the hangover Marshall was trying desperately to hide. He was the sickest he'd ever felt as he realized he'd made a mistake: he'd just given a goal, that he shouldn't have, to the visiting team. Through the fog of his hangover, he recalled what he thought he'd seen and realized the player had fouled. The call was already made, however. The crowd was already ravenous. The game was all but lost for the home team that needed the win for a shot at the World Championship.

"Oh, let me guess. You're a fan of theirs. Of course you didn't see the hand ball!" Olivia argued with her cab driver about the lost match that happened the day before.

"That may be true, but the call was the call. We won. You are simply going to have to get past it, love," the cab driver gloated.

Olivia was a staunch supporter of the team that was robbed of their shot at the World Championship. Half the contents of her large handbag were out on the seat next to her as she searched for her passport while she argued. The cab driver was having fun gloating and continued the argument he could have easily ended at any time.

"I'll tell you one thing. That man's career as a referee is over. And good riddance!" she passionately proclaimed as they pulled up to the drop-off zone at the airport.

She collected all the items from the seat and stuffed them back in her bag in a hurry. She'd gotten everything back into the bag except for the plug converter she brought with her on all her international trips. It had fallen on the floor and rolled under the driver's seat. She hadn't even noticed in the heat of their argument.

"The linen closet in the hall!" Jeremy yelled across the apartment to his house guest who was looking for a towel for her hair. She'd brought her own hair dryer, but couldn't plug it in to use it.

"Thanks!" Olivia yelled back as she grabbed a towel and shut the closet door as she murmured to herself, "I can't believe I forgot my plug converter. Or maybe I lost it in that damned cab with that damned driver."

"Hey, where's the kitten?" A half-hour later, Jeremy, dressed for his mother's birthday party, began to panic as he couldn't find his newly-adopted kitten.

"I don't know," a puzzled Olivia answered. "She was just wandering about a moment ago, I'm sure of it."

They searched the apartment, high and low, checked under the furniture and beds and in every room twice. They were running out of time as they had to pick up balloons and have them at the restaurant, where the party was being held, in less than an hour. The kitten was finally discovered asleep in the linen closet. They agreed she must have slipped in when Olivia opened it.

"I can't believe we actually made it!" Olivia laughed as she and Jeremy found the perfect parking spot in front of the restaurant.

"That was wild!" Jeremy agreed as he absentmindedly opened the back door of the car to get the balloons out.

In their haste to get to the venue on time, they failed to secure the balloons in the back seat. When Jeremy opened the door, they floated out of the car in a small, colorful cloud.

"Oh, they're having a bad day," Brian said to no one in particular as he watched the couple across the street desperately trying to wrangle balloons that were floating out of their car. He continued watching them instead of where he was going and ended up stepping on the heel of the man in front of him, making his shoe slip off.

"Oh, man. I'm sorry. I wasn't paying attention to where I was going," Brian apologized to the man who waved off the apology.

"It's fine. Happens to the best of us." The man chuckled.

Elliott shuffled toward the buildings, out of the walking traffic, to put his shoe back on. He put a hand up on the wall to balance himself as he pulled the shoe back over his heel.

"It should be here," Christina murmured to herself as she went around the man fixing his shoe. She checked the address she had written down and looked around for numbers on the buildings again. She might have seen the number she was looking for had it not been covered by Elliot's hand at that moment.

Claire walked down Main Street with no clear destination. She needed the walk and the fresh air after learning the terms of her contract that morning and then spending the most uncomfortable breakfast she'd ever had with Niran. She smiled politely at the young woman, about her same age, who was looking at the street numbers on the buildings in confusion. She would have offered to help, but they simply smiled at each other and kept walking.

Across the street, there was a small commotion as a couple scrambled to gather balloons that had floated out of their car.

"They've lost three already. Whoops. Nope. Four," Charlene said, more to herself than anyone else.

Claire acknowledged the commentary with a chuckle as she admired the bay window of the restaurant whose doorway the woman was leaning against.

"Are you looking for an apartment?" she asked Claire, abruptly.

"I'm sorry?" Claire looked around. "Me?"

"Yeah, you." The woman laughed.

Claire took a breath to consider her answer. She realized that while she did not have a destination in mind for her walk down Main Street, she did, actually, have a desire.

"Yes," she answered with a smile.

"Great. Let me get the keys, I'll show you the place. It's right above here. This is my restaurant and I own the apartment above it." Charlene pointed her finger up as she slipped back into the restaurant.

Claire looked up at the windows of the apartment and then back at the bay window she had been admiring. She turned and took in no particular part of her surroundings as she pieced together what was happening for her. Charlene returned, moments later, with the key and a quizzical look.

"You're not Christina, are you?" she asked with a smile.

"No, I'm not," Claire answered, realizing that Charlene must have been waiting for someone else who was going to see the apartment.

"Well." Charlene looked up and down the street. "First come, first serve," she said with a grin and a shrug of her shoulders.

Claire's new apartment, a second-story walk-up, was no bigger than the carriage house on her parent's property. It seemed pieced together with what little area was available, and almost better suited for being a large storage space rather than a living space. She had come to appreciate every unique thing about the apartment after her encounter with the delivery boy, who would never know what he did for her.

Early in the mornings, she could hear music and commotion from the kitchen staff of the restaurant. She was learning to sleep through it, but when the scent of their freshly-baked goods wafted through her bedroom, there was no more staying asleep.

It was in those morning hours, as she lay between sleep and waking, that she allowed herself to be consumed by the thoughts of her circumstances. Sometimes, she would dream of her life before and wake up with a sigh of relief, convinced it had all been a dream. Dread and realization sluiced the relief away as quickly as her new surroundings came into focus. It had been another three weeks since her first spark of appreciation and she was forcing herself, all day, every day, to appreciate anything and everything in which she found goodness, no matter how small the amount.

She hadn't done anything with her newfound good fortune and heard the ticking of her clock grow louder every day. Time spent making flower arrangements for the restaurant and filling her new home with personal touches gave Claire the illusion of normalcy she so desperately wished could return to her. Though she knew she might not have the time to fix what had broken in her, she repeated --like a mantra-- that she would focus every ounce of energy on only herself. She couldn't think of her parents yet. She knew she had to, but this wasn't the time - not when she was finally putting herself first.

On this morning, Claire sat at her too-big kitchen table, enjoying fresh pastries and freshly-brewed coffee from Charlene. The grateful landlady had insisted on them being her treat for another beautiful flower arrangement Claire just made for the big, bay window of the restaurant. She finished her pastries, just enough in the bag to fill her up, and had the last sip of her coffee, just enough to satisfy her caffeine craving. As she thought about how she might spend another day alone, she felt another gasp for air in the form of a strong desire for purpose and friendship.

Just then, the doorbell rang.

part three

destiny met

purpose and friendship

a thimble of revenge

"Everyone, out."

In her large vanity mirror, Lady Margeaux stared at the reflection of the quiet stranger who had just darkened her dressing room doorway. Her command to the other three ladies in the room needed barely be spoken above a whisper and they obeyed, squeezing past the stranger to exit. As the other ladies, in various states of costume dress, filed out of the dressing room, Lady Margeaux sat silently. Her eyes were transfixed on those of the man whom she'd known would come for her. She'd been preparing for this moment for months, but no level of preparedness, she realized, would stop her heart from feeling like it was going to beat out of her chest.

"Ms. Stone." Niran's voice slithered through the quiet and lay across Lady Margeaux's shoulders like a snake.

His presence kept her pinned to her vanity chair as fear replaced the air in the room with the thud of her every heartbeat. The sensation of her fear coiled around his face and ran fingertips across his lip as it teased him. He'd learned to control his appetite for it around those for whom he'd felt some respect.

Lady Margeaux had felt similar fear before, albeit none so great. She focused on her breath, feeling it pass through her nose and fill her lungs. She focused on the muscles in her face as they tensed under the weight of the deadened air in the room. She focused on her pride which spoke to her through gritted teeth.

You get off that chair and raise your chin to that man, right now. You didn't crawl your gangly ass out of suburban hell and become THE Lady Margeaux so some man in a two-season old button down could stand over you.

At this thought, this reminder of who she was, she raised her chin at the reflection of the statuesque man who still lingered in her doorway.

"That's Lady Margeaux to you. I'm so sorry, I didn't get your name," she said as she turned in her chair and faced the man fully.

Being addressed as "Ms. Stone" by anyone who wasn't her banker, doctor or lawyer was simply unacceptable. It wasn't about being informal so much as it was about addressing her outside of her title - like she was, indeed, nobility. That kind of familiarity was earned.

The stranger did not answer her. He merely glanced to the threshold of the doorway in which he stood and then back at her.

Lady Margeaux was not the same person she was thirty-five years ago when another stranger stood in that same spot with an offer that would change not only her life, but also her death. No, she certainly was not the same, as she stood from her chair, tall and proud, with a hand on her hip.

"You must have me mistaken for someone else," she dared him.

"Please excuse me. It's a pleasure to finally meet you, Lady Margeaux," Niran capitulated with a respectful bow of his head.

"That's more like it," she answered and when she decided he'd properly found his place, she finally invited the man in.

"Do come in."

The words, like the air, were heavy and uncomfortable to speak. She dropped the invitation from her glossy lips with not a wisp of breath more than was necessary for them to be heard. She waved a hand in the direction of a worn, brown leather couch which sat along the wall to the man's left - an invitation for him to sit.

The wall, starting at the door to the dressing room, was curved to form a quarter circle and ended at the entrance of the wardrobe closet. It would be a plain, unassuming white if not for being covered, from top-to-bottom, with thousands of signatures, greetings, well-wishes, one-sentence love letters, initials inside hearts, Polaroids thumb-tacked to it and even a section of chewed up gum. The welcomed vandalism was interrupted by three full-length mirrors that hung just outside of the wardrobe closet. A flattering, diffused glow emanated from the lights which lined the borders of the mirrors.

The wall to the right and perpendicular to the entry door was covered in framed photos of, what seemed like, every performer to have ever used that dressing room, going back decades. Lipstick kisses and signatures adorned some of the photos as well as trinkets hung from corners or notes and even cash tucked behind the frames. The back wall of the oddly-shaped dressing room was lined with five vanities. The center one was the largest with a mirror one-and-a-half times the size of the other four that flanked it. No surface was bare as all five vanity tops were strewn with every sort of make-up and tool for application their surfaces could hold. Hanging from the mirrors were all manners of underwear, stockings, scarves, ribbons, belts and other accessories.

It was from that center vanity that Lady Margeaux rose and waited for Niran to take the seat which she'd offered him. He did not sit. Rather, the pair stood before each other, assessing. There was only one other time, of note, that she'd stood before a stranger who seemed to know her more than she liked. It was with the woman whom she'd come to know and love as the sister she never had - Vera.

Staring at the stranger before her now brought her right back to the memory of that fateful meeting.

"You aren't looking for work, are you?" Lady Margeaux had asked with a quizzical look, taking in the beauty before her.

The women had been about the same height - Lady Margeaux only slightly taller. Where Vera's hair had been like prism-spun black silk, Lady Margeaux's had been naturally a cloud of tight curls that were almost always braided into neat cornrows to stay nicely beneath her wig caps. Both ladies had upward sweeping eyes that looked almost pushed up by their high cheekbones and full lips that made themselves a part of every conversation. Lady Margeaux had an athletic build and deep, brown eyes that were almost black. Her jawline, she'd brag, 'could cut you if you weren't careful' and she'd regularly passed for being fifteen years younger than her real age.

"Goodness, no!" Vera had laughed the response with a swish of her hair that shone like shards of obsidian. Her smile had been bright and curious.

"Then why, sweetness, are you standing in my dressing room?" Lady Margeaux had readjusted the stiletto heel she'd been about to take off and took a step toward the woman, rather unamused by the tone of incredulity.

With that, Vera's smile had become more subdued and she'd shifted her attention to the wall of photos. Her tone had become less flippant when she spoke again, and without invitation, she'd stepped further into the dressing room to admire the photos. Her back had been to Lady Margeaux as she revealed her reason for the visit.

"There had to have been a point where you were convinced that you were destined for more." She'd turned her head in Lady Margeaux's direction with a small grin, knowing this statement would elicit a narrow-eyed response of suspicion.

Lady Margeaux *had* been convinced she'd been destined for more. Her story was no different than any other young person's story who had discovered that the world was not only much larger than her neighborhood and the bus ride to school, but that she could also be a part of it in ways so significant, strangers would care - care about *her*. It wasn't that her parents or family didn't care; they'd supported her a great deal. Some could have argued it was so much that it bore an insatiable appetite within her for that same love and care from everyone. Her mother used to quip that she'd come into this world with that appetite, having brought it with her from a past life of royalty or stardom - born three weeks premature and, as the story went, a thousand times over, "threw such a fit to be a gift to this world, that waiting another three weeks was just unacceptable."

When Nicholas Alexander Stone told his parents that he was, in-fact, Nicole Alexandria Stone and a she, her mother's face had contorted with disdain. Her scowl, as if she'd taken a gulp of soured milk, formed itself around the name "Nicole" like the very sound of it had tasted of ash. She'd shaken her head, slowly at first and then resolutely before she'd demanded that her daughter *reconsider*. They'd bickered for a week over the name that she'd claimed she had every right to help choose.

"You're my baby, aren't you? Okay, then - I have a say in what your name is going to be," she'd said. Eventually, the mother and daughter had agreed on 'something pretty and French,' and she would, from then on, be called Margeaux Elise Stone. When the pair had announced the name to her father, he'd kissed her on the forehead and spent the rest of the day practicing how to say the name correctly.

Margeaux had known the profound privilege it was --and the sad truth that it shouldn't have been a privilege at all, but a given-- to have had the unconditional love and support of her parents. Had her dreams been grander, required more significant sacrifices on their parts or even taken her from their side, she'd known they would not only turn their own world upside down to help make it happen for her, but they would do it with great joy. Her dreams hadn't been very grand, however. They'd been big, to be sure, but not grand. Ever since she'd learned of the beautiful dancers at the famed, and even a little notorious, Aubergine Theatre, it had been her dream to become one. And so, she had. She'd done so with flourish and fervency. She'd done so with an attitude and truth that had earned her loyal friends and won her rivals. She'd done so, and then some.

Perhaps she would have done more, become more - but she would have had to want to. If there was anything of which one could be certain when listing the things one knew about Margeaux, it was that she'd only done what she wanted. She absolutely could have become a household name, but the only name she had been interested in having was: Margeaux, Lead Showgirl of Aubergine Theatre. She'd held the title for thirty years - thirty years after the three years it had taken her to earn it. That dream unfolded on the photo wall in front of which Vera had then stood. A picture of a much-younger Margeaux, small, and in the back of a group of dancers, had been juxtaposed with another, showing a more confident Margeaux standing with the dancers in front. There had been photos of her with the celebrities and well-known locals who'd visited the theatre. The most recent ones had shown her always front-and-center. She'd worn a proud smile in every snapshot of her realized dream.

"So, clearly, you found that destiny." Vera had turned around just in time to see Margeaux's face relax. Her small grin had stayed on her face as if it was just as much a part of this conversation as the words it carried. "But you've been feeling it again, haven't you? You've been feeling the restlessness that comes with destiny unmet."

The memory began to fade as Margeaux recalled Vera's penetrating eyes all those years ago. There had been something in them that compelled trust from anyone upon whom they fell. They compelled truth from one's lips - and not just any truth. It was that of desires unmet, dreams tucked away behind walls of priorities and circumstance, unrequited love. When those eyes, with all their magnetism, chose to connect with yours, there was no secret desire they could not uncover. Young Margeaux was no different, for she, too, could not help sharing her truths with Vera and that bright, inviting gaze of hers.

There was an emptiness to the eyes that met her own now, in this moment, nearly thirty years later. Where Vera's eyes --turned up by the smile that lived in them-- were full of possibility and promise, the eyes of the man before her now were as deep and dark as those nights where only a slash of the moon hung in the sky. There was just enough light there, a mere sliver, to let you know there was a bottom to what one beheld within them.

Just as his counterpart had walked to the wall of memories, so did Niran. He followed the easy tale the photos would tell of the woman he'd come to meet. His attention lingered on the photos and the changes in the story that took place once Vera started to appear with the young Margeaux.

Margeaux appeared a little older, front-and-center wearing a costume far more elaborate than those of the dancers sitting on the floor around her, amidst Great Gatsbyian affairs for birthdays and holidays. As the years went by, everything from the costumes to the celebrations to the furnishings of the theatre became more elaborate. There were many photos of her with the owner of Aubergine Theatre, even more photos of her with Vera, seemingly inseparable. The most recent photos included her sitting at the large desk in the owner's office - photos in which he had become noticeably absent.

The wall was started long before Margeaux's face graced its first photo. Before her, it was a collection of good times with good people. And while it certainly still was that, it had also become something of a mural for the odyssey of one woman in the life for which she had been born to live.

She stared at Niran's back as he studied the photos. She found it fitting that both Vera and now the stranger would open the conversation while taking in the chronicle of her life. It was fitting that she would, too, be standing in almost the exact same spot when he finally spoke and closed the circle that bound the three of them together.

"My name is Niran. As per your agreement with my associate," he said, as he turned to face her, "I've come to collect what you owe."

Muffled bickering could be heard on the other side of the door when Claire went to see who rang her bell. Through the peephole, she saw only a pinkish blur. It shifted around with every word from the animated voice she couldn't quite place.

"She guaranteed me that I would have everything exactly how I want, and I *want* whoever does those flowers downstairs - excuse me! You are stepping on my dress!"

The fussing and grumbles all stopped abruptly when Claire opened her door. There was Charlene with her usual sweet smile, and Niran, whom she hadn't seen since last week when she passed him leaving the bookstore. Then there was the resplendently-dressed woman who was adjusting the skirts of her half-tuxedo, half-evening-gown. She had on a pink fascinator of feathers and lace that complemented the fuchsia ensemble and jewelry that should have seemed gaudy, but she pulled off well. *That explains the pink blur*, Claire thought to herself.

"Claire, this is Marg- I'm sorry, Lady Margeaux and this is her friend, Mr. Niran," Charlene introduced with a warm smile. "Miss... Or Lady Margeaux came into the restaurant just now, because she saw your arrangement in my window."

She was interrupted by Margeaux's swishing and a little shove past Niran.

"Hello - Claire, is it? It is so wonderful to meet the woman behind the breathtaking floral arrangements I've seen, *thrice* now, in the window downstairs." She rolled the R in "thrice" as if she was pleased to have the opportunity to use the word. She held a silk-gloved hand out for Claire to shake, or maybe kiss - Claire didn't know.

It was held in front of her in lieu of just a mere handshake. Claire took the hand and shook it; albeit a little awkwardly. Margeaux gave no indication of whether Claire had returned the appropriate gesture. She merely drew her hand back in a graceful pull of her wrist and smiled as she gave the slightly-confusedClaire a once over. She had always seen Margeaux on posters, in advertisements, even once, from afar, when the glamorous woman hosted a yacht party at Ego Alley. Having her standing at her doorway now and in Niran's company, no less, had her unable to choose which question needed answered first.

"Hello, Lady Margeaux, it's a pleasure to meet you. I'm sorry, this is about my flowers? Oh, and please come in." She stood aside to invite her and Niran in as Charlene excused herself to return to the restaurant.

"Wonderful! We have lots of planning to do and not that much time to do it. Niran, darling," Margeaux beckoned to him without looking, instructing him to follow as she led the way upstairs.

The skirts of her gown filled the narrow staircase with the harmonized whispers of each layer of fabric and the distinct, self-assured striking of stiletto heels on wood. As Niran walked past Claire, she gave him a questioning raise of her brows. His eyes barely crept upward as if he caught himself about to roll them and stopped. She was surprised to see him standing there when she opened the door. Niran, her contract, the bookstore - she'd kept everything compartmentalized in her life since "the incident." Seeing him now, and being introduced by Charlene, felt almost like they'd soon be "caught" by the world; revealed for who she really is and what he really does.

From the top of the stairs, Margeaux murmured something to herself about the size of the apartment. With the billowing skirts of her dress, she managed to make the apartment feel smaller than it was. It could have also very-well been her personality that had the effect, Claire thought to herself as she took in the juxtaposition of Lady Margeaux and her simple, small home.

"Oh, I'm sure it's delightful, but not in this dress, thank you," Margeaux replied to Claire's offer of tea or coffee. She sat, straight-backed yet comfortably, on the couch. Her dress took up so much space, there was no room for anyone to sit next to her.

Niran had tea; no milk, no sugar. He seemed prepared to have very little to do with the conversation as he, without being asked, took a chair from the kitchen table and set it in the living room for Claire. With his cup of tea, he walked over to Claire's entryway bookshelf and browsed the titles. She had been learning, in these past weeks, to just allow answers to reveal themselves to her. Yes, there was a beautiful and elaborately-dressed woman in her apartment talking about needing her flowers. Yes, she was confused and curious. But, no, she wasn't going to worry about whether she got all the answers or if she even got them in a fair amount of time.

"We're planning my funeral and your floral arrangements are the only ones I'll accept for the occasion."

"I'm sorry. Your...funeral?" Claire asked.

"Yes, honey. You see, this one" --Margeaux said as she gestured to Niran, reading the back cover of a book-- "has come for me. And now I've only got three months to plan my funeral." She paused with a contemplative look. "And because I'm even able to say this to you, without my tongue falling out of my mouth, means that you..." She trailed off.

Claire's lips parted as she took in the woman again and for the first time. She took in the glimpse of her own future; the certainty and reality of it - sitting before her in all its theatrics. She also saw a choice. She saw a choice being made before her to accept one's circumstances with open arms. Lady Margeaux didn't avoid her fate. She didn't wallow in misery or self pity. She cat-walked toward her setting sun in sky-high heels and a ballgown. Claire found a spark of comfort in the thought that she, too, might make the same choice. Margeaux must have seen this all on Claire's face because she then saw something more familiar, more connected to her own circumstances. Margeaux looked around the apartment again and saw *it* with new eyes as well.

"You know," Margeaux began as she looked around the room, "you could have asked for, way...*way* more." She glared at Niran and then gave a more understanding look to Claire. "I see Mr. Niran failed to tell either of us we'd be meeting one of our own today."

"Mr. Niran," he said, to the back of another book he'd picked up, "didn't know it was *Claire's* flowers you were talking about until you dragged him all the way here at eight AM." He replaced the book and continued browsing without sparing a glance at either of them.

"You best watch your tone, Mr. Niran. Use your inside voice," Margeaux hissed. When he ignored her, as she expected he would, she turned back to Claire and continued.

"Mr. Niran, here, is a little grumpy because he's stuck helping me for the next three months and then has to babysit me for a whole week. He thought he was going to come up into *my* club and pull my number and make it back in time for dinner!" Margeaux laughed heartily and finished with a slap on her knee and a long, "*whooo*" that lilted into a satisfied sigh.

She was still giggling to herself and wiped away a tiny tear from her eye when Niran abruptly shut the book he was looking at. "I'm gonna grab a bagel from downstairs," he said, and left without another word. As he made his way down the stairs, Claire began to offer to call Charlene, but he was gone before she could finish.

"Why does he have to help you? And what do you mean when you say he has to babysit you?" she asked.

"It was a part of my deal - the same kind of deal you made. Although, sweet child, I cannot fathom what, in the world it must have been, you ended up getting out of it." Margeaux scanned her surroundings again and lowered her voice. "Did you have someone killed?"

"What?! No!" Claire exclaimed - answering almost too quickly and with too much conviction for it to be fully believable.

"Mm," was Margeaux's only response, and she continued, "I had some demands for my death as well as my life." As she spoke, she swept her arms open across the skirts of her gown, as if to flatten wrinkles only she could see.

"You can do that?" Claire asked the question of Margeaux, but looked in the direction of where Niran had been standing, as if to seek confirmation.

Margeaux rose from the worn couch as if it was a throne and walked into the kitchen where Claire had a pile of flowers waiting to become an arrangement. Though her eyes lay upon the flowers, her being seemed to have floated elsewhere as she spoke.

"You can bargain for anything from them. It all just boils down to a question of cost versus worth, sweetest Claire. In order to have bargaining power, you must be someone they want. If you're lucky, your personality will be enough. If it's not that, then you must be willing to do what they tell you to. And that's where it gets tricky. That's where you have to weigh-"

"–The cost of doing what they want against the question of if having bargaining power is worth it," Claire finished with a solemnly thoughtful tone.

"Exactly," Margeaux replied with a nod.

There was a brief pause and Margeaux continued where she left off.

"You see, my payment comes due in three months. So I need to make sure everything is all set for my funeral before I go. The last thing I needed to secure was a florist and here we are!" She floated her fingertips over the petals and greens. She savored the feel of them as if in recognition that she may not have the chance to experience this, and so many other tiny enjoyments, in the same way again.

"Due? As in... That's when you'll die?"

"Yes, another one of my demands was that I die peacefully and beautifully in my sleep. *But* I also get to attend my own funeral as a guest, so, I've got my people started on planning a great going away party for me as I am to journey away on a spiritual sabbatical. Of course, when they find my beautiful body, unexpectedly, that party will transition flawlessly into my fantastic funeral. Mr. Niran gets to babysit me for the week after, when I will be neither fully dead nor fully alive," Margeaux explained, and before Claire could ask another question, she continued.

"I need to know. If you didn't ask for someone to be killed, and you very clearly didn't ask for any discernible riches, then, for what, in this cruel world, did you enter into your agreement?"

Claire took in a breath with a look of resignation and a small shake of her head. She prepared to tell Margeaux the whole sordid story and quipped.

"How much time do you have?"

"Three months."

Claire winced at the curt answer and continued. Her story spilled from her and in a surprising way that made her realize she needed to tell it. She spared no detail, no thought or feeling. She bled her story onto the now captivated Margeaux like the wound that it was.

"It seems like only moments ago, I was in college, on my way to graduating and eventually owning my own floral boutique," she said with a glance toward the flowers on the kitchen table. "Then my dad got sick. Mental. He was having hallucinations, fits, things like that. And my mom couldn't take care of him by herself anymore, so I had to come home. I only had one semester left."

Lady Margeaux took in a breath and Claire only nodded to her with a resigned smile.

"So I took care of the both of them for the better part of two years. It was okay for the most part, but my dad's fits were only getting worse. My mom wanted less and less to do with him and I was just stuck in this endless loop of... I don't know. It just felt like this endless loop of having no idea when my time was supposed to come or if it would ever."

"I've been there," Lady Margeaux commented, more subdued than she had been all day. "There was a very long time when I felt that I was nowhere near where I was supposed to be; *who* I was supposed to be. It could drive you mad if you let it."

"I felt like it," Claire answered with all-too-knowing agreement. "It," --she paused, feeling a sting in her eyes-- "it was maddening. But I couldn't - there was no room for me to also go mad. My day-in and day-out was just taking care of the people who went ahead and did it and then counted on me to hold it all together." She shook her head and, as if practicing that very composure she spoke of, did not let fall the tears that stung her eyes.

"Was it to get away from that?" Lady Margeaux asked.

"No." Claire shook her head. "No. I would have done it in perpetuity; there was no question. It was actually my dad."

"Your dad?"

"Yup," Claire answered, with a faraway look that took her from the room in which they sat and brought her right back to her parents' house. "He tricked me into taking over his contract."

Lady Margeaux gasped loudly and without a hint of theatrics. It was a genuine gasp of shock. From the look on her face, Claire wondered how often Lady Margeaux actually experienced genuine shock.

"How?" Lady Margeaux barely breathed out.

"I don't really understand it completely, but I'm beginning to. He just wanted it to happen. And I guess, you know, this is how some of these contracts work. You want things to happen and then they do, I guess? He had his contract hidden in his office desk and had sent me to organize the office. I found the contract on my second day of organizing. It was stuck in a hidden compartment and I had to pry open the door with this letter opener. I sliced my finger open doing it. My blood got all over his contract and, apparently, then it was done. I had taken over his contract by blood signature."

Lady Margeaux only stared at Claire for a long moment.

"That rat bastard," she finally uttered.

"Niran came that very night. I found out that my dad had only six months left on his contract, which means I had only six months." Claire's eyes glistened as she continued to restrain her emotions, with difficulty. "I can't even describe..." She looked up at Lady Margeaux then, who, upon seeing the falling tear which did, finally, betray Claire, rushed to her in a loud swish of her gown.

"You don't have to," Lady Margeaux said, grabbing both of Claire's hands in her own and sitting beside her with complete disregard for her gown that had crumpled in the motion. "You don't have to do a single thing more that you don't want to. Do you hear me, girl?" she asked firmly, yet with so much care and understanding in her eyes that Claire broke down fully.

"One moment, please," Margeaux said, and continued to hold onto Claire with one hand while she reached into the bodice of her gown and pulled out an almost-comically-large kerchief which she placed across her shoulder like a baby's burp cloth. At the sight of it, Claire let out a surprised laugh through her tears and Lady Margeaux pulled Claire in for a tight hug, making sure her head lay on the kerchief.

For Claire, there was a mixture of relief, release and comfort that warred with an instinct to shrink away from the caring gesture. She couldn't bring herself to hug Lady Margeaux back, but allowed herself to be held by the angelic woman. They sat together as the last of Claire's tears fell and Margeaux rocked her gently.

"You'll be okay, Claire. I'll make sure of it for as long as I can. And if you don't want to see that Mr. Niran anymore, I can make that happen, too. Well, for the next three months, at least," Lady Margeaux cooed.

"It's okay. He's fine. He doesn't bother me," Claire said, her instinct to be as little of an inconvenience as possible answering for her.

"Well, you just let me know and I'll have that boy sourcing custom fabrics from India for the next three months," Lady Margeaux said with a small laugh as she shifted and held Claire by the shoulders to inspect her face. "Perfectly beautiful. As if you didn't spill a single tear," she said as she touched Claire's cheek.

"Thank you," Claire said sincerely, as she straightened and adjusted herself.

"This, my darling, now belongs to you," Lady Margeaux said, and plucked the kerchief from her shoulder with a forefinger and thumb, and held it out for Claire to take. They both laughed as Claire took the kerchief, that was soaked from her tears and runny nose, and set it aside.

The two walked back over to the table of flowers and Lady Margeaux chatted about the arrangements she'd seen in the restaurant window as Claire felt herself find balance once again.

Their chatting was interrupted by Niran who returned with a small bag of freshly-made bagels.

"Should we get going?" he asked, seemingly unaware of the emotional state from which Claire had just recovered.

"Let's. Claire, baby - you're coming with us," Margeaux instructed.

"Where are we going?" Claire said, looking down at her outfit and then to Margeaux's. "I don't have anything like that," she trailed off.

"You don't need to worry about that at all. *This*," Niran gestured to Margeaux, "is just how she dresses. I had to accompany her to a grocery store looking like this."

"And you were with the best looking person in that grocery store; you're welcome very much," Margeaux said in response with a flourish of her arms as she rose, her hands coming to rest on her hips.

Claire pressed her lips to stifle a giggle at how the two bickered. It made her feel less alone, somehow. And she realized that it made Niran seem the closest to being a normal person than she'd seen him yet.

"You've hosted me in your home, sweetness. Now you'll be a guest in mine," Margeaux answered as she swept past Claire with a wink. "Get your things, Claire. I can't wait for you to see where you'll be making magic for me!"

Claire didn't have many "things" to speak of, but figured she should bring the sketchbook and colored pencils she used for planning her floral arrangements. The two hadn't even gotten around to talking about the fact that she had been asked to do the flowers for the funeral of a woman who was still very much alive. Of two things, Claire could be certain: one, these would be no ordinary floral arrangements; and two, they would be exactly the kind of arrangements she'd love to do for her first--and possibly only-- big job.

Before walking out of her apartment, Claire folded up her contract, ignoring the countdown for the first time since receiving it, and stuffed it into her back pocket.

Just four streets over from Main Street, Aubergine was abuzz with a flurry of activity from every manner of performer and service provider preparing for the evening's show. They were none the wiser to the reason Claire was there to plan flower arrangements. In three months, she thought, these people will be much busier for a very different reason.

"I always wanted to ask if the owner of Aubergine loved purple that much," Claire said, a bit slowly, as she took in the space amidst the chaos - imagining her floral arrangements against this backdrop and that one.

"Oh, sweet heavens, no. I hate purple," Margeaux answered as she inspected and approved a combination of table linen colors that were brought to her.

"I just thought, because of the name..." Claire explained.

"Oh, I get it. We all get it. It was the very first owner of Aubergine that loved the color. Legend has it, she was a dreadful woman. This was all the way back when it was a proper theatre and not the heathen's den into which it has thus been transformed," she said with a laugh and a proud swish of her arm.

Claire had already begun scribbling notes and drawing little diagrams of the space in her planning sketchbook. The Aubergine's stage and its infamous bar were the only pieces of its original architecture. They stayed among the famous and infamous tales the locals told over generations.

"This is going to be the funeral to end all funerals," Margeaux said from behind the bar, leaning on her elbows and picking at her nails.

"I can't imagine it being anything less," Claire replied, half to herself and half to Margeaux, as she surveyed the organized chaos around her. She looked on at Margeaux in curiosity, awe, and respect as she acknowledged that casualness with which the magnetic woman spoke of her coming end.

"I've had a lifetime to live out this contract. I've had decades to take advantage of the life it's loaned to me. And I'll be damned, young Claire, if I go out with anything less than a bang heard around the world," she finished with a wink.

On loan, echoed in her mind. Her life, from the moment her blood touched that wretched paper, had officially become something loaned to her by the powers that seemed to rule this new world in which she lived. The grip she had on her pencil loosened as she considered the people working around her. She and they lived side-by-side but in two completely different worlds. It was only mere weeks ago that she hadn't even known this one existed.

"Did you get everything you wanted? Is that why this is all happening now?" Claire asked, hoping she did not sound too brazen for asking.

"I got what I needed from my contract, yes. But that happened many, many years ago." As she answered the question, Margeaux began putting ingredients into a cocktail mixer as if by muscle memory.

"And it was, all of this? I mean, your success and all?"

"Absolutely not." Margeaux stopped everything she was doing and her tone was hard enough that Claire straightened. They locked eyes and Margeaux made sure they had before she continued.

"Let me tell you something, Claire...

"...every success I've ever had here has been by my own merit, my own

blood, sweat, tears, meltdowns, starved days..."

She got louder and more dramatic with every sacrifice listed.

"... asses kissed, egos massaged, broken bones, cramped muscles, maxed out credit cards, hideous outfits and..."

She realized a small audience had formed around the two of them and paused long and satisfied at the undivided attention she now commanded before finally finishing.

"*Wigs*, honey!"

She finished with a dramatic toss of her head, sweeping to the left and to the right, then back again, with an upward and open flourish of her arms and splayed fingers in a perfectly delivered ethereal pose.

Claire smiled broadly and looked around her as those who gathered hooted and hollered in celebration of Margeaux: the woman --and as Claire was realizing-- the *legend*. Margeaux waited until the little crowd had dispersed before continuing both mixing the cocktail and speaking to Claire.

"Always remember that. I want everyone to always remember that. All of this was all of me and only me. No silly paper from no silly man in a bookstore was going to make my dreams come true for me," she finished.

"Incredible," Claire said, and meant it. It was incredible to her that Margeaux could have used the powers of her contract to fast-track her success and become this revered woman, but she didn't. But it also dawned on her to ask

Margeaux as she shook the cocktail mixer, "Well, then, so what was it? What could it have possibly been if it wasn't all of this?"

Margeaux set down the mixer, put both hands on the bar and studied Claire for a moment, as if deciding if she should know the answer to the question. She took in a cleansing breath and reached for a jar of cherries. She still looked at Claire as she casually held the jar out and it was taken by a man Claire hadn't even noticed had walked up. He opened the jar, handed it back to Margeaux and went about his business.

She still hadn't spoken as she poured the mixture into two martini glasses and then carefully chose two cherries to drop into the drinks, one in each. She kept one for herself and then slid the other to Claire as she finally spoke.

"Revenge."

"I had everything I could have ever wanted or needed. My family loved and supported me in every way. I was well on my way to becoming the lead dancer here. I lost track of all the men who loved me. My life could not have been more perfect for me and she hated it." Margeaux pointed over her shoulder with a thumb at a framed photo of herself, much younger, head thrown back in laughter, embracing another woman. Claire would have recognized that crystal black hair anywhere: "Vera."

Though Margeaux had to have been thirty years younger in the photo, Vera, at her side, looked exactly the same as she had, drawing a crowd around an oyster vendor only six weeks ago.

Margeaux launched into the story of how her life would forever become intertwined with that of the inspiring and baffling Vera.

"But you've been feeling it again, haven't you? You've been feeling the restlessness that comes with destiny unmet." Vera had turned to face Margeaux fully and had taken a step closer to her. The side grin she wore had been full of expectation and confidence.

Margeaux had taken a step closer to Vera whose very energy was so commanding, it had felt like falling toward the sun to be near her. In her wake had been the unmistakable scent of Chanel No.5 mixed with something else --something completely hers-- gardenia and fresh snow. Vera had grinned like a cat as Margeaux circled her, assessed her. The pair had been silent as Margeaux had found her way back to her vanity and taken in a deep breath.

"These fans get crazier and crazier every year." Margeaux had grabbed a photo of herself from a stack she kept on her vanity. "What's your name, angel?" she had asked as she opened a sharpie and had started signing the corner of the photo.

"I'm sorry. What?" The question seemed to have shaken Vera from what had seemed like a satisfied fog as she answered, "Vera."

"*Vera.* That's very pretty, sweetie," Margeaux had said as she finished her autograph and held it out to her.

"What?" Vera had repeated, her eyes widening as she flashed a surprised smile.

"*Someone, take this wheel...* Okay, Vera, sweetie, I've got a long evening ahead of me. I need to get ready. It was so wonderful to meet you, but it's time for you to go now." Her tone had been thick with condescension and impatience as she had gently guided Vera toward the door by the shoulders.

"No, you don't understand. I'm not here for an autograph. I'm here for you," Vera had said with a laugh and a wide grin. It had seemed as if she'd never been surprised before and was thrilled by it.

"Of course you are, darling. Okay, thank you so much for coming by. I hope I see you out there at our next show. Love you; mean it!" Margeaux had told her.

Margeaux sighed to herself at the memory she shared with Claire and Claire could not hear enough. She wanted to know everything.

"She had come around two or three times a week for about six months before I gave friendship a shot with her. I didn't know if I could trust her before that. When you're surrounded by people who are after this piece of you or that piece, you tend not to trust too quickly. And I didn't trust her. Ooh, and she hated it!" Margeaux laughed, much in the same way she did when she spoke of Niran's being stuck with her.

"I *absolutely* hated it."

Claire jumped, her pencil almost falling, as the sing-song voice fluttered through the air from behind her.

"Speak of the devil and she clops in on red-bottomed hooves," Margeaux trilled to and about Vera as she handed a drink over to her friend.

Vera took it so casually and sipped from it with such familiarity, as the two greeted each other, that Claire knew it was something they'd done a thousand times. For a moment, she could only look on at the pair of friends who looked and acted like they'd spent a lifetime facing the cruelties of the world together.

"Anyway," Margeaux sighed. "Yes, little Miss Witchyface, here, hated the-fact that I didn't just throw myself at her feet and beg for her services."

The three now walked together through The Aubergine as Margeaux told the story of her friendship with Vera with great flourish. They arrived at the dressing room where everything started, as Margeaux told it. As Claire sat in a vanity chair in the corner of the room and Vera draped herself along the couch, her head casually propped on a fist, Margeaux stood before the photo wall and continued her tale.

"This man here," --Margeaux said as she pointed at a photo of herself, much younger, with an older gentleman, both sitting on the edge of the stage-- "his name was Quinto Davide. We all called him Q." She smiled at the photo, seemingly lost in the memories it conjured up.

"He owned this place before I did. He's the man who gave me my start, my first chance at my dream. Everything."

She spoke of the man with such reverence and heartbreak that Claire sat up straight to the sound of it, wanting to hear every detail of the story in full.

"I walked through that door for the first time with bad makeup, bad clothes and a forty-dollar wig. Q took one look at me and walked me straight here, to this very dressing room, and told the ladies to do what they could with me." Her eyes started to glisten as she took a couple steps to a set of photos where she was a little older, she and Quinto obviously much closer.

"I started out as a waitress. Then he put me behind the bar. But he always knew I wanted to be front-and-center on the stage. He also knew I wasn't ready, no matter how much I fought him on it. He forced me to learn patience, which was definitely not my strong suit. I was here a full year before he let me rehearse with the other ladies. I learned so much from that man, fought with him, confided in him, tried to protect him, even. After my parents passed, he was there for every moment of it and he became all that I had. I was this bratty, little queen-in-the-making and he was this little, old Italian club owner who hated clubs and crowds and only kept this place going because he made a commitment to The Aubergine and he was a man of his word."

Vera had a look of sympathy and support on her face as she listened, quietly, to Margeaux's story. It made Claire wonder at what was to come in the tale.

"There's a man that's supposed to be here," --Margeaux pointed at another photo of Quinto with a man whose face was cut out of the photo-- "it was Q's brother, Severo." There was a clear note of disgust both in the way she said his name and looked at the hole in the photo. "Q did everything for Severo - gave him everything, and that man only took and took and took. He was so jealous of Q, but Q supported him, so he still came slithering back here week after week.

He was mean to us when Q wasn't looking. He'd say the worst things about us under his breath, steal from our tip jars, close doors in our faces. At least every other week, someone was crying because of him. None of us had the heart to tell Q that his brother was a deplorable waste of space. Q loved him so much. If there was anyone in the world who could teach unconditional love, it was that man. So we all just lived with it. We lived with this awful man coming here to take advantage of one of the best people we knew. Sometimes I'd catch Severo looking at Q and there was so much hatred, so much envy in his eyes, he didn't seem human." She looked at Vera when she said this. Vera only lifted her chin and breathed in deep as if she, too, was reliving the memories and was seeing what came next in the story all over again.

Margeaux lay on the floor, vision blurred, her own vomit on the side of her face and on the floor next to her head. She was starting to lose consciousness and had already lost most control of her own body. Sweat poured off her as she tried to get up, but she could not even turn to her side, having fallen mere steps from the dining table where she, Quinto and Severo had been eating only moments ago. There was pounding on the back door and then she heard it slam against the wall as it flew open. Steps came running down the hall and she saw a pair of stiletto heels halt by her. Vera fell to her knees before Margeaux and tried to prop her up.

"Mar. Mar! Okay, we gotta go, let's get up now. I need you to-"

"Q," Margeaux barely breathed out.

Vera looked over her shoulder, Margeaux still in her arms.

"Mar, he's not moving. I don't think-"

"Q. Save. Please." Margeaux used every ounce of the sliver of consciousness and energy to say the words.

Vera swore, thought for a moment and then laid Margeaux back down gently. She swore again and hurried to Quinto.

"Q! Q, are you with me," she yelled. It was followed by a silence that was so painful for Margeaux to hear that her eyes pricked with tears. Vera swore again and hurried back to Margeaux.

"Mar, I'm so sorry. He's not breathing. He's not moving. Mar!" Vera swore a third time and it sounded distant and muffled. She was fading fast and it seemed like there was nothing to be done.

"Damn it, Margeaux! Listen to me. Listen! Stay with me and listen!" She lightly batted Margeaux's cheek, forcing her to make eye contact. Margeaux could barely keep her eyes open and Vera was practically just a blur to her.

"Margeaux, you need to let me save you. There is only one way I can save you. Are you listening? Margeaux, all I need is for you to agree. Let me hear you say, 'yes!'"

"Q. Save." Margeaux barely whispered.

"I can't, Mar. I can't save him. I'm so sorry. I really am. But I can save you! Please, please let me save you! You just have to agree. I just need you to say, 'yes!'" Vera repeated herself earnestly.

"Sev-. Sever-" Margeaux tried to say, but could barely speak anymore.

"Listen to me, Mar! We don't have time. What do you want?! You can have anything, just agree. But you have to do it now. Margeaux, please. I can't lose you!" Vera began to beg.

"Pay. Sever- Severo. Pay. I agree." Margeaux dug deep within what was left of her to say the few words that she hoped would make sense to Vera. It was the only thing she wanted in this moment and the only thing that would make her agree to let Vera do what she needed to.

"He will suffer in a thousand hells, choking on his own blood for a thousand years, I promise you. I **promise** *you, Margeaux. Please, just agree. Just say, 'yes!'"*

Margeaux's eyes drifted to the other two figures on the floor. The brothers. The one she loved and cared for as if he was a second father. The one who, upon learning he would not inherit The Aubergine, but instead, Margeaux would, invited them to this fateful dinner. His plan was for it to be the last dinner any of them would have.

"Yes." She breathed out with the last of everything that was in her - strength, air, consciousness, self.

She felt Vera shift about, without hesitation, and then felt her shake hands with her, the cold of her signet ring against the side of her palm. Vera leaned in and whispered in her ear, relief and haste in her tone before everything went black.

"I accept the terms of our agreement."

Claire looked between Margeaux and Vera, both brought back to that terrible night in their memories as Margeaux recounted what she remembered. After a moment, Margeaux turned back to the photos, standing in front of one of her sitting at the desk in the owner's office. Vera looked on at the same photo from where she sat.

"What happened to Severo?" Claire asked, wondering if she should have, but needing to know.

"He is currently suffering in the fourth of his thousand hells. Choking on his own blood," Vera answered plainly.

"He died, sweet Claire. Neither he nor Quinto made it out of that dinner. The cops found a small grove of hemlock in a field by his apartment and several batches of tea in his refrigerator made with steeped hemlock. That, along with an assortment of other drugs, was in all the food we ate that night," Margeaux added.

"How did you know to go there and save her?" Claire asked Vera.

"While they are mostly just meddling gossips, the crows can serve great purpose when the need arises," Vera answered, knowing Claire was already well-acquainted with them. Claire took in a strange comfort that the crows might find a way to get her help if she was ever in danger.

It was Vera who continued the story then. Claire had set her sketchbook aside at this point and was quite literally at the edge of her seat, ready to take it all in.

"Mar, look at me. How do you feel? Mar?" Vera, for the first time, wasn't completely certain she had closed the deal. Margeaux lay so still in her arms, their hands still locked in the handshake that bound their agreement.

"Margeaux?" Vera said, far more quietly this time and held her breath as an unconscious vow not to take another breath until her friend did.

Margeaux lay in her arms, still as the death that surrounded them. Vera hugged her limp body to her and rocked slowly. Just then, Margeaux jerked. Vera pulled her away from herself, looking for more signs of life. Margeaux jerked again and then finally took in a breath. It wasn't a deep, life-giving breath, but a choked gasp that was interrupted by a gag. She rolled out of Vera's arms and began vomiting on the floor. She was on all fours vomiting what looked like the very death that tried to claim her. Vera got up onto her knees and ran her hand down her friend's back as she continued to vomit.

Footsteps sounded down the hall and into the room and Vera looked up to see Niran standing before them with a scowl.

"Over there," Vera directed. "No, the other one," she corrected when she saw Niran walking toward Quinto's lifeless body.

Margeaux's retching finally subsided and she slumped to her side, still weak, but with enough strength to roll away so her back was to the puddle of unearthly death and poison she emptied onto the floor. Vera went to her and stroked hair out of Margeaux's face as she made soft, cooing sounds, encouraging her to just rest for a moment and gather her energy.

Across the room, Niran was on a knee in front of Severo. He grabbed a napkin from the table behind him and used it to turn Severo's vomit-covered face toward him. He forced open an eye to look into it.

"How long has he been dead?" he asked Vera, as he studied Severo.

"Ten, maybe fifteen minutes," she answered. "Can you still do it?" she asked, absent-mindedly rubbing Margeaux's back.

Niran shifted Severo's body forcefully and without a shred of kindness, and positioned him so he could use both hands to force both eyes open. He searched them for something only he could find. There was another silence that was almost unbearable for Vera.

"Niran, can you-" She cut herself off as she saw Severo's eyes widen on their own. Niran grabbed his chin to keep their faces aligned as he roughly took Severo's hand to shake with him. The dead man's jaw dropped and his mouth opened in a soundless scream. He raised up on his own, sitting up halfway at an awkward angle as if it wasn't his own strength holding him up. Though his eyes were lifeless, terror swirled around within them.

"Mar, okay listen to me. We have one more thing to do. I can't make you completely better. We need to go and when we do, you need to call the police, okay? Can you do that for me?" Vera instructed, gently.

"Yes," Margeaux answered weakly.

Niran stood up from Severo's side, allowing his again-lifeless body to fall back to the floor with a thud, his face landing back in the vomit there.

"After Vera and Niran left," --Margeaux continued-- "I called the police. I spent a week in the hospital and planned Q's funeral from there. Q had already willed The Aubergine to me, so I took over shortly after his funeral. It was a beautiful memorial for a beautiful man. His brother was cremated and I took the ashes. We cleaned the toilets with some of them. Some were tossed in the corner of the lot where the drunks like to relieve themselves. Some went out with the trash and now rot in a landfill. I kept a tiny thimble full in the office so what's left of him had to see me living and owning this place every day."

"The rest, as you delightful creatures love to say," --Vera said in her sing-song way, getting up to stand at Margeaux's side-- "is history." She smiled and gripped Margeaux's shoulder.

Claire smiled slightly to see the bond between the two breathtaking women. It made Vera seem more human, less intimidating and like she might be able to grow comfortable around her.

"Can I ask what your agreement was?" Claire hoped that Margeaux would be willing to share. She needed so badly to know. The more she learned about Margeaux and her own contract, the less alone she felt.

"I had to go to Greece to meet with Jacob. That's where he was at the time. My contract negotiation took four days. He was livid by the end. He just wanted it to be over and done with," Margeaux said with a shake of her head.

"I didn't know you could negotiate," Claire said in a low voice, almost involuntarily.

"It's not normal practice," Vera said, rolling her eyes with a grin.

"I always had an idea of what Vera did, but as I'm sure you understand, I didn't quite believe it until it was right in front of my face. When she shook my hand..." Margeaux trailed off and her eyes looked off into that faraway place in her memories where that fateful night was kept.

"Anyway, I wouldn't let that Jacob finish my contract until we agreed on how things would end for me and what I was to do, you know," she flipped her wrist in the air and Claire understood it was a gesture toward what lay beyond when her payment came due.

"I would have been happy just to know Severo was rotting in circle-after-circle of hell because of me. Very happy. This little bonus is just icing on the cake. So now I have three months, a practically-unlimited budget, and a 'yes' for everything I want to be at my funeral. And *she*," --Margeaux said, pointing her slender, perfectly-manicured finger at Vera-- "gets to have me as a protege so I can eventually do what she does. That is my part in this forsaken bargain."

Vera simply nodded.

"There can be worse ways to spend the afterlife than being a globetrotting fashionista whose job is to make bargains with people who want to make bargains with you," Margeaux explained.

There was a look on Vera's face that was there and gone in a blink. Claire was sure she'd seen a flash of guilt when Margeaux said that. What could Vera have to feel guilty *about*, she wondered.

After an extended tour of the rest of The Aubergine, to give Claire a clearer picture of what her floral arrangement assignment was to be, the three ladies found themselves on the building's roof deck. It was late afternoon and the sky was brushed with jewel tones along the horizon as golden hour cast honeyed light over their meeting.

There weren't many opportunities for Claire to escape into a moment. This, however, had become one of them. All the familiar sounds of her town were dulled and far away. From that high up, she was forced to see her small world as a bigger picture and not the overwhelming details of which it was composed. She strode nearer to the edge of the building and took in the moment of peace as her mind emptied of everything but the chilly breeze on her face and the distance put between her and reality. Behind her, Claire could hear the murmurs of Margeaux and Vera in their own conversation as they moved chairs around. She turned to see Margeaux take an armful of blankets from an employee who brought them up and divide them between the three lounge chairs, arranged now for the group. They continued their chatting, ignoring Claire as if they knew she was having this moment to herself. After a while, she found her way to her chair and curled up under her blanket as she continued sketching her flower arrangement plans.

It was an unseasonably cool day made even cooler with the setting sun. Claire and Margeaux curled up in their lounge chairs under fluffy throw blankets while Vera lay out, as if to bask in the chilly air as one would under the summer sun. It was difficult for Claire to not study Vera's every move as if nobody in her life had ever basked before, or walked before, or sipped a drink before.

If Vera knew how closely she was studied by Claire or anyone else around her, she didn't show it. She wouldn't show it. She was cold, sitting in her lounge chair, skin prickling under the dropping temperature. The early evening air nipped at her flesh and slowly soaked into her bones. The chill stiffened her and it was uncomfortable, but she reveled in the feeling. She reveled in almost every feeling of discomfort she could steal for herself. They were like tiny broken rules in her life that was strictly governed by perfection. She collected these moments of stolen discomfort like treasures and secrets.

"Where did my nephew go?" Vera sighed in her basking.

"I let him leave for the afternoon. That boy can't wait for these three months to be over," Margeaux joked.

Claire looked up from her sketchbook. Her look of confusion and curiosity must have shown because Margeaux answered her unasked question.

"Our Mr. Niran. He's her nephew."

Margeaux's answer was so matter-of-fact that Claire decided not to ask any of the questions that immediately popped into her head. She decided, instead, to allow herself to enjoy this moment of warm comfort under her fluffy blanket. It was not lost on her that she might now allow herself the feeling of good fortune she could have for herself. She treasured the appreciation for her new job designing the most over-the-top flower arrangements she could dream up for a funeral that was going to be nothing but absolutely over-the-top.

part four

an important assignment

weeping magnolias

aswang

the beekeepers

It turns out, work gets done pretty easily and quickly when all your wishes come true almost instantaneously. It had barely been a week and Claire had already secured her team of florists, wholesalers, supply vendors and backups for all. She'd found herself redoing her sketches over and over until they all became a blur of one another. She'd even taken to asking if she could help in other areas of the preparations. That, too, was made into quick work as soon as she got involved. She was getting bored and it weighed heavily in her gut one day as she sat on a bench overlooking Ego Alley and people-watched.

"Well, there you are," came Vera's sing-song voice from behind. She took a seat next to Claire and held out a cup of frozen yogurt to her.

"Thanks. I was just thinking this was a perfect day for some froyo," Claire said plainly. There was the noticeable lack of surprise and delight that would usually be someone's response to thinking of something they wanted and then having it appear before them moments later.

"What is it, Claire?" Vera asked with a sigh as she spooned her own cup of frozen yogurt.

"I don't know what to do, I guess. I thought I'd be busy for the next three months helping with the flowers. But everything is done now. I tried helping with other things, but that just..." She trailed off and scooped her frozen yogurt that she hated to admit was delicious and, indeed, perfect for this day.

"My goodness. Then enjoy yourself," Vera exclaimed with a laugh. "What do you want? Would you like a little dalliance with a handsome man?" she lowered her voice to ask. Just then, a very handsome man, about Claire's age, started walking toward them, a map in his hand, about to ask for directions.

"No." Claire sighed. And the man found what he was looking for on the map and walked away.

"Claire Bear. This world exists for you now. You need only want and the universe will fold over itself to deliver your heart's desire. Luxuriate. Dally. Party. Travel. It's all for you."

"My parents did that. I tagged along for a lot of it. I'd just be doing the same thing they did, and look what good it did them." She watched a child throw a frisbee a little too high. It soared toward the water where the other children couldn't catch it, but as Claire looked on, a man walked directly in the path of the frisbee and it bounced off his shoulder. He tossed it to the awaiting children with a smile and a nod.

"You brood almost as much as my nephew," Vera sighed as she fished a peanut out of her pocket and tossed it high up. A crow swooped in and caught it mid-air. "I taught him that," she said proudly.

Claire smiled and shook her head. The crow swooped back around and landed on a statue to Vera's right. It gave a few caws and flew away. Vera looked contemplative for a moment while she took the last few bites of her melting treat.

"Well, this has been lovely, Claire. A little depressing, but mostly lovely," she said with a wink. "I've got to see a man about a horse now," she explained as she stood up with a little stretch and handed her empty frozen yogurt cup to a young girl who walked by, trash bag in-hand, wearing a 'Youth Cleanup Squad' shirt.

Another week after that and Claire felt the days pass in a sadly familiar way to how they had in the first weeks in her new apartment. She didn't feel quite broken, but the familiarity struck her. She just didn't know what to do about it. She desired nothing. She got up in the morning. Sometimes she put together a bouquet for the restaurant. Sometimes she helped around The Aubergine. Mostly, however, she just roamed around town. Time had never felt so short and so long before this. And for the first time in weeks, she'd felt herself needing to gasp for air again.

"Hello, Claire," Niran's voice, smooth and calm, stole her attention as she sat on another bench at Ego Alley, people-watching from another angle.

"Niran. How are you?" she asked him, a little empty in her tone.

"I am well. Vera said I might find you here. She requires our assistance at The Aubergine. Are you free at the moment?" he asked.

Claire looked around and then back to him with a small raise of her brow.

"Right. Well, shall we, then?" He held out an elbow for her to take his arm and for a brief moment, she remembered the terrifying man, who stood over her cowering father, darkness within darkness pouring from him. She took his arm, if slightly nervous.

"What does Vera need?" she asked.

"I'm not sure, but she did say it was something important for Margeaux," he answered. He casually removed Claire's hand from the crook of his elbow and stepped back to move to the other side of her. He was now on the street side of the sidewalk as he held his elbow out again for her to take his arm. As Claire took it once more, she gave him a questioning glance that he did not see.

"She also says you've been spending a lot of time --and this is me quoting-- 'doing not much of anything.'" It was as much a statement as it was a question when he said it.

Claire sighed, "It's hard to want anything when you know you can have everything. I don't know what to want," she said with a shrug. "In a handful of months, nothing I do now will matter. And before anyone gets concerned, I'm not saying I've given up or anything. I just," she trailed off, choosing not to finish and instead took a deep breath and closed her eyes as they walked.

She let him lead her as she kept them closed and let the late afternoon sun warm her face and make dancing, red-orange shadows through her lids. The thought crossed her mind that she might look strange to anyone who noticed, yet she relaxed into the pace set by Niran. She allowed herself to flow with his movements as they strode in wordless comfort. It was interrupted by Niran's gentle touch on the back of the hand she had in his arm. She blinked her eyes open and squinted as they adjusted to the light. They'd stopped at a crosswalk and when she looked up at her walking companion, his attention was fixed ahead.

"You don't have to want anything," he continued, once they crossed the street, as if there was no break in the conversation. "You don't have to take anything from this contract of yours if you don't want to. That's part of the benefit of it. You can do as you please and if you please, you can do nothing and the power of your contract will make sure that it is comfortable for you."

"What I would have wanted to do would have taken much longer than just six months," She said with a note of sadness and acceptance.

"I understand," he said.

She waited for him to say more; to offer advice o r consolation. He did neither and she didn't realize until that moment that it was all she wanted.

"Thank you," she said and truly meant it. "I know I'm supposed to feel like this can be the best six months of my life and I feel like I'm supposed to have some weird sense of gratitude for at least having the power of my contract."

"You are not supposed to feel like anything you don't want to," he interjected.

"You're not supposed to feel gratitude if you're not grateful, joy if you're not joyful. I told you that this could be the best six months of your life, but not that it should. The power of your contract and this time are owed to you. You do not owe them gratitude," he finished with a hard stare.

"Okay," she answered simply.

"And," he said, his casual tone having returned, "For at least the next several months, you can change your mind and whatever you want will be yours."

"Maybe I will," she said with a small smile. *Maybe I will*, she repeated in her mind.

The rest of the walk to The Aubergine was pleasant and Claire felt a little easier than she had at the beginning of it. She found herself talking about the time she'd spent people watching and commenting on the surroundings as they walked. Niran merely listened intently and offered his own thoughts on the now much lighter conversation.

"Are you ready for this? Whatever she needs, I don't think it'll be easy," he said, just outside of The Aubergine.

"I am," she said with humor in her smile as she slipped her hand out from the crook of his elbow before walking in.

"Oh, good! Claire. Niran. Margeaux is," --Vera made a distressed sound and waved her hands about her head-- "so I'm going to need all hands on deck for this. Well, your hands, specifically. More specifically, I need you two to hand-deliver these to this list of people." She gave Niran a large box of in-vitations and a list of names and addresses. "Listen to me. These need to be hand-delivered to each recipient, no exceptions. Those are the days and times each person will be available. She was very adamant about these instructions. Don't ask me why."

Claire examined the box. There had to be at least a hundred invitations in it.

"This will take weeks," she said. "And why us?"

"She asked specifically for a pair of beautiful people to deliver the invitations and since all her dancers are busy rehearsing and working on other things here, that leaves you two beautiful people!" she said with exaggerated sweetness. "And don't give me that look, Niran. You're just as much bound to this lunatic's contract as I am," she finished with a dismissive wave of her hand. "Okay, thank you. I'll see you later. Actually come back tonight. We're doing dinner here. Seven sharp. Thank you; bye!"

They stood there for a moment and Claire moved first, taking the list from the box.

"I guess we should get started," she said, reading the list.

Vera glanced up to see the pair walk out, murmuring about where they would go first. She smiled with all the satisfaction of a cat with schemes.

"We actually have the first one today, in just a couple hours," Claire said as she pointed to the first name on the list.

As Niran held the door open with his back, Claire sifted through the box of invitations in his arms and found the corresponding invitation to the name. Each envelope, though themed similarly, was different from the next - to suit each invitee's fancy, Claire assumed. The one she held now was wrapped in pretty, pink silk and was tied off with matching ribbon.

"This is the only one for today. I feel like the safest place for these will be the bookstore. We can drop all this off there and then head over," she planned, speaking more to herself than to Niran. It was the first bit of real work she had in two weeks and she was ready to dive in with full effort.

Hours later, the pair stood in the doorway of Madame Theresa's School for Exceptional Ballerinas. Claire clutched the invitation close to her chest as they neither wanted to fully enter the dance studio nor felt they could leave. A shoe whizzed past Niran's head and he instinctively pulled Claire behind him to shield her should the partner of that shoe follow. It did. He caught it mid-air as Claire peered around him with genuine fear for her safety. Hysterical laughter erupted from the dance studio from about a dozen little children, no older than five years. Some were bouncing around in a small semblance of co-ordinated dance. Some just ran in circles. One little girl simply sat in the corner trying to take her tights off. All seemed to have greatly overwhelmed the young lady, who was clearly their dance instructor, as she wandered around, unsuccessfully trying to corral them.

"Hello! Can I help you?" the flustered woman asked as she made her way toward Niran and Claire, a little boy clinging to her leg.

"Hi, I'm so sorry. We're here to deliver this to Madame Theresa," Claire explained, having to speak loudly over the raucous children who had now begun to take interest in the pair of strangers. She held out the invitation for the dance instructor to see.

"Oh, Theresa should be back any moment, she just had to run a quick errand. Would you like to wait here, or I can take that for you and make sure she gets it," the woman offered. "You can sit here while you wait," the dance instructor said, pointing to a child-sized table and two chairs. "I just need to get these little ones settled so we can learn a brand new dance called The Quiet Dance!" She said the last half of the sentence loudly and excitedly to the children within earshot.

Twenty minutes passed and it seemed to both Niran and Claire like it had been half the day. They'd been visited by each child at least once and there was a clear favorite in Niran. Claire stifled laughs as children had climbed onto him, asked him to show them tricks, sat in his lap, played with his hair and clothes. When Theresa finally did arrive, Niran had stood quickly, sending the child who was in his lap tumbling to the floor in a heap of giggles.

Theresa held a stick, seemingly used for instructing, and firmly tapped it, three times, against the wall beside her. The room fell silent immediately and every child, who had been uncontrollable only moments ago, rushed to the center of the dance studio and sat in formation. Niran and Claire looked on in awe, at the silent children, before they presented the invitation to Theresa.

"I trust my babies didn't give you any trouble?" Theresa said as she read the invitation. Niran took a breath in to say something and Claire gently gripped his forearm as she spoke for the both of them before he could.

"They were a delight. We're so happy we were able to meet them all," she said with a gracious smile. Hearing that, the children began laughing loudly and were, once again, stilled by the *tap tap tap* of Theresa's teaching stick.

After finally leaving the ballet school to a chorus of "goodbyes" sung around hugs and little waving hands, Claire and Niran walked in frazzled silence back to The Aubergine. Her hand lay limp in the crook of his elbow as they realized the peace of their walk with new appreciation.

"I'm sorry, you've got something just there in your hair," Claire said with a little laugh and a point to the side of Niran's head. It was a sticker and she reached up to pull it off him. He only looked down at her and saw the smile that started in her eyes as she tried not to laugh at his current state.

A little while later, they walked into The Aubergine and at the sight of them, Margeaux laughed, slapping a hand on a knee through the layers of her gown. She'd taken one look at Niran, who was normally smartly put together and known he'd been to her old ballet instructor's school.

"I see she still lets those little hellions run amok when she's not around." She laughed some more.

Margeaux explained at dinner that Madame Theresa was her favorite dance instructor and had been a significant influence in her early life. As she spoke, Claire couldn't help but notice that today had been the most human she'd seen Niran. She enjoyed it.

For the first week of handing out invitations, it had been more of the same for the pair. They met friends and loved ones of Margeaux's who were as varied and eccentric as she was. It seemed like every-other-day had been an adventure for them and it practically had been. Folks attending Margeaux's family-style dinners at The Aubergine had come to look forward to seeing what state the pair would be in when they arrived each time. It hadn't been a disappointment.

There was the day the doors of The Aubergine flung open to the sight and repugnant smell of the pair that wafted in and had caused several people to nearly gag. They had been filthy and smelling like farm animals. It was an alpaca farm, Niran explained. They had shown up when one of the alpacas was in labor. Claire had asked to help assist in the delivery and had squealed with excitement when she saw the cria being born. She could barely contain herself when she helped rub it down because it hadn't moved yet and she cried when it finally did and everyone cheered. In all her joy, she'd leapt out of the enclosure and thrown herself into Niran's arms for a celebratory hug. He'd hugged her back and paid no mind to the fact that everything that was on her was now on him. Margeaux refused to let them around anyone at The Aubergine until they'd washed and changed. They spent that dinner donning matching terrycloth robes while their clothes were in the wash.

There was the time they showed up in a gown and tuxedo. They'd had to deliver an invitation to a photographer who had been blocked for a new idea for a series until she'd seen the two of them and found her inspiration. After an hour of hair, makeup and wardrobe, the two of them had spent the rest of the afternoon ballroom dancing in a forest clearing for the photos. Margeaux had quipped that this would be the one and only time she'd allow anyone seated at her dinner table to outdress her.

It was after that dinner that Niran had begun to also walk Claire back to her apartment after Margeaux's family dinners.

Another time, Claire stormed into The Aubergine, letting the door close in Niran's face. She was clearly upset with him. He was somewhere between wanting to take things seriously and trying very hard not to laugh. When Vera and Margeaux saw Claire, their mouths dropped and they looked between Claire and Niran for answers. Claire stood before them, her usually free-flowing and silky hair then done up into a mass of curls and crimps with extensions and accessories. There were clips and pins and so much product in it, it was practically immovable.

"We walked in and *your* friend," Claire glared at Margeaux when she said this, "said he needed a volunteer to practice for some extreme hair competi-tion. I turned around and *this one*" --she pointed angrily at Niran-- "was gone! Poof! Just completely left me there!" Claire practically shrilled.

It had been too close to dinner time for anything to be done to her hair right away. The first couple mi nutes of di nner were in awkward silence as Claire seethed and nobody would make eye contact with her.

"Ugh! Fine! Just let it out!" she told the table as she dropped her fork.

The entire table had erupted into crying laughter. Someone produced a Polaroid camera and some took turns having their photo taken with her. By the end, Claire had found herself laughing along with them. The next morning, Niran had arrived to pick her up with apology flowers. Each type had been individually wrapped so she could create an arrangement of her choosing with them.

Together, Niran and Claire had worked out a routine of doing a handful of invitations every day. He'd pick her up from her apartment, they'd have a quick breakfast --usually at Charlene's restaurant-- and then get to delivering. At the end of each day, Niran would walk Claire back to either her apartment or The Aubergine. On occasion, they walked together to the bookstore to speak to Jacob. When they weren't delivering invitations, they were back at The Aubergine helping Vera and Margeaux with one thing or another.

There had been days where there were no invitations scheduled to be delivered. The days off were welcomed and she was grateful for the rest, but more than that, she felt herself looking forward to the following day of deliveries. She no longer woke up and lay in bed, pinned beneath the weight of concerns for the things she couldn't control. She rose with the morning bustle of Main Street, took time and care with dressing and preparing for the day and went down the stairs with a smile. The days she answered her door to see Niran awaiting her with a handful of invitations had become her best days; each better than the last.

"Where do you live?" Claire asked, as they made their way through town after breakfast at Charlene's. They had only one invitation to hand out this day.

"Where I call home is pretty far from here. For the time being, however, my address is the upper level of Jacob's bookstore," Niran answered.

"Do you miss home? You've been here so long," she asked.

"Not particularly. I've been pretty content here as of late," he replied.

Claire couldn't help gripping his arm a little tighter at the statement and the small smile he had when he said it.

As they neared the street where they'd be delivering the invitation, Niran put a hand over hers. She immediately understood why as they turned the corner onto the street where her parents' house was. When she squeezed his arm this time, it wasn't with the quiet joy it had been only moments ago.

"We can go another way. Maybe around and come up the other side," Niran offered.

"No, it's fine," she said, unsure of whether it actually would be.

As they neared her parents' house, Claire's breathing quickened and the peace, the small joys, the healing she'd begun to have the past month began to unravel. Seeing the house where she'd been lied to her whole life, where she learned of her father's betrayal, where her own life, as she knew it, had ended, caused everything else around her to fall away. The house seemed to grow to twice its size and it was all she could see. It was all she could understand. She let go of Niran's arm and distantly, she might have heard him say her name, but her focus was on the house as she walked toward it.

The towering magnolia trees in the front seemed to weep before her as she passed them. Over the last month, the thought of her parents was always in the back of her mind, like a dull toothache that hadn't yet crossed the threshold into pain that needed immediate attention. Now, it was as if that nerve finally got exposed to open air. She stood in the middle of the front walkway, looking at the bouquet of dead flowers in the living room window and stopped.

"Come out here," she said just above a whisper. Fists clenched and eyes stinging, she repeated herself, "Come out here." Not much louder, but more forcefully.

The door opened and there stood her parents who looked like they'd aged ten years. She hadn't realized, up until this moment, how easily it had been for her to just not speak to them or about them - to deny them space in her day and in her life. There they were before her and there was something so surreal about the moment that she had to turn around and make sure Niran was actually there. He was. He stood on the sidewalk, a respectful distance away, and was focused completely on her. She had to check. She had to make sure that it all had actually happened and she hadn't just woken up from some walking nightmare; that this wasn't just another day of caring for her parents.

The three of them faced each other with locked gazes so full of each person's thoughts and feelings that it seemed to cast a hush over the world around them. Nadine still dressed as if she was going to a garden party. Raymond still used his cane and seemed to truly need it now. They looked... She could barely allow herself to even think it, but in that moment, to her, they just looked pathetic. They looked pathetic to her in the purest sense of the word. They were frail and broken. The glint that had always been in her mother's eye that told the world she was a ruthless force to be reckoned with, was gone. Her father's face looked unwashed and his nails were too long. His outfit did not coordinate and the grip he had on his cane was weak. The two gingerly made their way to the bottom of the porch steps and did not take another step forward.

Claire could not bring herself to stay angry. She had kept a bubbling fury, just under the surface, just for them. It simmered, low and steady and it was partly responsible for keeping her moving forward, though futile as it may have seemed at times. When she could only think of them as the bastard who stole her life and the woman who let him, she could stay furious. In this moment, however, being in their presence, standing with them in front of the house where, for better or worse, they had raised her, she felt meek. She felt like she had only been pretending to be a person who was strong enough to carry the weight of anger toward her parents.

She felt so weak under the fact that she did not want to be angry at them. She did not want to punish them. She did not want to see them so pathetic. She could have, perhaps, held onto some vestige of anger had they walked out of that house standing stiff-backed and proud as they had her entire life. The shells of those people who stood before her now just seemed like people for whom anger and hatred would be a waste. No, she did not want to be angry. She did not want to know what else had to happen for her to be okay with having anger toward them. As she stared at them, she wondered if it was the same for every child of parents who had earned anger. Were they as conflicted as she was in this moment? For those children who were like her, were punishment and forgiveness both things they didn't want for their parents?

She didn't want to be angry with them. She didn't want to carry that with her anymore. They had, however, still done what they had done. That leaning, barely recognizable husk of man, made the decision to steal her life when he was of sound mind and able bodied; and she, whether out of selfishness or neglect, had given him the room and support to be the kind of man who would do that. With all of these thoughts, Claire stepped forward to finally speak.

"Claire, I-," her mother began.

"--No," Claire interrupted. "No. Just no. And never again," she said, feeling her throat tighten. Claire took another three steps toward them to make sure they could hear her clearly. She knew what she wanted to say, but started to feel herself change her mind. She started to feel herself shift to turn around and run from this. Not only did her parents steal her life, but their pathetic state was about to steal this moment from her, too.

Just then, she felt a warm hand gently touch the small of her back. Niran stood next to her, so closely that his warmth calmed whatever it was inside of her that almost made her run from this. She looked up at him and he only nodded at her. She felt the small movement of his hand on her back as a signal for her to do what she needed to do. She nodded in return and he took a few steps back to give her the space she needed. She turned back to her parents.

"I need you lucid right now," she said to her father. Instantly, he straightened, realizing where he was and that his daughter now stood before him. He opened his mouth to say something, but she cut him off.

"No. Not you either. Especially not you," she said with a shake of her head. With that, he closed his mouth.

"There was always a part of me that wanted to believe you were good - that your ruthlessness" --a look to her mother-- "and your charm" --a look to her father-- "were supposed to be admirable things. Maybe on other people, they are. Not on you two. You have always just been a cruel person. You were cruel to me. You were *cruel* to me," she said to her mother and repeated it as if she had to hear it repeated to believe it herself. "And *you*." She looked down her nose at her father, frail and pathetic. "Everyone loved you, didn't they? But not more than you loved yourself. I spent a little bit of time really wanting to know - how could you; how *dare you*. But the answer is so much simpler than anything that would even remotely make me feel better about any of this. You are just those kinds of people and I am someone who just had the profound misfortune of being born to you."

"You," she turned to her mother. "You. I know you only had me because it was a milestone you were supposed to reach in order to be a respectable woman in your society of," --a deep sigh-- "just *truly awful* women. I get that now. And everything you did for me from the moment I was born was certainly not for me. I know that much."

She turned back to her father. "There's still this annoying part of me that wants to demand an explanation - to know exactly why and what any of this truly meant to you, but... you're just too simple-minded a person for me to have any confidence that the answer I'd get from you --even if it came from the depths of your entire being-- would be, at all, satisfying to hear."

"That isn't true, Claire. There's so much--," her father began to say when a pebble under the foot of his cane rolled just so, and the cane gave way from beneath him, causing him to stumble and nearly fall. He slumped into Nadine, borrowing her for purchase. They both looked up at Claire.

"I wasn't done talking," was all she said in response to their look.

"And knowing all this, and seeing all of this for what it is and the two of you for who you are, has taken a pretty big piece of me...just out. And inside the space that piece has left behind is this image of the two of you. You," --to her mother-- "in your clothes and shoes, with your bags and hair and whatever else. You," --to her father-- "in your country clubs and important meetings and designer suits. The two of you in this house or on your trips and at your parties... paying for all of it, not with money *he made*," --she said forcefully with a jerk of her chin to her father-- "but with ***my blood***." She pointed to herself, to her heart, with the hand that shook under the feeling of her heart breaking all over again. Her eyes swept over her parents and then the house.

"I think a lesser person," she motioned a hand to the two of them, "well, people like you, would have sought to punish anyone who did something like this to them. But I can't necessarily wish for your punishment, because if I did, it would happen. Perks of the contract, am I right, Raymond?" she said, doing nothing to hide the tone of contempt.

"Like this," she said, and looked at her mother, just as the strap of the purse she carried on her arm --her favorite one-- broke, causing the purse to fall to the ground and spill its contents. "Or this," and she looked at her father who had winced in anticipation of what she might do to him. "Pathetic," she said with no shortage of disgust in her tone. She had to look away as her mother and father bent to pick up the spilled contents of the broken purse. It was humiliating and even now, after everything, she still couldn't stand to see them humiliated - especially knowing she caused it.

"You know. That's why I stayed away. That's why I wouldn't let myself think of you for longer than brief moments in faraway thoughts. I knew that if I let myself actually let the two of you creep to the front of my mind, this house would be burned to the ground and the two of you would be living under a bridge or something else unsatisfying like that."

At that, her parents shared a look of genuine fear. Upon seeing it, Claire only shook her head.

"It's not in me to be like you so you don't have to worry about any of that actually happening." She gave them a moment and continued. "But I'm only human. And while I'd like to believe I'd be strong enough and different enough from you to never wish for the level of punishment you deserve, I'd rather not have the temptation of having you near," she said and paused for a moment, as if waiting for something. Just then, a moving van pulled up in front of the house.

"So you'll be going now," Claire said, forcing all the strength she could muster into her countenance, though she felt her heart sink.

Both Nadine and Raymond seemed to remember something they hadn't been thinking about at all as the front door flew open and two men carrying full boxes brushed past the three of them toward the moving van. As Nadine and Raymond watched the movers busily working, they had a look of realization that this move had not been their decision.

Claire waited for a response and she silently admonished herself for even expecting that. When there was none, she took one last look at the house, nodded to her parents and turned to walk away. From behind her, Nadine finally spoke.

"Not everything was bad, Claire," she said, and it sounded more like a plea than a statement.

"You're right. It wasn't. But enough of it was. And the worst part is that it didn't have to be," Claire answered, sadly and turned back around. Niran was already walking toward her to take her from there.

"You can't tell me you didn't benefit from all this, too," Raymond said. His statement sounded accusatory but weak.

Claire wholly ignored him as she slipped her hand into the crook of Niran's elbow and began to walk with him.

"What? Are you with that freak now, even after what he did to me?" Raymond said loudly to their backs.

Claire whirled around, eyes darkened and focused on the man who had taken everything from her. Nadine backed up a step and watched her husband lose his balance again as his cane got caught in a crack in the walkway and snapped in half. He stumbled back, tripped on a warped floorboard of one of the porch steps and fell sloppily. Claire continued to walk toward him as he tried to pick himself up. Just then, one of the movers, carrying a large box out the front door, tripped over Raymond, losing his grip on the box, sending it and its contents crashing onto the walkway. Inside the box was Raymond's prized, antique vase that he won by beating out his rival for it at auction. It now lay across the walkway in hundreds of pieces. Claire stepped over the broken pieces, relishing the sound of them crunching beneath her steps. The mover tried to apologize, but she ignored him as Raymond finally stood and backed into the vestibule.

She felt a gentle hand on her shoulder. Niran. He said nothing, but as Claire took another step forward and the plaque above Raymond's head came loose from the wall, his grip tightened on her shoulder. It was enough to give her pause. She turned to face Niran and couldn't hide the deep sorrow and rage that warred within her. He only stood, a pillar of support should she need it. Without another word, she pushed past him and walked away from her parents and the house toward the sidewalk.

"Good afternoon," was all Niran said with a nod before turning to meet Claire at the sidewalk.

When he reached her, he held out his arm for her to take. She did, and gave one last look to her father as she grasped Niran's arm with both hands. A mover edged past Raymond through the door and he stepped aside just as the plaque above his head --the one he'd hung there to ward off his "demons"-- fell and landed at his feet. He stumbled back, then looked up to Claire who only raised her chin at him. For her mother, she'd only spared a glance. Claire knew there was nothing else to be said or done as she saw her mother weeping softly - not over her husband or daughter, but over the broken strap of her favorite purse as she tried, in vain, to reattach it.

Claire didn't speak for the rest of their walk to the next invitation recipient's home. She was grateful to learn all they had to do was hand the invitation over with nothing more than politely smiling and bidding them good day. The walk back to her apartment had been equally as quiet. It had been a silence that she needed. Though neither of them spoke, Claire somehow felt comforted, cared for and most importantly, understood by Niran. She felt his eyes on her for brief moments throughout the rest of the afternoon, and it might have seemed like he was going to speak, but he'd decided against it. It did not go unnoticed for Claire when Niran guided them along a much longer, yet, more peaceful route through town to get back to her apartment.

That evening, Claire did eventually speak just to ask Niran if he could let Margeaux know that she wasn't feeling well and could not attend family dinner. He'd obliged without hesitation and she'd merely closed the door and slowly trudged upstairs to her apartment. At the top of her steps, she could hear Charlene's muffled voice from outside her door.

"Oh! Mr. Niran. Hello. Are you looking for Claire?" she asked.

"No, I was actually just leaving. Have a good evening," he answered.

Claire stood at the top of the stairs, staring at her front door, and realized he'd been standing outside of the door long after she closed it.

With her mind fully occupied with every thought she'd ever had about her parents and every image of them her memory would serve her, Claire went through the motions of a nightly routine. As she showered, as she dressed for bed, as she prepared tea and curled up in the corner of her couch, she only thought of them. She had no care for time or place or anyone else or anything else. Though she knew her parents were going to live peacefully, with extended family, in the countryside --because that's what she chose for them-- she couldn't help but mourn them. She mourned them, in complete silence for the rest of the evening until a single thought of Niran entered her mind. It was the feel of his hand on her shoulder when she had been seconds away from making a wish for her father she would have regretted. It was his warmth beside her, reminding her that she was not alone - that she would no longer be alone in any of this. It was the winding path he took, up and down the prettiest streets of town and through little parks, instead of the direct route home. It was the silence he provided for her when it was what she needed most from him and from the world around her.

Claire realized she would always mourn her parents and the life she should have had with them. As they had been since the day she decided she would never return home, they would remain in the back of her mind. She would wish them peace and comfort. She would wish they had been so much better to her. She would wish them enjoyment and acceptance in their new life. She would wish all their luxuries turned to dust. She carved out the corner of her mind for her parents, back behind her new job with Margeaux, her new friendships and joys, her flower arrangements and experiences which filled her with gratitude when she thought she might never feel it again. She tucked them and all the thoughts and feelings about them into that corner and when she was done, she began to feel a different kind of emptiness. She didn't want this anymore. She didn't want to be alone in her apartment anymore. She didn't want her parents to steal another moment of joy from her anymore.

There were voices and commotion outside her door just then.

"I have a key. Hold on," said one of the voices.

"How do you have a key? I don't have one," said another, annoyed, followed by loud knocking. "Claire! We're coming in! I hope you're decent. My nephew is with us!" It was Vera.

"Aha! Here it is. Move!" Margeaux ordered as the doorknob jiggled and a key could be heard in the lock.

Claire's eyes welled with tears she quickly wiped away as the door opened and Margeaux and Vera spilled in, carrying what looked like baskets of food and wine bottles. She let out a small laugh as she watched the two beautiful women snipe and shove each other for space on the narrow staircase up to her. Niran was several steps behind them, focused only on her.

"Niran told us about your unfortunate afternoon, sweetheart. I told him there was no way you were spending this evening alone." Margeaux said, with a quick one-armed hug as she looked for a place to set down her basket of food.

"If you weren't feeling up to coming to family dinner at The Aubergine, then we were just gonna have to bring it to you!" Vera said, delighted and hugged her tightly.

Claire could barely contain the swell of her heart as she watched Margeaux and Vera unload their baskets of food and wine in the kitchen. They pulled out plates and glasses and anything else they could grab from the shelves and cabinets. They were determined to make the table photo-worthy for the dinner they brought. Niran made a single attempt to assist but was shooed out of the kitchen. He merely walked back to Claire's side with a shrug and she laughed, heartily this time.

"Thank you for this," she whispered to him when he joined her at her side. She took his arm and lay her head on his shoulder and squeezed for emphasis.

He didn't respond. Not with any words. He only breathed in deep and raised a hand to push a strand of hair out of her face. When she looked up at him, he exhaled as if he hadn't since he noticed the first pang of harrow in her at the sight of her parents' house. He opened his mouth to say something.

"Come eat this meal before it gets cold, you two!" beckoned Margeaux from the kitchen.

Claire rose up on her tiptoes and gave Niran a kiss on the cheek. He seemed stunned as she smiled broadly up at him.

"Let's go eat," she said sweetly, then gave him another little squeeze on his arm before going to the kitchen to sit where Margeaux instructed her to.

Niran didn't move for another several moments and Vera motioned for him to get to the table. With another deep breath, he found his way to his seat next to Claire.

Though it wasn't the raucous gathering of at least fifteen people that was the typical Margeaux family dinner, the dinner at Claire's had still been full of laughs, stories and the feeling of deep connection. Vera and Margeaux finished two bottles of wine between the two of them and by the end of the dinner, they were giggling and hanging onto each other as they stepped out onto the sidewalk from Claire's door, ready to make the walk back to The Aubergine. They each gave Claire crushing hugs before leaving and Vera had ordered Niran, over her shoulder, to help Claire clean up the mess they'd left behind.

He'd done as he was ordered without question or hesitation. Though it had only been the four of them eating, they managed to use every single dish in Claire's apartment, including all of the serving dishes and some of the pots. Vera and Margeaux had also left the kitchen in complete disarray and it was a wonder if they'd done it on purpose.

"I can't believe this whole mess was made by just the two of them in such a short time." Claire laughed as she turned on the radio and searched for a station. "This. This is perfect music to clean to," she murmured, pleased, as she turned the volume up.

A light song of acoustic guitar and easy vocals filled the apartment and they got to work. It was happy work, but like a compliment one was unsure if they should pay, the joy of the work they did together went unmentioned. Instead, Claire's smiles were shy and Niran moved around her as if careful not to seem as if anything was any different than it had been a day ago or a week ago. Everything was different, however, at least for Niran who had become keenly aware of every time they'd brushed by each other or touched fingertips when handing something to one another. Claire would shyly look away whenever they made eye contact for too long and he wanted to see it over and over again. They laughed so easily, conversed as old friends, and moved in sync. Where everything became easier for them and more familiar, it had somehow become monumentally more difficult for him to exist within it while remaining outwardly indifferent to it all. Every movement she made had become something of poetry and every word or laugh or glance had put that poetry to song.

An hour later, the apartment looked as if the dinner never happened. Niran was relieved; not because the work was done or because he didn't want to be there anymore. It was because he could barely be there anymore without feeling like he might say something that was beating at him from inside to be let out, but he had no idea what the words would even be.

"Are you okay?" Claire asked, concerned by Niran's shift in mood.

"I am perfectly fine. It's just late and I should get going. We have an early morning tomorrow. Invitations," he almost stammered.

"Sure," she answered reassuringly, "Well, thank you so much for staying to help me clean. Who knows how long this would have taken me if you didn't." She paused, watching him unfold his sleeves that he'd rolled up to his elbows to clean. "And thank you for today, too. I mean, for being there with me and," she paused, wringing a dish towel in her hands as she searched for the words, "and for being so good to me. I mean, I don't know if you even know that you are. Maybe it's just the kind of person that you are. Whatever the reason, I'm grateful for it," she finished with a smile.

He didn't answer her for an almost uncomfortable amount of time as he silently finished unrolling his sleeves and rebuttoning the cuffs. He still didn't answer as he seemed to try to brush out the wrinkles in them.

"If I found out there was a way to treat you better, I would do that," he finally responded.

It was Claire's turn not to respond, but it wasn't for lack of trying as she searched for anything to say that could touch how hearing those words, spoken in such earnest by him, made her feel.

"Oh. I," she tried.

"I'm gonna get going. We don't have to be out too early tomorrow, so you should still be able to get a fair amount of rest tonight once I'm gone," he said as he went to walk past her toward the stairs down to her front door.

"Okay," was her only response.

Claire followed Niran down the stairs, staring at his back, wanting to know everything else he might have said or thought. She held the door open as he walked out and though her mind screamed to her arm to just close the door, she didn't. She couldn't. She just watched him and could have sworn he had the same amount of difficulty taking those few steps onto the sidewalk.

"Well, goodnight," she said, her voice softer than she intended for it to be.

Niran turned around and stepped back into the threshold of the door, looking down at Claire for a moment before gently taking her hand and giving her a kiss on the forehead.

"Goodnight," he said as he pressed his forehead to hers and gave her hand a soft squeeze.

Claire let out a joyful noise and smiled bigger and brighter than she had since knowing him. Niran stifled a laugh of his own and instead let out a sigh of resignation as he shook his head and turned back around to leave.

"Okay, goodnight!" Claire said, giddily to his back.

Niran only raised a hand and she beamed again before finally closing the door.

XIV

Another week of handing out invitations had gone by and much to Claire's relief, it had been uneventful. She and Niran had grown accustomed to the eccentricities of Margeaux's invited guests. More and more, each day, Claire found herself appreciating each invitee's unique contribution to the world and the views and experiences they often shared with her. Margeaux's circle, Claire was learning, was full of people as different from each other as the outfits she wore for each show at The Aubergine. Though Claire felt true jealousy for the decades Margeaux had to curate such a group of people to enrich her life, she was equally as grateful for the opportunity to at least meet them and spend meaningful moments with them, however brief they may be.

She and Niran hadn't spoken about the night he stayed to help her clean, though she thought about it often. He hadn't kissed her on the forehead again since that night either, and she hated to admit to herself that she hoped he would every time he dropped her off at her apartment. Part of her wondered if she imagined different parts of that night and their interactions. She'd believe she had if not for the way the connection and familiarity grew between them - naturally, unprompted and without the slightest hint of discomfort. What this all meant for the rest of her short life and the role he played in it, Claire didn't know. She didn't want to know or think about it. She knew there would come a time when she had to, but for as long as she could help it, she would choose her joy, however small and fleeting, over all else.

"What are you doing?" Claire asked Niran, through a smile as she waved to the owner of the classic sports car they were about to get into.

"Getting into the car," Niran answered as he nodded to the same person.

The pair both stood at the passenger door of the sports car that the owner had insisted they take for a drive through town "to enjoy this perfect top-down weather," he'd told them. He stood at the railing of his porch, coffee cup in hand, and waved back at them while reading his invitation.

"I'm pretty sure he meant for you to drive, Niran," Claire said, confused.

"It seemed like you wanted to drive, so please, by all means," he replied as he nudged her to walk around to the other side of the car.

"Don't tell me you're scared to drive it or something," she said with a laugh.

"I'm not. I just haven't had very many opportunities to perfect operating vehicles of this nature. It would be better if you drove," he said as he slipped into the passenger side, avoiding eye-contact with Claire as he closed the door.

"You can't be serious," she mouthed to him as she walked around the car to the driver's side. "You don't know how to drive a stick?" she asked incredulously as she buckled her seatbelt and started the car. Her mouth hung open in sincere disbelief.

"You may be shocked to know how infrequently I need to actually drive, let alone a vehicle with a manual transmission," he tried to explain.

"Niran," she laughed as she put the car into gear and waved again at the owner before driving around the semi-circle drive onto the road. "You are a million and a half years old. How do you not know how to drive a stick?" She cackled as she asked him, genuinely shocked.

Vera, in one of their conversations from the past several weeks, explained that she, Niran, her siblings and their father were, in fact, immortal. She couldn't remember a childhood or doing anything other than what she'd been doing this entire existence and neither could her siblings. If her father could remember anything before them, he never spoke of it. Since then, Claire sometimes surprised herself with how casually she'd mention it - how readily she'd accepted it as something normal in this new world.

"Let's try not to be too facetious here. There are plenty of people who do not drive manual transmission vehicles," Niran continued.

"Right! But not all of those people were also around for when they were invented!" Her cackles practically turned to hollers.

"Well, I'm happy you're having fun with this, Claire," Niran said with half-hearted frustration.

"That's it. You're learning how to drive a stick today," Claire announced as she began scanning for an open parking lot where they could begin the lesson.

For a moment, she considered that this classic car was not the vehicle to teach someone in, but she quickly decided she would use the power of her contract to assure it would be unaffected.

"We will not be doing this today. Absolutely not," Niran stated firmly.

That evening, at family dinner, the table celebrated with a special toast, given in Niran's honor, for having finally learned how to drive a manual, thanks to Claire's lessons that day. Vera still wiped away tears from laughing at the story Claire told about how it was to teach Niran.

At her apartment door that night, Niran stopped Claire before she went in.

"Thank you," he said.

"Whatever for?" Claire asked with an exaggerated tone and a smile.

"Despite all the fun you had at my expense today," he started as she interrupted him with a dramatic gasp and hand to her chest, "and despite how absolutely unnecessary it was for me to have learned all this today," he continued, "it felt good to learn something new. I can't remember the last time it was that I just learned something new. It felt good," he repeated.

"Well. That could not have been easy for you," Claire teased and then answered sincerely, "You're very welcome, Niran. It filled me with great joy to do it," she finished with a smile and reassuring nod.

"Let's hope the last few invitations go much more smoothly," he said as he opened her door for her.

"I'm certain they will," she answered and bid him goodnight.

"I might have spoken a little too soon," Claire said under her breath, three days later.

She and Niran stood in the center of a crowded karaoke restaurant owned by a Filipino couple who seemed to be in their nineties and spoke not a single word of English. Their great grandson, no older than seven, acted as translator for the couple whom, he said, should be addressed as "Lolo" and "Lola."

"My Lola wants you to come eat," the child said as he grabbed both Niran's and Claire's hands and led them, through the crowd, to a table.

Claire attempted to give the invitation to Lola, but she did not acknowledge it. She, then, tried to tell the child the invitation was for his great grandparents.

"If you don't eat, my Lola won't take that," he said, waving off the invitation.

Claire and Niran exchanged glances as they were led to a table full of people already eating. They squeezed into two open spots in the bench seating. Lola brought over two plates of food and set them down before them. She pointed to the plates and walked away before Claire and Niran could thank her.

"Please eat everything my Lola gives you because she will be very mad if you don't finish her food," said the child as he sat across from them and began eating from his own plate.

Two more plates of food later, Claire started to feel sick. Niran sat at an odd angle as if to create more room for his full stomach.

"Please tell your Lola that I couldn't possibly have another bite." Claire practically begged the boy in as respectful and sorry a way as possible.

"I will let her know you are finished and would like some more," the boy said, starting to get up from his seat.

"No, please! No, that's not what we said," both Niran and Claire said, standing to stop the boy and speaking over each other.

A hush fell over the table and as they stood there, looking at everyone seated around them who all stared right back. It was the boy who broke first. He began to giggle and tried to hide it, slapping both hands over his mouth. Then, the whole table erupted into thigh-slapping, teary-eyed laughter as some of them pointed at Niran and Claire and made eating motions.

"What is happening?" Claire asked, wanting to laugh along with them, but wasn't sure she was invited to. Niran only let out a sigh and shook his head as if he completely understood what had happened and was frustrated with himself for not seeing it coming.

"It was a prank, Claire," he told her. "They told us to eat all of Lola's food and then kept telling her we were still hungry." He looked around and threw his arms up in surrender. The party-goers laughed harder.

"I can take that thing for my Lola now," the boy said, still laughing.

"You little brat!" Claire jokingly exclaimed, laughing, but also forcing herself not to laugh too hard because she was still very full.

Niran pulled the invitation out of the inside pocket of his jacket and held it up to the boy. "Now if you are done pranking innocent people, could you please make sure your Lola gets this?" he asked with a smile.

As Niran held the invitation out to the boy, it was smacked out of his grip by a withered hand adorned with chunky silver rings on every finger. The boy jumped back and the laughter fell silent. The woman looked like she might have been another great grandmother of the family, perhaps Lola's sister.

"*Aswang!*" The ancient-looking woman who was now pulling the boy behind her in a protective move, spat the word at Niran like it was a curse. "*Umalis ka dito, aswang! Umalis ka dito!*" She exclaimed again, and used her cane to forcefully shove the invitation across the table, making it fall over the edge to Niran's feet.

Both Claire and Niran staggered back.

"*Sinusumpa kita, aswang!*" The woman spat at Niran as she started to make her way around the table to him.

"*Pakiusap, Nanay! Hindi siya aswang, Nanay!*" many of the people around were saying as they rose to try to calm the woman and reason with her.

Niran had put Claire behind him in the same way the woman had put the boy behind her. She rounded the table and shoved past people who were trying to stop her. Though Claire couldn't understand what they were saying, she could guess at what was happening. She watched as the woman approached Niran, cane held out, still speaking aggressively to him. Before she could reach Niran, Claire moved swiftly from behind him and now stood between the woman and Niran. For a long moment, Claire and the woman only stared each other down.

"Please tell her that we mean no harm and have no ill intent," Claire said to no one in particular as she maintained eye contact with the woman, a hand held out to her in a calming gesture.

Someone from behind them seemed to translate what she said.

"Tell her that all we need to do is give this envelope to the kid's Lola and we'll leave. She never has to see either of us again. Please." It was translated again. She waited for the woman to respond, but there was none.

While still maintaining eye contact with the woman, Claire bent to pick up the envelope. Her other hand was still out in that calming gesture. She placed the invitation on the table and spoke directly to the boy this time.

"Kid. You're gonna give this to your Lola, right?" She spared only a quick glance to the child to see him nod and reach for the invitation.

The old woman moved then, seeming like she was going to try to prevent the boy from taking the invitation.

"No!" Claire moved to block the woman's way as she bought the boy the seconds he needed to collect the invitation. Niran remained silent behind her.

Unmoving.

"Can you please tell her that we're leaving and we're very sorry for the disruption?" It was translated again.

"Niran. Leave," Claire ordered him. He didn't move. "Now, Niran. I will be a few steps behind you." At that, he gave a nod to the people around who had apologetic looks on their faces and made his way to the door.

Claire checked one more time to make sure the boy had the invitation to give to his Lola and she made to follow Niran. As she turned, the old woman grabbed Claire by the arm, gripping her tightly enough to get her attention, but not enough to cause any pain. The woman got close to Claire's face, stared into the back of her eyes and murmured something in their language, she said it in haste and with great importance. She said it with fear and concern. Claire looked around for anyone to translate. The woman beckoned the boy to her side and repeated what she'd said to Claire.

"She said, 'Don't believe your own eyes. They hide the truth from you'," the boy translated and the woman stood straighter and gave Claire a stern and warning look before looking in the direction Niran had walked away and mocked spitting on the floor.

"I cannot take you anywhere!" Claire exclaimed to Niran with a laugh, once they were both outside.

"Thank you for that," he said, far more solemn than Claire was.

"What was she saying to you?" Claire asked.

"*Aswang*, in their culture, represent anything from werewolves to ghosts to succubi. It's kind of a blanketed term for evil, supernatural beings," he explained.

"How in the world did she know?" Claire began to ask. "I mean, not like how did she know you were an evil, supernatural being, but you get what I'm saying. How did she know you were supernatural at all?"

"Some people, especially children, and even some animals can see more than the average person can and they can see us for what we are," he answered.

"So much for these last few invitations being easy," Claire said with as much lightness as she could force into her tone.

Rubbing her eyes, Claire leaned on the threshold of her door and yawned as she tightened her oversized sweater around herself. She looked off into the distance where she knew the sun rose that time of year. It had barely crested the horizon.

"I thought we didn't have any invitations today. Why are you here so early?" she asked Niran who looked fully awake and like he'd been awake for hours.

"I have an errand I need to run, but thought you might want to join me," was his response.

"No. I don't want to run any errands if they involve my having to be up and ready to go at this forsaken hour," she answered with a rough shake of her head.

"There's a lavender field and you get to harvest honey from beehives," he clarified.

Claire gasped with an excited smile and bolted up her stairs to change her clothes.

"Wear something you don't mind getting a little dirty," Niran called behind her.

"Okay! Give me ten minutes," Claire called back to him as she dug through her closet.

A two-hour drive later, Niran and Claire rounded a bend in a long driveway that opened up to an expansive property. It had rolling hills, flower fields and was dotted with behemoth oak trees that looked to be hundreds of years old. At the end of the drive was a cobblestone cul-de-sac where stood three little houses. They seemed only big enough to have maybe one bedroom each and living space for one person. Though the homes were of a similar, idyllic countryside style, each had its own distinct personality - distinct, as it seems, as the three women who sat in the shade of the giant oak tree in the center of the cul-de-sac.

"You're going to meet my good friends, Lea, Faye and Jean," Niran explained as he found a place to park along the side of the drive. "They all live on this farm and tend the lavender fields over there and the honeybees over that way." He pointed to different areas of the property beyond the houses.

"Friends?" Claire asked.

"Don't look so surprised." Niran laughed.

"I'm sorry. I just didn't picture you having friends." Claire laughed, almost apologetically.

"I can't say I had much choice in the matter. The friendship was kind-of thrust upon me. You'll see what I mean when you meet them," he explained with a smile.

"This place looks like it's out of a fairy tale," Claire breathed as she took in the landscape before her.

"They're a little eccentric, but they do keep this place well," Niran agreed.

As they walked from the car, Niran slowed his approach to the tree under which the three women made several attempts to stand, trying and failing to help each other. At his side, Claire smiled and held in a laugh at the sight of the three women struggling, yet laughing to the point of tears as they did. She looked at Niran who studied the women with the start of a confused grin.

"Stop it. They're coming," one said.

"Wait. My shoe," said the other, breaking down into another fit of laughter.

"Shh. Be cool. They're here," said the last one.

The three women finally made it to their feet, one of them holding onto the tree as she fixed the shoe she had somehow lost.

"Niran!" they exclaimed in unison with bright, inviting smiles. One of them leaned against the tree, not casually, but clearly for support. One of them swayed where she stood, while the last one had given up and sat back down.

"Is everyone okay?" he asked with a raised brow and a suspicious once-over of each of them.

They all started answering the question together; each of the women telling a separate story. None of them seemed to acknowledge what the others were saying as they all casually dismissed any implication behind the question. Little could be gathered from what they each said as it sounded like commentary on the weather, something about a loose shoelace, a tale about a squeaky door hinge. Then, they all stopped with complete confidence that they'd answered the question in full. Niran and Claire were no wiser than before the three women spoke. He crossed his arms and gave them a tight-lipped smile, awaiting a real answer. For a moment, the women only stared back.

"Oh, damn it. Niran, we're high as shit," said the woman who had been using the tree for support. "We are blitzed out of our minds. I mean, I know I am. These two. I don't know," she finished. The other two women shrugged, making no attempt to deny it.

"Honestly, I'm shocked I'm still standing," the one sitting on the ground said.

Niran pinched the bridge of his nose. Claire outright laughed and threw a hand over her mouth.

"I'm so sorry, Niran. We forgot you were coming. Please, you and your friend, come sit," the last one said, attempting to be hospitable and in control as she helped the sitting one get to her feet.

Niran and Claire followed the three women as they walked at a comically slow pace to an area behind their three homes. Claire couldn't help but smile at the sight. When she turned her attention to Niran, he had been shaking his head, but with a smile of understanding and acceptance. She noted the difference in his attitude toward the women and how he had called them his good friends. Where Niran had little patience for the vices and follies of others, here, he seemed to not only accept this display, but find it endearing. It made Claire smile and feel more at home at his side somehow.

"The brunette with the big sun hat; that's Lea," Niran told Claire, leaning in to point. "The one with the gardening gloves in her back pocket; that's Jean. And the one with the three dogs and the cat following her everywhere; that's Faye. Lea and Faye are sisters. Jean is their cousin," he said with a smile in their direction.

Introductions were made with no shortage of laughter and antics. The cousins explained that Lea had been trying a new recipe for *special* muffins that morning. She had gotten some measurements confused.

"By decimal points, Niran. Whole decimal points," Faye had clarified to no shortage of snorting laughter from Lea and Jean.

Sat in an adirondack chair on the large, back patio that was shared by all three of the cousins' homes, Claire laughed and chatted easily with them. She learned that the cousins were known as the beekeepers and they were the sole providers of the candles used by another person who works with Niran, named Harena. The errand that Niran had to run was to pick up said candles for her.

"Harena," Niran explained, "is an extremely particular person who happens to need lots of candles for her work and she will only take the ones made here by the beekeepers," he finished with a little wave of his hand to his friends.

When they weren't making candles, the beekeepers grew lavender and harvested honey. Beyond the patio, the lavender farm was a sight as the wispy, flowered stems swished in the gentle breeze that blew over them. Close by the lavender was a long row of beehive boxes, all painted different colors with different patterns on each of them. Great, puffy clouds ambled across the sky, seeming to mimic the rolling hills over which they glided.

It had been about lunch time when the three cousins finally seemed to sober up from the incident, dubbed "the great muffin fiasco." Jean led Niran to the workshop where the candles were made, leaving Claire with Lea and Faye. They made lavender lemonade together, squeezed into the little kitchen of Faye's home. Claire awed at Faye's cat, Jerry, whom she could have sworn acted more like Faye's familiar. She used to read about them in stories about good witches and warlocks. Lea had explained that while she had the green thumb, it was Faye who could train any animal to do anything. Jean was the business-minded one of the three and she managed all the products once they made them.

They quickly felt like they could have been family and Claire caught herself wishing they had been. She caught herself considering how she would have loved a life like theirs had she been afforded another path. She tried not to let herself think about it. She was grateful she didn't have the space to as the sisters quipped and cursed and showed her what it was like to be unapologetically one's self. When Niran and Jean returned from the workshop, the group enjoyed lunch on the patio.

"I can see why you decided to bring our new friend, Claire, to spend the day with us," Faye said, as the group walked through the rows of the lavender field after lunch.

"What do you mean?" asked Niran.

"She means that Claire is just so lovely and it wouldn't bother us one bit if you brought her with you every time you came to visit," Jean said, giving Niran a pat on his behind as she took a spot by his side. "You picked a great one, Niran. We're very proud of you," she added.

"This isn't. I didn't pick her. I don't think you understand," he stammered.

"Ooh!" both Faye and Jean hooted with a laugh.

"Oh, you've got it *bad*," Faye said with a surprised, yet delighted smile.

Ahead of them, a couple of rows over, Lea showed Claire how to harvest the lavender. Claire gushed about how vibrant and unique they were. When she made a tiny bouquet from the handful of lavender she harvested, she held it up to show Niran. Her joy in the moment was radiant and Niran waved to her in acknowledgement. Claire's already-big smile grew and Niran's breath hitched to see it.

"Super duper bad," Jean offered in a loud whisper. Faye nodded in agreement.

"Please stop," Niran asked, already knowing the response he would receive.

"Never," they answered in unison.

Niran and Claire helped the cousins harvest lavender and then hang them to dry. Claire learned how to pull honeycombs out of the beehives and it had been particularly fun for her to learn how to don all of the protective gear for the job. Niran had fussed as he took it upon himself to double and triple check that it was all properly on. Inside the workshop, Claire learned how to harvest the honey from the honeycombs and then how to make a candle from the beeswax.

While they worked, the beekeepers shared stories about their lives that, more than a few times, caused Claire to gasp in shock or awe and sometimes both. They told stories about all the places they'd lived before settling on this farm and the trail of broken hearts they left in their wake. They'd been groupies and professionals, foodies and farmers. they were animal lovers, always; and role models, sometimes. As proud activists with "hippie hearts" --as they'd put it-- they were silent, never. Though she tried not to, Claire, once again, wondered at how she might have enjoyed a life as full as theirs. Though it took a little more effort than earlier that day, she managed to push the thought back.

"I can't believe we did so much in one day," Claire said as she stretched out in the same chair she'd sat in that morning.

Instead of the late-morning sun lighting the property, it was the early evening of "magic hour." The group only admired the setting sun as the work of the day caught up to them. They all rested in companionable silence as orange turned to indigo and then the glittered black of late evening. When it got dark, Lea flipped a switch that was on one of the patio corner poles. The warm, tungsten glow of tiny string lights lit up the lavender farm and the path leading to it.

"Claire, I think I see your little bouquet on the cart there in the lavender field," Jean said, pointing to the cart in the middle of the field.

"Oh! I thought I brought that back up here. I'll get it," she said, popping up from her chair and making her way down the path.

"It looks like it might rain tonight," Lea said, looking up at the clear sky.

"Definitely," agreed Faye.

"Niran, I'm gonna need that cart brought into the workshop. Do an old lady a favor, will ya?" Lea asked with a note of expectation and a sweet smile. Faye only looked up at him over the rim of her coffee cup.

"I probably left my gloves out there, too, if you can grab those," added Jean.

With a resigned sigh, Niran got up and made his way down the path behind Claire. Jean walked over to a set of hose spigots beside the patio. The three cousins watched as Claire grabbed her bouquet from the cart and turned to see Niran approach. It looked like he was explaining that they needed the cart and the both of them looked to the patio. Lea and Faye waved back with knowing smiles. Jean took a puff of her cigarette and as she exhaled, began turning the valves on the spigots. Then she waved as well.

"Oh, he's gonna be so pissed at us," Faye said as she continued to wave.

"What's he gonna do?" Lea laughed.

"I turned them on high," Jean said, taking her seat again.

The sound of rushing water and then a yelp rose from the lavender field as all the sprinklers around them showered Niran and Claire as they struggled to move the cart out of the field that was growing muddy.

"Hey, dorks," Faye said casually. The three dogs laying at her feet perked up. "Go get 'em," she commanded, then took another sip of her coffee.

All three dogs bolted for Niran and Claire and there was another yelp as they watched the dogs jumping at the pair, tails wagging furiously. Both Niran and Claire fell to the ground as the dogs climbed on them, licking and sniffing. Claire's laughter rang above the sound of the sprinklers and Niran's own voice trying, in vain, to command them to calm down. They rolled around in the mud with the dogs, having abandoned the cart and Claire's bouquet altogether.

"He's really gonna be pissed at us." Lea laughed again.

"Faye!" Niran yelled from the field through Claire's laughter.

"Fine." Faye sighed and then called for the dogs. "Dorks. Come on," she said loudly. All three of the dogs stopped immediately and ran back to the patio to lay at Faye's feet.

Jean turned the sprinklers off and they watched Niran help Claire up from the ground. They were soaked, muddy and covered in lavender buds. Claire laughed heartily and clung to Niran as he walked them out of the field. She slipped and Niran only barely kept them upright as she nearly pulled him down with her. She looked up at him, then. His face was covered in mud and he'd looked the worst she'd ever seen him. Her laugh filled his entire being as he held her and she picked lavender stems out of his hair. He found one in her hair and pulled it out as her laugh quieted and became nothing more than a sweet smile. They began to walk again and Claire made it only three steps and slipped again. Before she could right herself, she was being swept up in Niran's arms; one hand around her back and the other under her legs. She threw her arms around his neck with another helpless laugh and sank into him, laying her head on his shoulder.

"Thank you," she said happily.

"You never have to thank me," he replied without a second of thought.

From the patio, the scheming trio watched with satisfied smiles.

"I think we've done our good deed for the year," Faye noted.

"Still doesn't make up for almost killing us all, Lea," Jean added.

"We're still here, aren't we?!" Lea answered, throwing her hands up.

An hour later, Niran was loading boxes of candles into the car while Claire was saying goodbye to the cousins, wearing clean clothes that Faye had let her borrow. There were hugs all around and an invitation for Claire to return anytime she wanted to - with or without Niran. They'd said it loud enough for Niran to hear and he'd only sighed dramatically in response.

"I wish you two would just stay the night. You can have my house. It's very comfortable," Faye said with a mischievous glint in her eye.

"We'll be just fine making the drive. The three of you have done quite enough for us today. Thank you," Niran answered, giving a pointed look at Faye that let her know he knew exactly what she was trying to do. She only put her hands up.

As they were all saying their final goodbyes with another round of hugs, Niran held the passenger side door of the car open for Claire as she climbed in, holding a blanket that Lea gifted her. Niran closed the door and was about to walk around to the other side of the car when Lea made a loud, distressed noise. Everyone gaped.

"I have something I need to say!" she announced.

Claire rolled down her window and leaned over to listen.

"Well. And she's crying," Faye said, unsurprised.

"I don't care!" Lea said, wiping tears away. "I have something very important to say and I'm just going to say it and you can listen or not or do whatever, it's your choice. But I have to say it." She looked between Niran and Claire when she spoke.

"We know you don't have much time" --a look at Claire-- "and we know you are...what you are," she said, gesturing to Niran. "But listen to an old lady who has seen it all and has been through enough and knows things when she sees them," she said, huffing and wiping tears. "Not even your circumstances," she said to Claire, "or even yours," she said to Niran," are enough to not give love a chance where it so clearly wants to grow," She finished with a deep breath.

"Holy shit, we are never doing those muffins again," Faye said, under her breath with her jaw hung in surprise.

"I said it. I said what I said. Okay goodnight! I'm going to have a glass of wine and go to bed. You two have a safe drive home!" Lea said as she walked away to her house.

"Wow. She just...threw that grenade into the car and ran off, didn't she?" Jean said with a sorry, wide-smiled cringe. "Oh, wow. Have a *great* ride home. What is it, two hours?" she asked and both she and Faye laughed the kind of laugh that was also an apology.

"Thanks," Niran answered curtly.

"She's emotional. And she's a hopeless romantic. We all are. Please don't let what she said make anything weird. We just like to have fun," Faye said to Claire, reassuringly, making an attempt to ease the discomfort.

"Please, there is no apology necessary at all! Are you kidding me? This was the best day and I wouldn't have any of you any other way!" Claire said with a big smile, assuring her and Niran that it hadn't made her uncomfortable at all. She might have heard a sigh of relief come from Niran's direction.

The pair had stopped for gas only a couple of miles into the drive. Niran had filled the tank. Claire had gone inside the convenience store to get snacks.

"Ready?" He asked her, when they'd buckled in to leave.

"Mhm." She answered with a smile and a nod.

When they were about to pull onto the road from the gas station, Claire adjusted Lea's blanket so she could curl up in the seat and stay warm and comfortable under it.

"Niran?" she'd said softly over the low music that played. He looked at her, poised to do whatever she needed from him.

"Thank you for this wonderful day," she said with a yawn as her eyes began to flutter closed.

"You never have to thank me," he said and reached over to pull the blanket back up where it slipped off her shoulder.

He brought his hand back down to rest his elbow on the center armrest between them. When he did, Claire captured his hand and intertwined her fingers with his. They stayed that way the entire drive back as she slept.

part five

sand

the way time passes

an arrival

a new companion

Three days after the trip to the beekeepers' farm, Claire bounded down the steps of her apartment and flung the door open, ready to tackle another day of deliveries.

"Okay, we've got dinner at The Aubergine tonight again and you know how Vera gets when we're late so I'm thinking we should." She paused to see Niran holding up only one invitation with a knowing look.

"That's the last one?" she asked, having to put effort, now, into the smile she wore.

He nodded with a small grin.

"Oh! Okay, great! Okay. Um. Well, good, we did it," she said, having to put even more effort into seeming excited. "Are they close? Should we take the trolley," she asked, slipping her hand into the crook of Niran's elbow to walk with him.

"It's not far at all, actually," he said as Claire read the name.

"Charlene."

She smiled and silently thanked Margeaux for considering her. Her smile shrank a little as she looked up to Niran, realizing she hadn't thought of their task coming to an end.

"I'm thinking," Niran began as he turned them to walk in the direction away from the restaurant, "that there is no rush to deliver this one just yet."

Claire looked up at him again, her full smile returning, if not a little shyly.

"Because, you know," he said as he stiffened, "if Margeaux finds out we finished early, she'll only put us to work again."

"Right," Claire agreed sarcastically.

They delivered the invitation to a surprised and delighted Charlene later that day.

"Well! I'm not entirely sure what a dress code of 'like your life depends on it' means, but I will do my best." She beamed.

"All one hundred and twelve invitations have been hand-delivered," Claire announced to the table of gathered close friends and cohorts of Margeaux's. They clapped and toasted her as she laughed at Niran's side. He only rolled his eyes as he pulled her chair out for her to sit. She plopped down into it and food began to arrive on big trays delivered to the center of the table.

Margeaux told a very animated story about a time she and Vera got locked on the rooftop for two hours in the dead of winter. Claire absentmindedly stole bites from Niran's plate and his only reaction was to push his plate a little closer to her. Vera eyed the pair as she sipped her wine with yet another satisfied smile.

"Niran, I've got to see Harena today. You and Claire should come with me. Claire, it's beautiful down there, you simply must join us," Vera urged with a smile.

"Sure," Claire agreed, excited to finally meet the woman the beekeepers had told her about.

"Excellent. Bookstore after dinner, then, Niran," Vera instructed, and before he could respond, she went back to chatting with someone else at the table.

"You are all going?" Jacob asked when Claire, Niran, Vera and Reid made their way to the back room door at the bookstore later that evening.

"Yes, I'm taking the children on a field trip. Don't wait up," was Vera's only response with a wink and a grin.

"Reid, I will need you back up here when you are through with your business," Jacob ordered. Reid only nodded and opened the door, entering first and the rest of them followed.

"I didn't know what to expect, but when Vera said 'down,' she really meant it," Claire said as she, Niran, Vera and Reid descended a spiral staircase that seemed to go ten stories down, lit the entire way by hundreds of candles; candles she recognized. By the time they reached the bottom, Claire was winded and Vera was carrying her stiletto heels.

It took several moments for Claire's eyes to adjust, and when she was able to take in what was before her, in full, she grabbed Niran's arm and gaped, slack-jawed and breathless. They stood on a natural rock walkway that overlooked a colossal cavern below. Throughout, was every type of rock formation whose names she'd once learned in grade school. The enormity of the cavern and the rock formations within were staggering. She turned, still gripping Niran's arm, and looked back up the stairs, then back down into the cavern. It was lit by candles as well. There were thousands of them and beside every candle was an hourglass. Claire could not see far enough into the distance to see the end of the cavern and when she turned around, it stretched just as far in the opposite direction. The candlelight went as far as her eyes could see.

Niran bent to draw her attention to a spot in the rock formations just ahead of them. "Right over there," he said, their faces almost cheek-to-cheek. "Just watch."

Claire's grip on his arm loosened as she walked them both closer to the edge of the walkway, where only a wood-and-rope rail kept them from going over. She squinted at the spot he told her to watch and waited. Moments later, an old, wooden ladder thunked against the rock formation and up shimmied what looked to be a stout woman, carrying another hourglass. The woman made it to the top of the ladder and gingerly climbed onto the rock. She shuffled through a small walking path left open for her and delivered the new hourglass to a spot amongst the rest. She then pulled a small candle out of her pocket, lit it on another candle and then held the bottom of it over the flame. When the wax began to drip, she pressed the candle into the rock next to the new hourglass.

"That i s Harena. S he i s t he glassmaker," Niran informed Claire a s he walked her down a set of stairs carved into the rock.

They all followed Reid through narrow pathways formed into the stone and there was no sound but their footsteps and trickling water everywhere.

They wound around and went further down until the path opened up to a smaller cavern. Though smaller, it was still about the size of a large house with the ceiling at least thirty feet up. Within, there was the woman from earlier, the glassmaker. She squatted in front of a large pile of blankets and pillows digging through a sack at her side.

"That looks like a giant dog bed," Claire commented quietly and Niran only grinned.

No sooner than the words left her mouth, did Harena start pulling dead rats from the sack to toss them into the air over the blankets. They disappeared into the sound of smacking and chewing. A *thunk thunk thunk* echoed through the cavern as she tossed rat after rat. There was movement on the blankets, though nothing could be seen there. It startled Claire and she staggered back, searching for the source of the sounds.

"It's-"

" --Seir," Claire said, with a grin, at the same time as Niran, finishing the statement with him.

"Loud, smelly, and generally gross, but completely harmless," Vera added as they watched another rat disappear into the invisible mouth. "Well, harmless to us."

"Okay, that's enough, you greedy beast," Harena declared with a voice that seemed hewn from the very gravel beneath their feet. She stood up, turning the sack upside down where out fell another dead rat. It was gone in an instant and a moment later, the woman was batting at the air and stumbling back turning her head side-to-side seemingly trying to avoid getting licked.

"Seir. Relax," Niran and Vera said in unison.

Claire felt the thud of Seir going down, the *thunk thunk thunk* persisting.

It was his tail, Claire realized, wagging and hitting the floor. She admired the comfort and normalcy of having a giant, invisible hound among them.

"Niran, that beast of yours," said Harena as she straightened her simple, muslin dress and brushed silver hair from in front of her thick, tortoise-shell-framed glasses. "Where are my contracts? And who is this?" she said to no one in particular as she made her way to another side of the cavern where, Claire realized, was how the woman got her title.

It was as if someone carved a glassblowing furnace out of the rock, accompanied by various shelves and tables. All manner of glassblowing tools and equipment were strewn about and the room glowed bright orange in the corner where the furnace burned.

"Harena, meet Claire. She is a dear friend," Vera said sweetly. The introduction was noticeably void of detail.

Harena walked straight-backed and had obvious strength about her that made her move and act with far more youth than her years. She turned and stood with hands fisted on her hips as she studied her. Claire recognized her from her very first visit to the bookstore: she had been Niran's companion that day.

"Look at those eyes. Even on the most grumpy face, eyes like those can make it tolerable to look at. And she isn't just a dear friend. She's got an hourglass," Harena corrected Vera and then approached Claire. "I remember yours. It was an irksome thing to make. Would you like to see it?" She blinked up at Claire from behind those thick glasses with a glint in her eyes.

"Sure, I suppose," Claire answered politely, trying to figure out what having an hourglass meant.

"It's right over here. Let me show you. No, hold on. Where are my contracts, Reid?"

Reid stepped forward and pulled two, ribbon-tied, parchments from his pocket and walked them over to her. As she took them, she smacked Reid on the side of his arm. "Posture! You weren't gifted with great size just to be hunched over all day. It's ugly."

He immediately straightened and Harena gave him a gentle pat on the arm this time, "Much better." Reid smiled and pointed upward with a finger. "Yes, yes. You go back to taking care of that grumpy oaf. I'll see you next time."

"We'll see you when we're back up," Vera amended with a smile. "Well, out with it. Should I be wearing my party panties? What's the occasion?" Harena demanded as she opened the first of the two contracts Reid gave her.

"Harena, I wanted to chat with you about a few things," Vera began.

"This one will be easy," she assessed and then opened the other contract. "Mhm." She folded them, discarding the ribbons, and tossed them on one of the tables. "What was I saying? Ah. Claire. Let's go see your hourglass." She walked past the group and Claire made to follow, but was stopped by a delicate hand on her arm.

Vera scrunched up her face and then smiled, motioning for Claire to wait.

"Talk about what, Vera? Also, Niran, I've been meaning to tell you," Harena said as she turned back around to her work area. Niran merely waited with a hand in his pocket. "I need another pair of these gloves you got for me. They're feeling a little worn." She picked up the gloves in question from a shelf and brought them to him.

"Well, that particular glove-maker died half a century ago, but I will have another suitable pair for you next week," he promised.

"That's a shame. Should have given him a contract. I see we still haven't convinced my candle makers here," she said as she gestured to all the candles around them. "Oh well, what can you do? Oh, before I forget, perhaps a few more traps for the rats. You know I like Seir to have plenty of treats when he visits. The last time I didn't have treats for him, he cried and paced so much, I couldn't concentrate on my work. I was making an hourglass for a gentleman who needed a therapist more than he needed a contract, if you get what I'm saying," she said with a chuckle as she paused with one hand on a table and the other on her hip. The only sound was Seir's breathing, full of distant wails, as they all just stood there.

"Is it 'stare at Harena day' today or something? Let's go see this girl's hourglass before I have to turn it!" she barked and walked past them to leave the little cavern. "Well, come on, then!" she ordered again when nobody moved. There was a hissed exchange between Vera and Niran and Vera pushed him ahead of her after he tried to walk behind. He glared back at her as she stepped back and linked arms with Claire with a grin.

"Seir. Let's go," she said merrily. The sound of the hound rising to follow echoed throughout the cavern.

"You lot are at least a thousand years younger than me. Catch up!" Harena called from ahead. "Come look at this formation here. Let me tell you about, oh, Niran. Good. I've been meaning to..." Niran caught up to Harena and they walked together, Harena talked with her hands, going from subject-to-subject while Niran was unable to get a word in edgewise. The four of them and Seir wandered through the cavern as what sounded like great boulders over sand echoed throughout behind them. Every time Claire looked over her shoulder, the path behind was different. When she looked ahead, she could see movement in the pathways and rocks there, too.

"The paths change?" she asked Vera.

"Mhm. Only when Harena walks through them. If it was just you or I, or anyone else, for that matter, the cavern would stay as-is. It's like the difference between walking down a hallway with no doors and one with doors. Harena can go through any door and invite anyone through them, but only if she allows it."

"How big is the cavern, really, then?"

“The size of the world,” Vera answered with a sigh.

They made it to an alcove that was tucked behind a sixty-foot tall rock formation that looked like a stone icicle. Water trickled down and into a little stream that led behind it. The alcove opened up to a grotto that had a pond of water so still, it looked like a mirror. All along its edge, were hourglasses and candles that reflected so clearly in the water, it looked like another cavern rising from below. Harena picked up one of the hourglasses and handed it to Claire.

“Here it is. Do not drop it, or...” She swept her thumb across her throat and made a cutting sound. “If this breaks, so do you,” she finished with wide eyes and a slow nod.

In the soft amber of the thousands of candles, Claire watched a string of sands fall from the top chamber of her hourglass to the bottom. The bottom chamber had almost half of the sand in it and the sands that fell now drifted down so slowly, it looked like they weren’t falling at all. She held the hourglass up at eye level and marveled at the sand that represented a moment of her life that was passing, quite literally, right before her very eyes. Nobody spoke, not even Harena, for a change, who only sat on the edge of the pond, petting Seir and admiring her work. Vera and Niran watched Claire closely.

“It’s falling so slowly,” she said, almost as much to herself as anyone else.

“Each hourglass holds the exact same amount of sand. Not a single grain more or a single grain less. Right now, you are watching your sand fall for the amount of time you have left to live. When I turn your hourglass, once the last grain has fallen, then the sand will fall for the amount of time your soul has left to pay its due,” Harena explained.

Indeed, as Claire looked around, did she see all of the sand in all of the hourglasses around her, falling at different speeds. The candlelight glinted off each grain and Claire imagined them as tiny worlds floating in single sunbeams, in their own glass galaxies. She had questions, but she would ask them later, she thought, and gave herself the moment of peace and beauty. She watched these sands of her life make their slow journey to every other grain that held all the moments of the past almost-three months. At that thought, she looked up to Niran, her eyes welled with tears of realization. He took the hourglass from her, carefully handed it to Harena and pulled Claire into his arms.

“Seir. Let’s go,” whispered Vera as she, Harena and the hound left them.

He held her as the tears came, quietly at first and then the sound of her sadness drifted through the candlelight and sands of lives and souls. He held her in support as she curled herself into him. His embrace was all he could offer her and he offered it with everything in him and all that he was. Her pain became his pain as he realized her joy had become his joy. He held her and would hold her until the last grain of her sands fell if she asked it.

She asked for nothing. She only leaned into him, accepting his warmth, accepting his embrace and accepting his comfort. And she just cried because when that sand fell, and lay among the rest, in it would be the moment she truly and fully accepted her fate.

XVII

Outside the bookstore, Vera held Claire a little more tightly than she usually did when she hugged her goodnight. She made no mention of Claire's moment with her hourglass and she wouldn't. With a little squeeze of Niran's arm, she drifted off into the night humming a little tune to herself. Claire breathed in the perfumed night air and closed her eyes as she let out a long exhale. It wasn't a gasp for air; it was a breath of fresh, sweet-smelling air that filled her lungs and fed her another moment of the life she still had. When she opened her eyes, Niran was studying her profile as he stood silently beside her. She slipped her arm in his and they walked. They didn't speak for a long time as they ambled through the streets. She finally spoke as they walked past the food market.

"I think I know what I want to do," she said quietly, yet resolutely. Niran stopped walking as she turned to face him.

"I want to help people. I mean, not like ending world hunger or making world peace. Even if I had the time, I don't know nearly enough about the world to try to make those things happen without possibly destroying something else in the process. But I think I can help people in smaller ways. And I think it would make me happy to do that."

Niran took in the hope she exuded and concealed his profound relief behind a simple nod and smile. He had thought the worst, but didn't even know what the worst would be. He just knew, as he held her in that cavern while she cried, that he needed her to be okay. He thought she might tell him she wasn't okay and she might never be again. It made him feel like the darkness he brought to so many countless others would finally come for him.

"Okay," he said. "How can I help?"

She flashed a smile that nearly compelled him to blurt out, "Have anything I can give you," knowing the full extent of his power. He desisted, only hanging on her next word.

"Well," she said merrily as she continued walking, "I think whenever I see someone that could use a little help or something nice, then I will wish for it and I can just keep doing that until, you know, until I can't anymore." There was no longer sadness nor resignation in her voice when speaking of her fate.

"That sounds like as good a plan as any," he said, remaining as neutral as his self-restraint could keep him.

"It's the best plan," Claire proclaimed with a satisfied nod. "I can't wait to tell Vera and Margeaux."

The next day, Claire shared her good news with her friends.

"Oh. My goodness. I'm sorry, what?" Vera asked, with a laugh, as she looked to Niran for confirmation.

"I'm going to share the power of my contract with people," Claire repeated confidently.

"I'm curious. Which people in particular?" Margeaux asked, the words clipped and her face tight with forced placidity.

"Just people. Anyone I see who might need something nice. I'm not sure yet." Claire answered, a little more quietly, wondering if she should have taken more than just one night to wait to share her plan with the others.

Vera and Margeaux only stared at her for a moment. When that moment passed, both the resplendent women erupted in laughter. Margeaux's rose and crested into bursts of scream laughs. Vera's came from her gut in a high-pitched grunt, wheezing sound that she covered with a hand that looked too elegant for it. Claire, wide-eyed with jaw dropped, looked between them and just waited for them to stop. Niran merely looked down to his feet and then off and away in an attempt to control his own chuckle.

"Claire. There is a mega yacht out there, right now, that is headed to the Maldives. You could blink and have an invitation to the vacation of a lifetime," Vera tried to reason.

"Claire, angel, I spent two years coming home only once a month for a couple of days at a time. There isn't a country in which I haven't lavished.

Did you know you could lavish in Antarctica, because I've done it," Margeaux added.

Vera pointed her upturned hand at Margeaux with a wide-eyed and raised-brow look at Claire.

"Well, Niran thinks it's a great idea," Claire replied.

"Oh, of *course you'd* think her idea was great," Vera barked, throwing her hands up as Margeaux blurted out another laugh and turned to walk away.

"What's that supposed to mean?" both Claire and Niran asked in unison.

Vera only swished both hands in their direction with a roll of her eyes and a resigned smile.

"Leave them, Vera. She's made up her mind," Margeaux sighed as she sashayed out of the office.

"That went well," Niran casually said, after Vera left.

Surprise, followed by a celebratory squeal came from the table next to where Claire and Niran had lunch al-fresco, later that day, at the food market. The woman had won on the scratch-off lottery ticket she played as she sipped on a milkshake. Claire smiled and Niran shook his head. As Claire took a sip of her sweet tea, she watched an elderly couple stop to look at a street performer a moment before a distracted bicyclist zipped in front of them. Over the couple, a crow soared that swooped down to land on a fire hydrant near Niran. It cawed a few times, then waited. Claire watched Niran take his time finishing his last bite of food and then nod at the crow. It cawed again and flew away.

"It seems I'm needed elsewhere this afternoon," he informed her, while gathering up their discards to throw away. "I can only imagine the trouble you'll get into, but I'm fairly certain you'll be fine."

"Have fun," Claire answered, already scanning her surroundings for the next lucky recipient of her goodwill.

"Oh, I doubt I'll have nearly as much as you," he said as he strode off. As he crossed the street, he gave two quick whistles that sounded like chirps. Claire could have sworn that she saw a massive shadow appear next to Niran out of the corner of her eye - there and gone in an instant.

She spent the rest of the afternoon delightfully watching people have seemingly-random strokes of luck everywhere she went. There was the woman who won on a scratch-off ticket and the boy who got the last kettle corn before the vendor packed up to go home. There was the dog that sniffed out a ball from a bush and the baby who would have lost her pacifier when she threw it, but it landed right in her mother's purse. Claire hadn't realized all the tiny ways she could use the power of her contract or how each could be so different from the next.

Niran hadn't just been needed for the afternoon, he was gone for two weeks. Claire had asked, just once, about his whereabouts and Vera had told her not to worry, that Jacob was keeping him busy, but he'd be back soon. There had been a time when the mere thought of him nearly made her physically ill to consider who he was in her life - more so, who he would be at the end of it. These days, the voice of those concerns had become muffled behind walls of feelings with which she was not, and probably would never be, ready to reconcile.

During his absence, however, there was no avoiding the fact that she missed him. Her instinct was to feel sad about it and allow the doom to settle in, but if she had learned anything from Margeaux, from Vera, from the dozens of amazing individuals she'd met these past months, it was that she didn't have to allow it. She missed Niran. It was because they had shared reason to and it was good. In the beginning of this fateful journey, she thought she had no one and she could have easily made it so she *would* have no one. It would have been far too easy for her to do. The power she had wasn't just in what was offered to her by her contract. It was in the decisions she was still able to make for herself. This was one of them. She chose friendships. She chose purpose. She chose him. Now, with his being away, she missed him and she thought to herself that it was possibly the most beautiful thing she might have ever felt.

Claire couldn't be sure if it was coincidence or her own doing that her days were filled with more work than usual. She wanted to ask Vera when Niran would be back, but the look her friend already gave her, made her decide not to give the smirking woman any reason to make more of it. On an evening stroll with Vera and Margeaux, Claire didn't need to wonder because Margeaux finally asked instead.

"When is that boy coming back? He is contractually obligated to help me until my funeral, you know," Margeaux said around a lick of her ice-cream cone. She'd insisted they needed ice-cream at nine in the evening with no arguments from Vera or Claire.

"Soon. Maybe the next couple of days. Trust me, I know he's dying to get back here," Vera answered, eating from her ice-cream cone with a little spoon and giving Claire a playful side-eye.

"What?" Claire asked, almost dripping ice-cream on herself. Vera and Margeaux only rolled their eyes with knowing smiles.

As they walked down Main Street, every couple of minutes or so, there was someone with a look of joyful surprise or sigh of relief or even a celebratory dance. Vera eyed Claire who seemed to have half her mind on their conversation and the other half elsewhere.

"Claire. Baby, I love you so much, but you have got to tone it down. I feel like I'm living in a musical. It's like these people are going to burst into song at any moment," Margeaux pleaded.

Vera snorted, but said nothing.

"Sorry. It's kinda just habit now," Claire said with a shrug and a *mea culpa* smile. For the rest of the journey back to The Aubergine, nobody else around them got any surprise good luck.

"You've got some talent there, Claire Bear. I'm thoroughly impressed," Vera complimented her joyfully.

A few days later, Margeaux's gathered loved ones sat around another family dinner, passing dishes to each other, laughing, sharing stories and enjoying the fall, night air on the rooftop of The Aubergine. Claire laughed at some story about one of the dancers losing a wig in the middle of a show as she went to grab a fluffy blanket from a basket by the door. With her favorite blanket draped over her arm, she turned to go back to the table, but the blanket was pulled out from behind her. She whirled to scold whoever the trickster was and there stood Niran, casually draping it over his own arm.

"Niran!" she exclaimed and without thinking, threw her arms around his neck as she giggled and hugged him tightly.

"How are you?" he asked in a low voice. The sound of her joy rang through him and he squeezed her tighter and lifted her off the ground to another crash of her giggle over him. When he let her down, her smile was so broad, so full of joy, his breath hitched.

"Much better now," she admitted as he wrapped the blanket around her shoulders. She clutched it with another smile and took a step back, gesturing to invite him to the table where Vera had already cleared a seat beside Claire's.

"Welcome back, nephew. I trust all went well," Vera said as she gave him a peck on the cheek and beckoned for him to fill a plate for himself.

As the dinner carried on through to the last course of desserts and lattes, Niran listened to Claire regale her weeks of gifting good luck and good fortune to unsuspecting people. She talked about work that was done at The Aubergine and anything she thought remotely interesting might have happened while he was away. He listened like she was the only person there and as far as he was concerned, she was.

"Wanna see a neat trick?" he asked her, low and secretively.

Claire smiled widely. "Well, duh! Of course I do," she whispered excitedly.

Niran took a cupcake from in front of him and removed the wrapper as he looked around. Satisfied that no eyes were on them, he put the cupcake in her hand and pointed her hand to a spot on the roof behind where they sat - just past where the light fell off.

"Okay, toss it," he moved her hand slightly to the left, "right there. Just kind of up and over."

"What?" she chuckled. "Just throw the cupcake?"

"Yup. Right there." He leaned closer to her to point with his eyes.

Claire looked around to see that still nobody was paying them any attention and then tossed the cupcake. It disappeared to a familiar smacking sound and light *thunk thunk thunk.*

"Seir's here!" she exclaimed in a happy gasp.

"Yes. I know you kind-of met at Harena's, but I was hoping to formally introduce you sometime soon."

"I'd really love that." Claire beamed.

Later that evening, the pair took their usual route from The Aubergine to Claire's apartment. They chatted and savored the return to their unofficial routine as if Niran had been gone a month. Though her circumstances lay always in the back of her mind, and often visited the front, the joy she felt in this moment could have swelled to bursting if she let it.

"Do people tell you things feel different about the way time passes? You know, the other people like me?" she asked.

"There's no one like you, Claire," Niran stated as if he just said the day of the week. "As far as how people in your similar position perceive the passage of time, I have heard that the time, for them, can go very quickly or, conversely, very slowly. I imagine it depends on their particular set of circumstances. Why do you ask?"

"Because it felt like you were gone a month," she answered simply. He only looked at her and she only shrugged and continued, "I'm glad it wasn't really a month."

With a squeeze of his arm as they arrived at her apartment door, she let go to get her keys out. Niran stood by as he always did, waiting for her to go in and lock the door behind her. She stopped just shy of walking in.

"I'm happy," she blurted out. "I mean, I didn't think I could be, or that I would ever be again. But I'm happy, especially today."

"Well, I'm certain Vera and Margeaux would love to hear how you managed that without needing a trip to the Maldives on a megayacht," Niran answered with a smile.

"They can take some credit. I am happy because of them. I'm happy because of *all* the friends I've made along the way." She stepped out of her doorway and toward Niran. "I"m happy because I get to play with flowers every day." They both smiled at that and she took another step closer to him and took his hand. He immediately closed his fingers around hers when she did.

"And I'm happy because of you."

He watched her, as he breathed unsteadily, and she rose up on her tiptoes.

He wrapped his other arm around her to hold her closer and bowed his head to meet her where she raised her chin. She gave him a soft kiss on the spot on his cheek just next to his lips. He wrapped both arms around her and she brought hers around his neck, pulling him to her in an embrace that seemed like it couldn't be close enough.

"You have something of mine," he whispered with his face buried in her hair, hoping she could understand it. He, himself could barely understand it, but it was how he felt. She squeezed him tighter.

Unsurprisingly, the next two weeks they spent together, helping at the Aubergine, laughing through Claire's crusade of spreading good luck, Margeaux's family dinners and quiet walks through town had felt like they'd gone by in a heartbeat.

The annual Fall Flower Festival was off to a brilliant start. Claire thanked Charlene in a hurry for the coffee and croissant and made her way outside instead of eating inside as she usually did. She couldn't wait to stroll through the clouds of colors and textures that now lined both sides of Main Street and snaked through two side streets all the way down to Ego Alley. There had been a catastrophic water main break right in the center of town where the Fall Flower Festival was originally meant to be held. When Vera learned of the news and that it was going to be moved to their Main Street, she'd laughed and complimented Claire on her handiwork.

"Isn't this just delightful, Claire Bear?" Vera sang as she practically frolicked at her side.

Claire, sandwiched between Vera and Margeaux, tried desperately to take her companions and the day seriously enough to get some real work done. If she had to admit, however, she was having as much fun as she feared she would. Vera wore a dazzling fall ensemble complete with a flower crown she purchased from a vendor by the food market. Lady Margeaux, on Claire's other side, had settled on a Southern-Belle-meets-street-artist look that screamed for the attention she loved to get everywhere she went.

"Oh, I think I might want to add some of these to the arrangements for the funeral, what do you think, Margeaux, see any you want to add?" Claire asked.

"All of them. All of them, honey! Every last one!"

"We... I..."

"That means you have to decide for her. Remember, Claire Bear, if you ask our Margeaux to choose, she'll always choose both. Or in this case, all," Vera whispered loudly to Claire with a laugh.

"I heard that!" Margeaux sang to her companions.

The trio found themselves spilling into East Water Books & Antiques, giggling and dropping little flower petals in their wake. The bells at the door played a joyful and whimsical tune.

"No. Why?" Jacob protested their arrival.

Vera went straight to Reid for a hug which he was happy to give her.

"Not even your sourpuss face can ruin the fun of such a splendid day, dearest brother," Vera mocked, as she stuck a little daisy over Reid's ear.

The gentle giant touched the flower that looked positively tiny on him and smiled broadly. When he turned and found Jacob staring at him, unamused, he quickly took the flower off his ear and handed it back to Vera, closing it back in her palm with a smile. She shot a disappointed look at Jacob and he shot one right back at her.

"Brother, I am not taking 'no' for an answer, you *will* be joining us for dinner this evening in the square. They're supposed to have an amazing blues performer there and great food. I've already purchased a tent and table for us, so you needn't worry about your space or privacy," Vera detailed the order as she adjusted her flower crown in the mirror of a display case.

Claire and Margeaux had escaped into their own conversation, looking at Claire's sketchbook and going over designs and flower choices.

"And where is my nephew?"

"Working. As most people are wont to do in the middle of the day on a Thursday," Jacob replied curtly.

Both Vera and Margeaux gasped in unison at the reproval of their current activity. Claire only glanced up, and tried not to smile.

"He really did just..." Margeaux trailed off with a roll of her eyes, then returned to her conversation with Claire.

"I'll have you know, darling brother, that what we are doing today is hard work, and it's so much work that I'm tired and need a nap now," Vera said, with her nose pointed up.

"Please tell my nephew that he, too, will be joining us."

"Tell your nephew he'll be joining you where?" Niran replied, closing the back room door he'd just emerged from.

"Oh, good! You and your uncle are coming to dinner in the square this evening," Vera instructed, making final adjustments to her flower crown.

Claire looked up from her sketchbook, expecting to hear an excuse as to why he wouldn't be joining. She was in the middle of sketching something, her fuchsia colored pencil stopped on the page.

"What time?" Niran replied.

"Meet us under the blue tent at seven. I got us our own table." When he didn't answer immediately, she continued, "It'll be me, Mar, Claire, Reid, and your uncle."

"Okay. I'll see you there," he said walking toward the front door to leave. As he passed Claire, he paused to fix the flower she had tucked in her ear, that had begun to slip out. Like it was a habit, he put a gentle hand on the small of her back when he turned around to bid everyone goodbye and gave her a quick, little rub on her back as he turned toward the door. Claire could only watch him leave with a smile as the bells sang him a tune that sounded like a joyful confession.

Margeaux softly cleared her throat and Claire quickly refocused on the sketch before them. Margeaux shot a glance to Vera, who shot a glance to Jacob in turn.

"I am going to need you to clean up all those petals on your way out, Vera." Jacob merely said before returning to his ledger.

Hours later, Claire ambled slowly back through the busy streets of the flower festival. As she walked past the bookstore, she noticed the "closed" sign and most of the lights off and looked ahead to see Jacob pushed by Reid and Niran at their side. She must have only just missed them leaving. As if summoned by her thoughts, she saw Niran pause in his steps and then look over his shoulder. He didn't see her right away and stopped fully when his eyes fell upon her. She waved hello and she saw him say something to Reid, who stopped to look back. He waved hello to Claire and nodded to Niran before continuing on, leaving him standing aside to wait for her.

"Remember that time you said you wouldn't ask for much?" Niran quipped as he held out an elbow for Claire and looked around at the festival goers and flowers.

"Hey! I can't help it if your aunt taught me too well," she retorted as she took his arm.

They arrived at the tent to Vera and Margeaux drinking cocktails and eating fresh fruit while Jacob enjoyed the live blues band on his own. Reid noticed Claire and Niran first, looking up from his seat next to Jacob. He turned to Vera who nudged Margeaux as they all took in the smiling Claire with Niran, who looked far less broody than usual. Once in the tent, Claire took a seat on the other side of Jacob from Reid and Niran sat next to Vera.

"Do you enjoy blues music, Claire?" Jacob asked by way of greeting.

"I do. I can't say I can name even one blues artist," she admitted, "but whenever I hear it, I enjoy it."

"I like blues music, too."

Claire settled in, welcoming the small conversation.

"It might be different now, but there was a time when it was the music of the beaten and the downtrodden," he continued. "It was the music of the oppressed and often lacking in conventional instruments. I enjoy this artist for the homage his band pays to that. You see the guitar he has there, if you can even call it a guitar." He pointed with his chin at the makeshift instrument made of an aluminum box with a hole cut in it with three strings screwed into one end of the box and then at the end of a broomstick that came out of it.

Claire studied all of the band's instruments now, gaining a deeper respect for their talent as a group. The final lyrics of the song, as Jacob spoke, felt familiar though she never heard them before. They felt, to her, like they came from the same place she came from. Though the thought hardly made sense, how it felt had.

"*I'll never be sorry... I'll never say that I am... Me and you and those other two... We got words... And I'll have the last one...*" The lead singer sang this with a curt nod that seemed directed at Jacob.

"It was originally music for people who chose to pursue life on their own - a life of their own making," Jacob continued and paused to shift his head ever-so-slightly in Reid's direction. When it came time to applaud the band, Reid stood up and clapped.

"So, it has always been a very interesting concept to me when someone sells their soul and the thing they desire most is to be a celebrated blues musician," he finished, with a small tilt of his chin in Niran's direction.

It suddenly made sense why Claire felt the lyrics when she saw Niran stand up, roll his shoulders once and walk over to the band. As he approached the lead singer, the man sat straighter and set his makeshift guitar aside. Niran placed his hand, with his pinky ring that glinted, on the man's shoulder and bent to whisper something in his ear. The man's gaze became solemn and he looked up at Niran and nodded as he stood. The pair walked away toward a side street, Niran with a hand in his pocket and the man giving a nod to his band who waved back at him having no idea it would be the last.

"You need not worry, Claire. The man lived a long and happy life," Jacob told Claire, who sat with a stunned expression across her face.

Moments later, Niran emerged from the side street, fixing a sleeve and turning his pinky ring. Claire watched him as she suddenly felt foolish for ever forgetting who he really was to her. She hadn't thought about it in weeks, but there it was again, the memory of her father at Niran's feet. He looked up at her and she quickly turned away, unable to see his face without seeing that fateful night again. Vera pulled her into a conversation about flower arrangements and she was grateful for the distraction.

Another live band moved onto the stage to play covers of popular songs from the past several decades while the group sat around the table conversing. Claire had been quiet and unable to make eye contact with Niran. All she could think about was just how foolish she'd been. She hadn't noticed when Vera pulled Niran aside and they spoke in hushed tones away from everyone else.

The pair returned to the table, Niran having noticeably returned to his usual brooding form. It was the look of sorrow that gave Claire pause. They sat mere feet from each other, but it was as if a chasm had opened up between them. As the music and revelry played on, Claire weighed what felt worse in the moment. And in this moment, on this night where everything around her was her definition of perfection --from the mild weather to the flower strewn streets, to the peaceful and glad air about the crowd-- Claire could not feel the joy she would and should have.

She glanced in Niran's direction, seeing, again, only a sorrowful stare into the crowd. He must have felt her looking at him because he turned to her. It was then that she realized however badly she had been feeling in that moment, he was feeling worse. Whatever it was she would have to endure at the end of her contract, he would have to endure as well. No matter what, her contract would come to an end and she wouldn't want anyone else to be there when it happened. *He* wouldn't want anyone else to be there. She knew he wouldn't. She finally understood that this was his countdown, too. This was his burden, too. The pain he tried to hide said it all. Her end would, in a way, be an end for something in him, too.

With that realization, she closed the distance between them –and thus the chasm– never breaking eye contact. When she was close enough to touch him, she took his hand, which surprised her to feel was trembling slightly. He exhaled as if he hadn't been breathing and squeezed her hand almost too tightly. Claire smiled up at him and stepped closer.

"You'll be with me every step of the way, right?" she asked him, forgetting anyone else was there but them.

Niran nodded while taking a deep breath and straightening himself, squeezing her hand tightly. His exhale was shaky.

"Okay," she said, resolutely and reassuringly.

"Okay," he said and squeezed her hand again.

As if it was because she allowed it, lights, sound, music, laughter, a breeze, everything from the world around them returned to offer them this night to share. With Niran, once again, by her side, the evening ambled on and they enjoyed it together.

Several songs and several stories later, Claire leaned back on the table as Margeaux regaled the group with another story from The Aubergine. Vera confirmed her role in the antics and even Jacob chuckled once or twice. When she glanced over to see Niran, once again, relaxed and enjoying himself, never too far from her side, Claire felt a deep appreciation for this night with all of them.

"If I commissioned a biography, nobody would believe it," Margeaux said, sipping her wine.

"If you commissioned a biography, I'd–" Vera stopped mid-sentence as her attention caught on the crowd along Main Street.

"*Jacob*," she whispered.

Immediately, Reid stood in front of Jacob, as if to protect him. He did it out of instinct as he didn't even know where to look or from whom he was protecting his charge. Niran, beside Claire, stood up as well, standing slightly in front of her. Vera joined and now the three looked on at the crowd milling about Main Street, where Claire still could not see what had stopped Vera mid-sentence. She knew immediately when she noticed the crowd part.

It parted, but in a way that was like they didn't even notice they were doing it; and it was as if everyone in the street was told to be silent. There was nothing that drew the attention of the crowd. Nobody seemed to even notice how quiet it had gotten, but it had; eerily so.

In the wake of that unnatural quiet, towards them, walked three individuals. There were two women and a man whose presence was so dark, Claire could have sworn the temperature dropped. His face was severe and timelessly handsome with eyes that were like shadows cast by the moon. The quiet seemed to swell around him as still, no one seemed to even notice it was happening. He walked a step behind the two women, and they, unlike him, looked positively joyous with their surroundings.

They scanned the square with the wide, bright smiles of two ladies who were joyfully entertained. When their scanning fell upon Vera, the younger of the women, Claire assumed, exclaimed and pointed at Vera in delight. She seemed almost childlike in nature, but also seemed like she knew more of the world than everyone else in it. The other, a little taller and looking a little older, didn't land her attention on Vera, but on Niran, instead. She tilted her head slightly and smiled sweetly at him. Her presence seemed as deep and burdened as his. The man stopped and merely held his hands behind his back. Almost as if it was some cue, both Vera and Niran moved to join them, leaving Claire and Margeaux where they sat.

Claire watched on as Vera and Niran, followed by Jacob, pushed by Reid, approached the trio. When they did, it was as if the world was tilted, imperceptibly off its axis and had just righted itself. Vera approached the man first. She gave him a small kiss on the cheek that seemed insincere, almost forced.

"Sister!" exclaimed the youngest one, and nearly jumped into Vera's arms. They both cooed and hugged as the man only continued to look forward, perfectly content to have no part in this reunion. Vera affectionately touched the other woman's cheek and they smiled warmly to each other as the youngest one squealed at Niran. Niran merely dipped his chin to her with a smile as the oldest of the three women took him by both hands and studied him at arm's length before bringing him in for an embrace. He hugged her back and Claire realized she must be his mother.

Sister, Claire thought to herself. And, yes, now that she studied the group, did she realize that they acted like siblings, though they shared few physical similarities. The oldest, Claire was certain, was Niran's mother, though she did not look older than him by enough to be his mother. That was of no surprise considering their agelessness and immortality.

Reid, upon bringing Jacob closer to the group, was now standing in front of the wheelchair. All three sisters noticed Reid at the same time and he was met with hugs and happy greetings. The man ignored Reid completely. It was the youngest who beheld Jacob first, seeing him over Reid's shoulder as the gentle giant had to practically kneel to get low enough to hug her. When she saw Jacob, her smile, her joy diminished in the seconds it took for her to realize. She dropped her arms from around Reid's neck and stepped around him. Behind her, Vera held the oldest sister's hand as she, too, had faltered at the sight of him.

"*Ayn*, It is okay." Jacob said, reassuringly. There was a note of concern in his voice as he looked about the street as well as to her.

She only stood, staring at him. Something was unraveling in her and they could all see it. Not only that, it could actually be felt in the air around them. It started with a few people nearby sniffling and wiping tears. Then there were more and it got louder, the sniffling turned to crying, the crying turned to sobs. It spread with Ayn being the epicenter of this quake of sadness. Even the flowers around them began to wilt. Claire looked around and could almost see it spreading.

"Ayn. It is okay. I promise," Jacob tried again to reassure her.

"Dear, Ayn." A concerned Vera gently took her arm.

The sobbing spread further through the street and reached those who were sitting around Claire and Margeaux, both of whom seemed not to be affected. Still, nobody seemed to notice how terribly unnatural it all was as they continued to share in a sadness they didn't even realize wasn't their own.

"Ayn," said the man, sharply. Their father, Claire assumed.

Immediately, and as one, everyone stopped crying. Only final sniffles and shuffling about could be heard. Again, the sudden change went completely unnoticed as sound had returned to the square and Main Street behind them.

"Thank you," was all the man said.

After a few murmured greetings between Jacob and his sisters, they all, siblings and their father, approached the tent. It was as if they only existed in the blind spots of everyone there. People didn't move out of their way because they saw them nearing. They moved because they were going to move anyway.

They danced choreography they didn't even know they were a part of. Claire spotted florists casually replacing flowers that had wilted as if it was something completely normal that had just happened.

"Margie!" squealed the youngest one as they approached.

"Good gracious, woman, I don't know how many times I have to tell you not to call me that," Margeaux sighed as they hugged.

She hugged the oldest one next and then they all turned to Claire who had stood up, hands clasped in front of her, as she was unsure of what to do or what to say. She wore a polite smile and looked between Vera and Niran for guidance.

"Meet Claire," Vera said sweetly.

"She's in charge of all the flowers for my funeral which I am expecting all of you to be attending!" Margeaux demanded as she put an arm around Claire's shoulder as if she knew how nervous she was.

"It's a pleasure to meet you," Claire said, still taking in the family who now stood before her in all their great power and beauty.

"Indeed, it is," said the oldest one in a lilting voice, as she studied Claire and then Jacob and back again. She had a hand on Niran's arm, almost protective.

The youngest one greeted Claire with a tight hug before turning to the large trays of food that were brought out during their introductions. The man stared at Claire, unabashedly, saying nothing as the rest of them took seats at the table. He approached Claire with such a look of intent that she almost backed up a step.

"Has anyone ever told you that you have the most remarkable eyes?" he said with a tone that was meant to sound soothing and inviting, but felt like the most dangerous words she'd ever heard spoken to her.

She made herself not look down or away from his piercing study of her eyes. He didn't try to hide that he found something in them that seemed to go beyond just being a pretty shade of green.

Being in the company of Lady Margeaux and her best friend, Vera, had taught Claire a thing or two about being certain about one's self. Feeling Margeaux at her side and knowing Vera stood close by reminded Claire that she was someone who had no reason to shrink under anyone's gaze, not even this one. So she lifted her chin a little and gave the man her own penetrating stare, taking a step closer to him.

"Everyone does," she said with a little smile that was as kind toward him as his words were toward her.

"If they weren't attached to her, I'd steal them right off her for myself!" Vera said a little too loudly and giggly to be anything but an attempt to distract.

It was a tense dinner where the tension existed under the surface of every smile and casual conversation across the table. The man, who Claire had learned was named Ezra, was their father. Eyleth, the oldest, was Niran's mother, and Ayn, the youngest, seemed like the most carefree, yet also, the most cunning. When dinner was finished, Margeaux excused herself as she had a late show for which she needed to prepare at The Aubergine.

"If you need to get away from all of this, you come straight home, okay?" Margeaux whispered in Claire's ear as she hugged her goodbye. Claire knew she meant The Aubergine and could have hugged her even tighter for that, but only nodded in reply.

The next to excuse himself was Jacob who claimed he'd had enough of family time for one night and needed to be up early. Claire watched as Reid pushed Jacob into the shrinking crowd. When they were out of sight, she saw Niran stand and it looked like he was going to also excuse himself. She looked up at him with pleading eyes and a quick sideways glance to Ezra. Niran seemed to contemplate for a moment.

"Does anyone want a coffee? own Dock h as t he b est coffee an d they're open late," he said to no one in particular.

"I do. I'll go with you," Claire tried to say with as casually as possible as she rose to join him.

The pair were met with studious gazes from the sisters. After a brief decision, it seemed they all wanted some of this "best coffee" Niran mentioned. They all gathered themselves to walk over - everyone but Ezra, who stayed sitting with an ankle over a knee, people-watching.

Almost immediately after putting some distance between herself and Ezra did Claire feel light again. The walk to the coffee shop was enjoyable as she strode, now almost by habit, with her hand in the crook of Niran's elbow. Vera and her two sisters followed close behind. Their conversation was too low to hear more than just the makings of words here and there. The overall tone, however, seemed glad. Niran, though quiet, was content. Claire, again, felt like the night could not be more perfect.

"That dinner was so delicious and the coffee was the perfect after-dinner treat. But I think I'm going to have to call it a night. I know Margeaux is going to want to..." Claire trailed off as she squinted at a small family, across the street, walking with a stroller. The sisters and Niran followed her gaze and all started, wide-eyed.

"What is that?! Do you see that?!" Claire exclaimed and pointed at the family who seemed happy and oblivious.

Niran only took a few steps forward to make sure he was seeing the same thing. Claire let go of his arm to start walking toward the family. To do what? She didn't know, but she was compelled to go to them. Maybe she could warn them. The logical, reasoning part of her brain worked feverishly to make sense of what she was seeing and why the family seemed to be completely unaware.

"Claire, wait!" Vera shouted after her and grabbed her arm.

Claire took a couple more steps, but halted, terrified. She turned to Vera and Niran, pointing to the family and trying to articulate what she'd seen. Ayn had a look of concentration as they, now, like earlier, seemed to exist only in the blindspots of the people around them. Claire turned back around and made another instinctual attempt to go to the family to help them somehow, but was stopped by a hand on her shoulder. She started and turned around to find Ezra standing before her.

"Oh my," he said, looking past her at the family that still walked with whatever Claire was seeing.

"What has you so startled, dear?" he asked, placatingly.

"You don't see the thing over there?! It's huge! It's a... It's a *monster!* Don't you *see it?*" She looked past Ezra to the sisters and Niran who were standing calmly.

What she'd seen was inarguably monstrous. It was an abomination of the human body, only a mere idea of what a human body once used to be. It was as if every single one of its stretched bones was broken and disjointed. Its skin was covered in boils, some of it seemed like it was peeling right off of its face or whatever was left of the face as it had no jaw. Its tongue hung free and whipped about like it was tasting the air around the stroller. It moved unnaturally in every way, jerky and as if it barely had control of its limbs. It had on tattered scraps of what might have been clothing at one point, perhaps a shirt that once had colorful stripes, now threadbare and dingy. And it clung to the space around the stroller as if it broke its bones even more to do so.

"Father, stop it. Niran, get her out of here," Vera ordered as she stood in front of Claire to block her view.

"We have to help them! What's wrong with all of you?!" Claire exclaimed, nearly crying, trying to look around Vera.

"Claire. I promise you no harm will come to that family. What I need from you right now is to leave with Niran because you don't need to be around this. Can you please trust me right now?" Vera firmly, but gently explained.

Claire, breathing heavily and fighting back tears and adrenaline, only nodded. With that, Niran guided her, with a hand on the small of her back, away from where they all stood, still watching the family with the creature in tow. They'd only taken two steps when Ezra grabbed Claire by the arm, tightly enough to startle her, but gently enough to not be aggressive.

"You really do have the most remarkable eyes, don't you? And how, very remarkable it is that you could see one of our ferrymen," he told her, with a wild gaze that didn't hide how simply thrilled he was with this turn of events.

They stared each other down for a too-long moment before Niran finally guided her away.

XIX

"Why didn't you try to stop that thing? What is it doing with that baby? What the hell are ferrymen?" Claire was still in a panic as Niran hurried her through an alley toward one of the less-busy side streets. She grabbed his arm and wouldn't continue until she got at least one answer. They stood in the middle of the alley, twinkling lights in the shape of snowflakes hung overhead from one end of the alley to the other. They glowed a soft blue over Claire and Niran as she held tight to his arm and stood firmly in his path, demanding an answer, any answer.

"Niran. I might never sleep again after seeing what I just saw. Please, just tell me what's going on. Obviously, those things are some...*extension* of what you do. Right?" Her gaze was pleading now.

"Vera wasn't lying. No harm at all will come to that family or that baby. They will never know the ferryman was even with them. It was just trying to get back to where it came from. I'm sorry. It was a surprise to see it here. I'll answer all your questions," he explained, holding both her hands.

"Where did it come from and what did that family have to do with it getting back there?"

"It needs the baby's cradle. There are only two ways a ferryman makes it back home from here - either a cradle or a grave. The trip, from either, is similar. If they go into the cradle before the baby gets put to bed, or into the grave before the body is lowered, it's like walking through a door for them."

Claire looked past Niran in the direction of where they'd just come from as though she might see the family and the creature again. She pressed her back against the wall, some instinct of hers to ensure nothing could sneak up on her.

"Where home is for them requires a longer answer. Let me take you home and I will explain as best I can on the way."

"What? No! I…"

She looked so frightened that some heretofore unknown instinct had Niran wanting to make her feel safe again. He suddenly hated the look of fear in her eyes so much that he could barely stand to see it.

"Okay," he agreed without hesitation. "Where can we go?"

"The Aubergine. Margeaux said I could go there if I needed to. I won't be alone there."

Niran only nodded and put an arm around her shoulder as they continued walking. She was jumpy and clung to him tightly. He didn't like how it made him feel. The most recent time she clung to him that tightly was only a week ago. They'd walked down Main Street, a few steps behind Vera and Margeaux who had been bickering loudly over something he couldn't remember. Claire had gripped his arm as if it could help her suppress a laugh. This was no such moment. He felt her tremble and never wanted to feel it again.

"I know this might be difficult for you to believe right now, but the ferrymen are quite harmless. The relationship between my family and the ferrymen is strained for reasons we don't need to get into now, but I assure you, despite their appearance, they are completely harmless," he said gently.

She looked up at him, desperate for it to be true. He continued.

"The ferrymen play a very important role in what we do. There is a river where they live. It is where the ferryman you saw is currently trying to return. This river isn't like any you've seen or ever will see. It is as wide and as deep as the universe and as long as time. Its banks are at the edge of a forest so vast, going in means never coming out. From the river, you can sometimes hear the wailing of lost souls trying to find their way out of that forest."

"Lost souls?"

"Yes. Souls who try to run away instead of cross the river. The ferrymen live deep in that forest and only emerge to make their crossings."

"They don't do anything to the souls? Can the souls follow them out?"

"No and no. In the forest, they are invisible to the souls who get trapped there. It is only when a soul is on the riverbank that they can finally see the ferrymen." He stopped himself before continuing the thought. *Unless they're like you.*

"Wouldn't seeing the ferrymen make people want to run away?" she asked.

"Yes, sometimes. But when you're there, there's this sort-of understanding. You know you won't be harmed by them. You know you're meant to cross. You know all of these things, it's just sometimes a soul will ignore all of that and run. It would happen with the souls of children, as the sight of the ferrymen was more frightful to them. A long, long time ago, when the world was a fraction of what it is now, we thought we might try to resolve the problem by going into towns and villages all over and telling them they must pay a toll to the ferrymen. We told them the toll must be paid in the form of coins placed over the eyes, especially those of children. When the souls arrived, eyes covered with coins, they'd be blind to the ferrymen until they got into their boats. Once in the boats, the coins came off and whether they were frightened or not, it didn't matter because they couldn't leave the boat even if they tried to jump over."

Her trembling grip loosened just slightly as she contemplated everything he shared.

"On the other side of that river is another place. We've just always called it 'the other side.' But it's where every soul of every person who has ever lived and ever will live will go, eventually. I can't tell you if it's anything like what some of you consider to be heaven or hell or whatever else. It's just the place that's on the other side. The ferrymen - they're the only beings in the entire universe who can navigate the river. It is on their boats that the souls of this world travel from here to the other side." he continued.

"We all saw the ferryman. So why did Ezra say it was remarkable that I did, too?" Claire asked. It was as much a question as it was an observation.

"I think what he meant is that up until tonight and what just happened, the only people who could see them was my family," he said with a contemplative look, as if he had been trying to answer that question for himself this whole time.

"Why can only your family see them? And why is it that I could, then? And why did it look like that? Do they *all* look like that?" she asked with a small shudder.

"I'm certain we will be able to figure out why you could see it. And I promise you that as soon as we do, you will know, too. As far as why they look that way, I couldn't tell you. They've looked that way for longer than I can clearly recall. I do want to say I have very vague memories of them looking differently, but I can't be certain."

Claire had no answer and had no other questions.

While they walked and talked, they wound through streets, avoiding the direct path to The Aubergine. As it got later and there were fewer and fewer people around, Claire's fear began to return.

"You know. There's something else about the ferrymen that I've found amusing," Niran said with a bit of lightness in his tone.

Claire only looked up at him, with a look that asked what in the world could ever be amusing about them.

"There is only one thing in this entire universe the ferrymen will go nowhere near," he said, then made two small whistles that sounded like chirps.

Confusion was splayed across Claire's face as she waited, a little frustrated that he wouldn't just say what it was. Niran stopped walking, suddenly. She took another step forward before realizing and he pulled her back.

"What is-"

Thunk! A large tree branch the size of Claire's leg dropped in front of them. She staggered back with a yelp, looking around to see where it could have fallen from. Then she felt the warmth of big, panting breaths and whimpers so high-pitched, they were almost inaudible. Niran took Claire's hand and placed it in the crook of his elbow as he finally continued.

"Seir. They won't go anywhere near Seir," he said with a grin.

The branch rolled toward them as the panting and whining became more animated. There was shuffling about and the same smell that filled her parents' hallway was before her now. Claire gaped at the emptiness in front of her that was filled with scent, sound and movement. The branch rolled toward them again and his frustration echoed off of the buildings around them.

"Hold, please," was all Niran said as he bent to pick up the branch, needing both hands and a fair amount of strength to do so.

He flung it into the air in front of them and it disappeared, along with the sound and smell of Seir running after it. The space before them was as if the hound was never there. Claire inched back to Niran's side as she took in the silence that had returned. He did the two-whistle chirps again and right on cue, the branch returned with another clunk at their feet.

"No Seir. Put it away and come back," Niran ordered.

The branch didn't move right away, the panting steady.

"Seir. *Now.*"

Claire watched as the branch slowly lifted into the air on its own and disappeared again. A moment later, the smell and sound of Seir had returned.

"Good boy. Let's go," Niran said and held his elbow out for Claire.

As they walked, she could hear Seir padding next to Niran. Sometimes he'd walk away from them and return. Sometimes he even walked on her side, his scent and panting often the only indication that he was still with them.

"They truly won't go anywhere near him?" she asked quietly.

"They truly won't. They're scared of him - understandably. Seir took off one of their legs thinking it was something he could play with. I had to get it back, it was a mess."

Claire almost laughed. For the briefest moment, she actually felt something other than fear of the ferrymen. It was a little bit of pity.

"If you don't mind, I'll need a favor," he said, patting the air beside him.

"What is it?" Claire asked, wondering what she could possibly do as a favor to Niran.

"If you don't mind, it'd be a big help to me if I could leave Seir with you for a few days. I've got a lot of work to do that he'll just get in the way of and I don't want to keep leaving him with Harena. She overfeeds him. I could leave him at the riverbank, but he tends to cause trouble there."

Claire didn't answer right away, seeing exactly what Niran was doing. She knew it was not a favor she would be doing for him, but an enormous one he would be doing for her.

"The riverbank - is that where he disappeared to? Isn't that the same place that the ferryman is trying to get back to?" she asked.

"It is. Seir can come and go from the riverbank just like my family can. Much like dogs here love to roam and run for miles, so does Seir. He spends a lot of time in the forest. Doing what, I couldn't tell you. Like the ferrymen, he can go in and out without a problem. The ferrymen, I imagine, much prefer he stays out."

"Is he invisible to everyone? Or can you and your family see him? Can the ferrymen see him?" Claire asked.

"Yes, I can see him. My family can, too. But nobody else can, not even the ferrymen. But he will come when you call him and he will stay by your side until you tell him to leave or I call him back."

"Will he want to stay with me? What if he gets bored?" She paused and stopped walking altogether. "My goodness. What if he gets hungry? And where does he, like, go... to do his business?"

"You don't have to worry about any of that," Niran assured her. "Seir doesn't need food or water. He has been known to snack occasionally on his own, and he does his business in the forest, much to the chagrin of the ferrymen. And when he's here, well, I'm not entirely sure where he goes, but he is house trained. He just needs company. Like I said, it'd be a huge favor."

Claire agreed, knowing fully that Niran was doing this for her. As they walked, directly to The Aubergine now, he taught her some basic commands he used with Seir and she practiced them. The hound seemed to enjoy the lessons like it was a game.

About twenty minutes later, they arrived at the back entrance of The Aubergine. As Claire dug around in her bag for her keys, Niran gave instructions to Seir.

"You stay with Claire. Don't leave her side, you understand?" There was only panting and then Niran stumbled a step as it seemed like he was shoved. "Good boy," he told the hound.

Claire watched with a small smile, keys in hand. Niran pet Seir roughly and it looked so odd to her as she watched him merely waving his arms about the air in front of him, high above his own head and around widely.

"I'm not sure if I'll be back around tomorrow, but you've got Seir and if you need anything, I won't be far," Niran said, readying to leave Claire there for the night.

She only nodded and for the first time since the day she met him, she thought she might ask Niran to stay the night with her. Maybe it was because she was still frightened by the ferryman she'd seen. She was definitely still frightened and wondered how she would even be able to sleep. But there was something else there she wasn't ready to acknowledge. So she didn't. She didn't know what she was going to say until the words started to come out.

"Thank you, Niran," was all she could muster.

"You never have to thank me," he answered, looking up at her from the walkway, as she stood at the top of the steps at the door.

"Niran," she said. He looked down to his feet and then back up at her. "*Thank you,*" she finished and held her breath, waiting for his answer.

"You're welcome, Claire," he answered with a small, reassuring smile. She smiled back and watched him pet Seir one more time, whispering one more command as he did. "*Don't leave her side.*"

At that, Niran watched Seir pad up the steps to Claire's side. He bumped her legs and she stumbled back a step with a laugh and pet him, looking as Niran did, like she was just waving her hand over the air. Niran began to walk away.

"Niran," Claire blurted out.

He stopped, facing her silently, with a hand in his pocket. She had nothing. What did she do that for? Her mind frantically searched for the follow up that didn't exist.

"Have a safe walk home," she said and immediately felt her cheeks warm.

"Goodnight, Claire," he said, with a small dip of his chin that hid a smile from her.

"Goodnight, Niran," she replied quickly and turned to hurry inside, opening the door and holding it open for Seir to enter first.

Niran waited until he saw the door close and lock behind her.

After a brief explanation about what Margeaux was hearing and smelling at her side and a promise that any mess made by the beast would be thoroughly cleaned up, Claire trudged into the office carrying a set of pillows and blankets to sleep on the couch there. The Aubergine, as always, would have people in and out all night long and into the morning when daytime workers would arrive. As she hoped, she would not be alone.

Laying on the couch, a sleeping Seir laying right next to it, she replayed her conversation with Niran over again. She found herself strangely grateful for the very human feelings she was still able to have, even if they were for someone who was anything but. It surprised her and she imagined a past version of herself would even be impressed. She realized, with a sudden, sinking feeling, that no matter who he was to her or who she was to him, she could still find a way to embarrass herself.

"*Have a safe walk home*," she repeated in a tone mocking herself and couldn't help but throw a pillow over her face and make a low scream into it. Seir shuffled and groaned, then fell back asleep.

part six

a dangerous legend

a familiar face

light over darkness

the ferryman

Claire was pulled from her sleep by a quiet conversation across the room.

"Word will get out, if it already hasn't."

"What do you propose, then?"

"I don't know. Bodyguards?"

"Can I pick them?"

She was fully awakened by the sudden laughter after the question. It was followed by shushing that came too late as she shifted under her blanket and thought about trying to go back to sleep. She hadn't been able to truly fall asleep until daylight began leaking into the office.

"Oh, ew. Seir! *No! Down!*" Claire squirmed and protected her face with her arms as she shifted about under loud, disembodied sniffing and licking. She tried to remember all the commands Niran had taught her the night before and which one would get him to stop.

"Seir. *Relax.*" Vera commanded from across the office. The hound immediately thudded to the floor, a dense *thunk thunk thunk* sounding against the thick rug where his tail wagged.

"Thanks," Claire croaked as she sat up, pushing hair out of her face and wiping slobber, as invisible as the hound from which it came, from her cheek. "What were you two talking about?"

"Nothing that can get sorted this very second," Vera answered. "How are you feeling?"

"I'm okay. I didn't sleep great, but it was better than I thought it would be thanks to this guy," she said as she roughly petted Seir's head, the *thunk* of his tail sounded louder as she did. "Margeaux, thank you for letting me stay here last night. I just couldn't be alone."

"*Mi casa es su casa, sweetie*, but *that* thing - we're gonna have to figure out a situation for that. It smells." Margeaux shot a look of distaste at the space beside Claire.

An hour later, Claire was back at her own apartment to shower and change. Seir had already found a spot to sleep. In the quiet of her empty apartment, that second sound of faraway screams, in every exhale Seir made, was a reminder to her. Though he made her feel safer, and to the best of her understanding, Sier acted like any normal dog, he was still from *there*. It was the realm of the ferrymen and this invisible beast that now napped in a sunbeam in her living room. What else, she feared, would come from there?

When Claire returned to The Aubergine to do more planning work for the funeral, Margeaux had pointed a freshly manicured finger at the door she'd just walked in from.

"Nope. Today's your day off. Take that smelly thing with you and go enjoy the weather or play in the flowers. I don't care."

"Well, good afternoon t o y ou, t oo!" Claire responded w ith a furrowed brow.

"I don't care. Take a break, Claire! I'll see you later," Margeaux said with a swish of her hand, not even looking at her, as she went back to choosing linen colors. "*And give that thing a bath!*" Margeaux yelled as the door closed behind her.

She and Seir walked a little aimlessly through town until they made it all the way to the far end of the docks and started making their way back toward Main Street. She had nervously left Seir outside the food market while she went in to get lunch. As she waited for her wrap to be made, she kept looking over her shoulder, almost expecting to see people screaming and running, maybe even someone getting caught in an invisible maw. Nothing happened and when she went out to a secluded table to enjoy her lunch, she felt him brush against her. He'd done that several times during their walk to let her know he was still there.

From behind her, "*Claire Bear*" flitted through the air in the sing-song way Vera loved to say it. She looked over her shoulder, with a smile, to see Vera, shading her eyes, as she looked across the street at a group of children playing.

"He adores kids. I can't tell if he wants to eat them or play with them," she said, with a shake of her head.

Claire shot up, almost knocking the table over, ready to yell for Seir to come back, but she didn't even know where he was.

"It's fine. He just likes watching them. It's cute, actually," Vera reassured her. "Anyway, I'm here to collect you and the beast. We're needed at the bookstore. Prepare for dramatics," she said and rolled her eyes.

When Claire was finished with her food and ready to go, she let out two whistles and felt Seir brush up against her a heartbeat later. It was as if he could disappear from one position and reappear at another at will.

They arrived at the bookstore and were met with the "closed" sign on the door and the front lights turned off, even though it was the busiest time of day on Main Street. Vera stepped ahead and entered first. The song of the bells was drowned out by voices trying to talk over each other.

"They already know. It's happened. This is no longer a question of 'if,'" Eyleth said.

"What I don't understand is how they found out so quickly. It hasn't even been a day," Ayn replied.

"How do you think they found out?" Jacob asked sharply. "How did *you* find out? You did not come here with a question. You came here for confirmation."

"It's different, Jacob, and you know it. We all felt the same thing, but there's no way any of them did," Eyleth answered.

"Does the girl know?" Ezra asked.

"Does the girl know what?" Claire interrupted.

They all looked at her at the same time. She felt Seir brush her side as he swept past her to go to Niran who was standing against a bookshelf, brooding. She'd almost forgotten that was his natural state. The sight of him, being that way again, jarred her.

"Claire, sweetheart. Have a seat. We need to talk." Ezra's tone was so inviting and warm that it worried her. He moved a stool next to the bookshelf Niran was leaned against and continued talking. "Something has come up and it seems your safety may be of some concern."

"What? Why?" Claire asked, stunned. She looked up to Niran and he only shook his head, seemingly frustrated.

"We think–"

"-No. We don't think anything. You think," Vera spoke up, making her way to Claire's side.

"Okay. I think you should be moved to a more secure location, for the time being, until we know you will be safe," finished Ezra.

"I'm inclined to agree, sister," Eyleth followed up. Claire noticed Ayn nodded in agreement, though she said nothing.

"Why am I not safe?" Claire asked again. She felt Seir's head brush her thigh and she petted him, absentmindedly.

"There is a legend, Claire, and it has been shared among our kind for millennia. The details have been muddied since the first whisper of it started to spread, but one part remains the same. There are an infinite number of ways the souls may pay their debt to us when it's due. A select few do the jobs Vera, Niran and even Jacob, here, undertake. Others end up doing mundane or one-off tasks. A good many, and maybe the majority, end up paying their debt in quite undesirable ways. This legend is about a normal, human person who has the power to release all of these souls from the bond of their word. But in doing so, it would kill all of *us*." Ezra looked about the bookstore at everyone standing around. Claire, too, looked around at who might lose their life if there was truth to this legend.

"The normal human, the one who can set them all free, has the unique ability to see a ferryman. The ability, as told, only reveals itself once that human signs one of our contracts." He paused again to give Claire a look of concern.

"The part of this legend that puts you in some danger here, is that when that person is found, their soul must go into the river. The same river your Niran informed me he told you about last night. But," he emphasized, "The soul must go into the river voluntarily. Though, this little detail seems to never be shared when the legend gets told."

Still, Claire said nothing, waiting for the whole of the story to be told before she responded. They all studied her as much as she studied the information being shared with her. A small part of her mind snagged on the words "your Niran."

"Throughout the thousands of years this legend has been passed around, there have been the anomalous few who have fit the description - a regular human, bound by one of our contracts, able to see a ferryman. Those in service to their contract --who can come back to the world, or are already here-- have always come for that human and done unimaginable things to them. You see, Claire, the only beings in the whole universe who could ever separate a soul from a person's mortal body before its due time, are in this room. Myself, Eyleth," --a pause-- "and Niran.

"Without our ability, there is absolutely no way, whatsoever, that a human's soul may be separated from the body before its time. Some of them know this. Some of them don't. Some of them have come up with other legends of ways it can be done. It has never been, nor will it ever be, successful. The only outcome of their trying, and they do try, Claire, every single time, is the riverbank being littered with the mangled body of a human who was tortured in unspeakable ways. Sometimes the body remains in one piece. Sometimes, different pieces wash up from the river years later. Sometimes--"

"That's enough," Niran interrupted, pushing off of the bookshelf he leaned against. He stood partly in front of Claire as he continued. "She doesn't need the gory details. We just need to figure out how we're going to keep her safe," he finished.

"We know exactly how she can be kept safe. She needs to be moved to a secure location. Perhaps my home in the mountains. Nobody knows about it," Eyleth added.

"It's still risky there. We need somewhere more remote. Even though it is only the tiniest possibility that this legend might actually be real, we don't want to take any chances of anyone finding out," said Ezra.

"Who could we get to protect her there if anyone we task with the job could find out they stand to benefit from her death?" Ayn asked, finally join-ing the conversation.

"She has the power of her contract behind her. No harm will come to her. This is a completely moot point. I can't believe we're even discussing this," argued Vera.

Jacob was the only one who hadn't yet spoken, a silent observer to the conversation being had about Claire and her life, but didn't include her. He seemed to look only at Claire, glaring at her from behind those sunglasses, as if urging her. To do what? She didn't know, but their gazes were locked as the others argued around her. It was as if he was willing her to remember something.

"No."

The arguing continued.

"No!" Claire said more loudly, standing now. This time, silencing the argument. "I'm not going to some mountain house and I'm certainly not going to some 'more secluded' location than that. I'm not going anywhere. I have a job to do here. And I'm going to do it." She looked each and every one of them in the eye as she continued.

"I have a laughable amount of time left to live. And you promised me, you put in my contract that I could live exactly how I wanted to." She paused to compose herself. "*To live.* Now I don't know if you people can even comprehend what that means, and maybe you don't even care. But I'm only here because someone else decided to make an earth-shattering decision for my life and I will be damned if I let anyone else make decisions for what's left of it. So, no. I will not be going anywhere and you will not be doing anything that will make me feel less than absolutely, one hundred percent, in control of my life, however little is left of it."

"Claire, do try to understand," Ezra pleaded.

"I said *no*. You all figure out how to make it work. Or don't. I don't care. I feel for those other people like me who suffered because of this stupid legend, I really do. But they're not me. And I am certainly not any of them. If anyone wants to come for me, I dare them to try it." When she said this, she began walking toward the door to leave.

"*Claire!*" Ezra's dark and powerful voice bellowed through the bookstore. The lights flickered off.

She stopped and slowly turned around, glaring at Ezra from beneath her brow.

"*What?!*" she boomed back at him, her voice a freight train through the bookstore, hands fisted at her sides. The lights, again, flickered, but all turned on, even the ones out front.

Everyone was silent, even Ezra, who had a look on his face that carried so many different emotions, it was completely unreadable. Jacob, watching Claire, lifted his chin slightly and when she switched her attention to him, she could have sworn there was a look of pride in that upward angle of his chin.

She turned her fire-filled gaze back to Ezra. Eyleth and Ayn were stunned and it was finally Vera who spoke.

"Claire, honey. Let's go back to The Aubergine."

She didn't respond. She only continued to stare down Ezra.

"Very well," Ezra said, far more quietly than anyone expected, "If you will not leave to a safer place, then will you at least consider having one of us near you at all times? Niran, perhaps?" he offered, placatingly.

Her heavy breaths hitched for the briefest of moments when she remembered Niran had been standing there the whole time. Her fists loosened as she considered whether he would even want to do that. The look she gave him asked as much.

"I'll do it," he said, to her, not to Ezra, and gave her a reassuring nod. "I'll do it," he repeated, and finally looked to Ezra for confirmation.

"Then it seems we are in agreement." Ezra's suave tone had returned and Eyleth and Ayn relaxed as well.

"Seir. Let's go," Claire said, before backing up a few steps, then turning around, again, to walk out. Niran was on one side, Vera on the other.

Once outside and past the windows of the bookstore, Claire squeezed her hand into the crook of Niran's elbow and leaned into him fully. She felt drained, as if it had taken every ounce of energy in her to stand up to Ezra the way she did.

"When I told you to prepare for dramatics, Claire, I didn't think you would come ready to bring your own. Well done!" Vera beamed.

XXI

After declaring she would not be hidden away for safekeeping, Claire kept waiting for something to happen, or for someone or something to appear and try to do to her what Ezra had described. The first night had been the most challenging, in more ways than one, as she tried to will herself to fall asleep. Niran sat in her living room, reading, while Seir, with his unearthly snore, slept beside her bed. Though he was in another room, Niran was close enough to hear her if she said his name. She felt like he was too close and not close enough and the feeling filled her stomach with butterflies that fluttered for attention until dawn.

It was another two weeks of Claire constantly looking over her shoulder and Niran decided to try something different. He took her to an empty park, late one night. There, he'd shown her everything Seir was capable of doing when it came to protecting her. There was a headline in the local news the next day, reporting 'vandalism with some kind of heavy machinery' accompanied by photos of uprooted trees, trunks sheared in half, chunks of pavement ripped up from the parking lot, a light pole that was bent into a ball. Claire had been particularly impressed by that bit as she watched Seir rip the light pole from its concrete base and chew on it like it was a toy. When he was finished, he'd galloped to Claire and licked her and rolled onto his back as if to ask if she was proud of him. She was.

She stopped looking over her shoulder after that and she was, again, able to focus on living the rest of her remaining months. Over half of those months had come and gone. As expected, it felt like it passed in the blink of an eye. With funeral preparation going so smoothly after securing flower vendors, there wasn't much for Claire to do on most days, so she'd taken to sharing her wealth of good fortune around town. There was a dog who got loose from its owner and got its leash caught on a fire hydrant; the trolley driver who misplaced her glasses just long enough for the late couple, running to catch it, to get on board; the panhandler who was offered a job. On this particular day, a little cash was found by a group of children wishing for some ice-cream. Claire helped herself to some ice-cream after that one and Niran only shook his head as she chose her flavor and got a little cone for Seir to have when nobody was looking.

"Oh, ew! Seir!" Claire exclaimed as she wiped ice-cream slobber off her cheek with a sleeve.

"I told you he'd do that," Niran said a little smugly with a rough pat on Seir's backside.

"Does he have ice-cream on his fur? Margeaux will kill me, contract be damned, if I let him into The Aubergine with ice-cream on his fur."

"Nope. He put it all on your face."

They walked, as they'd become accustomed to, winding through town and enjoying the more crisp fall air. It was the most beautiful season for the town. And though she didn't enjoy how cold it could get, Claire still didn't want to think about how she wouldn't see the winter. Seir, according to Niran, enjoyed the walks immensely. It was typical for him to run off and come back with random objects on these walks, so it barely registered when he did just that and had something in his mouth to show off.

"Oh, goodness. What do you have now... Niran, what is that?" Claire was expecting another basketball or child's bike. She'd expected to tell him to put it back, but what she thought she saw sticking out of his mouth stopped her in her tracks.

"Seir. *Out*," Niran commanded. The hound did as he was told.

"Niran," Claire breathed. Panic began to rise in her, for what Seir had dropped at their feet was a forearm, seemingly separated right at the elbow. "Oh no, Seir what did you do," she gasped. As she examined the arm, she realized its bones seemed to all be broken, disjointed. Its skin had boils and there was a familiar striped pattern to the bit of sleeve that hung from it at the wrist.

"Niran, it's the ferryman!" she exclaimed at the same moment Seir seemed to happily trot off as if to go back and get more pieces to bring back to them.

They both ran after him, Claire following Niran's lead. Seir brought them to an alley beside a building that was closed for renovations. She immediately spotted the ferryman darting from one side of the alley to the other. It looked like it tried to scale the walls, with its one remaining arm, and when it couldn't, it tried to find a place to hide. At the sound of Seir's low growl, it cowered behind a small bin that barely did anything to hide it.

"Seir. Bring it here," Niran commanded.

"No! Seir! *Stay!*" Claire shouted. "Stay!" she said again to make sure he listened. The ferryman remained cowering behind the bin.

"What are you doing? We need to get rid of it," Niran insisted.

"Just, wait. He's scared. Can't you see?" With that, Claire began walking toward the ferryman. As she did, it began to dart around again, trying to climb the walls with its one hand.

"Where's the hand, Niran?"

"What? Where we left it."

"Can you please get it?" She looked over her shoulder with sad eyes.

"Claire."

"Niran."

With a frustrated sigh, Niran sulked away to retrieve the arm. She turned back around to face the ferryman who still tried to hide. It seemed to try to cover its hideous face and pull the scraps of rags over more of its body. With it mostly hidden, and with it being the middle of the day, Claire didn't find it nearly as frightening as it had been the first night she'd seen it.

"Are you trying to get back home?" she asked softly. She wasn't expecting an answer and wasn't surprised when she didn't get one.

"How did you end up here again?" Still no answer. "Let me help you get home, okay?" With that, it stilled.

She thought of how terrified she had been to see it for the first time at the flower festival. She couldn't sleep because of it. Now, though. It seemed pitiful and as harmless as Niran said it would be. That it seemed so scared broke Claire's heart and somehow allowed her to see past its nightmarish appearance.

"Here," Niran said from behind her, followed by a light thud on the ground where he dropped the arm.

Seir snorted and thunked his tail where he sat, still waiting to be released. Claire grimaced as she looked around for something to pick it up with. She went straight for a bucket of paint rags and old t-shirts left in a pile of contractors equipment.

"If I give him clothes, does that mean people will see the clothes?" she asked Niran while digging through the bucket.

"You're going to give it clothes?" Niran asked incredulously.

"Will people see them?" she asked again, with a look that rendered him a genuflect subject to the needs of her joy. *May she never know the power of that look*, he thought to himself.

"No," he said with a sigh, "anything it holds or wears becomes of it."

She held up a t-shirt that was stained with several different colors of paint and had holes in it. "It's not much, but it's better than what he's got on now. Do you think this is big enough?" She looked through the bucket again, finding a pair of worn khakis, covered in just as much paint and holes.

"Claire, I am not helping you with this. I am not playing dress-up with a ferryman," Niran insisted and looked away from her so as not to be captured by that gaze again.

"Fine. I'll do it myself!" she said with a light tone and a smile in the ferryman's direction. Its one good eye, clouded with cataracts, was focused on her as it still hid the rest of itself.

She picked up the arm using a paint rag and choked down a gag as she hadn't expected the flesh to be so loose and the bones so brittle. She walked towards the ferryman. Seir must have been thoroughly displeased as Niran had to tell him to stay again. As she neared the ferryman, it cowered even lower behind the bin and hid its face. She put the clothes and the arm down about ten feet away from it and backed away.

"There you go. I'm sorry Seir got your arm. I hope it doesn't hurt. And those are new clothes for you," she said with a soft voice.

It made no effort to leave its hiding place so Claire backed up even more, and told Niran they were leaving now.

"Seir. Let's go," Niran commanded and Seir trotted out of the alley, seeming to already have forgotten about the ferryman.

Claire took Niran's arm and walked them both out of the alley. He was still taken aback.

"What do you think is gonna happen?"

"*Shhh.* Let's just go. If he needs help, he'll find us," she said with a smile.

When she looked over her shoulder, she saw the ferryman slip from behind the bin to quickly grab its arm and the clothes she'd left for it. And she knew that the image of a ferryman would not keep her awake ever again.

"*What?!*" cackled Vera, later that evening, as she heard what happened.

"A ferryman! I promise you. She made me go back and get its arm and then gave it clothes!" They were in the bookstore, Niran telling Vera, Jacob and Reid what happened. Vera was practically in tears and even Jacob had chuckled at the part about the clothes.

"The poor thing was absolutely terrified of Seir and he already took his arm and I felt so bad for him! I just wanted to do something nice for him," Claire insisted. "He looked like he was lost, like he didn't come here on purpose."

"It did look that way," Niran said with a more serious tone.

"How do you suppose it keeps making it back here?" Vera pondered.

"I'm afraid we don't really have time to figure that out right now. Margeaux passes in three days. We've all worked way too hard on this funeral. Can we table this until after?" Claire suggested.

Niran opened his mouth to object and Vera was inclined to agree with him, but it was Jacob, this time, who spoke. "Allow me and Reid to find out what we can on this end. You three need to make sure that contract is satisfied."

XXII

Unsurprisingly, Margeaux did not acknowledge, for one second, that she was three days away from the end. She still barked orders to staff, sashayed through The Aubergine and carried herself like a queen holding court. When Vera practically begged her to allow herself, Niran and Claire to help with something, *anything*, Margeaux had finally agreed to let them help put dinner together.

The last family dinner Margeaux would have was just like any other. Her closest friends and cohorts gathered around trays of food that were just a little better than all the others. The table settings were just a little bit nicer. The stories were just a little bit more nostalgic and Margeaux was just a little bit more sentimental. All those subtleties went largely unnoticed, but that's how she preferred it to be. She wanted to remember every single one of these dinners in exactly the same way. She would not allow her memories of them to be tainted by even one dinner that was anything less or more than her closest loved ones sharing food, stories and their love for each other.

So often, so many of the people gathered around the tables of these dinners would laugh until they cried. Margeaux was especially prone to doing so. It would only make everyone around her laugh harder to watch her trying to wipe away tears without smudging her make-up. When the stories got told at this dinner and the laughter and tears ensued, hers flowed a little more freely and she worried far less about how her makeup looked when she wiped them. Claire watched the incredible woman hold it together through what had to be one of the most challenging roles she'd ever played - a woman who was certain she'd see all of her most cherished friends and loved ones again.

Three days later

The great Lady Margeaux was found exactly as she planned - in her most beautiful silk nightgown and robe, hair strewn about her head as if each strand was carefully placed, and laying as if she was posed. It was her best friend, Vera, who found her and called an ambulance. She also alerted their most trusted photographer and journalist friends. Margeaux's obituary looked like a luxury designer's ad campaign and took up an entire page in the local newspaper. News of her death spread, a wildfire that burned through the grapevine and brought fans from far and wide to pay their respects. There was already going to be a sizable attendance to her going-away party, but this news would make that look like an afternoon tea. As planned, her going-away party was swiftly transitioned into a funeral where her life would be honored and celebrated.

"You have got to be kidding me," Claire exclaimed as she stood before the ensemble Margeaux had commissioned for her to wear to the funeral.

"Where does this get put on the body? Like, where does this piece even go?!" The more she studied the outfit, the more she wanted to refuse to wear it.

"I'm pretty sure those are sleeves and this looks like it gets worn on the head," Vera said with uncertainty.

"*Vera*," Claire said.

"Mine is no better, Claire Bear!"

Claire lifted the skirts of the ball gown bottom, layers of tulle, silk and lace. Under it was, "Framework," she showed Vera, "Literal framework. Where does my body go," she exclaimed.

With the help of Margeaux's designer and a couple of dancers, who were all dressed just as elaborately, Claire made it into her outfit. This funeral, she realized, was to be the show to end all shows at The Aubergine; and every single attendee was to share the stage.

The street on which The Aubergine sat was closed for the funeral and, for the day, was renamed Lady Margeaux Street. Every side street leading to it had limited traffic to residents and shop owners and their employees. Every street lamp was heavy with Claire's floral arrangements, the size of small children, as Margeaux demanded. They engulfed the lamps at the top. Every manner of vine and weeping flower hung down from them, low enough that one needed only to raise their hand to run fingers through them. Guests began to arrive by the dozen, piling into the side streets, though not yet stepping foot on Lady Margeaux Street. Claire and Vera watched the awe-inspiring display from the rooftop of The Aubergine. Dressed in their overwrought ensembles and stood atop The Aubergine, they looked like some version of high fashion gargoyles keeping the gates to the castle.

"I've never said this, and I guess it makes sense that I would say it now, but this is better than I hoped it would be," said from behind, in an unfamiliar voice coming from a woman with an unfamiliar face.

She was dressed as they were, elaborately and without restraint. She was accompanied by Niran, who, when Claire beheld him, looked down at her own gown and then back to his tuxedo and saw they had been coordinated perfectly to each other. He noticed at the same time and only gave her a small shrug.

"Are we certain this is to be my protege? Hm," Vera assessed the unfamiliar woman and her gown. As she walked toward the woman, Niran walked to Claire's side.

"Don't you '*hm*' me. I've had to wear this body for the past week and I can't wait to get out of it!"

"Margeaux?" Claire blurted out.

"In the flesh," she said, looking down at herself with slight displeasure, "literally," Margeaux replied from the lips of the body that had, apparently, been loaned to her.

"Come see." Vera grabbed Margeaux's hand and brought her closer to the edge of the roof where she could see the growing crowd of people there to pay their respects and celebrate her. The four of them stood there now, looking down upon the crowd of people so fantastically dressed that it would not have been a surprise if someone had rode in on an elephant.

"It's time," Margeaux said with a heavy sigh, and looked to Niran who nodded and raised his hand above his head. Claire looked in the direction Niran waved and saw a man in the distance wave back. The street lights along the side streets and on Lady Margeaux Street flashed in much the same way theatre lights flash to signal the show is about to begin. Silence fell over the entire area and all that could be heard was the swishing of ballgowns and the shuffling of feet coming to a halt. Everyone turned to face Lady Margeaux Street. The man who waved back to Niran gestured to someone who was off in his distance. Moments later, the clock tower bells began to ring.

The doors of The Aubergine opened and from the side streets and breaking through the utter silence, rose up a crashing wave of keening wails and screaming sobs as the crowd lurched forward in plumes of colors and fabrics, statement headpieces, glittering accessories, masks. Their anguish was a woeful symphony bleeding songs in the minor key. The sound of their cries was thrown against the buildings all around and slid down, a deluge of tears in sound. News helicopters took turns circling above to capture the spectacle and throughout the crowd, were flashes from journalists' cameras. The group stood atop the roof for several moments just watching in awe. The sight and sound of it was breathtaking. As the crowd neared The Aubergine, Vera and Margeaux turned to head downstairs. Niran held out his arm for Claire to take and they followed.

"Will you be okay, Mar? This is where we leave you," Vera informed Margeaux as they entered the theatre.

"Quite alright, my dear," Margeaux, in her stranger's skin, assured Vera.

She hadn't been speaking directly to Vera as she answered, her gaze sweeping over the theatre hall and taking in all the decorations and perfectly-poised staff all around. She wished she could hug each of them and thank them for all their hard work. Her heart sank and her throat dried out as she wished she had another twenty or thirty years of this - that this wasn't the last show she would put on at The Aubergine. She wanted to rip this loaned skin off of herself and tell everyone she was alive and jump on the stage and dance and sing for them. The stage. She couldn't just jump on it and dance and sing because she, or at least her body, was already on the stage. Her open casket, a gleaming white with solid gold accents, seemed to float in a sea of flowers and greenery. Claire had unquestionably outdone herself, Margeaux thought. The arrangements which flanked the stage towered over Margeaux by at least five feet and seemed to stand tall and weep at the same time.

Claire looked over her shoulder as she, Vera and Niran walked away to the sight of Margeaux's eyes glistening. She couldn't help but consider that she would, soon, be following Margeaux. She thought of how much Margeaux would be leaving behind and wondered if she still thought the revenge was worth leaving all of this and all of these people. Though her own life was much, much shorter and far, far less grand, Claire couldn't help but think about everything she would be leaving behind as well. It made her cling to Niran a little tighter.

"Should she be alone for this?" Claire asked.

"Yes. We will find her after the service, but this, she needs to do alone," Vera assured her.

Only a portion of the large crowd was allowed to sit inside the theatre during the service. They were, of course, the best-dressed guests and most important to Margeaux. Claire recognized almost all of them as the invitation recipients. The rest of the attendees flooded Lady Margeaux Street and waited their turn to enter the theatre for their moment of respect at her casket. Velvet couches and chaise lounges were dotted around the street in front of the Aubergine. In other areas were long tables, heavy with decorations, and silk, padded chairs along them.

Everywhere one's eyes fell were Claire's flower arrangements. They'd nearly emptied the stock of three different wholesale florists in the region and had the rest flown in on two different shipments. Claire was given a team of twenty people to help with the arrangements and she needed every last one of them to pull off the job. She strolled through the crowd, inspecting the arrangements and taking in the looks of admiration on the attendees faces before making her way back inside The Aubergine to her seat with Vera and Niran.

"We're going last, so we've got some time before you need to worry about standing in that dress again," Vera instructed.

So Claire settled in. They had an excellent view of the entire theatre hall and everyone in attendance. Claire had no idea what to expect, so she just allowed herself the pleasure of taking in the almost-indescribable beauty and opulence that surrounded them. Just when she thought to herself, *there should be painters here to also capture this*, did she spy two painters in different corners of the hall, capturing what she was admiring.

As the last of the crowd settled onto Lady Margeaux Street and the side streets belonged to the town again, the clock tower bells rang once more. All of Margeaux's most important and influential guests sat inside the hall, silent now. Some wiped tears, some sobbed quietly. And, in an unassuming spot, by the stage, where she could see everything and everyone, sat Lady Margeaux in her loaned body.

The main theatre lights dimmed to almost pure darkness as flickering candlelight began to alight on the stage amongst the flowers. Towering candelabras were positioned throughout the hall as dancers, wearing bodysuits completely covered from head-to-toe in black Swarovski crystals, dramatically danced around the candelabras and lit them. From the ceiling, four enormous candelabra chandeliers were lowered along with dancers who floated around them on silks and lit them as well. How they managed to do so without burning themselves was part of the spectacle. With the dancers finished and the entire theatre hall lit to perfection, the service began.

Lady Margeaux's eulogy, as anyone would expect, was not spoken but sung in the form of a seventeen minute opera. At its conclusion, the soprano

--whose gown was made to resemble a Luna moth-- nearly swooned at the end of her fifteen-second long D6 note. Her sign language interpreter had tears streaming down her face and expressed agony with every sign. When they were through, they curtsied to the audience and bowed deeply to Margeaux's casket. It moved Claire to tears and she was nearly overwhelmed by the power of the song as she was swept away in its sorrow. She forced herself not to look at Margeaux from fear of the sight of her reaction causing her to break down fully into sobs.

A path was cleared through the flowers surrounding the coffin for attendees to begin stepping forward and pay their respects. There was no particular order in which these people approached, but when they did, it was in dramatic fashion.

There was a set of plump, busty triplets in jewel-tone gowns that were made so wide, they needed two chairs each to sit. The gowns, with their obnoxiously long trains, were similar, but not exactly alike. Each triplet wore a large fascinator with jeweled veils that glittered in the candle light. In unison, they rose from their seats, their sobs almost as operatic as the eulogy. They seemed to glide, as one, to the casket, everyone moving out of their way. All three threw themselves over the casket and their wails sent shivers down everyone's spines. The one in the middle was the loudest. She suddenly stood, upright, her mouth and chest to the sky and fainted in a cloud of her own dress. A man in a simple tuxedo and a plain, white mask caught her before she could hit the floor. Her sisters followed the man as he carried her away. Their wails faded and only the sigh of their gigantic skirts dragging across the floor was all that was left of their siren's song.

After them, walked up a trio of gentlemen. One was a lanky man in a blue velvet tuxedo. He had long, blonde hair and wore a mask that was just a veil of crystals cascading over his face, hanging from a crown of black antlers. Beside him, walked a giant Irish wolfhound that had fur so black, it dimmed the light around it. The other gentleman was dressed in traditional Moroccan formal wear. It was blood-red with gold stitching and accents. He had red, golden-tipped nails that were several inches long and filed to a point. His hair was slicked back like a classic film mobster. The shape of his mask was plain, oval for his face and eyes cut out, but it was made of four layers of gold, each cut to depict one of the seasons. Over his shoulders was an albino python that slept with its tail wrapped around the man's waist.

The third gentleman, one that didn't look like he belonged with them, was much older, short, a little hunched. He wore a simple tweed suit like you'd see worn by a newspaper editor from the 1920s. The first two gentlemen opened a path for the third, as he walked toward the casket, and then followed him with their silent pets. Once at the casket, the old man dug in his vest pocket and pulled out a golden coin. The other two men did the same, pulling out their own gold coins. They laid the coins down in a row on the casket, then the old man pulled out a pocket watch and dropped it on the ground. The man with the wolfhound stomped on it first, followed by the man with the snake. They three walked away, leaving the broken pocket watch on the floor in front of the casket.

One-after-the-other were these visits to the casket made and in equally dramatic and often perplexing fashion. A handful of times, Claire looked to see Margeaux's reaction and was met with a look of simultaneous delight and longing. While scanning the hall, Claire caught sight of Reid, dressed in a plain, black suit, wearing white gloves. He was the most plainly-dressed person in attendance. He had walked up to Vera, placing a hand on her shoulder.

"Reid, darling, where are you and Jacob sitting?" she asked him, as she watched a woman, wearing a gown that looked like panels of stained glass, open the bodice of her dress, pull out a glass heart and place it on the casket.

Reid stepped aside for Jacob to speak.

"They're here, Vera," Jacob said from where his wheelchair was positioned just behind Reid.

In the same way that laughter often precedes the arrival of children, or perfume, an elegant woman, an eerie and unnatural hush ushered in Ezra. He wore a black, brocade suit whose details could only be seen when light shone on it at just the right angle. His hair, white as snow, fell just past his shoulders and gleamed against his suit. His two stunning companions were dressed just as elaborately as everyone else in attendance, only their gowns coordinated perfectly with Vera's. Ayn's gown was wispy with tiered layers and puffy sleeves. Her platinum blonde curls were swept up in a hairdo as playful as her dress. Eyleth's gown was far more simple, the simplest of the three, but still managed to look elaborate in its own way with the two-foot train she dragged behind her. In lieu of layers or huge skirts were smoke-colored teardrop crystals sewn onto and dangling from her gown. They made her look like she'd been caught in a crystal rain. Her fawn colored hair was swept over a shoulder.

After a few murmured greetings, the family of dark immortality, more in their element than anyone around them could ever imagine, approached the stage. Atop Margeaux's casket, in the only open spot amongst the dozens of gifts, baubles, trinkets and flowers left there, the siblings left tokens of their own. Reid placed down a golden quill for Jacob. Ayn left a small embroidery of silk and gold. Vera left an ancient golden coin. Niran held his mother's hand in support as she was the last of the siblings to leave her token, a golden head of a wheat stalk. They parted to allow their father to leave his token. It was a signet ring that looked almost identical to Vera's, ancient coin and all.

Once everyone in the main theatre hall had visited the casket with their varying levels of drama and mystery, it was officially time to begin the reception. Those who waited outside would pay their respects throughout the reception which, according to Margeaux's instruction, would last until dawn crested the horizon and spilled its light over the darkness of their loss.

One after the other, performers danced, sang, contorted themselves, played every manner of instrument, strung illusions, recited poetry. If there was a way to express grief or celebrate a life, it happened just outside and within the Aubergine Theatre. Custom made, ceramic serving trays with mounds of food were positioned artfully among the flower arrangements which weighed down all the tables scattered throughout the street and inside. Guests imbibed on rare wines and liquors, drinking only from crystal glasses, as they watched performers or prepared for their own performances. From one end of Lady Margeaux Street to the other, candelabras dripping with wax provided light for the reception, along with globe lights strung between the buildings on both sides, creating an umbrella of softest amber and haze.

Claire reveled in the beauty and theatrics swirling all around her as she spent most of the evening at Niran's side, often accompanied by Margeaux in her borrowed body.

"Why aren't you with them?" Claire asked Niran, nodding to his family as they sat along a low wall, sipping wine and watching a ballerina perform her tribute to Lady Margeaux.

"I get plenty of time with them," he said with a sigh.

"I think it's great they all came here just for this funeral," Claire noted.

Niran didn't answer. He only looked down to his feet and then back out to the performance. She noticed, but said nothing. Instead, she changed the subject to remark on the awe of the funeral and everyone in attendance. They conversed easily and comfortably, often forgetting the theatrics around them.

As they chatted, Claire spotted Vera, Jacob and their sisters drifting through the crowd together throughout the night. As individuals, they were each captivating with undeniable beauty and presence. As the group, however, seemingly sharing in some power that knew them best together, they were devastating. It was as if being apart took from them and being together gave it all back with apology. Their father was no exception, though he remained several steps behind them, seemingly perfectly content with the arrangement.

Several performances later, Margeaux made her way back to Claire and Niran who still sat in comfortable company of each other. "This is the last performance," Lady Margeaux said softly, as she looked toward the east to see the setting night.

Just then, the crowd silenced as a little girl, no older than six or seven, was carried out by a behemoth of a man. She sat in the crook of his left arm as he walked her to a grand piano that was set up on a stage. The man lowered the little girl onto the stage and joined her, bent on one knee in front of the piano. She fixed her little, pink dress that looked like the petals of an orchid and then sat upon the man's knee facing the piano. Through the crowd, across the cleared street, came out two dancers.

"Claire. Whatever you end up doing with what's left of your robbed life, I implore you to keep your heart open to love," Margeaux said, having taken Claire by both hands and then touching her cheek with an affectionate palm.

"This" --Margeaux nodded in the direction of the dancers-- "is the last story of my life that needed to be told. I've saved it for last and perhaps it is being told far, far too late, but nevertheless, it is a part of who I am."

"What's the story?" Claire asked, honored to know it, to know the great Lady Margeaux.

The tiny pianist began to play. From her little fingers came a melody so full of hope, joy and love that Claire put a hand to her chest and looked to Margeaux in understanding.

"Is this-"

"--My love story? Yes," Margeaux answered. Her eyes were shining.

The little girl played and the dancers floated about each other in a way that looked new and hopeful, excited and a little nervous.

"We met when I just started at The Aubergine. I was nobody and neither was he. He was an artist. A painter. Q hired him to do some pieces for the main hall. I took one look at him and I knew I was in trouble."

One of the dancers took out a chiffon scarf and waved it about as if making broad strokes of a painting.

"When he finally worked up the nerve to ask me out, all either of us could afford was a couple of hot dogs from the market. We sat at the edge of the dock, eating our hot dogs and talking all night long. I spilled a bit of mustard on my shirt and he did his best to clean it off with a handkerchief he always kept in his back pocket."

The song became a whirling combination of chords into a melody that was overwhelming, but in a way that lifted the crowd to want more and more. The dancers fell into each other, completely in sync and completing each other's movements, their faces full of devotion to one another.

"It was a secret. And I can't tell you why I kept it so long. Maybe I was embarrassed and couldn't admit it. But he didn't care. All he wanted to do was love me and all I wanted was his love."

The song slowed. The dancers slowed. They fell out of sync. There was sadness on their faces. There was pain in their steps. The melody sank into Claire's gut and stayed there, turning over and over.

"They say ambition, unchecked, is a poison to love."

Claire began to tear as the song swept through the crowd, bringing about bowed heads and the feeling of final goodbyes. The dancers parted in their own individual waltzes of regret and longing. And Claire had felt the story and the dance and the music within herself, some kind of understanding she could never share. The song, the dancers, Margeaux, the crowd. It suddenly weighed on Claire in a way that made the tears spill from her eyes and onto her incredible gown. She swallowed hard and tried to control the tears, but they kept falling. The song kept falling. The dancers' movements looked like weeping from their hearts. Just as she was about to turn around and escape to be alone with her sorrow, she felt a hand take hers. It was Niran. She looked up at him, eyes welled with tears and couldn't help but shake her head and chuckle at herself. He adjusted his grip and pulled her closer to him, with his other hand, he wiped tears off her cheek with a thumb. She held his hand with both of hers and let out a cleansing exhale. He nodded to her and gripped her hand more tightly, his thumb making a soothing back-and-forth over hers.

At the end of the dance and the saddest song Claire had ever heard, the dancer who waved the chiffon scarf disappeared into the crowd and the other dancer laid on the ground, curled into herself. The crowd erupted into applause and tears. They threw flowers over the dancer where she laid. From the rain of flowers, a man in a tuxedo stepped forward; the tuxedo was covered in paint splatters of all colors. At the sight of him, Claire switched her attention to Lady Margeaux who had grabbed her arm and looked like she wasn't breathing. The man stood over the flower-covered dancer and reached into his back pocket. He pulled out an old handkerchief. From where they stood, Claire could see a distinct yellow-orange stain on it. Her mouth fell open as she watched the man place the handkerchief on top of the dancer.

"Niran- get me out of here," Margeaux choked as she watched the man disappear into the crowd as swiftly as he had appeared from it.

Niran and Claire looked at each other before letting go of each other's hands to lead Margeaux away. Niran guided her on one side and Claire gathered herself and fell into step beside Margeaux on the other. From across the way, past where the dancers continued, Vera, Jacob, Eyleth and Ayn all watched Niran and Claire. Ezra had been watching them all night. What they all witnessed now pleased him thoroughly.

A half hour later, as the dawn came to take away the sorrow, the funeral had come to its close. Sluggish guests poured back out into the side streets, some carrying half their outfits, some still proudly wearing theirs in-full, some having discarded theirs completely, wearing only scraps draped over undergarments. They all felt the loss of the great Lady Margeaux and wondered who could ever follow in her footsteps.

Margeaux hadn't wanted anyone to see where she'd be buried, as her plan was to be next to her parents, with a modest headstone, in a peaceful cemetery. She didn't want that peace disturbed by the rabble who would surely come to visit her. Lined up against the wall outside of the back door of the Aubergine, was Vera, Niran, and Claire draped in Niran's tuxedo jacket to fend off the early morning chill. They watched quietly as Margeaux's casket was loaded into the back of an unassuming hearse that would take her to her final resting place. Margeaux was inside The Aubergine, talking now with Eyleth who was instructing her on what was to happen next. She hadn't wanted to see her body taken away.

"It feels like I could just walk back down there and go about business, as if it was any other day. Like things should just be the way they always have been and all of this was just some fever dream," Margeaux admitted sadly. "It feels like I should be able to do that, right now, because I was able to do that every single day. And today should be no different because when you look around, it isn't, really." She, Vera and Claire, back in regular clothes, sat in lounge chairs on the roof of The Aubergine. It *did* look like any other morning.

"Everything that ever mattered to me and everything I've ever known is right here beneath our feet. It's still right here and so am I. But I'm trespassing on my own property. It's like I can feel her begging me to stay, telling me it was all a mistake and we can just go back to how things always were and ought to be." She took in a deep, sorrowful breath as tears fell from those unfamiliar eyes. Vera only reached over and held her hand. "I don't regret doing it. I don't. But how can I ever explain to my beautiful Aubergine? She'll never forgive me."

After a long morning atop The Aubergine, the trio finally made their way back down for the last time. Vera and Claire left first and waited outside. Margeaux cried rivers as she walked through the empty hallways, past her beloved dressing room, beyond her office and to the stage. She stood in the orchestra pit and walked to the stage, leaning her forehead on the edge where she'd sat countless times, her hands gently passing over the wood.

"I love you so much. I love you so, so, so, very much. Thank you for the life we shared. Thank you, thank you, thank you," she whispered. "Thank you." Her sobs echoed where her joyful laughter once had.

She finally gathered herself enough to walk away - every step taking from her very being, as if inside each footprint was a piece of her life and a piece of who she was. She plucked a matchbook from the bar - *The Famous Aubergine Theatre* printed on it. As she walked through the theatre, losing more and more of herself with every step, she chose a candelabra and her hand shook as she struck a match and brought it to one of its candles. "I'm so sorry," she said through her weeping, and she tipped the candelabra over.

When Margeaux stepped outside, she shielded her eyes from the sun and looked around. She had no idea where she was or how she even got there. There were two women standing on the sidewalk who seemed to have been waiting for her. One of them spoke.

"Margeaux. Hi. How are you feeling?"

"Okay, I guess. I'm not quite sure how I got here," she answered the stunning woman with impossibly long, crystal black hair and a pinky ring that glinted in the sun.

"That's okay, dear. I'm here to help you get settled in. This is my friend, Claire," the woman said with a broad, welcoming smile.

"Hi, Margeaux. It's a pleasure to meet you," Claire said with a smile just as warm and inviting.

"Where are we? Is that smoke I smell?" She turned around and it was, indeed, smoke she smelled as some began to seep out of the door she'd just walked out of. "Oh my goodness, I think there's a fire. We should call someone," she exclaimed, scurrying to the pair standing on the sidewalk.

"Yes, we've already called someone. We should go, so we don't get in the way of things when they come," the beautiful woman suggested, putting a hand out to direct Margeaux down the sidewalk.

As they walked away, Margeaux turned around to look at the building, flames and smoke growing bigger inside, and said, "What a shame. It's a very beautiful building."

"Oh, you would have loved it there. It really is quite a shame. I'm Vera, by the way."

As the three walked away, Claire and Vera gave each other a sad look before catching one last glimpse of the famous Aubergine Theatre.

The fire would not be noticed until it was too late to save the building.

A week had gone by since the funeral. Vera wasted no time getting started on teaching Margeaux all there was to know about "buying souls," as she'd once put it. She was optimistic and even excited about having a new version of the friendship they shared during her life. With the funeral finally over and work to be done with Margeaux, Vera suggested Claire should take the rest of her time to enjoy herself.

"If you're going to refuse to enjoy the big things, you might as well take the last of your time to enjoy the little ones, sweet Claire," she'd said with feigned disapproval and a wink.

Claire had watched them leave for Margeaux's lessons. Vera had hugged her tightly, yet Margeaux had only given her a friendly handshake. It felt wrong, and she'd shared as much with Niran as she slipped a hand on his arm and chose a direction for them to walk.

"She's still Margeaux," he explained. "She is only missing her memories."

"But our memories make us who we are," Claire countered, bothered and wondering if the same fate would befall her when her time came.

"What happens to a person in their life helps create the person they will become, yes. But once that person is created, removing the memories of that life will not change who they have already become," he clarified. "She will still want attention and adoration. She will still be inclined to being hospitable and fashionable. She'll still be kinder and more understanding to dreamers, relentlessly harsh to the entitled. She will still have a quick tongue and no patience for games. She will still be every bit Margeaux as she's ever been - all excellent traits of someone who is to be Vera's protege. She just won't have the stories to tell that explain how she got there."

"It's a crying shame," Claire said with a shake of her head. "Margeaux will never know the incredible woman she was, and the Aubergine..." she trailed off.

"She couldn't have been granted her wish and the position with Vera without sacrificing something that would have destroyed her to lose. The balance has to come from somewhere and what she asked for demanded its due."

"Will that happen to me?" Claire finally asked.

"I don't know," was all Niran could say.

They wound through town on no set path and with no set destination, adding themselves to the idyllic image of the town in mid-fall. Seir strode along with them, their silent and invisible guardian. Without the distraction of working on the funeral, Claire had become painfully aware of how quickly the last of her own time was passing.

"This is my favorite time of year," she shared, happy to change the subject from the sadness of Margeaux's loss or the thoughts of her own.

"It's about to get even better," Niran said with a smile and directed Claire's attention across the street. "Look over there, but don't make it obvious."

Across the street was a little girl who had just fallen off her bike. She cried as her friend tried to clean a scrape on her elbow. Another friend dug around in a backpack for a bandage.

"Um. I don't think little girls crying is supposed to make fall a better-"

"-No, look, Claire," Niran interrupted her with a grin.

"Oh my goodness! Niran, it's him!" Claire barely-contained her excitement as she saw the ferryman she'd helped appear at the side of the crying little girl.

They tried not to be obvious as they slowly walked by and watched the ferryman, who wore its paint-stained t-shirt and ill-fitting khakis, try to hand the crying little girl a flower. It seemed just as distraught as she was as it hovered closely, looking at her injury and then around for anything else it could offer her. Claire squeezed Niran's arm and watched the ferryman who held its detached forearm, tucked under the arm from which it was severed.

The friends found a bandage and the ferryman had a look of relief as the hurt little girl wiped away the last of her tears. As the three friends got back on their bikes to leave, the ferryman darted around them and looked up and down the street as if to ensure their safe departure. Once they left, it simply continued a leisurely stroll, even trying to pet a cat that was perched on a porch banister. The cat hissed and ran off and the ferryman only ambled along.

The next day, Claire had awoken, not quite adjusted to the slower pace, and feeling a little aimless. Niran had gone that morning, having left Claire with Seir and a promise he'd return in a few days. Curiosity got the best of her as she couldn't stop thinking about what the ferryman did all day long, so she decided to go look for him and simply find out for herself.

"Okay, Seir. I'm going to ask you to do something, but you have to promise me not to attack. Can you do that for me?" Claire asked the air next to her. She heard the familiar *thunk thunk thunk* of Seir's tail on the grass beside the bench where she sat. "Can you find the ferryman for me?" Before she could even finish speaking, she heard excited panting and shuffling as if Seir already stood, ready to do as he was asked. "Hey! But you have to promise me you won't attack him. No attack? Okay, Seir?" she tried to command but could only hope he'd listen.

It took no time for Seir to find the ferryman and to Claire's relief, he did not attack it. His restlessness showed, however, that he really wanted to.

"Oh, you're such a good boy! I'm going to tell your dad how good you were when he gets back," she told the beast while petting him and had to settle him when he nearly knocked her over with licks and gentle shoves with his head.

She spent the day following the ferryman around, watching what it did with its time and invisibility. Seir stayed by her side and after a while, eventually lost interest in the monstrous-looking creature. But it hadn't looked all that monstrous to Claire anymore. Somehow, witnessing its gentle nature and how it seemed to desire only to be a part of the world, had made it less and less difficult to overlook its appearance. The ferryman seemed to share in Seir's love for children, hovering around the ice cream shop and at the park. It was terrified of every kind of dog, big and small, and would dart away whenever it saw one. Just the sniff of an elderly Chihuahua sent the ferryman into a tree. That had made Claire laugh and feel bad for it.

Later that day, the trio found themselves lounging in late-afternoon laziness by a pond. Claire listened to distant wails in Seir's snoring beside her as she watched the ferryman by the water, reaching out toward a family of geese there. They were among the last to fly south for the winter. The sound of songbirds had died down and all the little creatures and bugs that gave life to the pond all began their transition to winter. Among them were a pair of chunky squirrels with cheeks full of food. They scurried slowly, under their growing winter weight, to get into the tree Claire sat under. In one moment, she was smiling at how cute they looked, in the next, the distant wails stopped, there was quick movement and the squirrels vanished into a familiar, invisible maw.

"Seir! No! Seir! Out!" Claire yelled, eyes desperately looking at nothing, waiting for the squirrels to be spit out. "Seir! Out, I said!"

The hound did not chew the squirrels as she heard muffled chittering and movement, but he did not spit them out either. She could only imagine the look on his face.

"Seir! I said *out!*" she tried again.

Just then, a disembodied forearm slammed into the tree, a boil-covered forearm with a scrap of striped shirt still hanging from its wrist. The squirrels --both wet and panicked-- stumbled out of thin air and rushed up the tree in an instant. The arm was scooped up into nothing and the sound of smacking and bones crunching turned Claire's stomach as she looked to see the ferryman darting nervously by the tree.

"Your arm!" she exclaimed to the ferryman and they both looked up the tree at the pair of squirrels, safely looking down at them. "Oh no, your arm, though!" she said, sorry and having no idea what to do. She could have sworn, with its jerky movements and disfigurement, that the ferryman only shrugged. There was the sound of Seir swallowing and Claire immediately ordered him to relax. The hound went down instantly; a huff and a groan sent the ferryman back a few steps.

"He won't hurt you. I promise," she said, wishing she could hug it, but deciding not to. "Do you want to sit with us?" she asked, the only thing she had to offer. She sat back down under the tree and ordered Seir to her side where he obeyed and soon fell back asleep. "You can sit right here," and she patted the grass next to her other side. It didn't sit next to her, but it did squat on the other side of the tree. The unlikely trio lounged together for the rest of the afternoon, watching the fall evening turn the picturesque pond into a living painting.

The next morning, Claire spotted the ferryman sooner than she thought she might as she and Seir left her apartment. Seir had become wholly uninterested in the ferryman and it seemed to become less frightened by Seir.

"Well, good morning. How are you today?" she asked it, as if it was just another neighbor. "Whatcha got there?" The ferryman had a pocket full of fallen leaves - yellow, orange, and red. In its hand was a napkin from the ice cream shop and it had a length of twine hanging from its neck in a loose, half knot that would come undone easily. “Are those souvenirs?” she asked with a smile and somehow she understood the odd, jerky movements of the ferryman, a sort-of “*yes*.”

“Does that mean you’re ready to go home?”

The ferryman jerked around and moved in as meaningful a way as it could.

“Hm. Okay, we’re going to have to find you a baby, huh?” Claire said.

The three walked along for half the morning, without a baby in sight. The ferryman only patiently jerked and darted about. As Claire passed by a children’s store, she was struck with an idea. “I don’t know if this will work, but we can try it,” she said as she turned to walk back toward a store that sold high-end clothes and furniture for infants.

Inside the store, Claire stood next to a cradle and tried not to look like she was speaking to someone as she gestured for the ferryman to go into it. The ferryman darted and jerked excitedly before stopping in front of Claire and the cradle. She smiled sweetly to it as it lifted a boil-covered, broken-fingered hand to her hair and touched it lightly. She looked around before tying a pretty bow into the end of the twine about its neck.

“You’re welcome. Have a safe trip home,” she whispered.

The ferryman climbed in and disappeared.

part seven

trick-or-treat

has anyone ever told you

first of their kind

"And just like that, it made it home?" Niran asked, two days later, a little surprised.

"Mhm. We're friends now," Claire stated plainly, as she and Niran sat outside of the bookstore handing out candy to trick-or-treaters. She'd convinced Jacob to let her and Niran participate in the Main Street Halloween Festival by handing out candy. She got an outright refusal when she took it a step further and asked if she could do a spooky book reading for the children inside the shop.

"I used to trick-or-treat here myself when I was a kid," Claire reminisced. "My mom would sit in the square with the other moms and drink cocktails and gossip while we came up and down the street twice to get double the candy. We never did the neighborhoods because this was the only place she could take me where she didn't have to walk with me," she finished with a wry laugh.

Reid's heavy, gentle hand patted Claire's shoulder softly; with a look of intent, he gestured inside the bookstore.

"He wants to see me?"

Reid nodded and smiled. Claire handed him the bucket of candy and he lumbered into the spot where she'd been sitting. A group of trick-or-treaters gaped up at him, mouths wide, as he towered over them and smiled broadly. To the chorus of "trick or treat," Reid carefully dropped candy into each of their buckets and bags and waved goodbye as they moved onto the next shop. He looked down the sidewalk to see the next group of children approaching and straightened. He checked the bucket to make sure he had enough candy for them all and waited, patiently.

Claire and Niran walked in to see Jacob positioned at a front window where he could watch the festivities. Niran gave her hand a small squeeze and then nodded to Jacob before continuing past to the back room door. Seir padded along. When the door closed behind them, Jacob spoke.

"You do not have much time left at all, yet you seem to be doing better than I imagined you would," he said with a curious look.

"What am I supposed to do? Cry? I've already done that. I already know there's no getting out of it, so that'd be a waste." She shrugged.

"If only everyone else in your position could come to the same conclusion when their time came. I imagine Niran's job would be much easier. Dealing with frightened people trying to run all the time has got to be exhausting."

"I'm not saying I'm not frightened. I'm terrified," she said, facing him. "It's just, what am I supposed to do? What *can* I do that would give me any other choice?"

"This is why I have called you in here. Nearly six months ago, you were told that you would be given a choice in what happens once your payment comes due. I would like to tell you what those choices are now. There are an infinite number of ways we can take payment on one's contract. Sometimes, the soul is needed for one, specific purpose and when that purpose is served, we are satisfied. Sometimes they are needed to perform a task that can take anywhere from a day to a century to several millennia. These individuals are never given the opportunity to choose what their soul is used for. However, given your unique circumstances, you *do* get a choice, Claire."

"Like Margeaux?" she asked.

"Sort of. Not everyone has this much bargaining power when it comes to these contracts. The vast majority of signees have none at all. It is wholly dependent on the person and what they can do for us." He answered. She only stared at him, so he continued.

"You can choose from four different jobs, as you might call them. You can carry the quill like me and write contracts, arranging the fate of the souls. You can carry the coin like Vera and what your friend, Margeaux, has been assigned, and broker the deals which bring us the souls. You can carry the needle and thread like Ayn and weave the tapestry of fate which makes all the wishes of the contracts come to fruition. And finally, you can carry the wheat stalk, like Eyleth or Niran, and collect souls of those individuals whose payments have come due."

Her heart was pounding. She had a choice and if she chose right, her future, however far outside the realm of what she once thought to be reality, might not be as bad as she'd feared it would be.

"Do I have to choose right now?"

"No. But you must choose when your payment comes due, which is soon, Claire."

"I understand. Thank you for telling me and for giving me this choice," was all she could say.

"For what it is worth, I believe you would do well carrying the quill. But I admit, I might just be biased," he said with the ghost of a grin; his sunglasses hid whether that, or any of his grins, ever started in his eyes.

"I'll think about it. I'll think about all of them," she answered with a smile.

She walked back outside, dazed from the news she'd just received, and took the bucket from Reid, who looked sad that his time passing out candy had come to an end. She absentmindedly handed out the candy as she thought about those options. Could she really decide the fates of people she didn't know? Or could she really convince a person it was worth it to sell their eternal soul for worldly wishes? Could she pull threads in fate's tapestry and grant wishes, good and bad? She took in a pensive breath as she wondered if she could empty unholy terror into the eyes of someone else and peel their soul from their life.

"*Claire.*" She heard her name called from down the sidewalk.

"*Claire. Can you come here?*" This time, she thought she'd seen Charlene duck into the snowflake alley.

"*Claire! Come see!*"

She curiously started walking toward the alley as she heard her name again being called. She was sure it was Charlene, but as she stepped into the alley, Charlene was too far ahead to confirm.

"*Claire! Over here!*" A shadowed figure stood at the other end of the alley, beckoning her with a wave.

She stopped, realizing something wasn't right.

"Claire, over here!" The voice only kind of sounded like Charlene's, and the more she thought about it, it sounded less familiar.

She turned around to go back to the bookstore, but ran into two large, masked men who stared at her with wild looks in their eyes.

"If it isn't the famous Claire," one of them said.

"We've heard so much about you," said the other.

She turned to run out of the other side of the alley, but her way was blocked by another pair of men, both masked as well. Before she could scream, they pounced. One grabbed her from behind and covered her mouth as she fought to get free, kicking and thrashing. Her muffled screams could not be heard over the music and laughter of the Halloween Festival carrying on strong on Main Street. She looked up to see a window-air-conditioner above them and locked her eyes on it. A rusty bolt loosened on its mount and the mount gave way. The air conditioner fell. She closed her eyes only to hear it hit the pavement - narrowly missing the man holding her, who had stepped in a crack in the pavement and stumbled aside just in time.

"We've got tricks, too, Claire," one of the men said, menacingly, with a mocking laugh.

"Don't worry. We'll take good care of you," another said.

The one holding her dragged her out of the alley as the other three concentrated on their surroundings. She knew that look and she knew what it meant, as she desperately hoped someone in the milling crowd would notice them. No one did as the five of them only existed in everyone's blind spots. They slowly made their way to the open door of a large work van parked nearby. Every way she wished for attention to be drawn to them, it was countered by things brought about by the other men. Tears streamed down her face as no amount of thrashing or screaming or using the power of her contract worked against the man overpowering her physically and the three others overpowering her will over their fate. She tried once again and felt a finger of the hand over her mouth slip down just far enough for her to take it between her teeth and clamp down with all the strength she had in her jaw. The man swore and let go of her mouth. She quickly gave two whistled chirps. She did it over and over until they covered her mouth again and began to run.

She was thrown into the van, her body slamming against the side. She got up and fought with everything in herself to get free. She kicked, scratched, flung her fists and screamed until one of the men got loose of her barrage of attacks long enough to backhand her with a mighty, closed fist. She saw stars and stumbled as he climbed in the van with her, her face now as bloodied as his. He finally took her down, wrapping her up from behind with his legs locked in front of her at the ankles. He had an arm wrapped around her neck and pulled on it tight enough to cut off her breath. She fought to stay conscious, feeling the burn in her lungs of lost air and warm, wet blood down her face. There was a struggle of fate's power as she concentrated her remaining energy on stalling the van.

The driver first dropped his keys and then found them.

The van wouldn't start and then finally turned.

The parking brake wouldn't release and then got unstuck.

The doors wouldn't close, then the front ones finally shook loose and shut.

The side door of the van was stuck; she focused all of her concentration on keeping it open while the last of the men tried with all his strength to close it.

It started to shake loose as she began to fade, the edges of her vision blurring.

She began to go limp as she watched the door of the van begin to close. It got stuck again --not by her doing-- and an earth-shaking growl, filled with the screaming wails of lost souls in a forest, reverberated off of the buildings and the van rocked with some invisible force. Not some invisible force: *Seir*. He'd heard her and had come for her.

The top half of the man at the door crumpled and disappeared with the sounds of gurgled screams, snapping bones and flesh tearing, thick and wet. The van rocked back as the bottom half of the man slumped in a pool of blood and poured entrails over the side, slopping onto the pavement. The man holding her shoved her off and tried to stand to get away. Claire weakly crawled away, gasping for air and coughing. She turned in time to see the man who held her fly out of the van, legs first. He grabbed hold of one of the legs of his half-eaten comrade and dragged the severed body with him. His screams were blood curdling as she watched him clawing and writhing midair, turned toward nothing and trying, in vain, to push himself out of the invisible maw. The cracking of his bones rang in Claire's ears as the man's face was covered in his own blood, drenching him as he watched himself be eaten alive. Shock overcame him as he finally flailed one last time, and his limp head and arm disappeared into the night with two final, crunching bites. The men in the front of the van were now trying to get out, but couldn't open the doors jammed closed as Claire, still gasping for air, focused on them. The front of the van dipped down and the windshield fogged with Seir's growled breaths, droplets of blood dripped onto the glass.

The men stumbled over each other to get to the back of the van; Claire backed up and stood weakly, but ready to take them both on and feed them to Seir. As she steadied herself to fight, she saw Niran approach the side door of the van, calmly. His eyes fell upon her, disheveled, coughing for air, and weakly holding a fighting stance with blood down her face and the front of her sweater. All the lights around them on the street went out. Claire's breath clouded as the temperature dropped around the van to near freezing. And Niran, still studying every hurt inch on Claire's body, turned his chin in an unnatural movement to crack his neck.

The night drew towards him as feral terror was released from his being, ravenous and searching. Claire loosened her balled fists as Niran's attention turned to the two men cowering in the van before her. They began to scream, high-pitched and panicked as they scrambled backwards, clawing at themselves and drawing bloodied lines down their own faces. One of the men beat at his own head and flailed about as if he was on fire inside his own body and was trying to get out. The other man stopped clawing his face and weakly sobbed as he seemed to fight his own body, crawling towards Niran who waited for him with a hand in his pocket.

When the man was close enough, Niran grabbed him by his open jaw and flung him out of the van. His doll-like body slammed against a building across the narrow street. As Niran walked toward the man, broken and struggling to get up, cracks formed in the pavement beneath his every step. The paint on the building before him peeled and flaked down onto them. Decorative plants wilted and crumbled to dust and the air became thick with the scent of millenia of death. He calmly stooped before the man and grabbed his jaw, jerking his head to face him. The man's guttural cries started anew and then suddenly stopped as the both of them became shrouded in darkness so thick, they were mere shadows. When the darkness lifted and Claire shivered in the rising temperature and lights flickered back on, Niran was standing before a drained husk of a body that looked like it had been dead for a century.

The other man started to get up as if to run and the van rocked again as Claire heard Seir jump off the hood to get him.

"Seir, relax," she said, in a whisper. "Relax!" she repeated with another cough, still catching her breath. "Seir! Relax!" she finally said with her full voice.

She heard the hound go down, but he continued to growl, snarl and paw at the doorway of the van as if his entire body fought against the instinct to obey. Niran stood beside him, clouds of darkness still clearing from around his eyes.

“Don’t worry,” --she spat at the last man-- “we’ll take good care of you,” she said, and booted him in the face, knocking him unconscious.

Claire turned to Niran, shaking, beaten, and bloody. She stumbled to get out of the van and Niran lunged for her, ready to carry her away.

"I can stand. I'm okay," she told him, reassuringly. She felt Seir's warm sniff s and little licks all over her as he bothered and panted at her side. "I'm okay, Seir. I promise. You did so good," she cooed as she pet him, as best she could with soreness setting in all over her body. "We need to find out what we can from him," she said to Niran, as they all looked at the unconscious man.

"Let's get you cleaned up, first, maybe get some rest, and we can come back to him later," he suggested.

Feeling the blood beginning to dry on her face and tattered, dirtied clothes, she agreed. Niran made quick work of tying up and gagging the man as Seir merrily lapped up blood and remains from the fight. They locked the man in the back of the van before making their way back to the bookstore. Upon seeing Claire, Reid had jolted and rushed to care for her. He abandoned Jacob in the teller's window and brought Claire a wet towel, made her some tea and sat her in the most comfortable chair in the bookstore. Meanwhile, Niran told them everything that had happened.

"You should find out everything you can and then get rid of him," Jacob Instructed Niran. "How are you feeling, Claire?"

She responded with a thumbs up as Reid fussed over her, offering her a new, clean towel, fresh tea, and crackers. "I need a shower and to change before we do any of that," and she looked to Niran who stood up, ready to take her back to her apartment. Reid nodded in agreement.

Back at her apartment, with the bathroom door closed and the shower to mask the sound, Claire sobbed quietly as she watched the blood and dirt wash down the drain. In her living room, Niran paced as Seir stood on high alert, ready for anything. Claire took her time getting out and getting dressed, pausing frequently to force flashes of what happened out of her mind.

"Let's go wake this guy up," she said, conscious of the cut on her lip and the blooming bruise across her cheek. The rest of the evidence of her ordeal was hidden under her thick sweater. Niran thought to object, recommending she rest and they tackle it in the morning, but the look she gave him made it clear she would not sleep until they got the answers they needed.

As they approached the van, Claire could already hear the man moving about, having woken just in time for their arrival. Seir gave a low, hungry growl, and Niran tried to restrain himself from thrusting horrors into the man's eyes for what he had done to Claire. When they opened the van door, the man was fully awake and trying to get free of his bindings. Upon seeing Claire and Niran, leaning on opposite sides of the door, he stilled. Claire tugged on the rag that stuck out of his mouth to let him speak. Niran removed his bindings, terror clouding lightly around his eyes.

"Seir, if he runs, you can have him," he said. Seir's growl, steeped in the wailing of the lost, confirmed he'd be happy to oblige.

"Your friends are all dead. You watched it happen. You'll die, too. I mean, that's just how it's going to be," Claire coolly informed him. "So it can be quick and relatively painless if you answer our questions."

The man spit on the floor of the van with a look of defiance. Niran tensed, ready to rip the man's soul from him and Claire put a gentle hand on his arm.

"Seir - take off his legs," she said.

"*Wait! I'll talk!* I'll talk," the man exclaimed, scrambling back, as Seir's growl reverberated through his whole body.

"Seir, relax," she ordered, and the loyal beast laid down, still growling.

"How did you know who I was or where to find me?"

The man started laughing hysterically. Claire worried he might lose his mind before he could answer all of her questions.

"How do you *think* we know? We *all* know! And we're all coming. All of us, from everywhere," he said maniacally, leaning toward Claire. "And we'll all keep coming, Claire, until your lifeless body is on the bank of that river and your soul is in that wat-" He began screaming, flailing and pounding at his own head, terror in his eyes.

"*Niran!*" Claire snapped. The man stopped screaming and slumped back, heaving for air. Claire sat in the doorway of the van and waited for him to calm down.

"Say her name again and I will make you carve it into your own skull," Niran warned.

Through sobs, the man began to speak again. "We know you're the one. Of everyone we've ever thought it might be in the past, it's you. It's finally you."

"What is it that's supposed to make me so different from everyone else?" she asked.

He sat up slightly and pinned her with an unhinged glare.

"Has anyone ever told you that you have the most remarkable eyes?" he crooned before his head hit the floor of the van and he flopped down on his back.

"Everyone does," she breathed out, trying to recall the last time those exact words were spoken to her.

"*Ezra.*"

The man winked at her and then chuckled to himself.

"He told us-"

There was a loud *clunk*, dulled by the inches of flesh, blood and bone the heavy piece of scrap metal had to go through before hitting the floor of the van. It had fallen from a rack on the ceiling and came down on the man's neck like a guillotine. Claire stumbled away from the van as she stared, mouth agape, at the decapitated body. She looked to Niran who only stared at him, scowling darkly. Above, a crow soared close enough to see inside the van and then flew away.

The next morning, after giving up on trying to sleep, Claire and Niran made their way back to the bookstore from her apartment. They were met by a familiar face that Claire didn't know she needed to see until that moment.

"Claire Bear!" Vera exclaimed, hugging her tightly. "I came as soon as I heard."

They explained everything that happened the night before to many gasps and sympathetic looks from Vera.

"Reid and I had to carry the head and body to Harena's furnace. As you can imagine, she was displeased," Niran answered, when Vera asked about the last man's body.

Claire sat quietly, mulling over the questions in her head. All night, she kept replaying the conversation. The man was about to tell them something Ezra had said. How did he even know Ezra and why would Ezra tell them anything when breaking their contracts meant killing him and his entire family? The man had to be bluffing. But if he was, why did he die so obviously by an act of fate? And whose fate, then, did it? He'd commented on her eyes with the exact words Ezra had used. That's how he must have told them to be sure it was her. But again, why would Ezra want Claire dead? Did he really believe in the legend he wrote off as stories shared between desperate souls bound by contracts? But her mind kept returning to the fact that it would be the end of him and his entire family.

"Has anyone ever told you that you have the most remarkable eyes?"

Distantly, she could hear bits of the conversation between Vera, Jacob and Niran. Niran rattled off questions. Vera only spoke of protecting her. Jacob's questions were around how much anyone else could know and who might come, what they might do.

"Has anyone ever told you that you have the most remarkable eyes?"

Reid made distressed gestures which they would sometimes answer. A plan to hide Claire away until her payment came due. Perhaps Harena could keep her in the cavern. Perhaps they could take her out of town, but the unfamiliar area could mean a bigger threat.

"Has anyone ever told you that you have the most remarkable eyes?"

She watched the four of them, deep in their discussion about her, her safety, who else might come for her. Vera, looking more subdued, dressed down from her usual finery. Niran, with that unearthly strength and power, looked like he could go again with another group of would-be attackers. Jacob, trying to stay in the conversation while he studied his ledgers that reflected in the sunglasses he wore - day or night, rain or shine.

"Has anyone ever told you that you have the most remarkable eyes?"

Claire studied Jacob more intently then. It was much in the same way Eyleth had studied Jacob and her when Vera first introduced them. Had she been comparing them?

"Even on the most grumpy face, eyes like those can make it tolerable to look at," Harena had said to Claire... and then later called Jacob a "grumpy oaf."

Jacob glanced her way as Claire then stared at herself in the reflection in his sunglasses.

"The only people who could see them was my family," Niran had said about the ferryman.

"Has anyone ever told you that you have the most remarkable eyes?"

Jacob spoke and she heard none of what he said. They all continued to speak and all she could hear was her heartbeat in her ears, thudding and gushing.

"Has anyone ever told you that you have the most remarkable eyes?"

She got up and walked between them and into the teller's window. Her gaze was locked on Jacob who hadn't noticed her yet.

"Has anyone ever told you that you have the most remarkable eyes?"

"Claire, wait!" Vera cried out.

She reached Jacob and tore his sunglasses off his face. It wasn't until she saw, that she realized she wanted to be wrong.

She wasn't.

He looked up at her with eyes she'd seen in the mirror her entire life - fiery emeralds with shards of jade and ice.

They stared at each other with those identical gazes as Claire's breaths quickened and her heart raced. His sunglasses slipped from her fingers and fell to the floor as she said, between heavy breaths, barely above a whisper...

"Has anyone ever told you that you have the most remarkable eyes?"

XXVI

Vera's mouth hung open with the intent to say something that could help or explain, but there was nothing. All she did was usher a stunned Niran and seemingly-ashamed Reid out of the store through the back room door.

"Seir, stay," Vera said quietly, and he obeyed.

"It seems there is a conversation we should have," Jacob began. "On the desk to your left, there is a box. Just behind that stack of parchment. What is inside will help answer some of the questions I am sure you have."

Claire ran her hands down her face and lay them flat on the desk before her. "Can you just give me a second?" she asked. After a long moment, calming both her breathing and her nerves, she retrieved the little box.

"That is the one," Jacob confirmed.

Claire opened the box and inside was another parchment tied off with another red, velvet ribbon.

"Open it," he instructed.

She did, and the first thing she noticed was that the shifting words on it were not in Reid's handwriting.

"What you are holding, is the last contract I ever wrote with my own hand. Fully capable and full of power. Such immense power," he said, staring at the contract. "What you have seen in my sisters, and even in Niran, has been a mere fraction of the power we once had. When the Greeks wrote stories of their Zeus, Vera had thought the character adorable and weak - such was our power."

Claire leaned against the desk, studying the contract as he continued.

"The Greeks did get one thing right. They understood the appetite that eternal and immeasurably powerful beings had for dallying with the mortal. There was something about the way your lives had beginnings and ends that gave us a thrill that no amount of universal power could. Ezra encouraged us, as any father would - to enjoy, so long as we did our duty, which was to bring the souls of your dead to him. He just wanted the souls and we just wanted to play. We were childlike in that sense, never asking why.

We could carry a thousand souls to the river bank in the span of a single thought, such was our power. We walked each and every one of them past the boats they were meant to go into. The ferrymen were agonized." There was a long pause before he continued.

"Each one of those souls went into the river where it could never come out, nor could it sink or drown. All it could do was cling to the soul that was thrown into the river before it. Men, women, children. Ezra would take the souls from us and drag them across the backs of the ones already in the river and toss them in."

"Are they still there?" Claire asked, barely able to imagine it.

"They are," he answered with a brief flash of shame. When Claire could only stare at him, he continued.

"One tiny soul belonging to a boy, barely a year old, changed everything. Eyleth brought this boy on the long walk past the boats to Ezra. She had walked a countless number of children to him, so there was no reason this time should have been any different, but it was. He had held her hand as, at the time of his passing, he had just learned how to walk. When he did, something happened in her that gave her pause. When they reached Ezra, she had begged him to let her keep the boy. 'As a pet,' she had said. Surprisingly, he allowed it. But it was under the condition that she share her power with him and teach him to do what we all did, which was to bring him souls. He even said that we each could have a pet if the same conditions were met."

"Niran?" Claire asked.

"Yes. Beneath all that brooding and that fearsome gaze is a mortal soul carrying immortal power."

"Niran was human? Mortal?" Claire, wide-eyed, asked for clarification.

"Yes. Your Niran was just as mortal as you are now." Jacob answered.

"And he just...grew up? Thinking he was like you all?"

"Such was our power, Claire. Eyleth went back to where he died. She found his little body, cold and starved. He had been abandoned. We do not know how long he was alone, but he had been dead for maybe only an hour when she went to retrieve his body. It was nothing for her to heal it, remove its mortal memories, and then give the body back to the soul. And that was that. Ezra taught Eyleth how to take of her own power and give to the boy through blood sacrifice. She gave half her power to him that would reach maturity when he reached maturity. When he did, it was drawn from us all like a blow to the chest, Eyleth took the brunt of it and was ill for a year. She still has never been the same since."

Claire let out a stunned gasp and Seir stirred with a grunt. She turned her attention to him and he shifted as if he felt her gaze on him. Jacob noted her glance to the beast.

"About the time he was, I want to say, six, the boy had developed a fascination with the wolves in the many forests of the world. He took one as a pet and it died, perhaps three or so years later. He was inconsolable. He cried day-in and day-out. I wanted to throw him into the river myself. Eyleth, desperate, actually tried to take a soul from that beast's rotting body and... *Such. Was. Our. Power*," he said, emphasizing each word.

"She dredged up this thing from that body that was the closest thing to a soul she could manage. First, it was enormous. And second, it was phenomenally hideous. The only one blind to his repulsive form is Niran. I guarantee you, if you could see him, you would never let that thing lick you again. That thing is held together by sheer will and another gift of power we agreed to give it for the boy's sake. Part of that power allows it to be imperceptible. Not by any of the five laughable senses offered to you mortal beings. That is, unless granted by Niran. The other power, you have already seen. He can devour anything of practically any size - alive, dead, mortal, soul. Anything."

Claire gaped, considering the great power Seir had shown just the night before. She tried to imagine how he could be *phenomenally hideous.*

"But he's such a...good boy," she said with a nervous smile.

"Of course he is. We went through great pains to train him, all of us. And all for that boy. He changed everything."

"How?"

"It started with Eyleth and did not take long to happen to us, too. Raising the boy and finally choosing the name, Niran, for him, and even helping to raise that beast… Claire, I am telling you it is a *monstrosity*," he clarified to her, again. "It made us all begin to think differently about mortal beings. We began to dislike bringing them to Ezra. Finally, as if we had awoken from a long dream, we began to ask why. Why were they not going into the boats? Why were they being thrown into the river and left to…" He trailed off, as if remembering what all those souls looked like, trapped in the river waters, clinging to one another for all of eternity.

"To suffer," Claire finished the sentence Jacob could not. He only nodded.

"And we finally asked him. At first he ignored our questions and demanded we continue to bring him souls. Vera decided to see what would happen if she brought a soul close to the boats instead of walking past them. One look into the eyes of a ferryman and the soul climbed into its boat. The first in millennia to go to the other side. Ezra was none the wiser, so we all started doing it. At first, it was all the children. Then we were giving the ferrymen anyone we thought remotely kind. Ezra would only receive the worst of the worst.

"As you can imagine, he learned of our scheme rather quickly when the souls had become so few and he saw ferrymen coming and going. He was enraged when he found out and instead of using his great power to punish us, he punished the ferrymen. That is why they look the way they do today. They were beautiful before. To see them was to see home. To be near them was to feel such peace, acceptance and trust that you would climb into their boats without question. Their nature is to love the human souls so much that they would brave the tumultuous waters of the great river to ferry them to the other side, protecting the souls with their entire being. For that love to be met with screams of terror and have children run away, I can't imagine how it must hurt them."

Claire's heart broke for the ferryman she had called her friend.

"Ezra demanded we stop bringing the souls to the ferrymen. It was Ayn who had the idea for a compromise first. She thought since we still had no problem bringing the souls of the wicked to Ezra, that we could push more of them toward wickedness. But even that felt wrong. We must have tried hundreds of different ways until it was Vera who said we should offer them use of our power in exchange for their souls. And it worked. Almost everyone we approached took our offer. We soon learned, however, that they would break that promise and run to the ferrymen's boats given the chance. So we needed to find a way to bind them to the agreement. Thus was rolled the first marble in the machine of mortal suffering that is these contracts and all the moving parts therein.

"We divided the tasks. Vera brokered the agreements. I wrote the contracts. Ayn made the wishes come true and Eyleth collected the souls. She, then, taught Niran how to collect them once he had reached maturity. And that - that worked. It worked quite well. Ezra was not getting near the amount of souls he wanted, so he told us we needed to work faster or he would no longer agree to the compromise. So we took from the souls who were meant to go into the river and gave them tasks to help. And then things were good again. Ezra was satisfied and we felt it was fair."

"Fair," Claire scoffed, with a shake of her head.

"You have to realize, Claire, that, to us, it was more fair than we ever needed to be or ever were. We had spent millennia seeing mortal beings as mere objects of enjoyment that would make more objects for enjoyment and then expire. But we did try, once things changed. Those who chose not to work with us went into the boats. Those who did, would complete their task and then go into the river. Like I said before, there is no winning."

She ignored his explanation. "So all these contracts are just for souls who do things for you and souls that will go in the river?"

"Yes. One such soul is our Harena, down in her cavern. Her hourglasses help us keep track of the number of souls we are working with. When we created her task, we had her retroactively make hourglasses for every mortal being's soul who worked for Ezra's cause. When we tasked her, she asked us if we were certain we wanted that. The task granted her knowledge - knowledge that, for the first time in our existence, was beyond our own. We did not think much of the question until she made the first five. "These are your hourglasses,' she had told us."

"Wait," Claire interrupted, but Jacob kept going.

"One for each of my sisters and me and one for Niran."

"Wait! What are you saying?" Claire asked, more forcefully this time.

"We told her that she was only to make hourglasses for those souls, who came from mortal beings, who were working in service to Ezra. She insisted that she understood the instructions and had done exactly as she was told. When we told her that she was mistaken, when we threatened to punish her, she did not falter. She only told us we should speak to Ezra."

"No. Jacob, no," Claire said and brought her hand to her mouth.

"So, of course, we did. We asked him why our glassmaker thought we should have hourglasses along with the rest of the mortal beings. And that is when he told us that she had not been wrong. The five of us together carried half the power as Ezra had, in the same way that Niran carried half the power as Eyleth and Seir carried a bit of all of ours.

"He chose us, myself and my sisters, at random, from the souls meant to go into the boats. He took our memories and by blood sacrifice, split his power in half and then that half into the quarters we all had. Such was that power: we truly believed we were like him. It was after he made us that the last of the mortal souls went into the boats, before they started going to Ezra and thus into the river."

"What did you do? How could you not- I would have killed him," she breathed.

"Out of all of us, Vera was the most distraught. She ran right into the river, thinking her power could get her to the other side. Ezra tried to stop her, but she did not listen. It was then that we learned why Ezra told us never to touch the water, not even to get our feet wet. Vera, the eternally powerful and immortal being that she was, almost died. It was Seir that went in after her and dragged her out, near dead. He barely made it out alive himself. We learned that river was the only thing in the entire universe that could kill us."

Claire could only gape as he continued.

"Eyleth tried to get passage for herself and Niran on one of the boats. The ferrymen refused her. They refused all of us and we could not touch the water. We were trapped and so was Ezra. And we realized the true purpose of his bridge of souls. He could not be taken in a boat and he could not swim it, but he could get there on the backs of those in the water. It destroyed everything we ever thought to be true and gave us such doubt that we had never felt before and had no idea how to manage. And then we just stopped. We stopped buying, granting wishes, collecting. All of it. Ezra went back to dumping every soul he could get into the river. We tried to put every soul we could into the boats. The pendulum of hope and horror swung so tragically."

"But why? Why is Ezra making this bridge to the other side?"

"That is its own story. But the short of it is he has his own deluded reason."

Claire only nodded, now contemplating what, in the entire universe, that reason could be.

"Ayn has always been loyal to a fault. She was the only one of us who wanted to understand Ezra and even find a way to keep helping him. She is the one who brokered the truce between the rest of us and him. She convinced us to go back to buying and collecting souls. She convinced him to stop taking souls who were meant to go on the boats. I cannot say things were good again, but they were not so bad anymore. But I... I just could not let it go. Where everyone else's hurt and frustration dwindled to practically nothing over the centuries, my anger only festered and grew stronger. I needed to do something about it.

I wanted to punish Ezra. I had no idea how I ever could because of that great power. I thought of how much I could do to him if he was without it. And that is how the idea came to me. I wanted to drain him of his power. I knew it meant draining all of us, too, but that was the answer. We could go to the other side if we were drained of our power because we had mortal souls. I just had to figure out how to do it so that he could not get it back. The irony was that I realized how I would accomplish this from millennia of doing what he had always urged us to. The answer was in every one of the offspring produced from my thousands of dalliances. In the same way I *denied* power to those offspring, I could *give* power to one through a form of blood sacrifice like Ezra and Eyleth performed. Unlike Niran or Seir, the power I give to my own offspring is forever tied to me by blood. I can control it. I can take it back. It is loaned to the bloodline or it is gifted. The choice and the control are mine.

"Claire, your bloodline has been born with, carried through life, and delivered my power to the other side of the river for centuries."

"How? I don't have any..."

"Of course you do not. It is not yours to wield. It is merely traveling from here to the other side through the blood within you and its connection to the souls of your ancestors and yourself. It has done so in the blood of everyone before you since I wrote that contract," he gave a pointed look to the contract still in her hand. "It was nothing for me to find one of my offspring and get her to agree to handing power over her lineage to me. In return, I think she got some goats, a farm or something. I can't remember. I made it so it would be a single line, one child born to each, no more and no less. Through the blood of each child would continue the flow of my power to the other side."

"And I am the last person in that bloodline."

"You are."

"Through my mother, I assume."

"Yes."

"So what happens to me if Ezra gets a hold of me?"

"He will try to put you into the river as you would then become a conduit to draw all the power from the other side back to him."

"Why hasn't he done that already?"

"For one, he had to be certain. I have thousands of bloodlines, but only one is currently draining power from him with every person born into it. Second, you are protected, in many ways, by the contract I wrote for you."

"How did Ezra even find out what you did?"

"Reid. Reid had been a good friend of my sisters. He was one of the few mortals for whom they cared deeply. They did everything together and they also told him everything. While I kept my plan from them, it was no secret that I'd taken a special interest in this woman. Reid was so naive and thought so well of everyone that he was not suspicious when Ezra invited him, now and then, for a meal and long chat. He had told Ezra of my particular interest in the woman who, by that time, had already given birth to her one child. Ezra had Vera bring the woman to him. He tried to get the truth of our agreement out of her, but I never told her the reason I wanted to control her lineage. She swore she knew nothing and thus could not help him even if she wanted to. He took her soul for it.

Vera confessed that it was she who brought the woman to Ezra. Reid confessed to having been the one to tell him in the first place. In my rage, I punished him for it. That brings us to his wordless service today."

"But, he didn't mean anything by it," Claire protested. Thinking of the gentle giant and how it must have been for him.

"Maybe he did not. And maybe I did not need to punish him. But this is where we are today and where he shall remain until I decide things should change."

"That's cruel, Jacob," Claire said, pained.

"You do not know cruelty, Claire," he said with no remorse. "Ezra thought killing the woman had put an end to whatever I had planned. The best thing

I could have done was to turn my back on the child, let her be lost in the sea of my offspring and their bloodlines and allow the contract to do as it would. And so it did. Every child took from us and we all felt it. When the first child reached maturity, it took the most from me, my physical being, mainly. There was no hiding what I had done, then, so I had to tell my sisters. It had been long enough that I could not find the child even if I wanted to. Ezra was enraged, as you can imagine, but there was little to be done. It did not stop him, however, from trying."

"Is that why you're in a wheelchair now?"

"It is. It is only our shared power that keeps me alive in this form."

"When did it happen? That first child?"

"No, it was a lot at first and then took from me in smaller increments thereafter."

"When did you end up like this?" she asked, realizing she could have asked more nicely or not at all.

"Seven years ago."

"Jacob. I..." She covered her mouth with a hand as she studied him, unabashedly now, counting back the years and knowing it had been *she* who took nearly the last of him. She could obsess over it if she allowed herself, but she had no time to think about this. She forced the thought aside and, instead, changed the subject after a long-enough pause to collect herself.

"So, it's working? Your plan?"

"It was. It would still be if your blood had not touched your father's contract. My power that was hidden in your blood instantly connected with the power of the contract and thus the rest of us. There was no denying that the bloodline had finally been found. Ezra had been searching, tirelessly, for hundreds of years. Every time another child, from the bloodline, reached maturity and took from us, his search became more desperate, more frantic. He was the one who started the legend of the mortal who could see ferrymen. It was he who sent contracted souls to retrieve anyone he suspected. He wrote contracts himself and hid language in them that might root out the bloodline. Ayn helped him weave threads of fate that might cross with the bloodline. He tried everything. And finally, a stuck door in a trick desk is what did it."

"You said I'm protected. How?"

"If I did nothing, if I let you walk out that door and leave me with your father's contract, they would have found you within the week and it would have all been over. You would be dead in the river."

"But... I-"

"I told Niran to transfer your father's contract to you. It was difficult, but

he made it happen. And the contract I wrote for you in its stead was your protection."

"And he's known this entire time," she realized sadly.

"He has not. I told him the transfer was legitimate. He knew nothing of the bloodline. This was for your protection."

"Why not just protect me forever," she asked, almost angrily. "Why only six months? Why not let me live and just hide me like you did the first child?"

"Because I could not protect your life. The moment your blood touched that contract, it was only a matter of time for your life. But I can still protect your soul by binding you to what is left of our power under the terms of your contract. The only thing more powerful than Ezra's ability to simply remove your soul and throw it into the river whenever he pleases is your contract. I do not have an explanation for why --none of us do-- but the bond of the word is stronger than all of us combined.

You may not be able to go to the other side, Claire, but I can at least keep you out of that river. It is why I gave you that choice. But you must make it to when your payment comes due or your soul is forfeit, all would be lost, Ezra would regain full power and all of this, every effort would have been for naught."

"No pressure," she said under her breath.

"You were never going to win, the moment your blood touched that contract, but if you let me, I can help you lose as little as possible," he tried.

"I have two weeks left on my contract."

"I am genuinely sorry that the last two weeks of your life have come so soon."

part eight

two weeks

the final sleep

reawakening

tempus est solucionis

After a long debate about what should be done, it was decided that Claire would stay in Harena's cavern, with Niran and Seir, until her contract came due. The cavern, with its ever-changing tunnels and pathways that only Harena could navigate, would be her best shot of staying safely hidden.

"Over here, girl. Follow me," Harena ordered Claire. "I had a feeling you would be trouble when I made your hourglass. Did I tell you about it? Irksome, really irksome, that one. But I'm happy with how it turned out. I always am. Each one of these hourglasses..." Harena's voice faded into the background of Claire's mind as she followed her through the cavern to where she would spend the last two weeks of her mortal existence.

Claire shifted her backpack full of essentials she had packed in a hurry and frowned at her surroundings. Niran noted the look.

"This is the safest place for you," Niran whispered to Claire, apologetically.

"I know. It's just... I'm gonna be in a cave with spiders and rats and it'll be dark..." She trailed off as the small tunnel they walked through became brighter the closer they got to the exit.

It got so bright by the time they reached the opening that Claire had to shield her eyes. When they adjusted, what she saw before her was anything but a dark cave full of spiders and rats. She looked up to see a bright, blue sky through a massive hole where the ceiling of the cave should have been. From the edges hung down all manner of vines and roots. Trees leaned over as if to peer at what lay within. When she looked down, there was a turquoise, blue lake into which a small waterfall splashed from the opening. All around the walls of the cave was lush plant life and trickling water.

"This way. Hold onto the rail. Don't dally. I've got hourglasses yet to make, though who knows if I will be making anymore by the end of all this. What a horrible, horrible- Anyway, come down here," Harena instructed.

Claire clutched Niran's arm and he pulled her aside as she felt Seir brush by her in a hurry. The wooden walkway which spiraled down and around the perimeter of the cave shook with his bounding gate.

"Beast! If you break my walkway, I'll make a new apron from your hide!" Harena yelled at Seir. Moments later, there was a loud splash in the water and around the large rings of the moving ripple grew a murky cloud of brown and red. "Niran! That beast of yours needs to be washed more than once a year. I've told you this. Look at my lake now! It's going to take all day for the water to clear."

"Nevermind. I can stay here for two weeks," Claire barely breathed out as she took in the rest of the paradise carved into the cave. "How is this here?" she asked as she saw tropical birds flying around, fruit trees, a small dock over the water, a little, white-sand beach along one corner.

"This is one of the undiscovered cenotes of the world. It's about as remote as we can ask for," Niran informed her.

"You'll be perfectly safe here, Claire. We are deep in the jungle of an island inhabited only by an uncontacted tribe. Great people, really great. I met them once and they let me have this place as long as I don't ever bother them. And I'm happy not to, really great people until you bother them, then it's..." Harena dragged a thumb across her neck with a warning look.

"An island? But where?" Claire asked as she allowed her senses to adjust.

"Ten steps down here can be a hundred miles up there, so we can be in the Mediterranean or at the North Pole. Judging by the weather, though, I'm thinking somewhere in the Pacific," Niran guessed.

When they reached the bottom of the walkway, Harena led them to a hut overlooking the lake. They walked a few steps up to a small, covered porch and Harena led them inside where there was a living area and kitchen area. Off the living area was a bedroom only big enough for the bed, chair and writing desk within. Claire set down her backpack on the desk and took in where she would be staying for the last two weeks of her life. Harena explained where everything was and how to use the wood-burning stove before leading her out to walk around the lake.

"You come see me anytime you need a break from these two fools," Harena told Claire as she started to make her way back up the walkway.

"Harena, thank you so much. This is so much more than I hoped it could be," Claire answered.

"I know," she answered with a nod and a grin. She started to make her way up, but turned back again. "Claire. I'm *going* to turn your hourglass in two weeks. And I am *going* to watch your sands fall however long they may take.

That is what is going to happen," she finished firmly and with a look in her eyes that asked Claire if she understood.

Claire took in a deep breath and nodded to Harena, understanding the statement to be a wish for her safe future.

The days went by without disturbance as Claire turned the tiny paradise into her home. She woke with the sun, bathed in the waterfall, bird watched and swam. She lay on the dock with Niran and Seir and stargazed at night. Harena brought them food every few days and sometimes Claire would cook for all of them. She and Seir would nap in the one sunbeam that came through the hole until it slipped away for the day. Some nights, she and Niran would sit on the little porch and talk about everything there was to talk about. When it was time for bed, Seir slept between the living area, where Niran often read all night, and the bedroom where Claire tried her best to sleep. It was as close as she could get to pretending they were just on a long, beautiful vacation. Every day that passed was too long and not long enough. The days crawled by, yet when Claire thought of the day she came down that rickety, wooden walkway, she realized the past two weeks had been an instant.

There were two days left on her contract and Niran had left Claire on the dock with Seir admiring the night sky while he 'fetched something from his pack,' he'd told her. Claire stargazed, leaning against Seir who, she thought, might be looking up at the sky, too. She tried to imagine him *phenomenally hideous*, but couldn't, in that moment, think of any way he wouldn't be the most handsome beast there ever was. She gently petted him and he shifted to lean against her more. And she thought to herself, that this might be one of those perfect nights. Niran returned holding a carved, wooden box, with a sheepish look on his face.

"What's that?" she asked as she and Seir stood to face the approaching Niran.

"I thought it might be a good night for this," he answered as he turned the box to reveal a winding key on its side.

"A music box?" Claire asked with a surprised smile.

"Seir, go lay down," Niran said, as he pointed to a corner of the dock near Claire. There was a shuffle and tired grunt as Seir laid down where he was told to. Niran then wound the music box until it couldn't be wound anymore. "I thought, perhaps, on a night as nice as this, we might also enjoy a little bit of music," he said, looking down at the box and then finally to Claire who only nodded to him with a sincere smile.

Niran opened the lid and as the music started playing, he closed the distance between them with two long strides. They both looked down at the music box that played a melody that seemed written for moments like these, shared between two people, and of the unspoken uncertainty of their future but certainty of their longing for it. Claire took the box and set it down on the dock as it continued to play its song of every word neither of them could speak. Niran could not take his gaze from her as she took one of his hands and stepped closer to him, placing it on the small of her back and put her hand on his shoulder. He then took her other hand and gripped it tightly, but gently, against his chest and they began to dance.

Claire laid her head on his shoulder as they slowly moved about the deck, in tune to the music that filled the entire cavern and seemed to cause the birds and singing bugs to answer the song with their own. He patted her hand down flat on his chest and let go of it to wrap his arms fully around her as they continued to sway to the music that filled the night air and rose to the star-filled sky above them. She curled into him and squeezed her eyes closed as he gently stroked her hair that lay over his arms.

"Thank you for this, for everything," she whispered.

"You never have to thank me," he answered and held her more closely.

She pulled away from him just enough to look up at him and he looked down at her. Ache was in his eyes and she felt it in the way he gripped her. She smiled up at him, wanting to take the ache away, wanting to see him smile back at her, wanting for only this very moment to be their only reality. He returned her smile and began studying every part of her face. She could barely breathe as she watched his eyes follow where he gently moved strands of hair from her face and tucked them behind her ear.

"Niran," she said, barely above a whisper.

His eyes switched to look into hers. She only swallowed, her lips parting.

"I-"

Seir let out a loud groan, filled with wails, as he stretched and the sound echoed throughout the cenote, startling even the birds that slept in the trees. It startled Claire, too, and she laughed, embarrassed. Niran laughed with her as she pressed her forehead to his chest and giggled some more to the sound of Seir letting out another groan before settling back down.

She still giggled as she pulled out of Niran's arms to look where Seir lay, but he pulled her back to him. He looked down at her and with a knuckle under her chin, tilted her face up as he bent to meet her there. He stopped himself and she felt his thumb brush her chin as she closed her eyes and rose up onto her tiptoes, closing the tiny space between their lips, and they kissed.

She brought her arms up to wrap around his neck and he wrapped an arm around her waist as his other hand gently cradled her head. They kissed for every time they struggled to leave each other's side; for every time they laughed together and had to look away; for every quiet goodnight and lazy good morning. They kissed, for every look across a room and every time they sought each other out. They kissed for every moment they had together and every one they knew they never would.

When they finally pulled away from the kiss, Niran held her closer to him than he'd ever allowed himself to before. He said the only thing that made sense to him when he thought of how he felt for her.

"You have something of mine," he whispered, like he had that night at her doorstep.

Claire answered by pressing his palm over her heart with both her hands. With her, Niran was as weak as he was strong. He ached to feel her joy, and in the bottomless pit which was his self-control, he found its floor in her pain. It was him watching himself long for her from up close, from afar, from the next room as she slept, from inside her grip on his arm as they walked. He knew, for longer than he would ever admit, that he would give himself in her stead, should a demand be made of her soul. He planned on it. He prepared for it. He knew what he would do for her and that she would always be okay if he had to give all of himself to make sure of it.

He kept his eyes closed, not knowing what he'd see if he opened them to look into hers. But he felt her. He felt her soft touch on his cheek and another soft kiss on his lips. He pulled her in closer as he kissed her again and he could feel her smile through it.

Her smile softened and it was her turn to press her forehead against his as she finally answered.

"You have what I have left to give," she whispered as she put his hand over her heart, with her hand atop it and began to sway with him again to the song of the music box.

They danced as the moon crept across the sky and Seir sang a howl from boredom and made Claire giggle into Niran's chest at the sound. They finally let each other go to be joined by the beast who licked and nudged between them. On the dock, Claire, wrapped in Niran's arms, fell asleep under a blanket of peaceful night and to the sound of Seir's soft snores.

XXVIII

Claire awoke to the cavern filled with early morning sun and waking creatures going about their morning routines. Niran had gotten up and was standing on the edge of the dock looking up at the opening. He had a look of concentration that made Claire sit up and try to see what he studied so intently. She even felt the low rumble of Seir's growl as he must have been seeing the same thing. As she stood, Niran took her hand and they both looked up. There was nothing but clear, blue sky and the occasional bird. For another minute, they waited, silently watching the opening and Claire was about to ask what they were looking for, but there it was. A single arrow shot across the opening. So faintly, it almost couldn't be heard, was the distant sound of tribal war cries. Seir began to growl louder as another arrow shot across the opening, and then another. The war cries were distinct now.

"What is that?" Claire breathed heavily.

"I'm not sure yet. It could have nothing to do with us, but we have to make sure," Niran answered.

There was movement in the trees that lined the opening. Arrows seemed directed there as two people began lowering themselves down by ropes. Seir started barking and growling, loud and ferocious. The arrows caught one of the people lowering themselves down and it was a breathless moment as their body fell, hurtling into the lake with a booming splash that echoed and sent birds flying. Above, tribespeople stood at the edge of the opening and shot arrows across at two more people who were lowering themselves down. One of the tribespeople looked down at Niran and Claire, and gestured with urgency, pointing across the opening.

"Niran?" Claire said nervously.

"Seir, let's go," he ordered as the beast let out a warning bark. The three of them ran for the walkway and did not hesitate to start going up.

From the top of the walkway, Harena appeared, as alarmed as they were. "*Get up here!* They found you! We have to go *now!*" she ordered.

They ran faster. Seir bounded up far ahead of them and kept pausing to let them catch up. Harena rushed them to the entrance of the tunnel. Before going through, Claire paused to say goodbye to the sanctuary that protected her and gave silent thanks to the tribe who protected it. Then they ran through as the tunnel closed off behind them, until it was only a wall of stone in the dark cavern.

"We need to get you to Jacob. This way," Harena ordered. They followed her through the ever-changing cavern for what seemed like miles of twists and turns. She suddenly stopped, and backed them into a crevice that opened up, just big enough for the three of them and Seir.

"Get in here, you stupid beast," she said to Seir. The crevice closed around them, leaving only a small slit low enough that they had to get down onto their bellies if they wanted to see out of it. Harena shushed them as a moment later, three sets of feet walked past that slit in the rock.

"They were just here. I saw them," said one voice.

"Try up there. They might have gone that way," answered the other.

"You two go ahead, I'll go back this way," said the third.

Harena harrumphed and turned around. The solid wall that was behind them a moment ago opened up before her to reveal another pathway. They followed her out as she paused to grab an hourglass from one of the rock shelves. They wound around, ducked into other crevices, went up steps and around rock formations that gave them cover. All around them were the footsteps of the people searching for them. Harena grabbed two more hourglasses, dropping them into her satchel.

"Okay, this way. The steps up to the bookstore are right up there," Harena directed.

They followed her and the rock formations became familiar as they approached the bottom of the spiral staircase. Harena stood by to let them go and Claire went first, heading straight up the stairs. From one side, she saw four more people coming toward her. From the other side, Niran came up the stone steps, that unholy dark already clouding his eyes. She stepped back down, not knowing what to do. Seir was at her front, growling at them and backing into her to push her back up the stairs. Below, she saw Harena faced with the three others who were giving chase earlier. She held up an hourglass from her satchel as the two groups squared off.

"Oh, let's get this over with already!" Harena exclaimed as she threw down the hourglass in her hand, shattering it on the stone floor. One of the men before her simply dropped into a pile of sand that glittered in the candlelight. She grabbed the other two and held them up. "Who wants to be next?" she dared.

All together, the four across the walkway from Niran and the two left in front of Harena lunged forward. Darkness fell around Niran and the sound of shattering hourglasses echoed as Harena threw them to the ground. Screams followed the breaking glass as Niran approached the four cowering figures, who now clawed at their own faces and writhed in agony and terror.

"There's no time! Claire, get up there! *Now!*" Harena ordered.

For a moment, Claire didn't move, waiting for Niran.

"Now, Claire!" Harena repeated and it sent her running up the steps.

She looked down to see two more people advancing towards them. They met their end swiftly as Seir tore them apart. She bounded up the stairs, not knowing if Niran or Seir would follow. She ran with everything that was left in her and she thought of nothing but making it up each step as fast as her legs could carry her. The back room door of the bookstore flew open and Claire landed in a heap, winded and gasping for air. She looked up to see Reid holding a chair over his head, ready to bring it down onto Claire, a look of panic on his bloodied face.

"Reid! It's me!" she shouted with her hand out.

He immediately let the chair down and gave Claire a sorry look. She looked around the bookstore - there were at least five bodies strewn about the floor. She looked for Jacob in his usual spot inside the teller's window and he wasn't there. Reid rushed back to the teller's window where he crouched down inside. Claire followed and saw him picking Jacob up off the floor and righting his overturned wheelchair. Jacob didn't speak for a moment as Claire thought the worst. Finally, he spoke.

"There is no time, Claire. You need to give me my answer now." He urged her, through huffed breaths.

She helped Reid get Jacob back into his wheelchair and when he was safely in, she looked over both of them for any major injuries. So far as she could tell, there were bruises and cuts on Reid's face and arms. Jacob seemed to have gotten away with only being pushed from his wheelchair.

"Are you two okay?" She asked between them anyway. Reid gave a swift nod and a dismissive wave of his hand and gently nudged her toward Jacob.

"What is your choice?" Jacob asked again.

She heard footsteps coming up the stairs behind the back room door. Reid picked up the chair he'd wielded earlier and stood in front of the door, ready to strike.

"Claire! Your choice! *Now!*" Jacob huffed.

The footsteps on the stairs came closer and she lunged for Jacob to tell him her decision. The back room door opened and Reid lifted the chair again, ready to bring it down. In stumbled a creature in a familiar stained white t-shirt and ill-fitting khakis. Reid lowered the chair, confused. He could not see the ferryman who now darted about excitedly and with great urgency. The sound of faraway screams and someone running up the stairs echoed through the back room doorway as Claire took a step back from Jacob. They both stared each other down with those twin emerald gazes.

"I accept the choice you have made for the terms of your contract," he hastily said, with a hint of dismay.

Claire quickly turned his pinky ring and shook hands with him. The sound of Seir's unearthly growl chased those footsteps up the stairs and then there was the sickening sound of crunching bones and sopping entrails. Reid took one look down the stairs and looked back at Claire with a horrified expression, gesturing for Claire to run. *Run where?* She had no idea what she was supposed to do. She looked around the bookstore and realized the ferryman she called a friend was darting about excitedly, trying to get her attention. She went to him and looked into his one good eye. He gently tugged on her shirt with that boil-covered hand and beckoned for her to follow him out.

"Go," Jacob said gravely.

"What if-"

"I said go!"

Claire looked to Reid for confirmation and he motioned for her to go. She turned to the ferryman and let him lead the way. He darted and jerked meaningfully, and then made his way to the front door of the bookstore. On her way out, she saw Jacob's sunglasses on the floor and picked them up. She looked at him as she put them on. He only nodded and returned his attention to the back room door, where more footsteps could be heard. Reid stood beside it, ready to protect Jacob with that chair and anything else he could use to fight.

Being back on Main Street was surreal for Claire as people still milled about as if there wasn't a care in the world and, for them, there wasn't. Main Street looked like it would any other lovely fall day with all the familiar decorations and hints of winter's approaching cold. Claire did her best to blend in and not look like she was running from something. The ferryman darted about, seemingly very sure of where it was going. It also seemed to understand that Claire needed not to stand out as neither were certain of who might be watching or waiting for her.

She walked with her head down and her hair covering most of her face as she followed the ferryman but also kept an eye out for anyone who might look suspicious. She put herself in everyone's blind spots as she walked and took comfort in only seeing backs or profiles. As she started to feel a little relief, she noticed there were several faces that were not turned away from her. As a matter of fact, when she looked over her shoulder again to confirm, they walked toward her, slowly at first, but began to pick up their pace.

"Are we close? I think we've been seen," she asked the ferryman under her breath. It looked around and noticed the faces as well. It began darting more rapidly and she kept his pace. The faster she walked, the faster the others followed. They were there for her. She knew it and they knew she knew it as they approached from half a block down the other side of the street. "We have to get wherever you're taking me fast. They're coming." The ferryman saw and began to dart more quickly. Claire hurried behind it, now unconcerned with being seen. The others across the street started to run, and she told the ferryman, "We have to run!"

He darted with Claire following at a running pace. The others were crossing the street and almost upon them.

Around her, people blocked their path, but then moved.

Car doors opened in their way, and quickly shut.

Groups gathered in front of them and then dispersed.

The others were close enough for her to hear as she broke into a full-on sprint. The ferryman finally ducked into a store: the baby store with the cradle she'd found for him before. She burst into the store and the only person inside was the cashier who slipped into the stockroom as she walked in. The ferryman went straight to the cradle. The door flew open behind Claire and she felt fingertips graze her back. The ferryman stopped suddenly and Claire ran right into its arms; it curled itself around her and pulled them both into the cradle. The last thing she saw were hands reaching into the cradle above her, and then there was darkness.

They fell. And they fell. And they fell for what seemed like hours or maybe it was minutes or seconds that only felt like hours. Wind beat around them as the ferryman kept Claire wrapped up in its body that seemed too frail, too broken and torn to survive the winds of this fall, let alone what the landing would be. She could barely breathe as she clung to it, feeling loose, rotting flesh and brittle bone beneath her grasp. They fell and the ferryman held her with that half an arm and used his one hand to pat her back gently as if to reassure her that she was safe. They fell and all around them was darkness so black, it seemed like light had never touched it and never would. Though everything around them was black, she could see glimpses of herself or the ferryman holding her, but nothing was around them for what seemed like eternity in all directions.

Finally, they landed. Rather, Claire landed as if startled awake from having only dreamed they had been falling. She jerked and opened her eyes wide and frightened as she clung, still, to the ferryman that lay with her in a shallow grave in the middle of a forest. Underneath them were the bones of small forest creatures, birds, mice, squirrels, something that might have been a fox or a raccoon. She felt her stomach turning over and over as if it was still falling and she quickly climbed out of the grave and stumbled a few steps to a tree nearby where she emptied her stomach onto the forest floor. Over and over, she heaved, coughing and spitting. In the forest, the ferryman moved gracefully - so gracefully, it nearly floated to her with gentle pats on her back as she spit up the last of her sick. When she was finally done, she stumbled over to another tree and sat up against it to catch her breath and try to regain her bearings.

"I'm sorry about the puke over there, I just... That fall was..." Claire gestured in a way that not even she was sure what it was supposed to mean.

From all around her came the most comforting and kindest voice Claire had ever heard in her life. It sounded like it belonged to someone's sweet grandfather who spent his days helping ducklings cross park roads. It didn't speak, but hummed in a gentle and loving way. Claire jolted and looked around and then to the ferryman who nearly floated in front of her.

"Is that you?" she asked, stunned. The ferryman made a graceful gesture of acknowledgement, and followed it with another gesture of urgency, and for her to follow him. "Okay, I'm just going to need a minute."

She sat for a moment longer as she caught her breath and drew back in every ounce of energy she could. The ferryman merely drifted about, seeming to take sentry as his friend rested. She was still a bit nauseous, but got up anyway, knowing she didn't have time to fully recuperate. So they began their journey, the ferryman leading the way and checking on her often.

The forest went on as far as Claire could see in all directions. It would have been peaceful and serene if not for the wailing. They were the same wails Claire always heard in Seir's snores belonging to the lost souls Niran had told her about. She could only see them out of the corner of her eye as they were, sometimes, far away or were so close, it made her cling to the ferryman. In those times, he gently patted her hand and hummed soothingly. As they hurried along, the ferryman would drift away and return with berries or nuts for her. Further up, he led her to a stream where she was able to drink. Whether it was from some deep connection between her and the ferryman or the direness of her current circumstances, Claire couldn't be sure, but she could feel how much he cared for her, even loved her.

Much like the two weeks she spent in that pocket of paradise, the end of their forest journey came too soon and not soon enough. The ferryman drifted in front of her and was engulfed in the light that shone down on him from beyond the canopy of the forest. For the briefest moment, Claire saw what he should have looked like, gleaming, ethereal, bathed in the light of the love he had for her and all mortal souls. She only stood at the treeline, unable to move forward and unable to step back.

"I'm scared," she confessed to her friend. "I'm scared," she said again and slumped down in front of a tree.

In an instant, the ferryman was back in the forest with her. He patted her shoulder gently and hummed his loving non-words. They sat together and stared at the vast uncertainty that lay before them. He did not rush her and he did not leave her side, though each passing minute may have brought her closer to losing her very soul. His love for her was a certainty, however. Claire felt it and clung to it. He had trusted her, and then he had risked himself for her, and then he had saved her. And right now, he stayed with her. That gave her the strength to decide.

"Okay. I'm ready," she said with more confidence than she actually felt.

The ferryman's sweet hum filled her ears and he rose to stand with her through whatever the next steps brought them. He held his hand out before he dipped his head, slightly turning away, and instead gestured for her to stand when she was ready. Claire noted his apparent shame and reached up to take his hand anyway. She gripped it tightly and he looked down at her, surprised, but with a renewed sense of purpose and joy. He held her hand and gently pulled her up to walk with him. She stood and without another thought, pulled the ferryman in for a tight hug.

"Thank you for saving me," she said and gave him a squeeze. "You are a dear friend." When Claire pulled away from the hug, the ferryman's one good eye glistened with tears.

The river wasn't just vast. It was unending in a way that Claire could have never known. Even the seemingly unending oceans of Earth disappeared over a horizon eventually. The river did not have a horizon to disappear into; it blurred with the sky that would never touch its edge. The ferrymen's boats rested along its banks and for as far as her eyes could see. Each one was different from the next. Some were row boats, others sailboats. Some were large, some small. Some seemed to come from a time when man just started to use tools. Some seemed to come from ancient times and through all the eras and regions of the Earth. All were captained by a ferryman whose appearance was as unfortunate as the next.

The pair walked to the riverbank, where the lush grass of the forest became a beach of river rocks all the way to the edge. Claire held the ferryman's hand tightly as they approached the boats and the gentle humming of her friend was joined by all the ferryman around them. At first, they stayed on their boats, unsure and wary. Then, one-by-one, they came ashore and the gentle hums became a chorus as it seemed Claire's friend explained something to them. More and more ferrymen joined them and they seemed to know something Claire and her friend didn't. They pointed down the riverbank with urgency and Claire understood that was where they should go.

She and her friend continued on along the riverbank and hundreds, if not thousands, of other ferrymen followed behind them. She saw the two figures ahead first and recognized them immediately. It was Vera and Margeaux. They saw each other at the same time and the two women began waving their arms about and ran toward Claire. She let go of the ferryman's hand and ran toward them. As she got closer, however, she realized their distress. She slowed down as she saw the both of them looking over their shoulders and then back at her.

Her ferryman friend caught up to her and grabbed her hand again, pulling her slightly behind him as Vera and Margeaux reached them.

"He's got Jacob. He got all of us. I can't find Eyleth or Ayn," Vera said desperately, taking in the horde of ferrymen behind Claire.

"I'm going to help however I can," Margeaux insisted. Even without her memories, her fierce loyalty and willingness to fight still shone through.

"Okay. I just need to shake with either Niran or Eyleth to close my contract, right?" Claire asked.

"Yes, but we have no idea where they are - and Claire, Ezra's coming. He was behind us, but I don't know where he went," Vera said.

Claire looked past Vera and Margeaux and saw nothing. She turned around and it was only the unlikely army of ferryman behind her. She was about to start instructing ferrymen to start a search party for the missing family members when she felt the low rumble of Seir's distinct growl.

She turned back around, anticipating that Niran would be nearby as well. Her relieved smile immediately faltered as it was not just Seir who approached, but Ezra astride him. Seir appeared to Claire, not fully corporeal, but no longer invisible. Vera and Margeaux backed away from Ezra to stand at her side as she seethed at what Ezra had done to Seir. He appeared as a swirling fog of shadows and sand, gnashing fangs and sinew. No part of him was recognizable for more than a second before shadow and sand swept over him as if he was bound by it. She had heard and felt this frustration from Seir before, when she commanded him to stand by instead of killing the last kidnapper in the van. When he was not growling, he was whining.

"Oh, *hush*, Seir. Aren't you happy to see your friend?" Ezra crooned. There was no agreement in the sounds Seir made. "And what do we have here?" he said as his eyes swept over the ferrymen behind Claire. "I don't suppose you know where our Niran is, do you?" he asked with a lazy smile.

"Why does it matter?" She asked defiantly.

"Oh, just a little loose end. We wouldn't want him to sneak up and shake your hand while I'm not looking, would we?" Ezra answered mockingly.

"Father," Vera nervously said. "This has gone far enough."

At the sound of Vera's nervous tone, a shudder of fear snaked down Claire's spine. She hadn't known Vera could even experience being nervous. For her to do so now made Claire feel keenly aware of her human fragility compared to these immortal beings.

"I will deal with you later. You're lucky I let you keep your pet," he chided, pacing in front of Claire and her makeshift army. "I don't like asking for things twice, Claire. Where is he?"

He leaned in closer to Claire and her ferryman friend drifted between the two of them. His hand was out, backing Claire away from Ezra who towered above him upon Seir's back. The humming of the ferryman seemed to urge her to stay behind him. Ezra only chuckled and turned Seir to step away.

The ferryman turned around to compel Claire to back up. His one eye was hopeful and his hum was reassuring. Suddenly, Ezra's arm burst through his chest, his spine fisted in that evil grip. Claire was sprayed with his blood, bone fragments, and pieces of his heart. She stumbled back in shock and horror, uselessly reaching out for him as he was briefly lifted into the air. Ezra pulled his arm back through the hole it made in the ferryman's already broken body; the one hand that had reached back out to her went limp. The last look in his one good eye, fixed on Claire, was still full of hope before the light left it. His body fell in a heap at Claire's feet as Ezra threw the ferryman's spineaside and shook blood and indiscernible bits of the ferryman's body off his hand with a look of disgust. All the air left Claire's lungs as she ran her fingers down her cheek to see blood on them. It was all over her and she fell to her knees before her friend's destroyed body, unable to speak and unable to think beyond the anguish and rage that both fought for control of her mind.

Pain tore through the assembled ferrymen with the realization of what had happened. Their gentle hums devolved into guttural screams of anguish that came from so deep, it woke something primal, something mortal that was buried within them. They surged forward as Claire stood with Ezra in her sights. Seir fought Ezra's control and pawed at the ground, growling his own hatred.

"*Heel*, you filthy beast!" Ezra roared. Seir let out a yelp of pain and obeyed. They turned and Ezra held up a hand with a smirk and snapped his fingers. From all around him, as if they came from his very thoughts, appeared his own horde of commanded souls. "Get her into that river," he ordered and then took off with Seir.

In a blink, Claire, Vera and Margeaux were engulfed in ferrymen. They formed a wall around them a dozen bodies thick. Claire only had time to bend down and close her friend's one good eye, making a silent promise that his death would not be in vain. Through the mass of shadowed souls and ferrymen's bodies, she saw Ezra's and Seir's retreating forms. She ran and the wall of ferryman ran with her. Ezra's souls were ravenous, wild-eyed - and while there is something to be said about the truly fearsome, they learn true fear when the peaceful turn to war. And on this day, the ferrymen, who had embodied peace, chose to bring war.

They picked off the commanded souls by the dozen, inflicting on them what had been done to their own. What few made it through their wall of protection were swiftly thrown back toward the blood-thirsty ferrymen by Vera and Margeaux, who ran alongside Claire, focused on reaching Ezra. The souls were ripped apart and thrown into the river. Some tried to escape into boats but were pulled out and dragged, screaming, into the forest. Some disappeared into a pile of ferrymen's bodies, only their muffled screams and then silence. The souls had slowed their attacks and then stopped attacking altogether as they were no match for the ferrymen. They began fleeing into the forest where the wails of the lost melded with the screams of the tortured as ferrymen gave chase. The other ferrymen looked to Claire for orders as they all realized the commanded souls were fleeing.

"Get every last one of them," she ordered, and continued to run. The remaining ferrymen split off to pick off the last of the souls. Claire, Vera, and Margeaux pursued Ezra on Seir, who ran far more slowly than Claire knew he was capable of. *Good boy*, she thought to herself as the three of them closed the distance.

Ezra looked over his shoulder once, with that same smirk and held a hand up to snap his fingers again. When he did, Margeaux slowed her running. Her face contorted into dread and agony as she stopped and grabbed her head, screaming. "*No! No! No! No!*" Over and over, she screamed and covered her eyes and grabbed her head. They all stopped.

"Margeaux, what is it?!" Vera asked, desperately.

"No! No! No! My Aubergine! No! My Aubergine!" Margeaux cried as her mind was suddenly flooded with all of her memories, starting with the sight of herself setting her beloved Aubergine on fire and then watching it burn. She collapsed to her knees, the pain of all her returned memories, pounded her mind like a sledgehammer to her skull.

Vera knew what was happening and told Claire, "You have to go on without us. I can't leave her like this. I'm sorry. Find Eyleth or Niran. You MUST shake with one of them. It's the only way to end all of this!"

Margeaux continued to cry and scream from the physical and emotional pain. Claire only nodded to Vera, gave a quick, sorry look to Margeaux, and continued her chase. Claire knew she had to find Eyleth or Niran, but she also could not help wanting to find Ezra first and do to him what he had done to her friend.

When she started to run, however, Ezra was gone. She frantically searched the riverbank and the treeline and could not see him, not even in the distance. So she continued, full of rage and desperation. There was still no Ezra in sight.

Up ahead, the water looked like it was moving, alive. It no longer reflected the light around it, but pulled it in and held it somewhere beneath the surface. As Claire approached, she heard the sound of choking, gasping and not the screams of being lost, but of being trapped. It was the bridge of souls. She looked down its length to find its end and could not see it from where she stood, but for as long as it was, the bridge was only about as wide as a sidewalk. There was a line of small boulders, on land, which connected to the soul bridge. Eyleth, Ayn, Jacob, and Reid were leaned up against it as if they'd been dumped there.

Claire stood with fists clenched as she noticed Niran was not among them. Reid looked badly beaten; his whole face was bruised and bloodied with one eye swollen shut. He held his right arm close to his chest and winced in pain when he moved it. His breaths were shallow and he could barely turn his face to see Claire approach. Jacob lay awkwardly half on the ground, halfway in Ayn's lap, a look of frustration and anger on his face. Claire lunged for Eylethto shake hands with her, but stopped at the sight of her right hand. She saw a bloody rag covering the space where her pinky had been. Eyleth only looked up at Claire with sorrow in her eyes as she opened her other hand to reveal her signet ring in her palm.

"Where is he, Claire?" Ezra asked impatiently from behind, with menace in his tone.

"I don't know," she answered forcefully, clenching her fists and teeth as the water of the river beside them swelled, and a boulder next to Ayn cracked.

Reid lifted his chin to the sky with mouth wide open as he arched his back painfully; Claire heard a bone crack as he slumped back down. He choked down a sob as Eyleth went to him.

"I don't need to hurt you to hurt you, Claire. Would you like to continue using that tone with me?" Ezra asked casually.

"*Stop!* Stop! I said I don't know!" she pleaded.

"Then it looks like we'll have to draw him out the fun way," Ezra conceded and raised his fingers to snap again.

Before Claire could react, two commanded souls appeared before her. She stumbled back and they grabbed her by both arms, heading for the river.

"Father, *stop!* Please, father!" Eyleth and Ayn cried.

"Bring her to the bridge," Ezra commanded the souls, ignoring his daughters' pleas. "It would be more poetic there, I think." Seir panted and growled beneath him. He pawed at the ground and whined, desperate, but unable to help Claire.

Claire fought as much as she could, but her energy was sapped from running and fighting. She had nothing left in her. As they approached the water, she looked down at the row of anguished faces that looked back up at her. They all clung so tightly to each other there was barely any water between them, and their sobs grew louder and rang through Claire's whole body. She was horrified at the sight and sound of these mortal souls – men, women and children. Even the two souls that held her stilled for a moment. The ones in the water were somewhere between solid and shadow as they sometimes melded together to make frightening images of four arms on one body or three faces on one head. The forms of babies seemed to grow out of backs or sides. Flailing legs cropped up out of the tops of heads or from bellies. A mouth would open wide in distress and from inside would stick out an arm and shoulder. As they clung to each other, they became each other.

"*Do it!* Or I'll throw you two in there with her!" Ezra commanded.

"I don't know where he is! *I don't know where he is!*" Claire screamed as the two lackeys took their first steps onto the bridge of souls. Ezra merely leaned forward on Seir, watching and waiting.

Upon the bridge, her captors had loosened their grip, unsure and wanting to be back on land as much as she did. The souls on which they stood bobbed stiffly in the water, neither sinking nor fully floating. It was a precarious balancing act to stay standing on their backs as she tried not to step on heads or faces. It was easy to lose footing and balance. All three of them tried to stay in the middle. Her captors had started moving more slowly as if they were getting stuck and unstuck. One of them let go of Claire and she fell back. She watched in horror as they tried to free themselves from a dozen hands that pulled on their legs and began slowly dragging them down. One of the commanded souls grabbed and held onto her left arm so tightly, she could not get out of its desperate grip. The other one was almost completely pulled into the bridge as it had already begun to wail like the others around it. The one that held Claire still had half of its form above the bridge and was ready to take Claire with it. She fought and kicked at it, and began considering what drowning in the river might feel like.

She gave one last desperate look to the riverbank and only saw Ezra still leaning forward on Seir with a look of curiosity and glee. Ayn was standing, both hands over her mouth, watching as Claire struggled. Though the soul had already mostly been pulled into the bridge, it still held tightly to Claire and her hand was inches from touching the water. She heard gasps. They belonged to Eyleth and Ayn. Niran had run past them and went straight for the bridge of souls. Claire almost wept at the sight of him as she still struggled.

Niran sprinted for her, and as he neared, she held out her right hand to shake with him. Clouds of nightmare gathered at his eyes and the soul that held her down cried out and let go of her hand. She ran towards him, her right hand stretched out.

"*Niran!*" she screamed, stopping in her tracks.

Ezra rode up beside Niran and grabbed him by the neck. He held him over the water with little effort as Niran struggled in his grip. All he had to do was let go and Niran would be dropped in the river.

"*Stop! Stop! You win!* Let him go!" she screamed. She put her hands up out of some strange mortal instinct. "You win! I beg you. Let him go!"

"Claire, *no!*" Niran protested through gasps of air.

"I win? I *win?!*" Ezra repeated. "Of course I win! Do you know who I am?!" he asked hysterically. "Did you ever think I *wasn't* going to win? I am the king of death! I am the final sleep! Of *course* I win!" His voice boomed over the wails of the bridge of souls. Beneath him, Seir groaned and whimpered, pawing at the bodies in the bridge.

"I'm sorry," Claire said more softly, "I'm sorry. You're right," she said, conceding. "You're right."

From behind Ezra, Eyleth sobbed and pleaded for the life of her son. She was being held back by Ayn and now Vera and Margeaux who had arrived at the bridge. They knew any new threat to Ezra might cause him to react. Their voices were distant from the two who were now in a standoff for Niran's life.

"I'll go in. But you have to let him go. There's no point in killing him, too." Claire said, on her knees, feeling the huffs of hot panting from Seir who stood so close to her, his body, again, fighting his will to obey.

"Claire, no," Niran tried again.

"I'll go in," she repeated, not looking at Niran. A calm washed over her, having finally accepted the loss.

"Was that so hard?" Ezra crooned and threw Niran down onto the bridge.

Niran coughed and choked for air as he stumbled back from the edge.

"Thank you," she said and stood.

"Claire, no, stop! We still have time," Niran tried again and she ignored him.

"You are the final sleep. You are the king of death." She said, a look of defiance in her eyes. Ezra only smirked at his words being repeated back to him.

"And soon, you'll be the king of nothing."

"Seir! *Relax!*" she ordered. And the hound obeyed.

As Seir dropped to his belly, Claire leaped for Ezra, who had no time to think as he wobbled off balance. She held onto him with everything left in her body, as they both fell, splashing into the river. The water burned of a thousand suns over her entire body as she held tight to Ezra. He beat at her arms and back and tried to shove her away, but she held on, curling her body over his. Bubbles, filled with the last gasp of air she took, floated up as she screamed in extraordinary agony. Ezra fought and jerked in her death grip as he, too, let out his last breaths in excruciating pain. Her entire body felt as though her skin was being shorn off with blades of fire, but she held on and would hold onto him until she could no longer. They sank lower and lower as Ezra stopped fighting her and she stopped holding him. The last thing she saw was his body sinking into the abyss of the river, as deep as the universe, before everything went black and she convulsed with the last of the pain.

There was a splash into the water above her and a large, hulking form swam beneath her. She had the distant feeling of rising as the body pushed her up to the surface of the water, where they were both met with air she thought she would never feel again. Beneath her, Seir swam, yelping in agony, gasping for air and struggling to keep his head above water. On the bridge of souls, Niran, Vera, Margeaux, Eyleth and Ayn all stood, yelling for them. The beast went under again and came back up, his yelping turning into screams as he tried again to reach the bridge, choking and yelping with every panicked paddle of his paws. The fire of the water washed over them, scalding hot, and Seir still continued to swim. He finally got close enough to the bridge for Niran to reach over and drag Claire off of his back. As he pulled her up, Seir went back under the water and they all screamed for him but he did not come back up.

"Seir!"

"No! Seir!"

"Claire. Claire stay with me." Niran grabbed her hand in his and choked out, "As per your agreement with my associate, I've come to collect what you owe." He shook with her. She didn't move. She didn't breathe. "I've come to collect what you owe!" He repeated, *"I've come to collect what you owe!"*

"Seir!" someone screamed.

The last of Claire's senses left her as the yelling, the pain, the entire universe,

faded to nothing.

"*Is she breathing? Niran, is she breathing?!*" As if through a thick wall, Claire heard Vera's panicked voice.

"*No! Help me! I've come to collect what you owe!*" She felt Niran shake her hand again and again, but it felt like it was through two pairs of gloves.

"*Seir! Seir!*" Ayn sobbed.

Claire dreamed of Seir or maybe she was remembering him. They walked along the pond and napped in the grass. He smelled of Earth and sun. He had brought her back from the depths of the river waters that meant to drag her to its unknown floor.

She dreamed of her friend who had been scared of her the first time they met. He gave her a flower and hummed for her as she lay lifeless in Niran's arms. He was beautiful, more beautiful than anything she had ever seen in her life. Then they were falling together again in that eternal dark of the cradle. It was different; like napping in the shade of a weeping willow as the breeze blew over her. When they landed, it wasn't with a jolt and it wasn't in a grave. They padded down gently on the banks of the river in front of his boat. The ferryman drifted off, humming something that she knew meant he would be right back and he disappeared into the river.

When he returned, he invited her onto his boat. All the other ferrymen, each as beautiful as the next, hummed around her, a chorus of love, peace and comfort. Her friend held out his hand for her to join him and she reached for it without question, without hesitation. She drifted into his embrace and felt such love it brought her to tears. He hummed for her again and she fell into a deep, light-filled sleep.

Sometimes she woke and she saw glimpses of water all around, and her friend who steered his little boat across it. Sometimes she slept and there were dreams and nightmares, memories and wishes. Sometimes there was only nothing and the nothing went on endlessly and was over in a moment. Often, she heard voices of people in her life.

"There you go! You've got it, baby! You're walking!" Her mother.

"Let's get matching dresses and be twins." Her best friend in the fourth grade.

"This is good work." Her father.

"I love what you've done with the place." Charlene.

Laughter. It was her own. Vera and Margeaux laughed along with her.

"You have something of mine." Niran.

Niran. She thought she might look over the edge of the boat and see them together, still on the bridge of souls, as he held her and tried to bring her back.

"I've come to collect what you owe."

She had made her choice. She had a debt to pay.

"I chose," she said, not knowing who she was saying it to.

The humming and sound of the boat slowly moving through the water started to put her back to sleep.

"I chose," she said again.

Her friend went to her side and gently stroked her hair as he had the day she helped him get home. His lulling response filled the air around her and she went back into that endless dark. The sound of water lapping against the side of the boat tugged her gently into another peaceful sleep. Her friend's gentle hum fell like the droplets of a light spring rain around her, and faded further and further away. She thought she heard her name in his loving hums.

Claire.

Claire.

"Claire! Claire, baby, hey!" Margeaux cooed as a shaft of powder-soft sunlight washed over her. "She's awake! Get in here, she's awake!"

Claire's eyelids felt heavier than they'd ever been as she tried to open them.

"*Margeaux*," she whispered.

"Ooh! She said my name first. That's right. All y'all can fight for second," Margeaux said joyfully.

It was joyful. Where was Ezra? If she made it out of the river, does that mean he did? How did she get out? The questions bounced around her head and slammed into her skull, her head throbbing. Then she remembered: it had been Seir who saved her. Seir. She felt the prick of tears as her heart broke.

"Move," Vera told Margeaux. "She only said it because you shoved your big head in her face. Claire, sweetie. How are you? It's Vera."

Claire didn't even have the energy to let out a humored huff. She couldn't even imagine giggling ever again as she still struggled to open her eyes.

"Perhaps you all should give her some space to breathe. She was out for two weeks, after all. I could be wrong."

"Shush. You are wrong, Jacob," Margeaux answered him.

Claire's eyes opened slightly, but she could see the blurry figure of Reid lumbering across the room to push Jacob elsewhere in his wheelchair. Her eyes opened a little more to see Vera and Margeaux, both misty-eyed by her side. And she loved to see them.

"Where is Niran?" Claire whispered.

"He's coming. He had to take care of some things, but he should be back any second now," Margeaux answered.

She closed her eyes and fell back asleep; Eyleth and Ayn were in front of her when she opened them again, hours later.

"Dearest Claire," Eyleth said, and held her hand sweetly.

"Hi, Claire. How are you?" Ayn asked, a bit nervously.

"Hold on. Let us help you," Eyleth said, gently helping Claire up. She was laying on the couch in some living room. Vera and Margeaux were in the kitchen, bickering over the meal they were cooking together.

"This is my house, we cook it my way! When we're in your house, we can cook it your way," Margeaux argued.

Ayn brought Claire a glass of water. "Oh goodness," she suddenly said. "Do you even want water? I can't imagine you'd want to touch it for another hundred years," she said with a wince.

"It's fine. Thank you," Claire said as she weakly took the glass.

The front door flew open and Niran burst into the room. Everyone paused what they were doing and watched as he lunged for Claire and kneeled by the couch to hold her. He buried his face in her hair and squeezed her tightly.

"Niran, not too tight. She's a little fragile right now." Eyleth giggled with a tear in her eye.

He loosened his grip slightly as Claire lifted her arms up to hug him back. So much was lost, but this moment made the pain bearable. They held each other long enough that everyone else went about their business around them. Jacob sat at the window, tasking Reid, who looked to be well on the mend, save for a few new scars to contrast his sweet demeanor. Eyleth and Ayn discussed a thank-you gift that might make Harena happy; a few souls contracted to help her in the caverns, they considered. Vera and Margeaux started plating the food they'd bickered about. And Niran only held her. She didn't think she would ever be held by him or anyone again. In the river, she'd given herself for them and through the fiery pain, a tiny part of her had realized that the grappling hold she'd had on Ezra would have been the last embrace she'd ever share. Even in what she believed to be her dying moments, she had hated Ezra even more for it.

"Hi," she whispered to him. It was the only thing she could think to say.

He chuckled lightly. "Hello, Claire," he whispered back, and she sank into him as he squeezed her.

"Excuse me!" Margeaux interrupted. "We didn't almost break this friendship up to cook this meal so all you people could ignore it! Claire, babe, you get soup today. Let's work you back up to full meals. Niran, come get this soup. She's not gonna make it to this table today," Margeaux said as she placed table settings. He finally let go of Claire to do as he was told and was happy to do it. They smiled at each other as he got up, and she shifted to sit up more comfortably for her meal.

"We need to open the back door. I told you that you burnt the butter, this place is all smokey now," Vera complained as she headed toward the back.

As she opened the door, she yelped and Margeaux and Niran yelled, "WAIT" in unison, a moment too late. Thundering came down the hallway as Claire looked up in confusion.

"Seir! Relax!" they all yelled as the thud of the beast going to his belly came only a second before he slammed into the couch.

"Seir!" she exclaimed. Tears immediately filled her eyes as he licked her and sniffed excitedly and she couldn't pet him and hug him enough. "Seir! Seir, you good boy! I thought we lost you!" She managed through her tears.

"Well, we lost some of him." Niran chuckled.

"Some of him?" Claire asked as she petted the empty air before her.

"He has fewer legs now. It's actually a little more convenient."

"What? How many legs did he have before?"

Jacob, Niran and Vera all answered, "Seven."

Claire let out a small laugh and then she heard one of the most splendid sounds she might ever hear.

Thunk thunk thunk.

During dinner, Niran quietly told Claire how her waking up was finally a bright spot in what had been an otherwise dark past couple of weeks.

"Though Ezra had been who he was in the end, he had still been father to my mother and her siblings. They still mourn him and they're still learning how to exist without him, for better or worse," he informed her.

"I can understand that," she said.

"I think Ayn has taken it the hardest. My mother seems to be okay and Vera has been so busy with Margeaux that I'm not sure she's even given herself enough time to process anything," he continued.

"Margeaux. How did she get her body back?" Claire asked.

"Ah, that. She doesn't have her body back. You can just see her true self - the way her soul sees itself, to put it simply. She's still in that borrowed body, but we see her true face."

"I'm happy about that," Claire admitted. "And what about Jacob?"

"He's Jacob. I can't say one way or the other how he's feeling about any of it."

"And you?" Claire asked, focused more intently on the answer to that question.

"I'm okay. I want my mother and the rest of them to be okay, too, but I understand it may take some time. But I'm okay because you're okay now," he assured her.

After dinner and in the peaceful quiet of the night, Claire smiled as she took in the room around her. Vera slouched uncharacteristically, but contentedly, in one of the dining room chairs, rubbing her full belly and quipping with Margeaux who stood in a regal pose using a butter knife as a mirror as she reapplied lipstick. Ayn and Eyleth chatted quietly with Jacob in another corner of the room while Reid sat cross-legged on the floor. At first glance, he looked to be sitting awkwardly without reason, but the sound of Seir's slow tail wags thunking on the floor beside him gave away that the hound had his head in Reid's lap.

Claire looked around for Niran who had stepped away. He was there and he was okay. They all were. It didn't feel real and it didn't seem right. She hadn't let herself hear the questions which hung like a cloud over the peace of this evening, but as everything began to slow down and the conversations quieted to murmurs, the questions became louder. She remembered the battle at the river. She remembered her friend, the ferryman, and the hopeful lookin his eye that stayed there even when the light left it. She remembered Ezra and going into the water. She remembered seeing the ferryman again, but he was whole, beautiful, breathtaking. And she remembered falling, but falling slowly, softly.

"What happened?" She asked quietly at first. No one seemed to want to answer right away, so she asked again.

"What happened? How did we all get back here? How are we all okay, but..." She trailed off as she turned her attention to Jacob who was still in his wheelchair. "Did it not work? What happened to the power?"

After a moment, it was Vera who finally answered her, sitting up straight again.

"We don't know, Claire. We were hoping you could tell us."

"Seir went in after you. We thought we'd lost you both. You were both in the water for so long," Ayn said, speaking softly through worry and distress over the memory of it all.

"Niran pulled you out of the water when you and Seir finally made it back to the surface. It took all of us to hold him back from jumping in after you. He almost fought us all off of him and would have if you hadn't resurfaced when you did," Eyleth added.

"So much was happening. Seir went back under when we pulled you out. We were trying to find him and Niran and I were trying to bring you back. You weren't breathing and we were nearly convinced we'd lost you both," Vera said as she walked into the living room to sit next to Claire. "We could barely touch you. The water that still soaked your clothes and your skin burned us like fire. Niran used his own shirt to clean it from your head and face. Even though it burned him, he held you and wouldn't stop trying to help you breathe until you finally coughed up the water that was in your lungs and started breathing on your own again. I don't know exactly when Seir made it back up, but as you can imagine, having you both back..." She stopped herself as if she knew another word would draw out emotions she wasn't ready to share.

"Harena found us," Jacob continued. "She used her own door to the river and was ready to fight with us and for us. She made sure each and every one of us knew the sheer depth of her disappointment over missing the fight. Seir was in bad shape and it was touch and go for you both the past two weeks. If not for Harena, I do not think Seir would have made it." There was a beat before he finished. "And if not for Niran, I do not think you would have either." Nobody disagreed.

"I was floating. Or falling. I'm not sure. And then I was in a boat with my friend, the ferryman. He was normal. I mean, he wasn't," Claire gestured to her face because there were no kind words to describe how he'd looked before. "We were going across the river, I think. And I told him that I needed to come back. I told him I made my choice and I was supposed to come back." Nobody spoke as she finally shared what she remembered. "And then I woke up here."

Jacob seemed to be turning over her words in his mind. Half his thoughts seemed to be elsewhere while still taking in what he was hearing. The rest of the group gave their own accounts of what happened at the river and the two weeks leading up to this night. Seir had recovered enough to seem himself again about four days before Claire woke up. They each took turns caring for Claire with strict instructions from Harena on what to do. For the first several days, she couldn't be moved from Harena's cave and after that, it was agreed that she'd stay with Vera and Margeaux at the house they now shared for the time being.

"But wait," Claire said. "Does that mean it's too late? I don't remember shaking anyone's hand. Niran or Eyleth."

"You did. I shook your hand when we pulled you out of the water," Niran answered, walking back into the living room. Claire only looked up at him, her whole body sagging as she exhaled a breath she didn't even realize she held for him.

"But I'm still here," she said, confused.

"I know," he said, quietly.

Everyone in the room seemed to take that as their cue to leave. Reid rose from the floor first, gently moving Seir's head from his lap. He made his way to Jacob's wheelchair as Jacob continued to study Claire, saying nothing. Both Vera and Margeaux gave Claire pecks on the forehead before making their way up the stairs. As Reid pushed Jacob out toward the front door, he placed a large hand on Claire's shoulder and smiled at her sweetly. Jacob only nodded at Claire who nodded back at him. Ayn shyly waved goodbye to Claire, still carrying the weight of the role she played to help Ezra. Eyleth made it a point to take Claire's face in her hands and touch her forehead to hers before standing up and giving Niran a warm, motherly embrace. Niran stood staring at the door his mother and Ayn had closed behind them when they walked out and Claire stared at him.

"Is it going to happen now?" she asked quietly, remembering the night she first met Niran and the horror of it all. Her heart raced and though she trusted Niran implicitly, she was still clenched in the grasp of her own fear.

"It is," he merely said, unable to make eye contact with her.

"I'm not scared."

"Yes you are."

"I forgot you knew these things," she said with a forced lightness to her voice that she hoped would reassure him.

He scowled at the attempt and still made no move toward her. It was clear across his face that he did not want to do what he knew he had to.

"Niran, I'm okay. We knew this day would come. I'm just grateful that it'll be you who does it."

Claire attempted to rise from the couch. She hadn't anticipated how weak her body would be and nearly fell over. Niran came to her in a heartbeat and held her before she could fall. She looked up at him with that smile that had haunted him since the day they met. He could only return a pleading look.

Claire noted the look and wondered if he'd ever pleaded with a person in his entire existence.

"*Niran*," she said, gently.

He could barely speak a reply.

"I don't know what's happening." He placed a hand, fingers splayed, on his chest and continued, "I already don't know how to say what happens here when I'm with you," and he patted his chest. "But this. Right now. This feels, in my whole being, like nothing has ever mattered or ever will. I don't want to do this, Claire." He looked at her with pleading eyes as if she could be his savior from what he had to do.

Claire touched his trembling hand. On his knees beside the couch, he slumped in his despair. He finally looked at her and she had a look of such understanding and kindness that all he could do was choke on his breath and pat his hand to his chest again.

With a nod, Claire placed her hand on top of his on his chest and he held it to him. Her tiny hand was engulfed by both of his before he wrapped her in an embrace he could not make close enough, long enough, big enough so the world could understand that what was happening was a tragedy of such profound greatness that nothing, and nobody, should ever be the same after.

"I know. It's okay. I know," she said so softly, so gently that it only served to further bury Niran in what was already taking the air from him.

Claire let herself sink into Niran's embrace as she gently pulled his right arm from around her and brought it to her lap between them. They stayed there for a moment as she gently stroked the back of his head and whispered; "It's okay. It's okay."

"No," Niran finally said as he looked down and saw Claire gently turning his signet ring toward his palm. He tried to pull his hand away from her, and she held it firmly as she turned the ring the rest of the way. "*No*," he repeated, choking on the word like a prayer he begged to her, his darkness and his salvation.

"We can do this together," she said as she pulled away just far enough so they could see into each other's eyes. She began to slip her palm into his. His hand trembled within hers.

"I can't," he barely made out, still refusing to close his fingers around her hand.

"Yes, you can. Please be the one to do this with me."

For another agonizing moment, they stayed there, palms against each other, only a grip away from the first handshake that he did not want to make,out of all the countless ones he'd had. Claire poured strength and understanding into him through her gaze as she nodded her head one last time before he finally spoke.

"As per your agreement with my associate, I've come to collect what you owe." And he closed his fingers around hers.

Silence fell over the room as it had the night Niran had come for Claire's father. A tear, nearly frozen in time, glistened on her cheek as she and Niran took each other in and left the world around them entirely.

At first, only bright white light surrounded them as Claire and Niran stood, hand-in-hand. She smelled them before she could even see them - flowers all around. Her eyes adjusted to the light and she found herself amidst a vast and endless sea of flowers. The land --gently rolling hills, as far as the eye could see-- went on until they met with the horizon in all directions. She stood barefoot on grass as soft as baby rabbit fur and all around her was every flower she had ever thought was beautiful in her life. Among them were also some she'd never seen before. She looked to Niran who smiled at her and held out a hand, inviting her to walk wherever she wished through the field.

As they walked, Niran bent to collect flowers, seemingly at random. Every time he plucked one, Claire felt it deep inside her chest. They walked as Claire took in the most beautiful sight she knew she would ever see in this life, or any other life she might live.

"There are no words --none-- for how beautiful this is," she breathed out, taken aback, yet full of such gratitude that she didn't even want to blink.

"No, there are no words at all," Niran said, looking only at her.

She only smiled at him as they continued walking and he continued picking flowers. It seemed like they walked for an entire day as Niran plucked flower-after-flower, yet the bunch in his hand never grew beyond a small fistful. He was quiet as she spoke of every flower she knew and when she'd first seen it in her life. There were ones from so early in her childhood that she could only remember a smudge of it from a foggy memory. There were others that stole her attention while out with friends or comforted her during the hardest times with her parents. As she told the stories, they walked and Niran plucked.

"Claire, I have to tell you something," he said, pausing as the sun began its descent below the horizon.

"Okay," she answered.

"There is one more thing about your contract that you might not have caught."

"What?" she asked curiously.

"There is a final payment that must be made on your contract before we leave this place and you move onto what comes next," he answered grimly.

"Okay. What is it?"

"The balance demands of you that which you love most. I'm sorry I couldn't tell you sooner. You weren't supposed to know before now." He looked down at first, and then to all the flowers that surrounded them.

She understood immediately and allowed her eyes to sweep across the fields. She strained to see as far toward the horizon as she could.

"My flowers?"

"I don't know for certain. This is one of the things to which I am not privy. But I thought this," --he gestured to the fields around them-- "I thought this would have been best for you. We can stay here as long as you want. We can look at each and every flower in this entire field if you want."

Claire's eyes began to well with tears. She thought of every joy she experienced with her flowers. She tried to remember every one she ever plucked and every arrangement she ever made. She thought of her dreams to own a floral boutique and how flowers had been her anchor to the love and joy within her that made her feel safe, free and a part of something profoundly beautiful. Through every uncertainty, every moment of self-doubt, every triumph and every failure, her flowers were her constant. She had never considered, not for a second, a time when they would not have a place in her life and in her heart.

"So, what will happen? Will I just hate them or something?" she asked through falling tears.

"I'm sorry. I don't know." He plucked the last one for the bunch he held in his hand.

Claire looked over the fields, part of her wishing to stay and take Niran up on his offer to look at every single one; another part of her wondering if she could find the strength to walk away even after that.

"Is it okay if we stay here a little bit longer?" she asked.

"As long as you wish."

Claire walked a little farther through the flowers, alone this time, and found what she thought might be the best place to stand so she could see all of them. Each flower held a moment of her life within it. Every moment-- the joyful, the painful, the mundane and the exciting-- was more beautiful than she could have ever been able to put into words. She stood among every choice she ever made and every outcome that came from them. She saw her mistakes and the accomplishments beside them and she felt love and appreciation for both. She took in the sum of her entire, short life, surrounding her and felt gratitude so deeply, it nearly brought her to her knees. No one, nothing, could have prepared her for the realization that everything within her mattered and mattered so significantly that only loving and embracing every single piece of herself would make her understand how it all could. She tried to imagine this field without her mistakes, without her losses, without her pain or uncertainties. It would not be the indescribably beautiful sight that it is now. She finally understood who she was in her shortened life and in the universe beyond it and all she felt was profound gratitude and peace.

The flowers were as much a part of her as she was of them. It made her realize something else and she searched for Niran who had given her the space she needed for this moment. Not her voice, but her heart called out for him and he was by her side in an instant. The flowers had told her every story of her life except for one. They'd shown her every reason to love every moment of her life and provided her the peace to let go. She realized, however, that she couldn't find Niran among them.

"Why aren't you in the flowers?" she asked him, holding both his hands as he stood before her. "You belong here. You belong with all of these beautiful memories."

"I belong with you," he answered, strained and with the weight of the world's cruelty on his shoulders.

Claire wrapped her arms around his neck and he bent to hold her with everything he had in him. She squeezed tears from her eyes as she looked at all of the flowers of her life from over his shoulder. She saw it, then - the way the whole field leaned in toward the two of them. She realized every subtle way their stems and petals pointed to him as they walked together. She saw how, now, the flowers closest to them seemed to weep.

She pulled away from Niran and studied him as they both realized at the same time.

"No! Niran, I lo-"

She opened her eyes with her forehead pressed against that of the man before her, their hands still entwined in the shake that hung over the last six months of her life. As she looked up she let go of his hand and sat straight, her heartbeat quickened as she scooted back from him. The man had a puzzled look on his face.

"Claire," he said, reaching out to her.

"Stop!" she exclaimed. "Stop. I-" She looked around and backed away from him as far as she could on the couch. "Vera," she said confused at first.

The man stood up and Claire jolted, calling for Vera again, louder this time.

"Vera! Vera! Where are you?" she said, never taking her eyes off of the man.

The man's face fell into an anguished look as he backed away from her slowly and looked up the stairs to see Vera and Margeaux come storming down them.

"Claire, what's wrong? Are you okay?" Vera asked, as she swooped down toward Claire on the couch. Margeaux was close behind.

The man only kept backing away, staring at Claire, agonized.

"Vera!" Claire said again, confused but relieved her friends were there now.

"Claire, sweetie, what is it?" Margeaux asked.

"Who is that? Why is he here? He was holding my hand. I think he did something to me," Claire said in panicked breaths, pointing a shaky finger at Niran.

pronunciations

Claire: KLER

Cielo: s-YEL-oh

Niran: NEER-ahn

Seir: SEER

Vera: VER-uh

Reid: REED

Margeaux: mar-GOH

Aubergine: ah-buhr-JHEEN

Quinto: KEEN-toh

Davide: DAH-vee-deh

Severo: SEH-veh-roh

Harena: ha-REH-nuh

Eyeleth: EE-luth

Ayn: AIN

Ezra: EZ-ruh

Made in the USA
Columbia, SC
28 July 2024